TOO FAR A DREAM

*For Breallyn
With best regards*

Too Far A Dream

Victor John Faith

Bearly Art Works
Chaska, Minnesota

ACKNOWLEDGEMENTS

Many thanks to my gentle readers, Claudia, Casey, Irene, Wendy and Terry—for your sake, I hope no error remains; to Russ and Rustin Rhone—the best green-breakers in the business; and to Jim Higginbotton, Lionel (Bud) Keen and all the other back-siders who filled divots in this story.

Bearly Art Works, Chaska, MN 55318
Copyright © 2004 by Victor John Faith
All Rights Reserved.

Printed in the United States of America

10 09 08 07 06 05 04   1 2 3 4 5

ISBN: 0-9755592-0-6 (paper)

Too Far A Dream is a work of fiction. Names, places, and incidents are a product of the author's imagination, or are used fictitiously.

TOO FAR A DREAM

1	A Hasty Promise	1
2	Fatal Daylight	21
3	Spy Games	59
4	Acceptable Terms	96
5	On the Mat	118
6	High Tea	122
7	Sweet Iron	161
8	Trickles	164
9	On the List	182
10	Schemes and Lies	202
11	The Baited Trap	227
12	Jump Up and Fly Away	261
13	Red Juice	283
14	The Dodgers Artful	291
15	Bob and Sid	325
16	The Hot Pepper Squirts	344
17	Riders Up	352
18	Twenty to Win	377

Epilogue   395

For Gabe Brisbois,
who saved a lad adrift

One: A Hasty Promise

"It's silly, Miss Phillipa, that's what I think. It's a silly, improbable dream. Do you know that every year in the United States, seven thousand, eight hundred and thirty people are hit by lightening? Does that surprise you? Well then, here's something that may not.... Out of all the horses born in the world every year, only one will win the Kentucky Derby—it's silly, Miss Phillipa, it's a silly, silly dream."

On the first Saturday in May, above the red oaks and gnarled junipers, bald eagles soar, whisked aloft on temperate thermals. Below the spring's first leaves, two teenagers, mounted on horseback meander at a walk, and chatter. The shuffle, and easy breathing of their horses is scarcely heard as sounds merge in the rush of an amiable breeze.

"He's so-oh cute," coos Morgan. "And he really likes me."

"He's a turd! He's just using you," Kallie grouses as the girls guide their horses nose-to-tail down a stony switchback. "I've seen the way he treats you.... You let him walk all over you. Wait and see, Morgan, you're going to cave and give him what he wants, and then he'll dump you."

"No he won't, Nash isn't like that—he's sensitive. Besides, he doesn't want to go that far. And quit calling him a turd."

"But that's what he is, a big old turd," retorts Kallie, the words whistling through a gap in her front teeth. "He's a boy—all boys are turds. Why would he be different? He calls you his squeeze, I've heard him; next he'll be calling you a skank." Kallie pauses, drawing her horse to a halt at an opening on the trail. The afternoon sun, filtered and benign sparkles from beads of perspiration on her thin neck. "Easy *Cashman*," she whispers, waiting for Morgan who's lagging behind. A shrieking jay skims, unseen, through the idle moment; Cashman perks his ears, stares apprehensively at the underbrush, and snorts. "It's just a stupid bird," she soothes him, rubbing his coarse black mane, "you saw a lot worse than that at the

1

Victor John Faith

racetrack—don't be such a scaredy cat." With her straight, blonde hair in a loose braid hanging out from under the back of her riding helmet, Kallie, un-tucks her faded blue T-shirt from her jeans, and uses it for a towel to wipe her face.

"Nice abs, girlfriend," Morgan comments, noticing Kallie's flat stomach. "If you ever get tired of being skinny, you can borrow some of my chub—I can spare you a bunch."

"You're not chubby, Morgan. God, you diet all the time."

"Nash says I am. He says he likes his women that way," she replies, urging her horse to walk, "but I'd rather be skinny like you." And then, glancing over her shoulder at Kallie, she asks, "What are you doing for your birthday?"

"After school, I've got to do chores," Kallie gripes, catching up to her. "And then, well, I don't know. Hey, Morgan, did you know that horses poop seventeen times a day? And they pee almost five gallons."

"No, get out!" Morgan guffaws in disbelief.

"Really, huge piles, and it's heavy too. Look at that..." Kallie flexes her bicep; Morgan stares in amazement as a hard mound of muscle pops from Kallie's arm. "Bigger than Nash's, huh?" she taunts. "The wimp, the only muscle he has is between his ears.... I kind of like doing the work though, and I love the horses, shoveling poop is just part of the J-O-B."

"Part of the J-O-B," chimes Morgan.

Emerging from the trail at the foot of the bluff, the two young friends walk their horses, in silence, over an arching, stone bridge. Built decades ago by the Civilian Conservation Corps, it shows its age like a neglected monument, but yet, it serves its purpose faithfully—those who cross it, arrive safely at a paved township road on the other side. Below the arch, a flood rushes; confined within its hewn channel, the spring tide surges against polished boulders, in their lee dart shiny minnows. Kallie and Morgan trot across the pavement to the opposite shoulder of the road and then resume their walk. Kallie breaks the silence continuing to answer Morgan's question.

"My parents promised to take me to some fancy restaurant for supper. Oh God, I hope the waiters don't go and sing that stupid happy birthday song. I'll be so embarrassed. Dad will probably put them up to it, and I'll have to blow out a candle on some puny cupcake." Throwing a raspy-voiced plea skyward, she yells, "Why do they do that? I'm going to die."

"Parents do such stupid things," replies Morgan. "I swear my mom is crazy." She pauses as if lured by a painful secret, and stares off pensively before continuing, "She thinks it's so cute when she does stuff like that—but it's just dumb. Parents just don't get it..."

"Sometimes..."

"Never, girlfriend," she scowls, "they never get it." But then her mood lightens, and teasing, she sings blithely, "Sweet sixteen, and never been kissed, NEVER BEEN KISSED."

"I have too," retorts Kallie. "I've done a lot of kissing—well—enough for me, anyway."

"Kissing your father doesn't count, Kallie."

"No, you dope, I've kissed boys. I kissed Katie's brother at the hockey rink last March. We were kind of dating then—see? I didn't like it much. It was kind of nice at first, but then he shoved his tongue in my mouth—I almost threw up. Who knows where that tongue has been? Then he grabbed my boobs and tried to feel me up. What a dink! I wanted to slug him, but he's so stupid he'd probably think it meant I loved him."

"Katie's brother?" Morgan screams in shock. "Katie's brother, Tim?" She sticks her finger in her mouth and pretends to gag. "UCK, GAG! Looser!"

"Looser," Kallie sings, slapping hands with Morgan in a high-five salute, "but not as big a looser as Nash." Morgan winces at the comment, but Kallie fails to notice the discomfort she's caused. Casually, she glances ahead at the open road and asks, "Hey Morgan, it's only about a half mile back to the farm, you want to race a little? We can trot the last quarter to cool out the horses... I don't want to miss the post parade for the derby."

"Yeah! Let's go for it girl," she yelps eagerly.

Kallie's horse bounds off at a wimpy gallop; Morgan's shuffles into an ambling trot, and then into a rolling, but lackluster canter. At a top speed of ten miles per hour, they bounce along the lane toward a white-fenced farm visible through the overhanging trees ahead. "Wee-ha,' yelps Kallie, "eat dirt, you slowpoke. Faster, Cashman, faster!"

"Ah, ah—oh crap," Morgan jiggles awkwardly. "Not fair, girlfriend. You got a thoroughbred; I'm riding a plow horse, and she's still pulling the plow."

Roadside, at the gravel drive leading to home, hangs a neatly lettered sign that reads: *Longview Stables*. The girls rein their mounts from the township road and careen beyond the chasing dust.

Relentless preening, and an aversion to weeds, makes this driveway the model for every pastoral study ever painted, or put into verse. Long, tediously long, edged in cut pile, and buttressed by gothic oaks, the driveway leads to a pristine, two story Victorian house that is skirted by a wrap-around front porch—a white-washed vision so dainty, it's precious. South of the house hides a single story, boarding stable—equally as cute as the house—large enough to accommodate ten horses. Arched, wooden doors hang in the center of the long side, and above the doors, protruding from the roof, is a gingerbread copula sporting a cockerel at its peak. At the front of the stable is an ample turnaround; in it, a cream colored, dual-wheeled pick-up with a matching horse trailer rests idle. On the driver's door, a placard reads: *Longview Veterinary Clinic, Regina Phillipa DVM. Trauma, Urgent Care, and Extended Lay-Ups*. The rear ramp of the trailer is down and a woman wearing blue jeans and a chambray shirt is backing a horse out. Kallie and Morgan, now jostling neck and neck, race up the drive. Hearing the clatter of the approaching horses, the woman turns, and greets them, "Hi girls, did you have a nice ride?"

The girls dismount short of breath. "Hi Mom," Kallie replies, puffing.

"Hi Reggie. It was so cool! We rode up to the top of Benning's Mill bluff. The eagles were all over, they were soaring like huge buzzards—they must be migrating—it was awesome!"

"We haven't missed the post parade, have we; we're not too late; it hasn't started?" asks Kallie.

Reggie glances at her wristwatch, and replies, "I think you still have about forty-five minutes…

"Great," Kallie chirps, "that'll give us enough time to cool down the horses, and toss their stalls."

"…and Kallie, your Uncle John is here, so run some water on your face. Please?"

"Sure Mom. Come on Morgan, I'm going to give Cashman a bath."

"Cool!" replies Morgan.

The two girls lead the horses by the bridles toward the stable. Reggie follows them, leading the horse she took from the trailer. As they pass through the arching doors, Reggie mentions, "I'm going to turn this gelding out in the first paddock. He has some nasty run-downs on his fetlocks. I'll 'bute' him, and check to see how he's doing after the race. See you gals at the derby."

"Is Uncle John going to make mint juleps?" Kallie quizzes as Reggie leads the gelding from the stable to a fenced paddock in the rear.

"He always does, honey. And don't keep him waiting, you're his favorite niece."

"I'm his only niece, Mom…."

With Reggie out of sight, Morgan gushes, "Mint juleps, awesome! This is so cool."

"There's no booze in them, Morgan, don't get too excited."

"Yeah, but it's so sophisticated sipping a cocktail and watching the Kentucky Derby—it makes me feel like a woman. My mom lets me have beer once in a while, but that's different; I like the bubbles, but it's not like having a cocktail with a man."

Kallie stares at Morgan and wonders what the difference could be. Morgan is three months older than Kallie, and more mature by years. She has a steady boyfriend—he's not her first—and she's eager to experiment with sex. In her life, Kallie has french-kissed one boy; it's not a lot of experience to draw on, and she replies puzzled, "Sometimes, girlfriend, I just don't know what you're talking about."

Victor John Faith

While Kallie and Morgan are busy in the stable, Reggie ambles the short distance to the house. On the front porch, she pauses, removes the barrette from her ponytail, and shakes loose her hair; it flows down her back in an amber tide. She sighs relief. Opening the screen-door, she enters her favorite room in the house: her very own Victorian foyer. Ten-foot ceilings, plated with sheets of embossed tin, form an enameled lid at twice her height. "I'm so glad we didn't tear out the tin when we remodeled," she whispers unlacing her paddock boots. And removing them, she kicks them atop a disorganized mound of loafers and tennis shoes gathered along the baseboard. "I should really make everyone take their shoes off outside," she thinks, making her way into the central hallway. To her left, a spindled staircase ascends to the upper floors. Against the wall beyond the foot of the stairs, leaning as if spent, is a rickety, federalist console table with a telephone on it. Reggie pushes a button on the answering machine, and listens to a recorded voice:

"Hey Doc, this is *Winston Chase*, I got a two-year old that come back sore from his work this morning. Can you stop out later and have a look? Might be a splint—I don't know—I might need some pictures took. I'm in barn 'C-6'. Thanks." The machine beeps and then a mechanical voice adds, "End of messages."

Reggie scribbles the message in her planner, glances at her wristwatch, and mumbles, "The races go on 'til seven—he'll still be there." Shuffling in her stocking feet along the hardwood floor of the corridor, she strains to hear a muted conversation coming from an adjoining room. Ahead on her right, an archway robustly trimmed in oak leads to a formal parlor. A hundred years ago, craftsmen wearing aprons and using hand tools, installed this millwork; through a thick patina of yellowed varnish, the wood boasts its noble beginnings in straight graining, and fresh lemon oil shows the tender regard in which its current owners hold it. "Hi everyone," Reggie announces, sneaking undetected into the parlor. Gazing from within the recess of a west facing bow window, opposite the archway, two middle-age men in stocking feet, and a woman, turn startled. The men clutch bottles of beer; the woman holds a dainty highball decorated with a sprig of mint. A television mumbles softly in the background. "Yeah, well, *Anthony*," Reggie scowls playfully, "don't rush over here and kiss your dog-ass-tired wife."

"I would darlin', but...."

Before Anthony can say any more, two overfed, golden haired dogs burst through the archway, and pounce on Reggie knocking her off kilter. "Ah, i-eee!" she howls, fighting to regain her balance. "Hi guys! Oh you bad boys," she giggles attempting to fend them off. Vigorously, she rubs their ears; they lick her face ferociously, and she pleads gleefully. "No more kisses, *Goldie*—ugh. Stop it. *Waggs*! Down boys, down..." The frolicking hounds ignore her until she barks an order they understand, "Go in the kitchen and lie down."

"Okay, we can do that, Reggie, but wouldn't it be better for us to nap on the couch?" jokes the man beside Anthony.

"John, John, John, is today going to be like that?" Reggie retorts glibly. "Your bad jokes, too much beer, and then you take a nap? Remember, you're an in-law here, not a boarder."

"But it's my brother's couch, and he invited me..."

Smugly, she notes, "It's my parlor, Johnny. And I think your stockings are dirty."

John reacts timidly; he draws up the legs of his khaki trousers, stares at his rag wool stockings and sniffs the air. "Did I put these on this morning," he wonders, "or was it yesterday?"

With John occupied, Reggie turns to the woman and greets her, "Hi, *Celeste*, that's a pretty dress. Is it new? Still pregnant I see. John, why don't you give *Seal* a break? You're like a freaking stud colt in springtime. We may have to geld you if you keep breeding like one."

"Ha! You're nuts, Reggie, if you think I'll be satisfied with a small litter..." replies John, still wondering if his socks stink.

"No, not my nuts John, yours," she hisses, displaying her index and middle finger mimicking the action of scissors approaching him. John shudders; he understands Reggie's meaning. "One little snip and you could sing in a boys choir. It's amazing how a man's attitude improves once he's gelded." While sauntering past John she whispers provocatively, "Snip, snip, snip," and as she passes Celeste, she winks and adds quietly, "I'll get that horny stud to behave." Anthony has been standing apart from the exchange between Reggie and John—near enough to be a reliable witness, but far enough away to avoid involvement. Impishly, Reggie sashays to her husband, smears his tanned cheek with a kiss, and whispers, "Yum," while reaching behind him to pinch his buttock. "Hey *Tony*, how's tricks?" she coos, and then, gesturing in the direction of the bottled beer Anthony holds below his belt, she asks, "You got one of those big boys for me?"

"I only have the one, darlin'," he drawls suggestively, "it's a long-neck, and it belongs to my wife. But I have another beer. You want one of those instead?"

"A long-neck is tempting, but I'm parched as a Mongolian salamander," she groans, "I think I'll take the beer..." but then, she pauses. Recalling that she has a later appointment at the racetrack, she adds prudently, "No, I better not, I've got to drive out to the track after the derby. Winston has a two-year old that might be popping a splint. No, I'll just have charged water on ice—at least it will fizz like beer. Could you get one for me Tony? I know you've got plenty in the fridge."

"Anything ya want darling," Anthony answers, but before he leaves the room, he turns back, glances at John, and jests, "No stallions living under this roof, hey John? Not even me. Anything she wants. I trot and get it. That's why the doctor likes geldings." With his stubby fingers, Anthony mimics the use of scissors. John fakes a swoon, and Reggie and Celeste laugh at John's antics as Anthony disappears through the archway.

While Anthony is busy in the kitchen across the hall from the parlor, the three adults gaze out the window at the Phillipa's band of horses running in a distant pasture, and engage in small talk. Celeste mentions that the cream-colored, organdy sash draped either side of the window, "really works with the mocha scarf." Silently, and unseen, Kallie and Morgan creep into the room—mischief motivates them. They sneak toward the occupied grownups. Stalking John, Kallie approaches him from behind; when she's at his heels, she nudges his leg—it buckles at the knee—and he drops yelping, but before he tumbles to the carpet, he recovers his balance.

"Ho! What the heck?" he shouts, wheeling round to see Kallie lurking behind him. "I almost spilled my beer—you little french fry—come here."

Kallie jumps back to escape John, but too late. He lunges, grabs her, spins her around and crushes her in a hug. Kallie screams, laughs and struggles to break free. "No! No, don't tickle, please Uncle John," she pleads, "I'm allergic to tickling."

"Then how about a snake-bite, ya little runt?" he growls, clutching Kallie's forearm in his hands, wringing it mercilessly.

"I-eee!" she shrieks in pain, "Uncle! Uncle! I give up, I give." John eases his grip; Kallie bolts free and taunts, "Just fooling, I didn't give—I didn't say uncle, I meant Uncle, JOHN!"

"Why you ornery wench," he laughs, "you better watch your back, I've got a bead on you missy." John raises his hands to his nose, sniffs, and then withdraws them in disgust, "Whew—do you stink!" he bellows. "Been rolling in manure again? My God woman, you got to learn what a shower is!"

Amid raucous laughter, Anthony returns through the archway carrying a tall glass of sparkling water and ice. Absent during the playful scuffle, he asks, handing Reggie the charged water, "What's going on in here? From the kitchen, it sounded like *All Star Wrestling*. No one got hit with a folding chair, did they?"

Reggie takes the glass, and quips sarcastically, "Hitting your brother with a chair isn't a bad idea."

Everyone turns, and stares at John... "Ah, um, nothing's going on," he protests feebly. "I was just loving up my little squeeze—right, French-fry?"

"Whatever," she moans. "Hi-ya Dad!"

"Hi-ya, shrimp," replies Anthony.

"Hey Mr. Phillipa," pipes Morgan from beyond the fray. "You got any money on the derby?"

Anthony brushes back his receding, brown hair, straightens to his full height of five feet, six inches and puts on the air of a gentleman. "Miss Morgan Marie Jasperson? Is that the woman whom I address?"

Morgan poses, stiff-backed, nose in the air, and responds in kind, "I am she who answers to that name, sir. But do not presume me to be less than a proper lady, or you are misled..."

"Then Miss," he continues soberly, "to answer your question, I am not a gambling man. Luck is the fickle muse the gods employ; she brings us ruin more often than joy."

Celeste scowls at John. "Repeat that again for my husband. Would you Anthony?"

"What? What?" he blubbers helplessly. "So I put a few bucks on the race—so? My horse is going to win—we're going to be rich." Celeste squints doubtfully. "You can shop as much as you want—buy shoes, whatever! Honey? Sweetie?" Celeste taps her foot. Everyone squints at John. He's looking for a diversion. "Ah, ah," he bumbles, glancing nervously for Kallie and Morgan. "Can I get you ladies a cocktail? Mint juleps for my little tulips?" Sternly, Reggie glares at John; he knows her meaning. "I know, I know—no liquor," he grouses, and then adds some advice. "You know Reggie, kids these days are a lot wilder than when you were young..." He pauses withering, he knows he's stepped on slippery ground. Everyone gasps an expectant, "Oh-oh." Cowering, John braces himself.

"What?" Reggie explodes. "When I was young? Why you foul-mouthed old cowboy."

"Oh God-oh-God-oh-God..." John whimpers, retreating.

"I'm half as old as you, twice as tough, and I've got a full head of hair!"

"Oh! Low blow, low blow," shouts the crowd.

"Penalty on Reggie!" cries Morgan.

"What?" John yaps, rubbing the top of his head. "I'm not loosing my hair!" John looks to Celeste—his eyes pleading for support. She's smiling with adoring sympathy, but nods her head in a gesture that says, "Yes you are sweetheart." John's jaw falls slack, his eyes grow wide, and he screams, "I-eee!"

"The judge rules no penalty," pipes Kallie. "The pugilist is vindicated. Sorry, Uncle John, even without hair, you're still really cute."

Everyone is amused except John—he moans. Muttering to himself, he shuffles to an elegantly crafted side table just to the right of the bow window. Old, but not antique, the table is stocked with glasses, a chrome-plated ice bucket, and an ample supply of liquor. He pours some liquid into two plastic cocktail glasses filled with ice. Then he picks up a bottle of bourbon, unscrews the cap, places his thumb over the opening, and pretends to pour…

"John Phillipa!" Reggie shrieks, making a fitful start at him.

John bolts, and holding up the bottle with his thumb still pressed over the opening, "Ha!" he laughs, "just kidding Reggie. They can think it, but they can't drink it…" Then with a sigh of regret, he moans, "But you know, it just isn't a julep without a bit o' bourbon."

As the party laughs at John's prank, the sound of a trumpet squawks from the television at the far end of the room; like cowboys hearing a distant dinner bell, everyone turns their attention to the TV. Reggie dashes to a tartan plaid couch facing the TV, bounds over the rear cushions, and plops lightly down in the middle. Celeste, careful not to crease her dress, sits gently down on Reggie's left. Anthony scrambles to *his* recliner at the left corner of the couch. Kallie and Morgan scuttle, and sit on the floor near the couch's right armrest. John, lingering at the bar, turns to see where Kallie and Morgan are seated. He whispers, "Psssst…"

Both girls turn and look at him. Ready to pour, he holds the bottle of bourbon above their glasses, and nodding his head, he asks silently, "Want some?" The girls glance quickly at the seated adults—they're occupied watching the TV. With a muffled giggle, they nod back to John eagerly. He pours a splash into each glass, screws the cap back on the liquor bottle, and brings the drinks to Kallie and Morgan. When he hands the girls their drinks, he steps behind the couch, and sure that Reggie can't see him, he raises his finger to his lips to gesture "secret," and winks. Kallie and Morgan wink back approvingly. His mischief complete, John returns to the bar, and retrieves his beer; he ambles to the couch, and plunks down on the open end next to Reggie. "Squeeze a cheek, ya runt," he slurs, grabbing Reggie's thigh just above her knee and pinching.

"I-eee," she shrieks kicking her leg free, "that hurt, you turd!" And then she retaliates by jabbing her elbow in his ribs.

"Ouch!" he howls, grabbing her again.

"You're asking for it, you skinny asshole."

"Mom!" scolds Kallie.

"Ooo—a sassy Reggie always brings me luck. Keep it up ya pint-sized runt; your bony elbows ain't hurting me."

Anthony looks at Celeste who concurs with his disapproving glance. Then he glares at Reggie and John who continue to tussle on the couch. He shakes his head, side to side, and purses his lips, "Children, if you don't behave," he scowls playfully, "I'm going to have to punish you—I'm serious. Now be quiet and watch TV."

Reggie and John heed the warning and quit wrestling. Kallie and Morgan sit quietly, listening to the voices of expert commentators coming from the TV:

> *"...Thanks, Jim. Thank you for that very kind introduction. First of all, I'd like to welcome our viewers to the annual running of the Kentucky Derby, an event unlike any other. Unrivaled for its history, unsurpassed in its tradition, and unequaled in the drama that is sure to unfold, in this, the most prestigious jewel in horse racing's Triple Crown. In today's field, are the finest fledglings of thoroughbred racing—"*

"A fine field of fledglings," scoffs John. "Enough with the alliteration, get to the race already. God, these morons can blab." John fidgets, and sips his beer; the others remain quiet, their eyes fixed on the television...

> *"Fourteen, three year olds will enter the starting gate, but only one will cross the finish line ahead of the others. That horse, will it be Crushing Rage, Forever Gone, or the odds on favorite Twiddledundee, that horse will swell the ranks of previous champions.*

Their names are legend, War Admiral, Seattle Slew, Affirmed, to name just a few. And now, for a rundown on today's field, let's go down to the saddling paddock, and Calvin Winthrop. Calvin, the money on the track seems to be favoring Twiddledundee. Is that where the smart money is today?"

"Well, Sidney, before I answer your question, let me say that you could be wrong about only one winner. It's not unheard of for a race, with horses of this caliber, to finish in a dead heat..."

"Right you are, Calvin. I stand corrected."

"...And I do think the smart money belongs on Twiddledundee. He's had four races coming up to the derby—all respectable stakes races—and he's won three, decisively. The other race was his first outing and he finished second by a head. He does have boasting rights. He's talented, pugnacious, and the fans love him."

Anthony glances at his wristwatch and groans, "These talking heads will be jabbering for another five minutes. Anybody care for some snacks? I can rustle up some chips, or maybe nachos. How about some beef jerky?"

"Yeah, sure, I'll have some," is the general reply.

As Anthony gets up from his recliner, Reggie mentions, "There's some dip in the back of the fridge, I don't know how old it is, so smell it first Tony."

"It's called sour cream, because it is soured cream..." he jibes sarcastically.

"Need any help, Anthony?" Celeste offers, making a feeble effort to get up from the couch. "I'll be glad to help."

"Thanks Seal, you relax. I can handle it. Heaven forbid that Reggie would enter a kitchen."

"Watch it, cowboy," Reggie grunts as Anthony swaggers from the room, and then she nudges John, and asks, "Why'd they blow the trumpet before 'riders up'?"

13

"Drama, runt," replies John. "To get everyone to rush to the tube for a stupid commercial."

Calvin Winthrop's voice drones in the background:

"And now, let's pause for a word from our sponsors."

"See, what did I tell you? Works every time. Watch me, I'm going to get another beer."

John gets up by pushing off of Reggie, and hustles out of the parlor. Kallie, Morgan, Reggie and Celeste glance at each other and groan disgustedly, "Men." From the kitchen comes the noise of clanking beer bottles, clattering dishes, muffled conversation, and masculine laughter. The women giggle, make faces and mocking gestures that are meant to mimic Anthony and John, but an abrupt call, "*Riders Up!*" blares from the television, and their interest shifts from teasing to the broadcast. On the sound of hurriedly padding stocking feet, Anthony and John burst through the archway and into the parlor. Anthony carries an enormous bowl of potato chips, and a platter heaped with nachos swimming in cheese. John lugs a sack of beef jerky, and two bottles of beer. Anthony thrusts the platter to Reggie, grabs a beer from John, and clutching the potato chips, sinks back into his recliner. John squishes in next to Reggie. "Won't be long now, kids," he bubbles, sloshing his mouth full with beer. "When Kangamaster crosses the line, I'll be on easy street."

"Huh," asks Anthony, "you've got money on Kangamaster?"

"Just a few bucks," replies John.

"I bet you put twenty across the board."

"Yeah, so?"

Celeste leans forward and glares at John over Reggie's lap. "You were supposed to put half of that money on my horse," she grouses.

"Sorry Seal, but Kangamaster is a sure thing."

"Good bet, John, if he finishes, but he won't," Anthony says, contradicting him. "My money's on Climbaboard—now that's a for sure. Blue blood and jingle all the way."

"Sir!" Morgan interrupts. "You assured me that you never wager. Ah, oh!" she moans swooning. "To keep company with a gambler. I'm disgraced!" Morgan pretends to faint; her antics arouse approving laughter from everyone. Just then a voice, thick and dark as melted toffee, comes from the television. It's the track announcer:

"*The final horse is entering the starting gate.*"

An audible pause follows his words; the Phillipa parlor swells with pregnant silence.

"*They're all in line, but the number three horse is acting up. We wait on Climbaboard—he's steady now...*"

In a wink of time, John snipes, "Climbaboard ain't gonna do it, brother."

"Wait and see..."

Still hearts and held breaths abide the moment. The starter's bell rings. The gates blast open. The field explodes.

"*THEY—ARE—RACING!*" growls the announcer.

In three strides the horses are at full speed. "*A clean start for all with Twiddledundee taking the early lead to the clubhouse turn...*"

The roar from the television is so loud the floorboards in the parlor shake. Ice cubes jump from the bucket on the bar. The Phillipas stand and stomp their feet as the announcer calls the race, updating positions every eighth mile:

"*Twiddledundee, unhurried, sets the early pace; and then it's a length back to Kangamaster who vies with Crushing Rage, and Forever Gone...*" At the far turn, the announcer's voice crackles with tension. "*Blue Gloom is moving up to test the leaders...*"

15

"Where the hell is Climbaboard?" howls Anthony.
"Not even close!" taunts John. "He's running the other way."

> "Rounding the final turn and heading for home it's Twiddledundee giving way. Matching stride for stride and taking the lead are Kangamaster and Crushing Rage outside; Forever Gone is gone."

"Kangamaster, go Kangamaster! I told you, I told you."
"SHUT UP JOHN!"

> "Not out of it yet, Blue Gloom is raising a challenge…"

"Where the hell is Climbaboard?"

> "From out of nowhere, making an unstoppable late bid along the rail, Climbaboard is flying…"

Anthony gasps and leaps gleefully. On his tiptoes, he shuffles like a prizefighter, spars with the ceiling, and yelps, "Holy-moly! Yes!"
John crumbles to his knees and pleads, "Oh please oh please oh please!" Celeste clutches his arm. "I can't watch," he moans groveling.
The screeching voice of the announcer is high enough to be soprano:

> "It's Kangamaster by a head, neck and neck with Crushing Rage; Blue Gloom is there too; Climbaboard is a rocket on fire! Climbaboard is zooming on the inside. It's Climbaboard. Climbaboard by a neck, by a half…"

Too Far A Dream

Propelled by pounding feet and thundering hooves, the TV polkas across the room as the horses flash past the finish line. The announcer shrieks:

"It's Climbaboard, no one can catch him today! Climbaboard wins it by two!"

Dancing up the walls, across the ceiling and down again, Anthony shouts, "YES! YES! YES!"

John writhes on his belly, his hands clasp behind his head; sobbing in the plush, burgundy carpet, he whimpers banefully, "No, no. No—it can't be!

Reggie scampers to Anthony and coos as she hugs him, "Good job big boy, how much did we win? Enough to buy your brother a toupee?"

"I can't stand it," John sobs, rising to his feet. "Turn that damn thing off, I can't stand the humiliation!"

"There, there," Reggie chuckles, offering jeering comfort, "You poor baby, mommy will turn it off—NOT! We have to wait until they announce the pay-outs..." She stares anxiously at the TV. After a tense moment, the tote-board flashes on the screen. "Yes," she shouts, "twenty-two, eighty. Let's see, you usually bet fifty on the nose. Don't you Tony?" Anthony nods, yes, and grins. "That figures out to be... Five hundred and seventy dollars! The long-shot paid off." Reggie jabs her hand in front of John's nose and rubs invisible money between her fingers. "Read 'em and weep, Johnny-boy," she hisses, gloating. "We got easy street, and you got the poorhouse—ha!"

John staggers dejectedly and withers onto the couch. As the excitement of the race fades, and the rest of the party returns to their seats to watch the video replays, Kallie announces, "I'm going to be in the Kentucky Derby someday; I'm going to be a jockey and ride at Churchill Downs. I've made up my mind. I could do it—you know?"

"You're small enough, French-fry," teases John, reaching down and mussing her hair. "I'd put my money on you. You're a scrapper, just like your dad."

"That'd be awesome," blurts Morgan. "That would be so cool!"

17

Victor John Faith

From the expression on Anthony's face, Kallie can see that he has doubts. "What about college?" he asks, frowning. "Your mom went to college, now she's a doctor. You don't want to grow up to be like me, do you?" Anthony holds up his hands for Kallie to see. They are thick and pulpy, his fingers are scared and crooked, and every knuckle appears to have been broken more than once. Morgan gawks. "Look at those things," he continues sternly, "I can barely hold a pencil."

"That trick won't work, Dad. You went to college too—on a scholarship. Your hands look like that because you were a boxer. Besides, you've seen my grades, they suck. I'd never get into a college. I really want to do this—I love horses."

"It takes a lot more than loving horses to survive in the race game," he advises, "It takes experience—racing is dangerous. And it takes a lot of money—a hundred and fifty thousand for a supplemental nomination to the derby. You may be a little short of both. I don't think so, Kallie..."

"But Dad, I've thought about it. I'm going to do it—somehow."

"Your father is right, Kallie. I don't think you know what you're up against." The sound of resentment enters Reggie's voice as she continues, "I had to work like hell just to get into vet school, and that was nothing compared to what you'll face. Jockeys aren't just little people, they're men, and racing is a man's game. There's still a lot of discrimination out there. They'll fight you every step..."

Kallie's mood grows serious; she squints soberly at Reggie and asks, "Have you looked at me lately, Mom?" Reggie replies with a puzzled stare. "I'm homely, and I'm a shrimp. Uncle John calls me French-fry because I'm skinny and small—I think I know what I'm gonna face." The comment jars Reggie, and leaves her without a reply.

"I don't mean it that way, Kallie," blurts John, apologizing.

"You're cool Uncle John, I know you don't." And then winking, she adds, "Besides, I like the name."

Usually quiet about her opinions, Celeste intervenes on Kallie's behalf. "I think you're wrong, Anthony. She's young, and it sounds like she's thought about it. Why shouldn't she try? The most that could happen is she could fail..."

"I won't!"

"A lot worse than that could happen, Seal," Anthony replies grimly.

"Maybe," she agrees, "Kallie could get hurt. But she can always go to college. If she really wants to be a jockey, she has to start now, when she's young—it's not something she can learn when she's twenty-five, and I say, go for it girl." She glances at Kallie, and smiles approvingly when she advises, "If you don't go after your dream now, you won't get another chance—you'll get old, and be very sad and bitter." John appears uncomfortable at hearing Celeste's remark; he stares and wonders, "Is she unhappy?" But his momentary doubt vanishes when Celeste adds, "I chased my dream, and look at what I got, a husband who's a wonderful father. And your mom? Well, she got your dad." And then, with a naughty giggle, she concludes, "Maybe not every dream works out after all..."

Reggie giggles too, and whispers, "You got that right, Seal."

"Thanks a lot, Celeste," Anthony comments dejectedly. "Thanks for the support. I'm just the voice of reason, that's all. Don't anyone listen to me. I might as well be preaching to the dogs. I can see I'll never win this one, and I've never entered a fight I couldn't win. You're as bull-headed and stubborn as your mother, Kallie. After twenty-four years of marriage, I've learned that some deals need to be negotiated, so—we'll see. That's not a yes, and it's not a no. Just a we'll see."

"And my college money, Dad," Kallie bubbles, "can I use it to buy a racehorse?"

"Don't push it, shrimp. You can't spend one penny of that money on another horse. Maybe you can get a part time job this summer, and take some riding lessons—maybe. I want you to go to college, that's what I want. So—you're going to have to earn your own money if you want to be a jockey..." Anthony looks quickly at Reggie; she nods her approval. Secretly, she knows his sternness is bluster.

"I really hate to butt in on your negotiations," Reggie interjects, glancing at her wristwatch, and getting up from the couch, "but I have a vet call at the track to get to, and I have to check on that gelding I brought in earlier..."

19

"Hey Reggie," interrupts Morgan, "can I catch a ride home with you?" Her eyelids flutter when she looks at Kallie, and gushes, "Nash said he'd call me at five; he gets pissed if I'm not there."

Kallie shakes her head, and flexes her bicep. "Let him get pissed," she snarls, "Girls rule!"

"No trouble," Reggie answers, digging in her jeans pocket for the van keys. "You going to ride along, Kallie? I've got to take the van, it's out front, it has my X-ray equipment in it." Kali nods, yes. "Good, let's get going then."

"Hey, what about supper?" Anthony pesters Reggie, disappearing through the archway. "We have guests!"

"Unless you feel like cooking, toss a frozen pizza in the oven, that's good enough for your mooching brother. Sorry Seal, we won't be long—couple hours, tops," she replies from the foyer just before slamming the front door shut.

"Frozen pizza?" John scowls. "Tony, I'm your kin, ya gotta do better than that."

* * *

Two: Fatal Daylight

The township road fronting the Phillipa property meanders cautiously below yellow limestone cliffs, turns in and out of steep-sided canyons, and then, plunges onto an alluvial plain where Longview Township Road intersects State Highway 25. Five miles farther on is the Interstate. During a weekday rush hour, the drive from Longview Stables to Dorchester Downs takes forty minutes, late in the afternoon on a Saturday it takes twenty-five—even allowing for the time it took to drop Morgan home. For twenty-five minutes, Reggie has endured Kallie's effusive warbling. "Maybe Kallie. It's possible, dear. Yes Kallie, but I don't think that's what Dad and I meant," she'd reply, vainly trying to deflect Kallie's chatter. Now, with the backside entrance to the racetrack just ahead, Reggie anticipates deliverance. She signals her exit from the interstate; Kallie chatters on. She whizzes onto a frontage road; still Kallie chatters. She turns the van left and rolls along the fenced-in, backside access route. Along the route signs warn: No Trespassing; Restricted Area; Licensed Personnel Only; No Unauthorized Visitors; Violators Prosecuted. While reading the signs, Kallie stops chattering. Coming into view ahead, she sees dormitories, rows of stables, and the security checkpoint that guards them. Two, chain-link gates, one in and one out, both sporting razor-wire coronets, control the traffic that comes and goes. And hunkered ominously between the gates, a single story blockhouse gives grim assurance that the warnings are genuine. Reggie slows the van to a crawl on approaching the blockhouse; a security guard, wearing an arsenal, a white dress shirt, necktie, and navy blue slacks with yellow piping, steps from inside. Fumbling, Reggie digs in the front pocket of her jeans, pulls out her racing commission license, and holds it out for the guard's viewing. With a squint of his eyes, a suspicious nod, and a chilly wave of his arm, he motions her to pass.

    The backside of Dorchester Downs is a structured community of named boulevards, and secondary lanes that branch from them. Straight ahead, as Reggie accelerates, is Bold Ruler Boulevard—main street—and it's as grand as Park Avenue. Curbs and gutters line either side; quarantined lawns of sculpted fescue extend from curb to stable—stable? These are kingly halls for pampered bluebloods. Holding the middle ground, and patents to the surrounding acre of prominence, these robustly opulent mews house royal hooves that never labor, except to race. Reggie drives three blocks and passes six palaces before turning left from Bold Ruler Boulevard onto Nearco Lane. Here the rents are lower, but still require a flush wallet to pay them. Two blocks more, and Nearco Lane ends at a maze of squalid alleyways—the curbs and gutters are gone and so are the street names, and the haphazard way is paved with pit-run sand instead of rosy dolomite. Reggie pauses before entering the maze, and wonders, "C-6. Right, left, or straight ahead?" but before she can decide, a golf cart, driven by a scarecrow in a security uniform, putters from the center alley, and slowly approaches the van. The late afternoon sun glares from the windshield, and as the golf cart rolls by, the guard shields his eyes with his hand and squints at the van to see who's inside. Reggie offers him a friendly smile, and then accelerates into the maze. "They all loop around and end back here," she jokes to Kallie, "We can't go wrong going right down the middle."

Gawking at the humble shed rows, Kallie giggles in reply, "Mom, you gotta get a better class of customers. This place is a slum." And then, noticing a gas powered washing machine and attached hand wringer settled wheel deep in mud, she adds soberly, "Morgan's trailer is a castle compared to these shacks."

"Not much to look at; they call it Tent City," she replies. "Cheap claimers mostly, but the guys who work back here are pretty good—good horsemen. Winston especially." Glancing left, she spots the stable she's looking for. "There, that's it," she yelps, turning the steering wheel abruptly and veering toward an open-air stable. A stenciled sign labels it: C-6. Long and narrow, it has no exterior walls and no paint. On both long sides, twenty-four stalls with dutch doors face outward. A common wall that runs down the center of the building's length separates the rows of stalls. Overhead, a corrugated roof of rusted tin covers the feeble structure, and extends six feet beyond the stall doors providing a covered walkway around the building. At the west end of the stable, two wet horses, attached to a mechanical hot walker trod endless circles, but determined to not resign to drudgery, occasionally they kick out, buck, and fart defiance. "They must have run today," Reggie notes, stopping the van near the hot walker and a weathered placard that reads: *Winston Chase Racing Stable.*

Glancing at the horses just in time to see one leave a juicy trail of manure, Kallie observes quietly, "That filly probably didn't run too well carrying a load like that." And then, diverting her attention to a lanky, middle-aged black man, wearing a rumpled Stetson hat, a plaid, polyester shirt, faded blue jeans, and cowboy boots, she thinks, "I bet he spent a week's wages on a loosing ticket today..." Then she notices a wizened Hispanic man dozing against the doorjamb. He's dressed like a rummage sale, and a leather lead rope with a chain-link shank drapes vigilantly around his bronze neck. Sympathetically, she adds, sliding out of the van, "...and your paycheck too señor." But before approaching the two men, Kallie turns back to Reggie, and asks, "You going to need anything from the back? Do you want me to help with any of your stuff?"

"I'm just going to take a look-see first..." she replies, walking around the rear of the van to join Kallie. "Evening Winston," she says with a wave as she and Kallie amble toward the seated man.

Winston rouses himself from his chair and walks forward to greet them. "Hi-ya Doc," he answers in a voice pure and musical enough to be operatic. "Thanks for stopping out..."

"Sure Winston, not a problem. Did you run anything today?"

"Yeah, I sent out a cheap claimer," Winston replies dejectedly. "We beat a few horses, but we got no check."

"Too bad. Next time, maybe. Hi Juan!" The Hispanic man waves a sleepy response. Kallie jostles Reggie, eager for an introduction. Reggie is peeved by her impatience, but doesn't show it when she says, "Hey Winston, this is my daughter Kallie, she'll be giving me a hand today—crazy girl wants to be a jockey. Hope you don't mind, I thought I'd give her a hands-on view."

"A jockey?" he laughs, reaching to shake Kallie's hand. "I'd say you're puny enough now, but let's hope ya don't grow up none. How old are you?"

"Almost sixteen…"

He winks at Reggie, and whispers aside, "They heal fast at that age." A momentary shudder grips Reggie. Winston realizes that she's uncomfortable with Kallie's enterprise, and he reassures her, "Don't worry none Doc, she's young, she'll be fine."

"Yeah, that's why I'm out here looking at one of your babies," she smirks, contradicting him. Reggie allows Winston a moment to dwell on the irony of her comment, and then she suggests, "Well, let's have a look at that two-year old of yours."

"You bet," he replies, eager to change the subject. And signaling to Juan with a wave, he adds, "He's in stall eleven, I'll have Juan take him out."

Juan shuffles past Winston, Reggie and Kallie; as he passes them, the cuffs of his oversized trousers scoop spoonfuls of sand from the walkway and spill it with his next stride. Calm and nonchalant about his work, Juan pulls the leather lead from around his neck while walking the short distance to stall eleven, and appears oblivious to the horses that stare vacantly at him. One bay horse yawns, a second scratches the outside of its stall door with its teeth, another nods its head, and another cribs releasing a tedious belch. Reggie and the others watch as Juan, finally enters the stall.

Approaching C-6 from some dead end alley of Tent City, a scruffy pony rider mounted on a few-spot leopard appaloosa, comes into view, and announces his arrival by singing:

"I got a happy feelin', a feeling about you; you're a magic racehorse, with lightning studded shoes…"

Wearing tattered chaps over his jeans, his willowy legs dangle down to western spurs at his heels, and topside he wears nothing to improve the lower unit: a soiled, sleeveless sweat-shirt, a protective riding vest scuffed by hard falls, and a steeplechase helmet made before he was old enough to put it on. But his voice is unexpectedly mellow for a man of such coarse appearance. As he sings:

> "...You're entered at a mile, and gonna come in first; I'll join you in the test barn, where beer will quench our thirst!"

Kallie's attention is drawn to the spindly thoroughbred filly that he leads. "Nothing but legs and muscle," she thinks studying the animated filly. "Now that's a horse to bet a paycheck on—wow." The pony rider whistles the melody while moving on, and as the sprightly tune fades, from midway down the shed row comes a sudden, WHAM!

Winston, Reggie and Kallie yank their gaze from the pony rider back to where the noise originated—stall eleven. Again the huge noise comes, WHAM, BAMB, and then a mournful, "I-eee," and several angry words in Spanish. An instant later, the stall door crashes open; out zooms a snorting thoroughbred dragging Juan—limp and helpless—on the end of the lead rope.

"Juan, Juan!" Winston yells, catching sight of his foreman on his belly behind the agitated horse. Still groggy, Juan summersaults to his feet and gives a desperate yank on the lead rope; the horse stops abruptly, squarely on all fours, and stares menacingly at Winston, Reggie and Kallie. Juan moans, "Ah—I-eee," raises his right foot, and curses in Spanish.

"Did he kick ya?" shouts Winston.

"N-ooo, he step on my fooo-t," he replies painfully.

"Here, I'll help ya," says Winston, approaching cautiously. Reggie and Kallie follow at a safe distance. Winston takes hold of the lead rope, and Juan begins to walk, but he limps badly. Winston passes the lead rope to Reggie, and takes Juan under tow, but the two struggle to maintain balance.

Seeing that Juan needs more help than Winston can provide, Reggie hands the horse to Kallie, saying, "Here Kallie, hold the horse..." Kallie takes the lead rope, gives it a sharp jerk to get the horse's attention; it responds as if stunned, and then stands quietly attending on Kallie's every move. Reggie goes to assist Juan and Winston. She takes hold of Juan's arm, and the three hobble back to the chair near the tack room. As she and Winston place Juan in the chair, Reggie leans over him, and asks, "Am I going to have to put you on the twenty-one day vet's list, Juan?"

"Nooo Señora, I be fine," he groans, removing his shoe. The toe of his stocking is stained red; he whimpers, slowly peeling it off to examine his mangled toes, "Ooo—Mister Winston, they look bad..."

"You should have a doctor look at that foot, see if anything is broken," Reggie advises.

"Yeah, Juan," adds Winston, "I'll take you to the infirmary when we're done with *Pennyante.*" And then, he whispers aside to Reggie, "I'm glad you brought help... He's a good hand—hate to see him laid-up."

"I can come back later if you want to take him to the doctor now..." she suggests.

"Nah, Juan's a tough one, let's get this done while you're here."

Reggie and Winston return to stall eleven where Kallie still holds Pennyante. Reggie walks to the frozen gelding, looks it over and asks, "The right front? Do you think it's the carpal joint, or the medial splint?"

"Don't know for sure," replies Winston. "Looks like it could be the knee, it's a little swollen, and it has some heat—you're the doc."

Reggie stands next to Pennyante and readies to palpate its right knee. Lifting the limb from the ground, and holding the hoof between her thighs, she kneads the small bones of the flexed joint. Next, she returns the limb to the ground and slides her fingers up and down both the inner and outer surfaces of the shin, and then she checks the flexor tendon. Finally she places her cupped hand over the front of the knee, holds it there for a few seconds, and says to Winston, "The joint feels clean to me, couldn't feel any floaters in it, and he showed no pain response. There is heat here though, and some swelling, but the swelling is more toward the medial, you know, the inside. I think he's got a minor separation—he's popped a splint—nothing serious. I can take X-rays if you want, but they won't show much—too early. You can put it off for a few days. We'll get a better picture then."

"Hum," he shrugs.
"Let's see how he jogs, okay? Kallie, trot Pennyante up the shed row, and then back…"
"Okay, Mom."

As Kallie walks Pennyante away from Winston and Reggie, the security guard in the golf cart that passed them earlier comes into view. Like a keystone cavalry of one, he bounces tenuously on the seat, and the police hat he's wearing, wobbles low on his forehead. Kallie begins to trot the horse away. With a casual glance, the security guard sees her, stops his cart dead, and surveys her intently.

Focused on the horse, Reggie doesn't notice the security guard, but Winston does. Swallowing deeply, he leans over to Reggie and whispers, "Oh-oh, the Hawk…"

Reggie replies quizzically, "Who?"

"Jim Peterson—the Hawk."

The guard leers a moment more, and then he drives up near Winston and Reggie and parks his cart on the grassy edge of the alleyway. Getting out, he saunters toward them. He's six feet tall. A skinny man, whose uniform fits poorly and hangs loosely over his shoulders. Strutting nearer, he says nothing. Reggie smiles at the narrow mustache protruding below his nose. "A bad attempt at hiding those lips," she giggles quietly, "No lips, just a beak." Then, she sees his most striking feature: thick, round glasses, through which his eyes appear like huge chickpeas, and she giggles aside, "Presbyopia too—bad luck for a hawk."

As Kallie begins the return jog from the far end of the shed row, the security guard stops, and stands motionless, silently observing her. Kallie brings the horse from a trot to a walk, halting by the assembly. Winston backs up sheepishly when the Hawk clears his throat, and asks, "Ah, Doctor, when ya ran the gate, ya didn't sign in your guest. Can I see your license, please?"

Surprised, but compliant, Reggie reaches into the hind pocket of her jeans, and pulls out her racing commission license; she hands it to the Hawk who squints at it closely. "You're current," he grumbles, handing the license back to her, and then he squints at Kallie. "An' what about the kid? Ya didn't sign her in."

"She's helping me out, I didn't know I had to sign in my daughter," replies Reggie.

"She's helpin' ya out, huh? This your first meet on the backside, Doc?"

"I just have a few clients here, my daughter is interested in racing, she wants..."

The Hawk cuts her off, turns to Kallie and barks, "What's your name kid?"

"Kallie Phillipa..."

"Ya got a license Kallie? Ya want to show it to me?"

"No..."

"No?"

"No, I don't have a license," replies Kallie.

"How old are you, Kallie?"

"I'll be sixteen in two weeks..."

"Oh-oh," scowls the Hawk. "This isn't good, this isn't good." He looks at Winston, who's face now reveals worry. "Winston Chase," he barks, "Ya know the rules, don't ya Winston?"

"What rules?" interrupts Reggie.

"State statutes, the 'Rules of Racing,' the law. They're printed in the back of every condition book. If ya want the whole set of laws, the Racing Commission will be glad to give ya a copy, so ya don't break the law. An' ya did, didn't ya Winston? Doc? You're using unlicensed, underage help."

"Ah, come on Jim," he pleads, "give Kallie a break. Here Kallie, I'll take the horse."

She stands firm and holds onto the lead. "I've worked with horses all my life," she states defiantly. "What's the big deal?"

"Look kid," the Hawk retorts, "I'll be glad to write ya up and report you to the stewards. They'll call you all in and fine the whole bunch of ya. It isn't gonna break my heart if ya get some days and a fine..."

"Kallie!" Reggie scolds.

The Hawk reaches in his pocket, takes out a tablet and pencil, and begins to spell, "K-A-L-L-I-I..."

Kallie thrusts the lead rope to Winston, and folds her arms across her flat chest. Winston returns the horse to the stall, strolls up to the Hawk, and asks, "Jim, can I talk to you for a minute?" His tone is more pleading than inquiring. The Hawk nods, and he and Winston step aside to converse in whispers. "Look Jim, no harm done," he grovels. "Juan got beat up by that two-year old of mine—maybe busted his foot. The Doc's kid just helped out a little. She's a good hand—we didn't even think. She wants to be a jockey—shees! Nobody knows better than me the crap she's gonna take. I started out as a muck-sack, an' I had to work twice as hard as anybody—she's a woman—the guys out here are gonna have her for breakfast..."

The Hawk nods agreement, the two shake hands and return to Reggie and Kallie. "Winston just told me that ya wanna be a jockey, kid. That takes a lot of guts—ya shouldn't waste them being smart to the guys who look after you, because jockeys get busted up enough on the track." He casts a scolding glare at Reggie and advises, "What ya did, Doc, is very serious, and I was serious about the fines. The rules are there to protect all of ya, jockeys, trainers, owners—all of us." He slides his enlarged eyes back to Kallie, and continues, "And Kallie, if ya really want to be a jockey, ya gotta learn the rules, and ya gotta live by the rules. I'll give ya a break this time—as a favor to Winston, and because he asked real politely." As the Hawk puts the tablet and pencil back in his pocket, everyone sighs relief. He spins on his heels, walks to his golf cart, turns back to Kallie and warns her, "You remember what I said about studying, kid." Then, getting into his golf cart, he mutters, "A jockey? Ha! Not today kid."

As the Hawk drives away, Winston leans over to Reggie and whispers, "He coulda' nabbed us—that was close..."

"Thanks, Winston for talking him out of it, we appreciate it. Don't we, Kallie?"

"Yeah, thanks Winston." And then she asks irreverently, "Are all the security guards turds?"

"Kallie! Knock it off!" scolds Reggie.

"He's not a turd, Kallie," Winston assures her, "he's a pretty decent guy. Racing is a hard life. You may need a friend someday, maybe you made one today—maybe not." Winston pauses, he reaches in his shirt pocket, takes out a tin of fine-cut snuff and digs out a two-finger dip. He replaces the lid, and holds the tin tenderly in his hand. "Now what about the horse?" he asks Reggie while packing the snuff inside his lower lip.

"Like I said, I don't think it's serious, just a small separation. The splint isn't broken... I'd hand walk him for the next few days, and stand him in ice. Do you have any *bute*?" Winston nods, yes. "Give him ten milligrams tonight, and again tomorrow morning... I'll stop back on Tuesday; we'll be able to tell more by then. Okay?"

Winston nods, yes, and reaches out to shake hands. "Thanks, Doc," he says with specks of tobacco marring his smile.

Reggie shakes his hand, and replies, "You're welcome Winston. You going to need any help getting Juan to the infirmary?"

"Nah. I'll throw him in the back of my pickup..."

"Yeah, thanks a lot Winston. Maybe tomorrow you'll win," adds Kallie. And as she and Reggie amble toward the van, she glances back and apologizes, "I'm sorry for being rude, Winston."

Just five minutes after leaving Dorchester Downs, the cell phone attached to the dash of Reggie's van rings. Reggie grabs it from the holster and answers, "Hello, this is Doctor Regina Phillipa..."

"Hi Doc," the voice in the phone starts, "this is Mike Reynolds."

"Hi, Mike. What do you need?"

"Well," the voice continues, "my mare seems to be colicky again. We've been walking her for two hours, and nothing—I can't hear any gut sounds. She's due to foal anytime now; she's all sweated up—I'm kind of worried we might loose the baby. Can you stop out?"

"Yeah, I'm just headed back from the track," replies Reggie glancing at the dashboard clock. "I can be there in about half an hour. Keep her walking, and don't let her back in her stall."

"Okay, Doc—hurry."

"Yeah, bye." Reggie presses the *end* button on the phone, and hands it to Kallie. "Here," she says, "I hate driving and talking on that thing at the same time. Can you call Dad and tell him we'll be later then I thought?"

Kallie takes the phone and presses the speed dial function, it rings and a man's voice answers, "Phillipa's..."

"Hi, Dad. Mom wanted me to tell you that we're going to be a little late. Somebody called—we gotta make a house-call."
"Mike Reynolds," Reggie interjects.
"Mom says, Mike Reynolds. We're going to stop by his place and have a look at his mare. You making pizza?"
"I've got a pot of basil pesto cooking," replies Anthony over the phone, "we'll have it with linguini. Is Mom handy?"
"Yeah, she's right here," she chirps, handing the phone to Reggie.
"Hi Tony—you know I hate to use the cell when I'm driving…"
"I know," he groans, exasperated at being scolded, "but I need some cabernet for supper, and some rosemary breadsticks. Can you stop and pick some up?"
"Could you send John?"
"Seal would have to drive him…" he replies.
"Okay. I'll stop at the liquor store, and there's a bakery next door. Anything else?"
"No. That's it, see you soon—I put a ton of garlic in the pesto—bye-bye."

Ending the call, Reggie hangs the phone on the dash, and remarks dryly, "Short detour, Kallie, this isn't going to take a minute—we have to get some stuff for supper." A few miles farther on, Reggie pulls the van into a strip mall. There's a twenty-four hour grocery, a liquor store, a bakery, a coffee shop—she wheels into an open parking space in front of the liquor store, and squeals to a halt. She turns off the ignition, hands Kallie a ten dollar bill, and says, "I'm going to run into the liquor store and get some wine. You run over to the bakery and get a dozen of the rosemary breadsticks—okay? We'll meet someplace in between."

Reggie and Kallie bound from the van and head in opposite directions. Reggie darts into the liquor store, grabs a waiting sales clerk, and they disappear among the wine racks. At the same time, Kallie rushes to the bakery door, swings it open, roars to the counter, places her order, and hands over the money. The clerk hands her change, she puts it in her pocket; he hands her a bag of breadsticks, and she zips from the store. Reggie zooms from the liquor store. The two rush toward each other and the van. They are about five feet from rejoining, when the door of the *Dangerous Grounds* coffee shop swings open, and out steps a regal gentleman, directly in their path. The three screech to a halt just before colliding. Coffee splashes from the cup the man carries, and a breadstick crashes into his tie.

"Oh! I'm sorry, Regina. Excuse me," bleats the startled man. He's in his late middle age, and his graying hair is manicured as perfectly as his fingernails. Glancing down at the fresh olive oil stain on his navy blue, linen necktie, he groans, "Oh, this will never do…"

Kallie, panicking, bends down to retrieve the breadstick, and when she begins to rise, she notices the man is wearing full seat riding breeches that blouse above the knees, and brown hunt boots with swan-neck spurs. "Oh-oh," she gasps.

"Ah, ah, excuse me Baron, we didn't see you…" Reggie apologizes breathlessly. "You alright?"

"Yes dear," is his terse reply.

"Good, good—bill me for the tie—see you Baron, sorry…"

Reggie and Kallie bolt for the van, leaving the startled man soiled and bewildered. They jump in, toss their groceries in the back seat, back up, and patch out. As they drive past the row of parked cars leading to the parking lot exit, Kallie sees the gentleman walk to, and enter an antique, black, *Jaguar* sedan. Reggie and Kallie pull out of the parking lot and onto the interstate toward Mike Reynolds' farm. The sun is fading. As they drive, Kallie asks, "Who was that guy, Mom?"

"What guy?" Reggie replies evasively.

"Hello-oh! That guy we almost killed; the guy with the coffee that you're gonna buy a tie for."

"Oh," she laughs, "that guy. He's a client—nobody important."

"A client? He called you dear; you called him baron, kind of cozy for not being important. Does he have a name? I'm not going to see you in the tabloids confessing a secret life, am I?"

"Yeah sure, me and the Baron—like *Lady And The Tramp* in reverse."

"What's his name?" Kallie pries. "And what's with this baron stuff—he looked more like one of those Royal Canadian Mounties."

"I really don't know," replies Reggie, pausing. "His name is *Albert Verrhaus*. He has that farm with the Queen Ann cottage off of Gleason Road. It's called 'Spring Ridge.' I really don't know much about him. I've never really talked to him—except on the phone. I've never seen anyone talk to him…"

"Suspicious," mutters Kallie.

"I've heard that he was the illegitimate son of some rich German nobleman, and that he got run out of town because he had an affair with his cousin."

"Wow! Now we are talking cool dirt."

"I also heard that he was a guard at Buckingham Palace," Reggie continues, "and when the Lord Chancellor was assassinated, he was badly injured, and left the army—I don't know, those are the rumors. I know he's a very private man, and really eccentric."

"Awesome…"

"Not awesome, odd-some! Get it?" quips Reggie. "Odd-some?" The two laugh at the pun, and drive on for half an hour in a silence, broken occasionally by Reggie singing to the oldies on the radio. Kallie nods into a cat-nap until Reggie announces, "We're here," as she turns from highway onto a humble, gravel driveway marked only with a mail box on which the name, *Reynolds* is hand lettered.

The Reynolds' driveway is lined on both sides by a three wire fence; the metal fence posts that support the wire are badly rusted, and the wire hangs loose from them here and there. Behind the fence, lay wide pastures that stretch to distant trees. At the far end of the drive, glowing red in the setting sun, is a crippled barn—like most midwestern barns its ridge pole has broken and the roof sags. Next to the barn, piled unrecognizably are the remains of a grain silo. A short distance from the barn and silo, an unassuming rambler crouches beneath a forest of weeping willows.

Reggie pulls the van to a stop in the open yard near the barn. Alone in the twilight, a frumpy woman in her late thirties struggles, encouraging a reluctant mare to walk. A woolen cooler that appears to have been a home to a family of mice hangs over the mare; it's wet, and steam rises above it from the horse's back. Faintly showing in the dim light, a well-worn path is trod in the gravel—clear evidence that the two have been walking the same course for a long time. As Reggie opens the door of the van to get out, the screen door on the rear of the rambler slams, and she sees a man approaching. It's Mike Reynolds and he walks briskly toward the van. "Hi, Mike," she says greeting him. "We got here as quick as we could. How's the mare doing?" Mike stares blankly, and doesn't answer.

"Not too good," Shelly Reynolds replies, catching her breath.

Reggie hustles to the rear of the van and lifts open the hatch grabbing a plastic tote from a veterinary trunk inside, then reaching back, she takes a stethoscope from the trunk, and hangs it around her neck. Kallie walks to the path Shelly and the horse have worn in the gravel. She stops, and watches the pair curiously. The mare's head is down, its every step seems labored; sweat drips from its fetlocks, and it groans mournfully.

"She's been like this for the last two hours," Shelly reports, holding back tears. "She started showing signs of colic about four o'clock—nothing serious—we started walking her right away. At six, she started to get worse."

Reggie has come from the van, and now stands next to Kallie. Mike joins them, and watching the activity, he comments, "Rotten luck. All the way through this pregnancy the mare's had trouble. Cheap horse is going to have one expensive foal."

"They don't always go the way we plan them, Mike," replies Reggie. "Stop her walking a second, Shelly, so I can have a look." Shelly stops the horse and steps to its shoulder where she waits. Reggie walks to the horse, places the tote on the ground next to its flank, and removes the blanket handing it to Shelly. Placing her hand on the horse's back, she strokes the mare tenderly toward the withers and pats its neck, whispering, "Pregnancy sucks, doesn't it Boo-boo?" Reggie takes the stethoscope from her neck and examines the horse in silence. First she listens for intestinal sounds, and then she listens for respiration and heart rate. "Hum..." she murmurs, removing the stethoscope from her ears, and hanging it around her neck. Next, she takes a small flashlight from the tote, and walks to the mare's head to examine its eyes. "Try to get her to lift her head, Shelly," she instructs. Shelly gives a short jerk on the lead, and the mare raises her head. Reggie reaches a hand to the mare's half closed left eye, she holds it open with her fingers and shines the beam across the pupil several times, and then does the same to the other eye. "Her eyes are clear, but she's in a lot of pain. Let's check her gums." Reggie clinches the lighted flashlight in between her teeth, and then, standing in front of the horse, she rubs its nose, and lifts its upper lip. She touches the gum with her index finger, and watches closely. "Slow response, and not much color... She's impacted pretty good."

"Is it worse than the other times?" asks Shelly.

"Yeah. I'm going to have to get some oil in her. Hope it works."

"Think her gut's twisted?" asks Mike, pleading desperately for a positive report.

"No—I can't really tell for sure. You haven't let her lie down, or roll, have you?" Reggie asks, turning to Shelly.

"She went down a couple of times, but she didn't roll."

"Good. Kallie? Will you get the stainless steel bucket and the injector pump from the van? Mike, I'm going to need a couple buckets of warm water..."

Kallie scurries to the van; Mike hustles to the barn where several buckets are stacked outside the door. He takes two, and jogs off toward the house. Reggie turns to Shelly, still holding the mare, and says, "She'll be fine, Shelly. We've been through this before with Boo-Boo..."

"God! Why does she colic so much?" Shelly asks weeping.

"First foal. A lot of mares have trouble with the first one. If men only knew what they put us gals through..." Reggie comments, patting Boo-Boo's neck. And then, rubbing Shelly's shoulder to console her, she adds, "Men don't have a clue."

"Yeah, let one of them get pregnant," replies Shelly, laughing through her tears, "the world would screech to a stop to hear them cry!"

"Why don't you keep her walking, it'll make you both feel better."

Shelly starts to walk Boo-Boo around the path again. As they walk together, she asks Reggie, "Do you think the foal is okay? She's so close to delivering..."

"I could hear its heartbeat, that's a good sign. She's fully waxed, and she's lactating—it should be fine. We'll tube her and see what happens. The oil should loosen her up."

"God, I hope so..."

"But just in case," Reggie continues, "have Mike hitch the trailer. If we don't get something to pass in half an hour, I'd like to ship her to the clinic—just in case."

"That won't make him happy—he's been grumbling for months that this broodmare thing is a mistake—we had no idea how much all this stuff cost. All he could think of is making a killing at the track."

"We'll work something out on the bill, Shelly..."

"Mike's been off work since January," Shelly mentions, beginning to sob again. "And there's no sign that the union will settle anytime soon. We'll be able to pay you when he goes back to work—we've been living off our savings, and what I make at the daycare..."

Just then Kallie returns from the van with a stainless-steel bucket, an injection pump that looks more like a grease gun than a medical device, a length of clear plastic hose, and a container of mineral oil. Overhead, a yard light flashes on, and illuminates the barnyard. "Is that everything you need, Mom?" she asks, gesturing to the bucket.

Reggie surveys the equipment, and nods, yes. Then she whispers, "As soon as Mike gets back, we can tube her. Can you help me out, Kallie?"

"Yeah," she replies. "Same as last time?" Reggie nods, yes. "Okay, I'll get the twitch."

While Kallie is rummaging in the van for the twitch, Mike is walking toward Reggie, Shelly and the mare. He carries two steaming buckets that he sets on the ground near the walking path. When Kallie returns with the twitch, Mike asks, "Need anything else, need me to hold the horse?"

"Thanks, Mike, but Shelly can handle it," replies Reggie. Then, she suggests, "Stand still, Shelly, and keep a strong hold on the lead rope." She gestures for her to stand near the mare's left shoulder, and then she nods to Kallie to apply the twitch to Boo-Boo's nose. Kallie slides the chain of the twitch over her right wrist; grabs hold of the mare's nose, and gently twists. Then, in a quick motion, she slides the chain from her wrist, over her hand, onto the mare's nose, and twists the handle to snug the chain. The mare jerks her head and tenses briefly. Reggie, who is standing in front of the horse, has been filling the injection pump with oil. She hangs the ready device on a loop connected to her belt. As the next step in a choreographed dance, she takes the clear plastic hose and begins to insert it the mare's right nostril.

Shelly looks away grimacing, and mentions, "Mike, Reggie asked if you could hitch up the trailer? We might have to ship Boo-Boo to the clinic…"

"What? No way! We can't afford that!"

"Just a precaution, Mike, we probably won't have to ship her," replies Reggie.

"We're into you for more than twenty-seven hundred bucks now," Mike shouts gesturing with two fingers. "That's twice what I paid for her!"

"If we don't get a stool out of her soon, you could loose her, and the foal—I don't think we should take the chance," Reggie responds emphatically.

"God, Mike!" Shelly pleads through renewed tears, "Is that what you want?"

"Get a grip, for Christ's sake, Shelly—of course I don't want that. I don't want to get so deep in the hole that I won't get out, either!"

"Quiet! Please!" snaps Reggie, irritated by the quarreling. "I've got to hear if I'm in the stomach or the trachea…" Reggie has the open end of the inserted hose held close to her ear; she listens carefully, gently sliding in the hose inch-by-inch. She pauses, and probing to feel her location, she says quietly, "Good, there…" and quickly inserts the rest of the hose into the mare's nostril. Reggie then reaches for the injection pump, connects the nozzle to the hose, and using both hands and all her might, she depresses the plunger. "That's never easy…" she grunts as she disconnects the pump and refills it with warm water. She repeats the process several times. "Let's hope this is all she needs."

"Yeah," Mike agrees, kicking at a dirt clod. "You still going to need the trailer?"

"Just hook up the damn trailer, Mike!" Shelly scolds, her voice now clear and free of tears. With his head down and shaking it side to side, Mike walks away grumbling to himself.

"Loosen the twitch as I take out the tube, Kallie. Be ready Shelly, she's going to cough some. Okay? Everyone ready?" With that, Reggie, in one quick move, withdraws the tube from Boo-Boo's nostril. Kallie releases the twitch and steps away cautiously. The mare drops her head, and begins to gag and cough frantically. "Start her walking again, Shelly. Don't let her stop," Reggie barks. "Kallie, could you clean up my equipment, and then give Shelly a break?"

"Sure Mom."

"Shelly, can I use your bathroom? I've had to pee since I left the track."

"Do you remember where it is?"

"I think so. Just off the kitchen, by the back door?"

"Yeah."

"I'll be back in a jiff..." Reggie says, glancing at her watch, and then she makes a hasty jog to the house.

Kallie cleans the equipment and returns it to the back of the van. Shelly continues to walk Boo-Boo. "Do you need a rest, Shelly? I can walk her if you like."

"Those are the kindest words I've heard all day, Kallie—yeah," she replies, and then adds, "You know, I'd kill for something cold to drink..."

"Hey, I got a soda in the cooler. Do you want it?" Kallie reaches into a small plastic cooler in between the front seats, and takes out a bottle of soda pop. "Here," she says, walking toward Shelly, and handing her the bottle.

Shelly stops, gives the lead rope to Kallie, and takes the pop. "Phssst!" it fizzes as Shelly opens the cap. She pours back a quenching drink, and then sighs gratefully as she says, "Thanks, Kallie. Your mom's saving Boo-Boo's life, now you're saving mine. Will you be okay if I run up to the house for a second? I have to pee too."

"I'm pretty good with horses, Shelly," she answers. "You don't have to worry—go take a pee..."

Too Far A Dream

Moments after Shelly walks to the house, the kitchen light, and the back porch light come on—night is falling. Under the glow of the yard light, Kallie walks alone with Boo-Boo and talks to her in soothing tones, "Not feeling so hot, hey girl? Don't worry, we'll take care of you." She rubs Boo-Boo's neck affectionately. "You're gonna be a mommy soon—you're gonna be the mom of a little racehorse..." Kallie sighs and looks skyward at the faint twinkling of the evening's first stars, and breaths the words, "maybe a derby winner..." She sighs again as she looks at Boo-Boo's glazed eyes, and then, leaning forward as she walks, she whispers, "You have this baby, Boo-Boo, and I'll ride it." Just then, the mare groans to a faltering stop, and collapses on her right knee. "No, Boo-Boo! Get up, keep walking!" Kallie commands worriedly. "No, no!" She gives a firm tug on the lead rope, but the mare is determined. Reaching forward with her left forelimb, the mare squats on her haunches, and falls onto her side. "Get up Boo-Boo!" Kallie shouts, tugging on the rope with all her strength. The mare throws back her head. Rubbing her neck in the gravel, Boo-Boo groans, catching shallow gulps of air as she thrashes. Mike comes from behind the barn, walking at first, and then, seeing Kallie struggling with the downed mare, he breaks into a panicked dash toward her.

"Kallie!" he shouts, "Get the horse up—don't let her roll! Get up you stupid mare! Doc, Shelly!" Mike grabs the lead rope from Kallie and yanks desperately. Reluctantly, Boo-Boo briefly lifts her head, and then flops it back on the dirt.

Kallie runs behind and grabs the mare's tail. She tugs, swats its rump, and shouts, "Haw! Get up, haw Boo-Boo!" The mare lifts her head, rolls upright, straightens her forelimbs in front of her, and rises to stand on all fours. Mike gawks at Boo-Boo in disbelief. Her right side and back are covered in slime, mud and sweat. "Damn it Mike!" shouts Kallie. "Get her walking, don't just stand there—hup, hup, hup Boo-Boo!"

"Christ, kid, don't bark at me. You're the one who let her go down!" Mike jeers angrily as he pulls Boo-Boo into a labored walk.

"Mike! Mike, what happened?" Shelly cries, running to confront him.

"She went down and rolled," he answers, casting a blameful look at Kallie.

"Mom, I couldn't stop her—honest, I tried." Kallie's lower lip begins to quiver. She's angry with Mike for blaming her, and anxious about Boo-Boo's prospects.

"It's okay, Kallie," Reggie says, comforting her. "Mike, let me check her over again. Then, go pull the truck around, and drop the ramp…"

Mike stops walking Boo-Boo. As Shelly approaches and takes the lead rope, Mike shuffles into the darkness behind the barn. Reggie removes the stethoscope from her neck and listens to Boo-Boo's gut. "Nothing," she mutters as the mare drops her head and groans—her knees buckle and she threatens to go down again. "Up! Up, stay up," Reggie shouts while slapping Boo-Boo on the flank. The mare obeys, and stands languid and still. Quickly, Reggie shifts to Boo-Boo's head; she lifts the mare's upper lip checking its gums. "Shit," she whispers, "they're white, and the tongue is turning blue; it looks like peritonitis. Shelly, this girl's in trouble. We have to ship her—now."

Shelly starts bawling, "Are we going to loose her? What if she goes down in the trailer?"

"Shelly," Reggie advises, trying to calm and reassure her, "we need you, we need you to be tough. Colic or not, this mare has got to have this baby soon. Otherwise it doesn't have a chance—we could loose them both."

"You're right, Reggie," replies Shelly, holding back her tears. "How can I help?"

"When Mike brings the trailer, you load Boo-Boo as fast as you can. Make sure you tie the lead off on the upper hook. That way she can't go down…"

"What do you want me to do, Mom?" asks Kallie, her voice quivering nervously.

"Get behind the mare, and push…"

The urgent roar of the truck and trailer plunging from the darkness cracks what brittle calm the moment reserved. Pebbles jut from its arrested tires as Mike slams the truck to a stop. Its motor idles unevenly. Mike leaps out.

"Mike! We have to ship this mare now. Drop the ramp..." Mike runs to the rear of the trailer and drops the ramp—it thuds to the ground, lifting a cloud of dust. "Shelly, get her going... "Kallie, follow me." Shelly leads Boo-Boo to the back of the trailer; Reggie and Kallie follow behind the mare. Turning to Kallie as they walk, Reggie speaks emphatically, "Kallie, when Shelly gets Boo-Boo to the trailer, we'll link arms behind her butt. I'll get on her left; you get on her right. Remember how we do this?"

"Yeah, Mom..."

"Hold onto my arm tight, don't let Boo-Boo back up. We may not get a second chance." Shelly and the mare approach the open trailer. Reggie and Kallie link up, and using their arms as a guide rope behind the mare's haunches, they urge her forward. Shelly enters the trailer, followed by Boo-Boo. Mike's posted beside the trailer ready to assist. Halfway in, the mare hesitates. "Mike," Reggie shouts, "slap her on the ass!" Mike slaps. Reggie and Kallie push. Boo-Boo budges inward.

"She's in, Reggie!"

"Great, tie her off quick, Shelly, and get the hell out—she might start thrashing. Help us with the ramp, Mike." He dashes over to Kallie straining at lifting the ramp—they lift together. Reggie grapples with the other side and latches it. Shelly bounds from the front escape door of the trailer as if launched from a slingshot. She hits the ground flat with both feet, wheels back, and slams the door shut. "Good! Let's get this girl on the road," Reggie yells, wiping her hands on her jeans. Shelly runs to the passenger's seat of the truck cab and jumps in; Mike gets in the other side to drive. Reggie and Kallie jog to the van.

"Should I go first, or follow?" Mike quizzes anxiously from his rolled down window.

"You lead, Mike," Reggie shouts back, "We'll follow behind to make sure the mare doesn't get loose and go down."

Mike pulls out slowly, and then accelerates down the driveway. Reggie, driving the van, follows close behind. After only seconds into the trip, Reggie asks, "Kallie, could you reach in the glove box and get me a napkin or a tissue—I'm sweating like a pig."

Kallie opens the compartment, and searches. "Here, Mom," she says, handing Reggie a crumpled napkin.

"It smells like ketchup," Reggie complains, sopping sweat from her cheeks, and then, casting the napkin to the floorboards, she reaches for the cell phone.

"I'll get it, Mom," Kallie says, pulling the phone from its holster on the dash. "Who do you want to call?'

"Dad. I need him to set up the birthing stall in the clinic—tell him to put down straw, not shavings. And tell him to take the colostrum from the fridge and put it in warm water."

Kallie dials the phone; a man's voice answers, "Phillipa's."

"Dad?"

"Yeah…"

"It's Kallie," she says, speaking slowly, "we have an emergency. We're shipping Mike and Shelly's mare to the clinic. Mom needs you to do some things for her."

"It's pretty serious, Kallie? You and Mom okay?"

"We're good, Dad…" Kallie continues. "She needs you to put straw in the foaling stall. Dad? Got it? Straw, not shavings."

"Straw," Anthony replies over the phone, "okay."

"And she wants you to get the milk from the fridge—the colostrum—and start it warming up."

"Tell him to get John to help with the straw," Reggie interrupts. "Tell him we should be pulling in," she glances at the clock on the dash, "in about twenty minutes."

"Did you hear that, Dad? Mom said, to have Uncle John help you, we'll be there in twenty minutes."

"Got it Kallie. Anything else?"

"Anything else, Mom?" she relays to Reggie.

"Tell Daddy, that when John's done helping him, make sure he and Seal go back to the house—this delivery could get ugly real fast."

"Did you get that? Mom doesn't want Aunt Seal and Uncle John to see this…"

"Got it Kallie," Anthony responds. "Drive swift and safe, there's a severe weather warning posted—we could see some thunderstorms later…"

Too Far A Dream

"Thanks Daddy, we will—love you pal."

Kallie presses the *end* button on the phone and reaches to hang it on the dash.

"Don't hang it up yet," Reggie says, stopping her, "I might need some help with this. Call Carl Kassman; see if he could stay by his phone in case I have to rescue the foal. His number is in my address book—I'll need to talk to him."

Kallie checks for Doctor Kassman's number in the menu, she hits speed-dial, a man's voice answers, Kallie hands the phone to Reggie. "Carl, this is Reggie. I'm shipping a pregnant mare to my clinic—she's showing signs of a severe colic. Carl," Reggie pauses, clearing her throat, and then continues in a lowered tone of voice, "I'm not sure, but I think she may have twisted the gravid uterus. I'll try to correct it rectally when I get to the clinic, but if I can't, I'll have to do a caesarian to rescue the foal. I may need your help. Can you be ready to come over if I call?"

"Is she showing any signs of dehydration?" Carl asks. "Have you noticed any uterine congestion?"

"None, no outward signs. I just don't like the symptoms she's presenting."

"Does the foal appear to be in distress?"

"No. I'm pretty sure it's okay, its heartbeat seems steady."

"Good. I'll wait by the phone Reggie, call me if you need help."

"Thanks Carl—I owe you big time," she says, ending the call and hanging the phone in its dashboard holster. Kallie's attention is focused on the trailer ahead. Illuminated by the headlights, Boo-Boo's tail swishes, buffeted by the back draft as Mike's truck speeds into the dark.

Overhead at Longview Stables, comforting yard lights defy the crushing night. The arched doors of the boarding stable that also houses the veterinary clinic are swung open, and all the interior lights are lit. Anthony and John are in the trauma theatre making preparations for Boo-Boo's arrival. The theatre's interior walls are white—white, spotless white. Off center in the room, an overhead, swing-arm winch, with an attached sling, dangles from the ceiling, and below the sling, a huge, stoutly built stainless steel table waits ready, should its service be needed. An X-ray machine, like an egret on one stilt, props nearby. Along two walls are cupboards stocked with pharmaceuticals, bandages and other medical supplies. Occupying the third wall are twin box stalls. The door of one of the stalls has been removed, and inside Anthony and John work. "That good enough, Tony, or should I get another bale?"

Anthony fluffs the straw several times with a pitchfork. "That should do it," he replies while nodding to John to leave the stall. Anthony follows him out, and carries the pitchfork to the side of the stall, hanging it from a tool rack above his head. Then, glancing at his wristwatch, he mumbles, "It's been more than twenty minutes—they should be pulling in any second now." He glances over to John, and suggests, "Why don't you head back to the house and get the pasta ready—just enough for the three of us, I don't think Reggie and Kallie will be eating for a while."

"What about the breadsticks and the wine?" John pesters.

"For Christ's sake," he replies perturbed, "I'll get them from Reggie when she gets here. Now get going. She said she doesn't want you hanging around—she may have to operate. Go!"

As Anthony and John leave the trauma theatre and walk down the center aisle toward the arched doors, they pass several stalls with horses in them. When they reach the archway facing the turnaround, Anthony stops, and stares out toward his manicured driveway. John leaves him there, and disappears into the darkness in the direction of the house. Two sets of flickering headlights grow brighter as they approach; when they enter the turnaround, the truck and trailer lead. Desperation rages inside the trailer—the sounds of kicking and stomping report as evidence. The truck and trailer screech to a halt, followed closely by the van. Reggie and Kallie jump from the van and rush to the rear of the trailer. Mike and Shelly burst from the truck and join them. Seeing Anthony standing in the doorway of the stable, Reggie quizzes hurriedly, "Is everything ready?"

"Good to go Doc, need any help?"

Too Far A Dream

"Not right now—thanks Tony, you're a saint. The groceries are in the back seat of the van—don't put anything on for me." She wrenches free one of the latches to the ramp…

"Shelly, did you have a bucket of water in the trailer," Kallie interrupts, pointing below the tailgate. "What's leaking?"

Everyone's attention focuses on the ground at the back of the trailer, a puddle is forming. Reggie lifts Boo-Boo's tail, a thick, white amnion sac is visible protruding from the mare's vulva. "Oh shit! She's broken water," she squeals, "the sac is protruding; this girl's going to drop her foal right out the trailer. Mike, undo that latch. Anthony! Anthony! Run in and take the door and front panel off the stall…"

"Already done," he shouts back.

Shelly wails hysterically. Reggie glances at her, and advises her sternly, "Shelly, stand back," and then she turns to Kallie, and orders, "Kallie, get in the trailer and undo the mare—Mike, you and I are going to drop the ramp. Kallie, get Boo-Boo out fast!"

Kallie runs to the escape door of the trailer, opens it, and climbs inside. Her voice comes as a raspy yelp exclaiming, "Ready Mom!" Just then Boo-Boo starts to kick, and jostle violently. "Drop the damn ramp, Mom," cries Kallie, "I can't hold her. She's coming out!" Reggie and Mike drop the ramp, and leap out of the way as the distressed mare scrambles backward dragging Kallie along with her. "Whoa girl, whoa." Kallie pleads, tugging on the lead rope. Boo-Boo obeys and stops, and then attempts to lie down. "Hup!" cries Kallie, jerking on the rope.

"No, no, no!" yells Reggie frantically. "Get her in the clinic, Kallie! Run, run!" To urge her, Mike spanks Boo-Boo on the rump; Kallie yanks at the lead rope, and Boo-Boo staggers forward—her head dragging, moaning. "Shelly," Reggie says, clasping her arm tenderly, "maybe you should go into the house for a while. Celeste and John are there; have some coffee; keep an eye on things for me…"

"Okay Reggie," she sobs. "Please try to save the baby…."

"Yes, yes," Reggie replies, attempting to soothe her, and at the same time not betray any urgency. "I'll do everything I can—trust me. Oh, if you want to help, could you grab the wine and breadsticks from my van, and bring them up to the house?"

"Sure," replies Shelly, recovering enough to answer.

"Thanks. Mike, you're with me!" she barks, diverting her attention from Shelly to Mike, shooing him into a jog toward the stable.

It takes what seems like endless moments to encourage Boo-Boo from the turnaround into the sterile trauma theatre. Once in, Reggie snaps out orders, "Kallie, put her in the stall, if she starts to go down, stand clear and let her. Anthony, call Carl Kassman. Tell him I need his help. Mike, stay the hell out of the way unless I need you."

Kallie leads Boo-Boo into the open stall. The mare groans, paws at the straw, sniffs it, and then splaying her limbs, she crumbles heavily down. Kallie takes off her halter, coils the lead rope around it and tosses it over the stall partition into the next stall. Then she kneels next to Boo-Boo's head, and says quietly, "Remember what I said girl, you have this baby, and I'll ride it…"

Boo-Boo starts to thrash and groan. Across the theatre, Reggie puts on a turquoise, surgical smock and plastic gloves while Anthony talks anxiously on a wall phone. Reggie goes to the cupboard beside the fridge, and takes out a roll of white elastic bandage; she walks over to the stall, lifts the mare's tail, gathering the loose hair into a tight skein, and wraps it in the bandage. Then she kneels to examine the amnion sac, and what appears to be one small hoof protruding from the vulva.

"Carl will be right over, Reggie," Anthony shouts from the phone.

"Thanks, Tony," she responds. "Kallie, check her gums, what color are they?"

"They're white—maybe yellow, and her tongue is blue."

"Shit!" Reggie curses, putting her stethoscope on, "I was afraid of this…" She presses the diaphragm to the mare's gut, and listens—the gravity of her expression intensifies—then she listens to Boo-Boo's failing heart. "Anthony, wheel my instrument cart over here. Mike, maybe you should run up to the house for a while, you might not want to watch this." Mike paces indifferently, ignoring her advice.

Too Far A Dream

    Anthony pulls the stainless steel cart from its docking station under the countertop that separates a bank of overhead cupboards from the base cabinets below; heavily stocked with surgical knives, forceps and other instruments, swabs, and antiseptic vials, it's cumbersome to move, and Anthony struggles. Boo-Boo moans painfully; gasping for breath, her head jerks convulsively, blood oozes from her vulva. When Anthony delivers the cart to her, Reggie removes the stethoscope and tosses it to Anthony. She pushes the rolled cuff of the plastic glove over her right garment sleeve, inserts her arm, probing the mare's rectum, and reports, "It's twisted," she probes deeper, "and the foal's inverted." And then, withdrawing her arm from inside Boo-Boo, and stripping off the glove, she concedes, "the baby isn't coming out this way." Her anxiety is growing; she can't conceal it, and she wonders aloud, "Where the hell is Carl?"

    Just then the lights blink off momentarily; thunder rumbles in the distance, and shards of clay, thrust from the turnaround by an impatient wind, scour the clapboard siding outside. "Shit! Just what we need..." Reggie growls, going to the cart and putting on clean, latex surgical gloves. Without ceremony, she walks to a cupboard above the docking station, unlocks it, takes out a hypodermic needle and a vile of liquid. She fills the syringe and returns to the mare. "Kallie, kneel on Boo-Boo's neck for a minute. Keep her from moving," Reggie advises, "I'm going to have to sedate her." Kallie kneels across the mare's neck. Reggie, squats opposite her, and pats on Boo-Boo's neck to raise a vein. Kallie grimaces. Reggie inserts the needle in the mare's neck, and injects the sedative.

    "What are you doing?" Mike asks, hovering anxiously.

    "Knocking her out..."

    "What the hell for? The foal's hoof is showing."

    "Wrong hoof, Mike. I'm going to deliver the foal by caesarian section."

    "By yourself, why? Can't you wait?"

    "Sorry Mike," she replies, "Boo-Boo's uterus has twisted, the foal is malpresented and trapped within the birth canal."

    "For Christ's sake! You can reach in and correct the position—they do it with cows..."

"Normally I could, but not with the uterus twisted, this is serious. If I wait any longer, the foal will suffocate."

"Reggie," Anthony interrupts, "she's really bleeding bad. You should have a look at this."

Reggie springs from beside the mare's neck and goes to its haunch. Blood flows in steady pulse from the vulva, like quick magma, it advances in a crimson sheet that spreads beyond the stall. "Christ! She's hemorrhaging. Mike?" Mike has turned away from the sight, he wretches as if he's about to vomit, and staggers from the room. "Worthless asshole." Reggie mutters. "Anthony, you're going to have to help me lift the foal out when I open up the mare. Kallie, keep kneeling on her neck, the sedative hasn't had enough time to work—keep her still, but be ready to get over here if we need you."

Tears fill Kallie's eyes, and her nose runs; she sniffles, "Okay Mom."

"You okay with this, Tony?"

"I better be..." he replies. "Should I put on a smock?"

"It ain't gonna help, honey..." Just then, WHAM! The stable shakes as the wind slams the archway doors closed. Kallie cringes at the unexpected sound. The growl of thunder preys nearby. "Let's hope the lights stay on long enough to get this done," Reggie says, going to the instrument cart. Selecting a scalpel from among many on a tray; she returns to Boo-Boo who now lays gasping—her breathing uncertain and irregular. Reggie studies Anthony's face, she's seen his expression before—he's worried. As calmly as she can, Reggie describes the procedure: "I'm going to have to make a couple of incisions, Anthony. One in the side of her abdomen to get to the uterus, and a second to open the uterus up, it's going to be messy..." Anthony nods that he understands. As Reggie kneels, poised to begin the operation, she whispers, "Say a little prayer for Boo-Boo, Kallie. I'm not going to be able to save her... Is everybody ready?" Anthony nods.

Whimpering, Kallie crouches over Boo-Boo's head; shielding the mare's eyes in a grieving embrace, she prays, "You'll race with the clouds, Boo-Boo," and then, her held-back tears burst in a sobbing torrent. The only other sounds are from the wind harassing the trees, and thunder, muted by the bluffs.

Reggie edges closer to the mare's abdomen; she reaches with her left hand, feeling for the base of the rib cage. In her right hand is the scalpel. She works deftly, making a long incision from the sternum back to Boo-Boo's hip. Anthony kneels beside; his attention fixed on Reggie's hands. She makes a second incision, deeper, to penetrate the abdominal wall. The viscera extrude. Blood spills. Feeble kicking jars the mass of exposed organs. Reggie puts the scalpel aside, and reaches in. "Anthony," she says, "Before I open the uterus, I'll try to free the foal's head and limbs from the birth canal, when I pull, reach in behind me… See this?" she asks, indicating by nodding her head where he should reach.

"Yeah," Anthony replies.

"That's where the foal's hind limbs are. Grab hold and lift when I tell you."

Anthony reaches to where Reggie instructed and waits; Reggie probes deep within the mare's body cavity, and then yanks powerfully. "Now, Tony," she grunts, "lift now!"

"Ugh," he groans straining to pull the organ clear. "Got it—oh shit—it's slippery. I'm going to drop it!"

"That's okay Tony, don't worry. Just lift it out of the way—there!" Reggie exclaims as Anthony flops the enormous organ aside. The amnion is pale white; and now, there is no movement visible from within. "Move it a little farther away," advises Reggie, "I'm going to need room to work." Anthony drags the pale sac away from the mare—the umbilical trails behind. Reggie crawls to it, and feels along the slimy surface orienting herself to its internal features, "There, that's the head," she says, grabbing the scalpel and cutting away the sac to expose the foal's head. The foal is not breathing. Reggie lifts its head, and peers into its nostrils. "They're full of mucus, grab that suction bulb from the tray, Anthony," she orders frantically.

Anthony jumps up, grabs an instrument from the tray, and hands it to Reggie. "Here. Is this what you need?"

49

Glancing at it, Reggie nods, yes, and inserts the suction bulb in the foal's nose. She draws out mucus, and then repeats the same operation on the other nostril. The foal is not breathing yet. Reggie enlarges the incision and frees the foal from the uterus; lifts it up from under its belly so that the hind legs are off the floor, and the head and neck are lowered. "Pat it on the ribs, Anthony, use the flat of your hand and pat rapidly on his ribs."

Anthony pats the foal; water runs from its nose.

"What's happening, Mom?" Kallie asks, kneeling upright, her face is pale; her expression vacant. "Why isn't it breathing?"

"This happens sometimes, Kallie. Its lungs are full of fluid, I'm draining them now, I'll have to do some resuscitation…"

From outside the stable comes the thump of a car door closing, followed by the sound of rushing feet. A breathless man appears at the door of the operating theatre. In his hand, he carries a tote bristling with surgical devices. He scans the horrific scene quickly. "Holy cow, Reggie!" he exclaims.

"Carl! Thank God, you're here."

"I drove as fast as I could. The wind is getting really bad out there, and they've upgraded the thunderstorm watch to a tornado warning. What do you need me to do?"

"I've got this part under control, but the mare is suffering," Reggie replies. "Her gut is twisted, and she's hemorrhaged a lot of blood—we can't save her; we need to put her down."

Kallie jumps up and erupts in tears; she covers her eyes, and sobs.

Carl takes a syringe and a small vile of clear liquid from his tote. Preparing a lethal dosage, he walks over to Boo-Boo, who now rests somberly; he kneels beside her neck, and inserts the needle. "Kallie," he says, returning to his feet, "step back a little, she may kick some—she's not in any pain, it's just a reflex to the medicine."

Kallie weeps as she leaves the stall; with her head bowed, she shuffles to where Reggie and Anthony are treating the foal. Boo-Boo exhales loudly in the background; she thrashes mildly and quits. Kallie knows what's just taken place behind her back—the mare has died. Sniffling, she watches her mother. Reggie has laid the foal back on the floor, and now holds its nose in her hands. With one, she pinches the foal's lips; with the other, she supports its head. She places her mouth over the foal's nostrils and blows deeply, pauses, and does it again for several breaths in succession. "Carl," she asks, "could you check its pulse—see if we have a heart beat?"

Carl takes the blood-spattered stethoscope that lies beside Anthony, puts it on, and listens for a heartbeat. "Got one Reggie," he replies, "keep breathing. I'll cut the umbilical." Reggie continues the resuscitation, while Carl clamps a forceps on the umbilical, and then cuts the cord. Reaching into his tote, he takes out a gauze pad and iodine, swabs the severed navel, then glances at Reggie and asks, "Do you have any colostrum here? The foal is going to need it soon."

"There's a nursing bottle set up in the sink, it's heating up, it should be warm by now," Anthony replies.

Just then, the foal's hind limb twitches gamely, Reggie removes her mouth from its nose, it snorts, spewing mucus all over Reggie's face, and then it gasps to life.

Exuberant, Kallie shouts, "Yes! Holy cow, it's breathing. It's alive!"

Anthony, still kneeling, clasps his hands together in his lap; he looks at Reggie, and beams proudly. Their eyes meet. His deep brown eyes fill with tears; he blinks to hide them, but they flow down his cheeks, glistening. With the foal's head cradled in her lap, Reggie smiles at her husband adoringly. She leans forward, wiping the mucus from her lips, and then, she wipes the tears from Anthony's cheeks, and kisses him. "Tony," she whispers, "you're a saint—and a real softie. And, you're really brave."

"Shoot darlin', it weren't nothin'," he drawls, humbly.

Carl returns with the nursing bottle. "This should be warm enough," he says, handing the bottle to Reggie. She shakes a drop of milk on her arm and nods agreement. "Should I close the mare up, or just put a sheet over her?"

"A sheet is fine—thanks Carl," she answers, and then, placing the nipple in the foal's mouth, it begins to suckle. "Well that's a good sign," she sighs, "it has a good appetite."

"Mom," Kallie interrupts, "you haven't checked to see what sex it is."

Anthony lifts one of the foal's outstretched hind limbs, glances in and announces, "It's a colt, Kallie, it's a hungry little boy."

Just then, off in the distance, a warning siren wails over the rumble of nearing thunder. Anthony stands up. Looking at Carl he asks, "Hear that Carl? It's either a severe thunderstorm, or they've issued a tornado warning."

"Springtime," sighs Carl, "snow one day, and the next, tornados. I better make a run for it, Reggie. You going to need me anymore tonight?"

"No Carl," she replies. "Go on, get out of here—give Trudy a hug for us. And Carl, thanks."

Carl dashes from the operating room, and down the aisle that leads outside. The storm confronts him at the door. Lightening hacks through the night sky, opening wounds of fatal daylight; immodest gusts defile the Sabine oaks; twigs, like tangled webs spun by wooden spiders thatch the ground; the sirens gasp, then wail no more. Hiding his worry, Anthony turns to Kallie, and suggests, "Kallie, run up to the house and stay there. Tell everyone to be ready to head to the cellar. Mom and I will be up as soon as we can."

"What about the baby?" Kallie asks desperately.

"He needs to nurse a little more," Reggie reassures her. "Dad and I will get him cleaned up and bring him into the basement with us—God I hate tornados."

"Go on Kallie," he repeats sternly. "Get your butt up to the house."

Kallie runs down the aisle and out of sight. Anthony goes to a stainless steel washbasin, fills a shallow bowl with water, and wets a towel. He returns to Reggie, and wipes her face tenderly, and then he sponges the foal.

In the living room of the house, the television is turned on, and a weather report is in progress. John and Celeste are seated on the edge of the couch anxiously watching the telecast. Mike props against the armrest of the couch; Shelly stands next to him. A strident voice comes from the TV:

> *"The National Weather Service has just issued a severe thunderstorm warning for all of Redwing County, and portions of Goodhue County in the southeastern part of the State. These thunderstorms have a history of producing tornados, high winds, hail and heavy rains. Be prepared to seek shelter..."*

The front door swings open, and inside bounds Kallie pursued by savage gusts. The door slams behind her. She runs into the living room, the dogs rush to greet her, but slink away when they smell the scent of the blood staining her clothes. "Hey everybody," she announces fitfully, "Dad said we should be ready to go to the basement!"

"We are," replies John. "We've been glued to the TV for the last fifteen minutes. They say we could get tornados. How's it going in the barn?"

Kallie pauses, taking time to recover her breath. "Mike, Shelly," she starts, "Boo-Boo had a little stud colt, Mom will tell you the rest when she comes up here."

"A colt," Mike grumbles, "all the good races are for fillies. Shit, we'll probably have to geld him just to get him to run."

The lights flicker, and the TV picture changes to snow.

"He's really cute, Shelly," Kallie says, ignoring Mike's complaint. "Mom's going to let him spend the night in the house, so we can nurse him..."

"Nurse him?" quizzes Mike. "What the hell's the matter with the mare?"

Kallie realizes she's said too much; she drops her head, stares at the floor, and mumbles, "Nothing..."

"She's dead isn't she?" Mike yells. "The goddamn horse went and died. Great, just freaking great!"

Shelly bursts out bawling, and sags limply on the couch...

"Jesus, Mike," John snaps, his voice showing irritation and contempt, "you have about as much compassion for that horse as a fox has for a chicken. Look at your wife, she's bawling her eyes out!"

Celeste puts her arm around Shelly's shoulders, comforting her with a hug.

"Who the hell are you?" Mike asks, rebuffing John. And then he goads him, "Just mind your own goddamn business, Phillipa!"

"Stop it, both of you!" Celeste scolds. Her eyes are fixed menacingly on Mike; he escapes further confrontation by looking away.

At that moment, a numbing flash of lightening illuminates the room, the instant report of thunder shakes the windows, and the house goes dark. The front door flies open, and in rush Reggie, followed close behind by Anthony who carries the foal wrapped in a blanket. The house lights flicker, and then come back on. "Wow! That was a close one," shudders Anthony as he enters the parlor. Reggie has paused at the door to remove her shoes. "We have some more company for the night." Anthony says, putting the cumbersome bundle down in the middle of the room. Waggs and Goldie come up and sniff at it. The blanket moves suddenly. The dogs jump back, and out of the blanket appears the head and neck of the baby horse. "Cute little bugger, isn't he?" asks Anthony.

"Oh," sighs Celeste, "he's darling."

"Looks kinda puny," scoffs Mike. "A dead mare, and now a puny colt. Promise me that there's some good news here."

"I'm afraid not," says Reggie as she joins the company in the living room—her blue-jeans and blouse are stained with blood, but her white, sweat socks are clean. She squints at Anthony and grouses, "Tony, honey, could you take off your shoes, you've tracked a mess all the way down the hall."

Anthony looks down and notices the bloody footprints he's left behind. "Crap, sorry darlin'," he replies apologetically. "Excuse me folks, I'll be back in a jiff."

As Anthony leaves the room to clean up, Kallie kneels beside the foal and cuddles it. Just then, the sky ignites as lightening slashes through it; the lights go out; Kallie counts off the seconds, "One thousand one, one thousand two…" Her calculation is arrested by a thunderclap that rattles everyone, and leaves Waggs and Goldie cowering. "Two seconds, about a quarter mile away," she predicts, and then she adds, "Listen, it sounds like the wind has stopped—it's way too quiet out there."

"The calm before the storm," Celeste interjects. "John, maybe we should all go to the basement. I'm frightened. Where's Anthony?" In the dark silence, breath is the only wind that stirs; the only sound that's audible. And then, an indistinct thumping comes from the center of the parlor.

Anthony returns with a flashlight; shining the light around the room, he asks, "Is everyone alright?" The soft thumping comes again. Anthony's attention is drawn to it. Perking his ears, he shines the light toward the source of the sound. The light falls, first on Kallie, and then he hears a soft whinny, and a high-pitched squeal. Anthony casts the light in the darkness that surrounds her, and there, wobbling on all fours, is the foal. "Would you look at that—the tyke is standing," Anthony exclaims, holding the beam steady. "I think he likes being in the spotlight." The foal leers at its distorted shadow that stretches across the carpet in front of it. Apprehensively, he cranes his neck to sniff it, but the shadow changes shape. Startled, he snorts; the shadow snorts. He snaps back his head, puffs up defiantly, snorts again, squeals, and strikes out at the shadow with his tiny hoof...

"What the heck is that?" laughs John. "What kind of antics is that little guy up to?"

"He's dancing," suggests Celeste.

"Nah," Kallie interjects, "I think he's afraid of his shadow."

"He's sparring, Kallie," Anthony muses, "the little tyke is shadow boxing." The foal jabs ferociously, and Anthony adds, "I wish I'd had a wicked punch like that when I was boxing."

"Gosh, Dad," Kallie shouts, "you're a genius! What a great name—that's gonna be his name: *Wicked Punch*."

"That should work," adds John, "not too many letters, the Jockey Club shouldn't have trouble with Wicked Punch. Let's hope it's not taken..."

"You can't name a horse you don't own, kid," says Mike, scowling. "It's my horse, and when it gets a name, I'll give it to him."

"But it's such a perfect name, Mike." Shelly says as she moves toward the foal for a closer look. "Just look at him, he's so small and clumsy...." But before Shelly can finish speaking, Wicked Punch teeters, and plops into Kallie's waiting lap.

"I am looking at him!" Mike crabs as the house lights come back on. "He's a clumsy, little runt with a crooked leg and big knees. Not much point in even naming him—that puny sucker's never gonna run."

Everyone's gaze turns to Wicked Punch's outstretched forelimbs. The knees seem awkwardly large, and the left limb has a noticeable bow.

"The leg can be corrected with a brace," Reggie replies calmly, "it won't be a problem..."

"Yeah, you'd like that, wouldn't you?" Mike snaps at Reggie. "Six or eight weeks in a brace—what a waste of money! You should have let him die..."

"That's an awful thing to say," cries Shelly. "You don't mean that?"

"That really stinks..." John mutters aside.

"What's that, Phillipa?" he blurts, glaring at John.

While the tension inside is rising, the storm, advancing outside, resumes with a muted growl.

"I said your attitude stinks, Mike," John repeats, but this time, his voice is clear and well understood. "You don't deserve to have a horse. All you care about is the money you lost."

"You privileged little punk!" shouts Mike, lurching aggressively at John. "You've never lost any money—rich bastard—you should try it sometime, see how you feel inside. I've been out of work for five months..."

John edges nearer, but Celeste restrains him. "We all know you're out of work, Mike, and that you're suffering..." she interjects, hoping her words will calm him. "But think about how this little foal is suffering—no matter what happens, his life won't be easy. He just lost his mother."

"Yeah, well the mare was insured," Mike comments dryly. "But that puny thing," he says pointing at Wicked Punch cradled in

Kallie's arms, "he don't even weigh a hundred pounds. What's that worth to the knacker? Fifty bucks?"

Kallie, who's been nursing the foal and listening to the bickering, has come to the end of her patience. Riled by Mike's harsh words, she glares at him and blasts ferociously, "Mike, you're a real asshole—you know that? If you don't want to take care of this foal, then I will—you selfish asshole!"

"Kallie!" Reggie scolds, "watch your language."

"Yeah, real smart mouth kid," Mike retorts, "the two of you would be perfect for each other—you're both runts!"

"I'm no runt," she snarls. Then, under her breath, adds, "asshole."

"Reynolds!" growls Anthony, standing solid as a prize fighter—his arms stiff at his sides, fists clinched—trembling with anger. "You're standing in my house. You're talking to my family, and you've talked enough." Mike shrinks at the challenge and treads back. "And Kallie, don't ever call a guest in this house an asshole, or any other dirty name. Is that clear to you, Kallie?"

With Anthony's stern words, the edge is taken off the moment, and Mike's aggression begins to fade. The storm outside intensifies—the sound of hail striking the roof fills the room.

"I'm sorry everyone; I didn't mean what I said," Mike recants, offering an apology. "Things have been kind of rough lately—I'm just frustrated. I shouldn't take it out on you." He turns to Kallie and adds, "I'm sorry Kallie…"

"Me too…" she replies.

A strong man will quiver when his spirit is broken; Mike stammers when he confesses, "I want the horse, but can't afford to raise him. Your vet bill alone," he looks at Reggie and purses his lips, "will take months to pay off. Before the strike we could do it, now we can't…"

"Mike," says Kallie, interrupting, "I can buy him."

"No you can't…" Reggie says in an attempt to cut her off.

"No Mom, I can, I've got some money. How much do you want?

"Kallie, your mother doesn't think you should…"

"But Dad, it's my money—savings—not my college money. It'll be my horse. I can train him. I'm almost sixteen; I can get my license. Dad, I can do this."

Mike looks to Shelly standing beside him, the two pause, considering Kallie's proposal. Mike nods, yes. Shelly smiles, giving her consent, and replies, "Kallie, the stud fee was five hundred dollars, if you can pay that, I'll give you the stallion's breeding certificate, and the blood test on the mare—you'll have to file for the papers yourself."

"That's a done deal!" Kallie shouts.

Shelly reaches down to Kallie and shakes her hand.

"Kallie, this isn't a game," Reggie says, cautioning her, "Shelly and Mike are serious."

"I know that, Mom," Kallie acknowledges softly, staring at Reggie with maturity and reassurance in her expression, "I'm not playing a game—it's my career." Kallie looks back at Shelly, and continues, "I can go to the bank on Monday. Can I pay you then?"

"Just make the payment to your Mom," Mike suggests calmly. "Is that alright with you, Doc? Will you accept that as a partial payment on our bill?"

Reggie pauses; she ponders Kallie's face, and realizes, for the first time, that her little girl is ready for responsibility. Then she glances to Anthony; he smiles, and nods, yes. Reggie sighs in resignation, and answers, "That's fine, Mike."

Before anyone has a chance to utter another word, Wicked Punch struggles to his feet and nickers. Kallie steadies him in a hug. "Thanks Mom, thanks Dad," she says. Then, fondly squeezing the foal, she whispers, "Your name is Wicked Punch; you're going to be a racehorse; you're going to be the fastest racehorse ever."

* * *

Three: Spy Games

Four weeks later. It's a sunny warm day, just before noon. In a paddock behind Longview boarding stable and clinic, a fleshy, bay gelding gobbles its lunch indifferently. In the paddock next to him, sheltered from the sun by over-hanging oaks, a paint mare has worn a deep path along the front fence boards by pacing anxiously. From across the way, comes a high-pitched whinny, and Kallie's laughing voice. The mare studies the nearby activities with keen attention. Bounding around in the paddock, Wicked Punch is running in tight circles just beyond Kallie's reach; she chases gamely, but two legs are no match for four. "Come here you little rascal!" she shouts, laughing while making a diving grab for a lead rope that dangles from Wicked Punch's halter. Kallie misses the attempt, and stumbles into a sprawl on the ground. Wicked Punch snorts and squeals; extending his neck, he whizzes away. Kallie raises to her knees, dazed. Pulling the front of her T-shirt from her jeans, she examines the fresh, indelible grass stains, and grouses, "I put this on clean this morning—ugh, turds!" And then, she pauses before getting to her feet. Wicked Punch's nimble hooves are a blur. "Not so clumsy now, are you?" she muses, admiring his fleet and steady stride. "You're the fastest little bugger I've ever seen." Pausing a moment more before resuming her mission, she whispers her plan, "If speed isn't going to catch you, maybe brains will."

Kallie flops on her stomach, sprawls spread-eagle on the ground, and remains motionless in the middle of the paddock. Wicked Punch runs a few more circles around her, transitions to a trot, turns in and approaches her. As he nears Kallie, he squeals defiantly, breaks into canter and leaps like a hurdler, resuming his circling. Kallie does not move. Wicked Punch slows down to a trot, and then to a walk. He approaches Kallie a second time. When he reaches her, he stops, probes her head with his nose, sniffs cautiously, and satisfied that it's safe; he begins to nuzzle. Kallie rolls from her stomach onto her back and the two meet nose to nose. "You see, *Punchie*," Kallie says, deftly reaching for the lead rope, "you may be fast, but you gotta have brains too."

Kallie and Punch continue to nuzzle as Kallie climbs to her feet. Just then, from the stable, Anthony calls, "Kallie! Hey, shrimp!"

"I'm out here Dad," she shouts back as she leads Punch to the gate, "I'm in the paddock. What do you need?"

"Mom has to make some deliveries, she thought you might want to drive the van for her..."

As Kallie leaves the paddock, leading Punch to the stable, she quips to Anthony, "Sure Dad, but isn't that how it always goes? You get your license, and then you gotta drive everyone everywhere."

"Oh, you poor dear, you're such an abused baby," Anthony chides her, "you're going to make me cry. You better not count your chickens too soon, maybe Mom just wants some company."

When she and her colt pass by, the paint mare leans heavily against the paddock gate and nickers fondly to Wicked Punch. Puffing up his narrow bay chest, he prances, swishes his tail, answers with a childish whinny, and an unexpected cowkick. "Hey, you rascal. Quit that. *Quilts* is just being friendly." Reaching the rear entrance of the stable where Anthony is waiting, she asks, "You heading back to the house?"

"Uh-huh..." he nods as they go in together.

"Could you tell Mom that I just have to make up some foal mix for my kid here, and then I'll be ready to go."

"Yeah—sure."

Walking down the center aisle to his stall, Wicked Punch is a frugal slice of bay bologna, sandwiched between Kallie, and Anthony. "The little bugger is doing okay, huh?" Anthony asks, gently stroking Punch's back and rump. "From what I see, that crooked leg doesn't seem to hold him back—I saw you guys playing in the paddock—he's got some fight in him. It was his right front, wasn't it?"

"No Dad, it was his left..." she corrects him.

"The bigger he gets, I guess, the less you can see it—my mistake, Kallie."

When they reach the stall, Kallie leads Wicked Punch in, and removes his halter and lead rope in one motion. Anthony leans sluggishly on the doorjamb, but steps quickly aside as she comes out and closes the door. "Could you keep an eye on him, Dad? I'll get his chow from the feed room."

"That's okay Kallie, I can feed him. You'll let me do that, won't you? I think Mom wants to get going…"

"Daddy," she coos, "you're a big boy—I trust you." And then she scolds him, playfully threatening with a clinched fist, "But you better not screw up, or you'll have to answer to me!"

"Your bad side is one place I don't want to be, shrimp," he replies, watching Kallie jog up the center aisle and disappear out the archway. Then he peers through the bars of the colt's stall and whispers, "Champions break records, Punchie, not little girls' hearts." He lingers thoughtfully, and after a prolonged pause, he clears his throat, and advises, "She has big dreams for you—Kallie's the only dream I've ever had—take care not to hurt her."

Coming from the stable, Kallie moseys, taking time to enjoy the color that greets her. The garden surrounding the turnaround is in full summer bloom—sweet williams, stunning to the eye with pink and crimson hues; regal petunias, blowing scarlet and lavender trumpets; shasta daisies, mere petals on a pike, all full with nectar, add their scent to the fragrant breeze that blows from across the grassy meadows. Kallie wonders, making her way to the van, "How does he do it? How can an old fighter like Dad know anything about gardening?"

At the house, the front screen-door slams and Reggie bounds down the porch. Dressed in a canary T-shirt, blue jeans and a baseball cap—her hair, in a knotted bun, protrudes above the clasp on the back of the hat—she walks, deliberately, toward the van, one hand stuffed in her hip pocket the other in the front, her head down.

"Hey Mom," Kallie shouts, seeing her jabbing at her tight pockets, "Ready to go?"

"Just about, I just gotta find my keys…" Approaching the van from opposite sides, Reggie pulls the keys from her hip pocket and asks, "You want to drive? I have to enter some billing on my laptop"

"Sure, you bet Mom..." Reggie tosses the keys over the van to Kallie who leaps, making a one-handed grab. "One hand, YES!" She clutches the keys to her chest, puts her head down, reaches out her right arm, and charges the van like a football player. "Eat your heart out, *Randy Moss!*" she shouts. When she arrives at the door of the van she stands tall and erect, lifts her arms and dances a victory pirouette, "Yeah, hurrah, the crowd goes wild, hurrah! There's a rumor of a signing bonus!"

"Just get in the van and drive, Randy."

Reggie opens the passenger door and gets in. Kallie jumps in the driver's seat—they put on their seat belts, and Kallie asks, "Where to, boss?"

"The track, and then a couple of quick stops." Kallie starts the van, and then tromps the accelerator in several quick bursts to rev the motor; she looks at Reggie and smiles impishly. "You better not try it Kallie..." Reggie warns.

Kallie laughs and chides, "Yeah, girlfriend? You don't scare me, I got the wheel."

"But I've got the power to punish. Need I say more?"

"Message received commander, loud and clear. Kallie out!" Ever so lightly, she presses on the accelerator, and pulls out at a crawl. Playfully, Reggie slaps the back of Kallie's head. "Okay, Mom, new message. Got it." Kallie speeds up, and they disappear down the drive.

Thirty minutes later, at the Dorchester Downs backside security gate, Kallie drives the van alongside the gatehouse and stops. The Hawk, squinting at a computer screen just inside the door, hears the idling vehicle, and looks up. "Hum, looks like trouble..." he thinks, adjusting his eyeglasses, pushing them snuggly onto the bridge of his thin nose. "Let's have a little fun with the kid."

"Afternoon sir," chirps Kallie, leaning out the window as the Hawk approaches the van. "Can Doctor Phillipa sign me in?"

"Hi-ya kid, long time no see. Been keeping your nose clean?

"I try to, but it keeps running..."

The Hawk chuckles at her comment while handing a clipboard and pencil in to Reggie. Reggie scribbles her name, and hands it back to him. "Still a little smart aleck, ain't ya?" he asks, resting his arms on the window sill, and leaning his head inside the van. He's within inches of Kallie. She can see magnified crow's feet accenting his eyes; his breath is stale, and his aftershave, bargain brand. He's too close, but she's trapped, and he knows it. Menacingly, he hisses, "I ain't stupid, ya know. I know what ya guys call me behind my back: the Hawk. That's okay, kid, as long as ya remember why ya call me that—'cuz I always got my eyes on ya..."

Kallie is startled by his accusation, and shrinks with guilt.

Reggie stares at him in blank embarrassment, and protests, "You're wrong Jim, nobody calls you that. Not us—nobody!"

"Sure they do, Doc," he replies, sneering. "Now get outta here, and kid, ya better not be any trouble. A troublemaker is just as bad as a smart aleck."

Kallie presses the accelerator nervously—too quick and too hard—the tires spin; the van jolts ahead and then screeches abruptly to a halt. "I-eee," she groans before regaining her composure and driving carefully onto Bold Ruler Boulevard.

"He's got your number, doesn't he Kallie?"

"Gees Mom! Every time I meet that guy, I end up in deep crap!"

"Maybe you should work on your people skills," she says, glancing up from her laptop. Then suddenly, gesturing frantically, she yelps, "Here, here! Turn right here—yeah that's Fred Berkley's barn. Pull up and park by the dorm entrance."

Kallie drives the van into an open parking space at one end of a splendidly kept, mission style, adobe building, and stops. Pressing her nose against the windshield, she gawks, reading a sign, wrought in sand-blasted relief, that announces the proprietor: *Fredrick Berkley Stables,* and the restrictions: *Runners for Turf and Route*, *Visitors by Appointment Only*. She blinks hard and whispers, "Holy crap, Mom does have some class clients..." Then she gazes at the structure: an enormous, single story stable made of stucco, painted to look like southwestern adobe—even the full timber logs supporting the fake tile roof above the stalls are made from cement, but look real enough to burn—and connected at either end of the stable are dormitories— two story, fake-adobe block houses—that serve as home to a hard-working staff. An exercise rider speeds by on a bicycle distracting her, and when Reggie finishes typing on her laptop, Kallie asks, "You going to be in there long? You need my help?"

"Why?" Reggie replies inattentively, closing her computer and placing it on the console between the seats.

"I want to run over and talk to Winston—congratulate him..."

"I've got a couple more stops to make, so take care of your business, and I'll swing by and pick you up. Okay? Oh—Kallie, the keys..."

"Cool, Mom... Here."

Kallie hands Reggie the keys, and bounds from the van; she dashes around the dormitory toward Tent City. A moment later, she enters the maze. Ahead, she sees Winston standing on the cement pad in front of his tack room; he's holding a hose and spraying water on the shins of a napping gelding. Standing in front of the horse, a groom dozes, a lead rope hanging slack in his hand. As Kallie approaches, she breaks from a jog to a walk, and shouts, "Hey Winston! Winston the winner!" Winston lifts the brim of his cowboy hat, and squints to see who's calling. Kallie saunters up and greets him with a growling, "Wa-zup *Winman?*"

"Kallie! Not much, same crap, different day," he answers, exchanging a 'high-five' handshake with her. "What's up with you?"

"I hear you had a couple of winners last weekend. Nice tag too. I hope you had some of your own money on them—long odds, big payday!"

"Fifty on the nose," he replies, smiling so broadly that the snuff in his lower lip spills onto his chin. "No feather soup this week, this week we're all eating chicken."

While Winston packs the tobacco back into place, Kallie glances down at the shins of the horse. They're noticeably swollen, and she asks, "Did the baby shin-buck?"

"Yeah," he replies, "not too bad though, just some swelling, and a little heat in them." Kallie stares closely at the front of the cannon bones; she knows that a shin-bucked youngster can be laid-up for a month or more, but the injury appears minimal. "Too bad. He shows a lot of promise," Winston adds, continuing to spray cold water on the horse's shins, "he came real close his first time out—ran up to the lead rounding the final turn, then he quit. I guess you gotta expect the babies to buck their shins."

"Are you going to pin fire him?" she quizzes.

"Nah, I really don't believe in that old race track voodoo. I'll give him some time off and keep icing him—nature cures best."

Kallie glances up at the groom, and then back to Winston, "This your new man?" she asks.

"Yeah, this is *Lupé*."

Kallie reaches out her hand to shake; Lupé looks at her puzzled, then shakes her hand and mumbles: "Que' hubo?"

"He only speaks Spanish," Winston advises, "not a word of English..."

"That's something else for me to study," Kallie grouses. Then, looking around the shed row, she asks, "Where's Juan? I haven't seen him since Pennyante stepped on him."

Winston turns off the nozzle of the hose, gestures to Lupé and says, "Bueno, vamos. Stall number two."

At first, Lupé appears perplexed, but after a pause, he responds, "Si, numero dos?" Winston nods his head indicating, yes. Lupé leads the horse from the wash pad, down the shed row to stall number two.

Winston turns back to Kallie and replies to her question, "Juan still works for me—he mucks out stalls in the mornings. He's up in the kitchen playing pinball, and having some grub. Next week, when he gets his cast off, he'll be back full time walking hots and grooming." After having put the horse into its stall, Lupé moseys to the tack room, hangs up the halter and lead rope, and then plunks leisurely onto a metal, folding chair outside the door in the shade. Winston watches him, and then suggests to Kallie, "I think Lupé has the right idea." He takes off his cowboy hat and wipes his brow. "Let's go and sit where it's cool, it's hot as a tamale..."

"Chili today, hot tamale..." quips Kallie, walking toward the shade.

"Chili today, hot tamale, that's pretty good—hey what's this I hear about you getting a horse?"

Kallie glows with excitement at Winston's question, her movements become animated, she skips and dances lightly as she says, "Yeah! You wouldn't believe it, Winston. It was great—and really horrible, too. And it's kind of a long story, but anyway..."

The two have reached the tack room. Winston reaches inside the door and grabs two folding chairs. He sets one out opposite Lupé and gestures for Kallie to sit. Then he places the other next to Lupé and sits down, exhaling an exhausted groan. "We've got time to listen," he says, pushing his hat back from his forehead, "but not all night, so give us the not-so-long version—Lupé isn't going to understand anyway...."

"Okay, the not-so-long version. Well," Kallie bubbles, "where do I start?" She pauses to think a moment, and then begins, "Remember when the Hawk busted us?"

"How could I forget?" answers Winston.

"Anyway, on the way home, Mom got a call from this client with a pregnant mare. The mare is sick—colic—and has to be shipped to the clinic. Mike—that's Shelly's husband—he's whining that they can't afford it, 'the mare's been nothing but trouble,' he hollers. And Shelly, she's bawling her eyes out ' cuz she thinks she's going to die, and Mom's thinking that she's twisted her gut—not Shelly, the mare—so into the trailer and off to the clinic we go."

"Sounds serious..."

"Not the half of it, Winston. We get home, and the mare's broke her water, what a mess! So we run her into the clinic, and she plops down. Anyway, my Dad and his brother and Mike are running around like they're crazy. But Mom stays real cool and tells everyone to get out—except for Dad and me. Then she delivers the baby by cesarean! There was blood all over, it was so gross, and then Boo-Boo—the mare—died." Winston is listening intently; each of Kallie's words seems to recall a memory in him. Lupé appears confused, but he watches Kallie's gestured speech with interest. "Did I mention that was the night we had the tornados?"

"The night of the derby?"

"Yeah! Anyway, we had to take the foal to the house to spend the night. When Mike saw it and figured out that Boo-Boo was dead,

Too Far A Dream

he went ballistic! Yelling that we should have let the little runt die, screaming at Mom that he was going to go broke—he called Dad's brother a privileged punk!"

"Then what happened?"

"I've never seen my Dad get so mad. I thought he was going to knock Mike on his butt, right there in the living room, but then the lights went out and the wind started to shake the house…"

"Your dad should have knocked him down—what an asshole…"

"That's what I said!" she shouts, and then continues: "Anyway, by this time, Shelly is blubbering like a baby, both Dad and Uncle John are really pissed and ready to go at with Mike, but then Mom, I think, told them all to cool it—she's pretty tough."

"Worse than a cat in a sack, I guess…"

"When the lights came on again, there was this little horse standing in the living room dancing around, and I named him Wicked Punch. Everybody thought it was a cool name, and since they couldn't afford to raise the foal, Shelly and Mike decided to sell it to me! That's pretty much the end of the story."

"Good story, I like the part about the storm," Winston says, rocking his chair back, and clasping his hands behind his head. "I like the name too—Wicked Punch—good name for a racehorse."

"It's a dynamite name," Kallie shouts. "He's so cute, and fast too. You should see him run around the paddock. I can hardly wait until he's old enough for me to train."

"Train?" Winston asks surprised. "I thought you were going to be a jockey…"

"I am. I'm going to be a jockey, and a trainer. I've already got the horse."

"Can't do it Kallie," Winston advises her soberly.

"Sure I can—it's my dream, and I'll make it come true!"

"Kallie," Winston replies, unclasping his hands from behind his head, and leaning forward to rest his elbows on his knees, "you didn't take the Hawk's advice, did you?"

"What? What are you talking about?"

"You haven't read the rules, have you?"

Kallie appears stunned and confused. "What does that have to do with my being a jockey?" she quizzes.

"Kallie, it's against the law for a jockey to own, or train a racehorse..."

"Bull crap! That doesn't make any sense."

"Sure it does. Jockeys ride, they could fix the races..."

"Are you sure? It's against the law?" Winston nods a confident yes. Kallie is agitated, incredulous at hearing Winston's report. "Like heck," she yells, disbelieving him, "you gotta be wrong. I don't believe it—they gotta make an exception!"

"No exceptions Kallie, the rules protect racing from becoming corrupted."

Aggravated, Kallie jumps up from her chair. "Where are these rules? I want a copy, I gotta see this for myself."

"Commission office in the grandstand."

Kallie paces nervously, she slaps at her hips with her hands, and yells, "Ugh!" After a moment she recovers her composure and growls defiantly, "Well, I'm going to ride Wicked Punch come hell or high water—nobody better try to stop me."

Winston gazes off into space; he is considering Kallie's options. Stretching out his legs, he scrapes the worn heels of his cowboy boots across the pavement to dislodge mud that's stuck to the cleats, and then he similes—he's found a loophole. "You know, Kallie," he suggests, "you could transfer the horse into your dad's name."

"What good would that do, and why Dad's and not Mom's?"

"She's a track vet. She has the same problem as you," replies Winston. "The rules prohibit a veterinarian from owning a horse, too."

"But Dad could be the owner? That would be legal?"

"Well, unless he's a convicted felon," Winston replies, chuckling. "Anyway, your name wouldn't be on the horse's papers as the owner, and if I understand the rules right, it'd be legal. Then you could hire someone to train him, and go and get licensed as his jockey."

"That's a great idea, Winston," Kallie shrieks, and then she begins to pummel him with questions. "If I do that, will you train him? How much does it cost? What do you charge? How long will it take?"

"I'm cheap Kallie, and I get forty dollars a day per horse, and that doesn't include the vet, farrier and shipping."

"Forty bucks? You get forty bucks a day? That's…"

"Twelve hundred a month," says Winston interrupting, "not including…"

"I know, vet and farrier. I don't have that kind of money. How come it costs so much?"

"Man's gotta eat, and I have to pay for Lupé, Juan, feed, equipment, everything you see around here."

"I could get a job," she muses, staring off, "maybe I could walk hots—I can earn forty bucks a day…"

"Better if you win the lottery," Winston jests. And then, his voice takes on a consoling tone when he adds, "It looks to me like you have to revise your plans…"

Kallie continues to stare off, pondering, "Forty bucks. Car insurance, gas, feed, tack…" One by one, she considers her expenses, but before she can arrive at a final sum, a distant shout distracts her.

"Kallie, Kallie! Gotta go girl."

"Oh damn!" she mutters, turning to see Reggie's van coming to a stop in front of the stable. "I can get a copy of the rules from the Racing Commission?" she asks, returning her attention to Winston.

"Yeah, in the basement of the grandstands—and study them."

"Will do, Winman…" she replies, bolting toward the van.

"Hi-ya Winston," Reggie shouts, leaning out the driver's window. "Congrats on your wins!"

"Thanks Doc," he yells back. "You gotta have a talk with your daughter about her career choice."

Reggie appears confused by Winston's comment; Kallie opens the van door and jumps in. "What did Winston mean by that?" she asks Kallie while driving off.

"He just told me that the rules don't allow jockeys to own racehorses."

"I didn't know that…" Reggie muses. "It makes sense though—looks like you got a problem to solve."

69

"Maybe not, Mom. I think Winston's come up with a way to beat the system. Could you stop by the grandstands?" Reggie looks at her watch and nods, yes. "I've got to get a copy of the rules—there might be a loophole—they aren't going to keep me from riding."

Far across the grounds, opposite the backside, are the grandstands. On a race day, the distance requires a long walk, but today, it's a short trip by car. Reggie steers the van into a reserved space near the frontside entrance, and stops. Kallie bounds from the van and runs through the gate toward the grandstands' main entry, she yanks open the doors and rushes inside. When she enters the building, her attention is drawn to an immense mural that covers the second story wall ahead of her—it is a head-on view of racehorses charging frantically down a grass track to the finish line. She pauses, and stares at it with wonder and amazement. It's rendered so lifelike that the horses seem to be running right off the canvas; moist, steamy breath blasts from their inflated nostrils, the jockeys jostle for position and flail with their whips, clods of turf hang in the air; if there were noise coming from the painting, it would be thunderous. Kallie whispers awestruck, "Holy shit!" And then she glances at the artist's signature, it reads simply: *Charles Foxx*. Kallie shakes her head in admiration, admitting, "Charlie Foxx, you can really paint!"

Sprinting off toward a stairway leading to the lower level, only one thought is on her mind—get the rules. She leaps down the stairs, covering them two at a time. At the bottom of the stairs she bursts through stout, double doors, slamming them forcefully into an elder gentleman who is knocked backward, and teeters precariously from the blow. He staggers, fumbles to adjust his eyeglasses, but before he can speak, Kallie reaches to steady him. "Sorry, buddy," she apologizes grabbing hold of his shirt sleeve. "You okay? I didn't see you…"

The man shakes his head, mumbles, "How could you?" and looks at Kallie with a condescending glare. Then he cautions her gruffly, "You had better slow down, Miss; it could well have been a child that you injured."

"I'm so sorry—really," she stammers contritely. "Do you know where the racing commission office is?"

Too Far A Dream

The man points to a door on Kallie's left; it has a window in its center covered by several posted notices. Above the door, a sign reads: *Racing Commission.* Kallie glances at the sign, then back at the man. An embarrassed smile creeps across her lips when she adds, "Oops. Thanks Mister."

As Kallie opens the door and enters the room, the elder gentleman lingers outside, scowling. His crisply starched, white shirt sleeve bears a dirty hand print; the double windsor knot of his red silk necktie is ajar, but his wool khaki trousers still hold a neat crease. Above his shirt pocket is an engraved, gold name badge that reads: *Mr. Maxwell Heppner, Chief Steward.* Straightening his tie, he mumbles, "I'll remember that face…"

A short while later, back in the van, Kallie is seated in the passenger's seat; her attention focused on a weighty, blue covered book resting open on her lap. Reggie is driving, and singing to the oldies that play on the radio. The countryside through which they travel is a flat summit above the river valley. The road winds through fields of sprouting corn and oats. Far off in the distance, the bluffs on the opposite side of the river are visible, but indistinctly—looking more like a herd of porcupines than ramparts above a river gorge. Overhead, enormous cumulus clouds float; they reflect the warm hues of the afternoon sun. The road begins to descend into the valley, and Kallie groans, "There are more than two hundred pages of rules in this damn book." Reggie glances from the road to the book on Kallie's lap. "I think if you fart, they have a rule for it—and it's probably against the law."

"Was Winston right about being a jockey?" Reggie asks.

"I don't know; there's all this legal stuff. Paragraph this, and subsection that, I can't figure out what most of it says. What a bunch of crap."

"Well, don't worry about it now," Reggie says to reassure her, "you've got all winter to study. Punch has a lot of growing to do before he's ready to race. You'll find a way to make it work."

Kallie closes the book and places it by her feet, and then she asks, "Much farther Mom? Do I have time to catch a few 'Zs'?"

71

Victor John Faith

Reggie yawns, "About twenty minutes. I could use a nap myself..."

As Kallie nods off, the van continues its descent into the river valley. The road winds around an outcrop, then switches back into a narrow canyon overhung with oaks and wild grapevines. Flashes of sunlight plunge through the canopy only to be swallowed up by the deep shadows of the dense overgrowth. The van descends, precipitously, into the craggy ravine before the road reverses its course and leads back out of the canyon on the opposing wall. At the foot of the bluff, the river's expansive, green floodplain appears. Soybeans in hump-backed rows, and meadow grasses, spread in wide carpets, stretch from the bluffs to the river's distant edge. Farther on, the road merges into another and Reggie heads south along the shaded western base—above the van, jut high plateaus, spiked pinnacles buttressed by talus piles, and the eroded clefts and cliffs of the bluffs. Reggie yawns, making a noise like a snow goose honking, and then with one hand on the wheel, she reaches into the cooler beside her, takes out a soda and gulps a long drink. "Ah," she sighs, releasing a rattling belch, "that felt good." She takes another sip, and drops the soda back into the cooler. She shudders as if seized by a chill, and grouses, "Come on Regina, wake up!" Just then, she passes a mailbox, "Oh shit, that's it!" she yelps, squealing the van to a halt—Kallie pitches forward, but she's restrained by the shoulder harness. "Sorry girlfriend, nap over—we're here..."

"Here?" Kallie asks, half asleep, "Where's here?"

Reggie shifts the van into reverse and backs up to beyond the mailbox; there is no name on it, only an address: 12848 Gleason Road. She drives forward making a right turn onto a cobbled stone driveway. Right away, Kallie senses she's intruding on a very private domain. On either side of the entry to the drive, a gate pillar made of cut limestone blocks four feet wide, stretches to a height of twelve feet. Wrought iron lanterns, looking like wine barrels missing two out of three slats—years ago lighted by gas—cap each top and now rust from disuse. In the shade around the pillars, horsetail ferns and variegated hosta thrive. Reggie navigates the van into a leafy cloister drenched in an iridescent green hue. For a distance of fifty yards

Too Far A Dream

ahead, all that can be seen is the straight profile of a security fence that time and vigorous growth has covered in a tangled mass of creeping charlotte and wild grapevines. One can sense, however, that beyond the walls of this living fortress are open parks and manicured lawns—it's a feeling hushed in secret. Kallie's eyes grow wide as the van nears the end of the long corridor—her nap has refreshed her—ahead lays a whimsical sight. Roses of dazzling and varied color grow in tidy gardens walled by stone. A time worn, and mossy statue of *Bucephalus*, the warhorse of Alexander the Great, reigns defiantly within a fountain that splashes faceted sunlight.

"Whoa," Kallie gasps in disbelief, "where the hell are we?"

Joking, Reggie replies, "Nice shack, hey?"

She drives the van onto a circular drive in front of an enormous Queen Anne style country mansion that is set back, almost pressing, against a cantilevered scarp of Saint Peter limestone—like a beneficent colossus, the cliff is shepherd to the house. The first level is constructed of yellow limestone blocks, laid in courses bound with mortar. The windows are tall, narrow slots of leaded glass. The front door—hefty oak planks, weather worn and gray—is embowered in an arched recess; above it hangs an iron lantern—a cousin to those rusty kin crowning the entry pillars. The second level is constructed of rough-hewn, half timbers that stand vertically; each file separated from the next by a yard of tan stucco and wattle. Closing the house to the sky, is a gabled roof of terra-cotta shingles—slabs of lichens have ensconced themselves within the sheltered cloves between the tiles. Kallie gawks, whispering, "Yeah, this is a pretty nice shack...." Leaving the circular drive, Reggie turns the van onto a narrow lane that wanders into the secluded meadows beyond the house. An afternoon breeze drifts past; sniffing, Kallie asks, "Mom, what's that smell?"

Reggie inhales a long breath, "Lavender," she answers, pointing out what appears to be a kitchen herb garden planted next to a side entry of the house. "No, that's rosemary and basil, I think. Maybe all three." She glances at the thriving herbs, and remarks, "I wore a perfume that smelled like that when your dad married me—he couldn't keep his lips off me—he kept asking me if the lace on my gown was made of linguini."

Reggie drives a furlong's distance down the lane; ahead is a carriage house and adjoining stable. With two imposing stories, its architecture matches that of the house. To their right is a wide meadow—tidy as a golf green—a compact band of horses grazes placidly in the distance. The lane approaches the carriage house from its business end. Two, massive, chevron timbered doors with iron hinges, are swung open, and in the dim light inside, Kallie glimpses the outline of a familiar car, and she gasps, "That guy; the guy with the coffee. The baron...." And then she notices, fronting the stable, a broad open lawn; in its center, harrowed with a comb, is a sandy riding arena fenced within knee-high, white kick rails, and marking each corner, is an urn stuffed with roses. As Reggie stops the van in front of the open doors of the carriage house, Kallie stares at a showy man riding a horse in the arena—the lapels of his canary vest are trimmed in ivory silk, and his English boots reflect the afternoon sun. She reaches for the door handle to get out...

"Wait in the car, Kallie," Reggie orders, reaching her arm to restrain her.

"I just want to go and watch that guy ride."

"No, you have to wait in the car." Reggie says a second time.

"What's the big deal, Mom? I'm not going to step on the flowers or steal anything."

"Kallie," Reggie says, her voice betraying irritation, "that's Albert Verrhaus..."

"The Baron? I knew it," she gloats confidently. "Then that's gotta be him riding, right? This is his joint?"

"Yes..."

"Wow, this is so cool! What's he like, Mom—besides being filthy rich? Is he crazy like you said?"

"I never said that," Reggie replies as she opens the door of the van and steps out. She pauses a moment watching the Baron riding a trot half-pass across the arena. His agile horse glides along the diagonal with poise and grace; its fore and hind limbs cross and splay like a ballet dancer's performing echappe. And then, as she leans into the back of van to get a parcel, she adds, "I've never really met him, except for that time when we bumped into him outside the coffee shop."

"You mean sandwiched him, don't you?"

Reggie smiles, recalling the Baron's startled expression as she and Kallie crashed into him. "He seems nice enough on the phone, always polite, and he pays his vet bill on time—I could use more customers like him." She glances through the side window and watches a moment, and then remarks, "Maybe he's shy…"

"Dressed like that? I think, maybe he's weird, or hiding something—maybe the rumors are true."

"I don't think so, Kallie. Whenever I come here he's either riding, or in the house. If he's riding, he waves to me; if he's in the house, he stays there. He never comes out to talk, and I've never seen anyone else around—I just drop off his order and scram."

"Is he married, does he have kids?"

"Like I said, I've never seen anyone…" Reggie pauses thoughtfully. When she stands up, she tucks the parcel under her arm, and observes wistfully, "I imagine he gets lonely though—I would. It seems like a big place without a family." As Kallie hangs out her window to get a better view, Reggie taps on the roof of the van, her voice filled with purpose, she barks, "Back in a jiff—stay in the van, I mean it."

Reggie walks from the van toward the carriage house, the Baron waves to her, she waves back, and then he continues performing. He rides the centerline from C to A, and turns right. At K, his horse begins to canter the change of rein from K to M, but to Kallie's amazement, at X, the horse performs a canter pirouette to the right before resuming the change of rein. At M, it does a flying change, turns left up the centerline at C, and begins canter half-pass left four strides, flying change of lead, canter half-pass right eight strides—zigzagging back and forth, four times before finishing with another canter pirouette. Kallie giggles, delighted, she claps softly, "Yeah! Wow." Just then the driver's door swings open…

"I'm back," says Reggie, leaping into the van.

"Mom," Kallie asks excitedly, "have you been watching this guy ride? Holy-moly! I can't see him giving any cues. How is he getting his horse to do that stuff?"

"You're talking to a gal that rides in a western saddle. That dressage stuff is beyond me. Kind of fun to watch though…"

Reggie starts the van and puts it into reverse to back up and turn around. The Baron, now walking his horse on a loose rein, waves good-bye as Reggie and Kallie pull out. Kallie ponders quietly while Reggie drives the van down the long cobbled stone driveway. "I wonder if he could teach me to train Punch," she muses aloud.

"Who?"

"The Baron," replies Kallie. "I wonder if he could show me how to ride that good."

The van has come to the end of the drive; Reggie turns left onto the main highway and accelerates. "I thought you wanted Wicked Punch to be a race horse."

"I do," she replies, "but I'm not a good enough rider yet, and I really don't know anything about training."

"And the rules," Reggie interrupts, "don't forget about the rules."

"Please Mom, don't ever mention them again—not even joking."

"I won't—I promise.

"The Baron must have trained that horse, and I don't know anyone else who can ride like that." Kallie pauses thoughtfully. "Just imagine if I could teach Punchie to do that skipping thing—changing his lead—he'd never get boxed in, he could always stay out of trouble."

"Yeah," says Reggie, reaching in the cooler for her soda "that might help, but I don't think he takes any students." She takes a drink, and then hands the bottle to Kallie, saying, "Besides, all the trainers I know at the track ride western."

Kallie takes a drink, hands the soda back to Reggie, and groans, disheartened, "Another set-back! The rules won't let me be a jockey, hiring a trainer costs more than I make in a year, and now this crazy old Baron doesn't give lessons." Kallie looks up; dramatically she raises her hands as if to pray, and pleads, "Hello-o! Can I get a little help down here? Are you listening?"

Too Far A Dream

"It's not that big of a deal, Kallie. You're always in too much of a hurry—things will work out."

"They better Mom, I'm getting older by the day—look at my eyes. Am I getting bags under my eyes? I think I am..." Kallie reaches for the sun visor, opens the vanity mirror and then examines her eyes closely, "Ahhh!" she exclaims. "Oh-my-God, I am. Bags!"

Later that evening. The front porch light on the Phillipa house glows a soothing invitation to any traveler waylaid by a flat tire, or bad luck. Crickets chirp in the rural arbor beyond the house; mourning doves coo faintly from the shadowed limbs above, and from somewhere, across meadows and miles, a cow moos. Wags and Goldie snooze on the entryway carpet—asleep, but vigilant, they're ready with a friendly pounce and lick. In the living room, the television mumbles quietly; its droning mutes the intimate conversation coming from within. Kallie is in her bedroom upstairs, sitting cross-legged on the floor at the foot of her single bed. The bed is a wrecked car, with crumpled upholstery, hogging a junk yard. On either side of the bed are second-hand night stands with third-hand table lamps; both lights are turned on. Kallie is wearing a jumbo sized, red T-shirt, and white sweat socks that are rolled down around her ankles. Resting in her lap is the book of rules she got from the racing commission earlier today. Around her, on the floor, strewn akimbo, are other books: a picture book of horses, a book on veterinary science, and two manuals on horsemanship. Kallie is jabbering on the telephone. "Me and mom went out to the Baron's house this afternoon. And wow, Morgan, you wouldn't believe this place!

"Where'd you go?" Morgan replies over the phone.

"Out to Albert Verrhaus's. He lives in that old mansion on Gleason Road. I almost expected guards to come and boot us out—the place is huge!"

"I've never heard of the guy," Morgan says. "Who is he?"

"Albert Verrhaus, the Baron," Kallie reiterates, shifting the phone from one ear to her other. She tosses the book from her lap, uncrosses her unshaven legs, and continues, "I told you about mom and me almost killing him. You know, he's that weird old guy that hangs around the mall reading, the guy in the riding boots… I pointed him out to you last week."

"The fossil that dresses like the guy who saved the white stallions—Patton?"

"Got him!" she yelps, "That's him—that guy."

"He's rich?" Morgan asks over the phone, "Why'd you go out there?"

"Mom had to deliver some stuff. Anyway, there he is riding this big horse—pitch black—and he's doing all these fancy steps, you know like when we went and saw the *Royal Lipizzaners*."

"Cool."

"No Morgan, it was awesome," she gushes. "He did this spin thing where the horse turns around, and he did it at the canter. And then—this is so great—and then he made the horse go skipping off around the ring, zigzagging from side to side."

"Sounds neat…"

"I'm going to try to get the beater tomorrow. I'll tell mom that I have to go to the mall and do some school shopping." Kallie lowers her voice to a hush as she reveals her plan. "I'm going to sneak out there and see if I can watch him ride some more…"

"Are you crazy?" Morgan interrupts, "What if he catches you—you're the one who said this guy is weird."

"No Morgan, listen. There's this ridge behind his house, I'll sneak up there and watch with dad's binoculars. He'll never see me."

"Yeah girlfriend," Morgan replies with a sarcastic laugh, "smart move. If you do that, we're going to see your face on a milk carton." The thought causes Morgan to shudder fearfully.

"You want to come along? You should see this guy ride."

"Oh yeah, I'd love to end up floating in the river—dead!"

"Come on Morgan," she pleads, "no harm no foul. It'll be fun." Kallie clings to the phone waiting for her to reply.

A stretched moment passes, finally Morgan says, "Really, I'd like to, but I can't. I've got a doctor's appointment tomorrow."

"Your physical for the soccer team?"

Too Far A Dream

Apprehension is clear in her voice as she says, "No, it's something else..."

"You got to be tested for rabies or what? Come on Morgan, what is it? Tell me."

After another elongated pause, Morgan whispers, "I'm late..." Kallie drops the phone. Two words—paralyzing news. Morgan calls desperately, "Kallie. Kallie are you there? Girlfriend?"

Kallie jabs her arms upward in shock, "I-eee!" she shrieks, and then stares blankly at the phone resting in her lap.

"Answer me, girlfriend. Kallie..."

Kallie grips the phone and presses it close to her mouth and ear. "Yeah Morgan, I'm here," she mumbles.

"I missed my period," Morgan repeats shyly. "I took one of those home pregnancy tests and I think it was positive."

"How could that be, Morgan?" Kallie asks, her voice conveying shock and trepidation. "Who did it? I always thought you were a virgin."

"God Kallie, where'd you get that idea?" she replies derisively. "I'm sixteen, I'm not a nun. You know, you're not the only girl that Tim felt up."

"Katie's brother? But I thought you hated him!"

"I do—what a looser!" The inflection in Morgan's voice betrays contempt when she huffs, "A minute man, that's Tim; a sixty second wonder. Screwing him was like holding a little perch—he'd wiggle and flop and then go limp! He never got me off—he was," she clears her throat and continues ruefully, "the first boy I ever did it with."

"What? No! Tim? You screwed Tim, he's the father?"

"Kallie, you're such a nerd sometimes," chides Morgan, "Nash is."

"That asshole!" roars Kallie. She yanks the phone from her ear and strangles it. "I'll bust that little prick's ass." Kallie yells, slamming the phone back to her ear and quizzing angrily, "How'd he get you to give it up, did he force you?—I know he did. That asshole. I said he was no good."

"He didn't want to do it..."

79

"You don't have to protect him," Kallie rails contemptuously, "He raped you didn't he?"

"No—God no. Nash didn't want to do it. He said he wasn't ready; that he believes in abstinence, and wanted to wait. I told him he'd better start putting out, or I'd be looking for a man who would. He thought about it and figured I'm worth it, so he did the deed." Kallie is squeezing the receiver tight enough to squirt milk from it when Morgan continues. "I like having sex. Its not like it's dirty or anything—cripes, even worms have sex. I wasn't going to wait until I'm an old hag. I'm pretty now—I say, use it or loose it—and having sex proves that a guy loves you—it's wonderful."

"I don't even know who you are Morgan..."

"Don't pretend to be so shocked, Kallie, like you don't think about it. You're not so innocent. It's just plain dumb for you to hold on to it. You should go out and get your share."

The strident tone of Kallie's voice affirms Morgan's charge. "Sure, I think about doing it," she snarls, "I'm not afraid of it. I could go lay some guy. I'm not a prude, but..." and then she speaks with certainty, "I don't want all the emotional crap that comes with having sex, and a boyfriend. I mean, think about it Morgan, you're sixteen, it's our junior year and you're pregnant—you'll be fat as a cow! Don't you think Nash is going to be looking around?"

"Nash really isn't like that, Kallie. I had to force him to have sex. He was clumsy at first, but now he's getting really good at it, I'm a good teacher—he won't be bringing home any strays."

"Don't believe it Morgan, he's a man, it's what they do..."

"Not my man," Morgan replies confidently, "he gets more than he can handle from me."

"God Morgan, you sound like a nympho!"

"Yeah, I'm a regular sex kitten..." laughs Morgan.

Kallie joins the laugh, but she's less jocular. After a moment, she presses the phone against her lips and asks in a whisper, "Have you told your mom?"

"No..."

"Are you going to?"

"I'm going to wait until I know for sure. She doesn't have to know until then—she'd just freak."

"What if you are, what if you're pregnant?" The sound of anguish enters Kallie's voice. "What will you do? Will you be able to graduate?"

"Nash says he'll support me, he doesn't want me to get an abortion—you know he's Catholic, don't you?" Kallie listens anxiously as Morgan continues, "I can still go to school, and after the baby's born, they have a daycare room. Nash and I will be there to take care of him—cool huh?"

"No Morgan, it's not COOL." Kallie rebuts harshly. "I think it's dumb, I think you should consider the consequences…"

"Duh! I have…"

Just then, there's a knock on Kallie's bedroom door. Kallie clutches the phone to her chest; Reggie asks from outside, "Kallie?"

"Yeah Mom?"

"It's ten thirty, you probably should get to bed…"

"Okay Mom, thanks." Kallie takes the phone from her chest, and returns to Morgan, "Just my mom, Morgan," she grouses, "I got to go now, but I want to talk to you when you get home from the doctor's—in case you need anything. We're still girlfriends aren't we, girlfriend?"

"Best girlfriends Kallie, the best. See-ya."

"Yeah, see-ya, Morgan. Call me."

Shortly after noon the next day, a clanking, sub-compact automobile winds its way along Gleason Road. Exhaust smoke, a wisp of trouble, puffs from the muffler. The car stops at a driveway marked 12848 Gleason Road; Kallie is behind the steering wheel. While the car idles, she leans across the center console, and avoiding the stick-shift lever, she studies the sheltered driveway quickly. She puts the car in neutral and engages the parking break. Getting out, she props against the car, and surveys precisely: the fortified limestone portal; the cloister of hedge and vine inside, and sun drenched canopy above; the high cliff rising to a breathless altitude, and then, at its summit, she notices a transmission relay tower penetrating the upper wind. "Yes! There must be a maintenance road," she squeals, hopping into the car, slamming the sprung door twice to close it before driving off to search for a maintenance road.

The road leading to the relay tower overlooking the Verrhaus estate is hidden at the rear of the bluff. It is nothing more than a single lane cart path that winds its way, precipitously, through the gnarled conifers on its way to the summit. Leaving Gleason Road, Kallie drives cautiously. The route is not easy, switching back and fourth across the bluff to attain a passable grade, traversing wash outs and detouring around fallen rocks. Reluctantly, the car chugs ahead. It takes ten minutes to scale the jagged road. Finally, Kallie reaches the top. Before her, assuming prominence in a park-like setting, the transmission tower stands. She squeaks the car to a stop on a flattened driveway beside the tower, and turns the ignition off; opening the car door, she grabs her worn backpack, gets out and whispers, "Careful Kallie," then closes the door silently so as not to betray her arrival. She glances around. Many paths diverge into the stunted junipers and spiny buckthorns obscuring the rim of the cliff. "Hum," she sighs, "that one looks promising." Walking ahead, into what appears to be a boundless sky held to earth by hedge, she navigates a tangled route into the shrubs. Along the way, she notices beer and soda cans, bits of litter, a scorched fire pit filled with trash, and a cast off, folding beach chair—she isn't the first visitor to enjoy this overlook—and then, after a few steps more, at the scary edge of the cliff, a view of the Verrhaus estate expands far below her. A breeze, soft as air moved by a dove's wing, fluffs a loose curl at her temple; she adjusts her ball cap, tucking the loose hair inside. A streak of sweat marks where her spine lays beneath her red T-shirt. "This is okay; this is cool," she muses, dropping her backpack, and then sighing, she squats cross-legged on the ground, and notes, "The old fossil really has it made. Look at this place…. That stable is big enough for three of our houses."

Eagerly, she waits an hour for something to happen below, nothing does. A second hour is passed in restless discomfort as Kallie discovers why the little red ants around her buttocks are called 'fire ants.' At five past three, she hears a far away sound— a door banging

Too Far A Dream

closed. She grabs the binoculars from her backpack; lifts them to her eyes; she adjusts the focus on a lone man walking from the house toward the stable.... "It's the Baron," she whispers gleefully.

In the herb garden far below Kallie's perch, the Baron swaggers along a paving stone walkway that connects the enormous house with the agrarian occupations of the estate. With a prideful smile—a self-satisfied, but not a smug smile—he enters the carriage house where his Jaguar is stored. There, he pauses a moment to admire his car before striding to the rear of the carriage house, and passing through a timber-framed, doorway that provides access to the attached stable. Lofty, open to the rafters, the airy, stable quickens as startled pigeons rush a slat-sided copula in the gabled roof high above. Acknowledging that he's intruded on their napping, the Baron calls out, "Sorry children. It's only me. Come back..." One by one, the pigeons return to their roosts. The Baron waits for them to settle before marching down the wide, center aisle of the stable. Paved with umber and yellow colored bricks laid in a herringbone design, the aisle stretches sixty feet to an exit that leads to the grazing meadows beyond—roomy stalls line the aisle on either side. Above the stalls are brimming haymows. Stacked with fresh, green bales of first crop timothy and orchard grass, the scent from the mows wafts downward and mingles with the odor of urine and manure that fills the cavity below. To a horseman, the resulting aroma is a cherished perfume. As he enters the only occupied stall, the Baron murmurs, "Whoa, Mouse. Easy boy. That's my good *Fledermaus*." Kindly, he strokes the giant's slick black neck, and comments, "Today, my little Mousy, you wear the double bridle..."

Just then a second voice enters the stable, and inquires, "Albert? Albert, are you in here?" It's the voice of a woman. She is approaching determinedly.

"In here *Charlene*, I'm in with Fledermaus," he replies.

As the woman enters through the passageway from the carriage house to the livery, she pauses to inquire again. "Where, Albert?" The impression she gives by her appearance is that of a refined foreigner, but her voice betrays no accent. She is in her late middle age. Her hair is variegated—brown, with streaks of gray—parted in the middle and drawn back at the temples where it is held in place by tortoise shell combs. She wears a generously sized, floral print dress that hangs loosely over her portly frame and reaches below her knees. A canvas apron protects the dress; it's dappled with myriad colored stains. Charlene looks around the livery and, in a tone that intends scolding, she says, "Albert, you left your pills on the table after tea…"

The Baron emerges from the tie stall and saunters toward Charlene; his saddle-brown riding boots ticking off strides like the sound of a lazy ratchet. She observes him fondly. His whitening hair is waxed in shiny waves. His aging face, richly stained by the sun in hues of tarnished copper, glows with a summer tan. In the unwrinkled space between his sparse gray eyebrows and his hairline, she could lay her hand and touch no follicle; his angular mandible juts proudly forward. Approaching, he pinches the open collar of his white shirt closed—a pretentious gesture of gentility performed by habit. He stops before her, smiles—his lips forming a narrow slit framed by upturned curls—and then, as if addressing his sovereign, he asks while rolling up his shirtsleeves, "Again? Have I forgotten my medicine?"

Sympathetically, she nods yes, handing the pills to him; and, noticing that his shirt tail has formed an unsightly gather in the waistband of his khaki breeches, she smoothes the wrinkles, and coos, "Is that better, Birdie?"

"Thank you Charlene, much better," he replies, rolling the medicine like dice in his palm. "You know," he adds, "it's not like I'll die if I forget to take them…."

Charlene tweaks his chin and warns him, scowling, "I've given you forty-three years—you old bastard. You'd better not even think about dying. Besides, there'd be too much celebrating in the old country when the news got there."

The Baron winks agreement, walks briskly to a water hydrant that protrudes from the wall of the tack stall abutting the doorway, lifts the handle, tosses the pills into his mouth, bends down, and slurping, he swallows. "There," he says, standing upright, wiping his mouth with his linen handkerchief, "that should keep the old country wondering—will the bastard live, or will he die?"

"I think you'll live," Charlene replies, laughing, "but just in case, you should repay my keeping you alive with a token of good will. Birdie, you didn't kiss me after lunch..."

"Ooo," he groans, feigning protest. Charlene puckers. "Okay, but Fledermaus gets jealous," he says, gesturing to the tack room, "step in here so he won't see us...." When they exchange a loving peck, a loud "WHAM!" reverberates from Fledermaus' stall.

"How does that old beast know what we're doing?"

"He probably heard our lips smack," replies the Baron. "Next, he'll smell your perfume on my breath, and expect me to share the treat." An impish glint shines from his eye. "Come on," he teases, mischievously tugging on Charlene's dress sleeve, "let's go and give Fledermaus a big smooch..."

Charlene struggles—the fullness of her dress and covering apron make the Baron's grasp tenuous. She cries out, "Let me go you old bastard, I'm not going to kiss your horse!" The Baron tugs some more. "No, no I won't! I'd give my kingdom not to kiss your horse!"

An impudent snort issues from the end stall—a hurricane of pollen is propelled by the exhaled wind.

The Baron lets Charlene loose. She jumps away. He growls and frowns in mock ferocity. Fledermaus snorts again. "Don't get him mad," he warns, "Don't hurt his feelings. I'm the one who'll suffer; he's going to take it out on me."

"So sorry, Birdie," she chides, dashing away, and with a return glance, she adds, blithely, "Don't forget, it's ribs and kraut for supper tonight."

As Charlene darts through the passage leading to the carriage house, the Baron ambles down the aisle to Fledermaus. When he enters the stall, he whispers, "Baked ribs and sauerkraut—*das ist gut*."

Kallie is waiting impatiently for the Baron to ride. She rests the binoculars on her lap; her eyes are fixed on the carriage house below. She shifts fitfully from one side of her buttocks to the other—the ants

85

are at work—she scratches at them with mortal intent. An osprey shrieks from the lofty drafts above. Kallie peeks skyward. There, among the craggy clouds she sees air-filled wings outstretched on pillowy currents. Motionless, the raptor soars. Another sound intrudes from far below. Kallie jerks her gaze downward. She holds her breath. Her prolonged hush is interrupted when she utters softly, "It's about time...." Anxiously, she awaits some action; silently, she squirms in anticipation. The sound grows louder—the clip and clop of steel horseshoes clicking on hard stone drifts from under the blazing, terracotta roof. She leans forward; she squints. A tiny man leads a giant horse onto the bridle path leaving the far end of the stable. Unhurried, the two walk side-by-side to the riding arena where they halt. Kallie raises the binoculars to her eyes and focuses on the Baron's horse; her enlarged view provides detail. Straining, she sees an enormous stallion more than sixteen hands high. His coat is black as a bat's eye at midnight. He is lean with deeply cut muscles. His haunches are full and low; his withers broad and high. His neck, arched at the poll, soars elegantly from strong shoulders; his ears are peaked, and his head tapers like poured liquid splashing into a kind smile. "Now that's some fancy horse," she giggles secretly.

Outside the arena, preparing to enter at A, the Baron tightens the girth, pulls down the saddle irons, slides the double reins over Fledermaus' neck, and mounts—the giant stands still and square. At once secure in the saddle, with the reins looped over his forearm, the Baron pulls out a pair of brown leather riding gloves that he's had tucked under his belt behind his back. He puts them on smoothing each slender finger like a surgeon before making a first cut, and then, he takes up the reins. Although Kallie knows that the Baron must give an aid to urge his horse on, from her perch, even with the enlarged view provided by her binoculars, she sees none given. The Baron and Fledermaus enter the arena as if by common consent, and begin their warm-up, walking 'long and low' around a twenty-meter circle, then a change of rein at X, followed by another circle.

"Is that all he's going to do?" wonders Kallie. Unconsciously, she scratches the growing welts on her buttocks, and grouses,

Too Far A Dream

"Cripes, I can do that good on Cashman. Come on, gramps, do something great."

After concluding the second circle, the Baron releases the right rein and gently strokes Fledermaus' neck—perspiration, oozing from his obsidian pelt, dampens the Baron's leather-clad palm. Then, taking up the rein again, he muses aloud, "Ah, my little Mousy, shall we ride the kür today?"

The elegant giant murmurs approvingly, and nods in a way that would imply that he understands the performance before him. Wistfully, the Baron speaks what he imagines to be Fledermaus' reply: "The master's heels close on my flanks; I feel his spur—a tender caress—first on the left, and then on the right. He sits deeply into the saddle, I round my back, and explode into collected trot; haunches lowered, chest thrust forward, my head high, I move gallantly into the bit. At X, I ram to a square halt; I don't twitch; I don't flinch—I am muscle made of stone. He tweaks my mane invisibly—so the judges can't see—and he applauds my sure-footedness, whispering, 'That's my good little Mousy.' Of course we'll ride the kür. Let's get on with it! I love the passage; I live for the canter half-pass, and the pirouette—there isn't another horse as excellent at it as me. And although it seldom happens, I'm devastated if I flub the changes: the four time, the two time, the tempi. And piaffer? Perfect every time! Yes, I am that good—I'm not boasting idly—watch me, see for yourself."

And Kallie does. For thirty-five minutes she witnesses the duo perform without flaw. The choreography is faultless; the transitions, seamless; the collected trot changes to piaffer imperceptibly; piaffer to passage, perfect as a cloudy day giving way to sunshine. After a final halt at X, the Baron puts Fledermaus on a long rein, and allows him to walk at liberty; the horse stretches his elegant neck downward, relaxed, his muzzle glides inches above the sandy footing. The Baron relaxes too, nodding his head side to side; arching his back; alternately rounding and squaring his shoulders—sweat marks the underarms of his white shirt—he removes his feet from the saddle irons, reaches in his hip pocket taking out his handkerchief, and swabs his forehead. Just then, off in the distance, he hears the sharp chirping of a cellular phone. He glances to the scarp above the house and sees a flash of reflected light—Kallie's binoculars are trained on him, the sun shines from the lens. The Baron halts his horse; he stares suspiciously at the rim of the cliff. The chirping comes again. He trains his ears and eyes with pinpoint accuracy on Kallie's location; her red T-shirt, bright as a matador's cape, reveals the lair. "Well, Mousy," he ponders quietly, "what have we here? Have we discovered a trespasser, is there a spy in our woods?"

   Dropping the binoculars to her lap, Kallie struggles frantically to find the cellular telephone ringing in her backpack. Pertinacious, she's a terrier digging for a rat; she claws determinedly. Finally, she finds it, yanks it from hiding, and crouching, she presses the phone against her lips as she whispers, "Hello, this is Kallie."
   "Kallie, Kallie." the voice on the phone responds, "It's me, Morgan. Where are you? You okay, girlfriend?"
   "Shush! I don't want him to hear me. I'm up in the woods behind the Baron's house, I've been here…" She glances at her wristwatch. "…I've been here almost three hours."
   "Are you nuts, girl? You said you were going to do it, but I didn't believe you—shit, you'll never guess what happened today."
   "Shush! Not so loud," Kallie says, repeating the caution. She glances down, worried that her conversation will alert the Baron—he's a motionless speck in the middle of the arena, and without the binoculars, she can't see what he's up to. "Give me a second Morgan, I'm going to turn down the volume on this phone." Kallie takes the phone from her ear and adjusts the volume. She returns to her conversation with Morgan. "There," she continues in a hushed tone, "that should do it. What happened, what are you talking about?"
   "My doctor's appointment this morning."
   "God, Morgan," Kallie exclaims in an excited whisper, "I forgot. What did the doc tell you? Everything okay? Are you pregnant? Where are you, are you at home?"
   "No, I'm over at Nash's—he went with me this morning, we both talked to the doc."

"What? What? Tell me, Morgan."

"Well, we had like this long talk, the three of us. She was really nice. She didn't bitch at us or tell us we shouldn't be screwing, it was like a counseling session..."

While she listens to Morgan, Kallie stretches to peek at the Baron below. He's dismounted his horse and is walking Fledermaus back to the stable. She sighs in relief as she pulls at the crotch of her jeans. "I have to pee like a racehorse, Morgan," she interjects, "but at least I can talk now, the Baron's done riding. Go on."

"Well, she told me that I did the test wrong. That I should have taken it in the morning, so she told me to go into the bathroom and pee in this little cup—you know—like for our soccer physicals, and then she drew some blood."

"Yeah? Then what?" Kallie pries anxiously.

"She gave them to Andrea, her nurse, and said she should send them to the lab STAT. That means, like right now."

"Is she going to call you and tell you if you're pregnant?"

"No," replies Morgan, "the lab's going to send me results in a few days, but that doesn't matter, I already know..."

"How? What happened?"

"*Rosmah...*" Morgan starts,

"Who?"

"Doctor Levi-Schmidt, she said we could call her Rosmah. Cool huh? Anyways, she did a test right there in the office..."

"What did she say, are you pregnant? Ouch!" cries Kallie as she scratches at her rump. "Sorry Morgan, I sat in an ant hill and the little buggers are chewing my butt to shreds."

"That's got to hurt, girlfriend," Morgan laughs, imagining the pain Kallie must be in. "Your skinny butt's going to swell up like a melon!"

"But you, are you?" Kallie quizzes.

Morgan pauses; she's teasing Kallie and trying to heighten the drama before saying: "No, I'm not knocked-up."

"That's great news, Morgan!"

"Maybe. I don't know—maybe not."

"What do you mean?" Kallie asks, confused by Morgan's evasive answer.

"I was sort of looking forward to getting a check," Morgan replies, her voice betraying regret. "Last summer, when Sandy got pregnant, after she had the baby, social services sent her a check for five-hundred bucks every month, and she got a bunch of other stuff, too. Now her mom takes care of the baby, and she's out partying. I thought it'd be kind of nice—you know?—it'd be cool to get that much money every month—I wouldn't have to spend my weekends waiting on the dorks at the diner."

"Morgan, that's a crappy attitude," Kallie scolds her. "You'd be a welfare mom. This can't be you talking—you don't really mean it. You sound just like a slut when you say stuff like that."

"A slut? Are you calling me a slut?" Morgan shouts over the phone.

"I didn't mean it like that, Morgan…"

"Yes you did! You think I'm a slut, don't you?" she rants angrily. "Just because you never get laid, just because you're still a virgin. That's a bogus thing to say to your best friend."

"Morgan, I'm sorry, I didn't mean it."

"You meant it Kallie—you're such a priss, so perfect, always the perfect little Kallie. You never did like me going out with Nash. You hate him. You think I'm trash." Morgan's tone grows more harried and irrational. "Just because I'm chubby, you think the only way I can keep a guy is to screw him…"

"No, Morgan."

"And because I'm not rich…"

"Neither am I," whimpers Kallie, "My folks aren't rich…"

"Bullshit! At least you have a dad, and your mom's not a drunk—you don't know anything about me. Well, that's it, Kallie. I don't need this shit from you. We'll see who's a slut, girlfriend." And then shouting, she adds sarcastically, "Ex-girlfriend!"

Kallie jerks back in shock as Morgan hammers down her phone ending the conversation. She shakes her head in disbelief, closes the faceplate of the phone and stares at it, wondering, "What am I going to do now? Why'd she get so mad?" She tosses the phone in her

Too Far A Dream

backpack and whispers earnestly, "I didn't mean it, Morgan." As Kallie straightens her knees to get up, she leans forward to see what is happening at the stable; when she does, the binoculars slide from her lap. "NO!" she squeals in alarm, making a frantic grab for them, but it's too late. They bounce on the ground, summersault once, and tumble over the edge of the cliff. "I-eee!" she shrieks, stunned by the misfortune. An instant later, she hears the sound of snapping twigs as the binoculars plummet through the canopy, and then a dull thud as they hit the ground below. "Those were dad's; those were dad's expensive 'nocks,'" she groans. "Kallie, you're dead. You are so dead, girl." Mindlessly, she pulls at her groin to free the jeans from her crotch. She rubs her buttocks feverishly; she trembles while doing a two-footed jig and exclaims, "And I got ants in my pants—ooo, ouch!" And then comes an ominous sound. The sound of a car starting, but not just any car, it is the unmistakable sound that no other car makes, it's the sound of a Jaguar growling to life. Kallie quits fidgeting. She stands petrified as she looks toward the roundabout outside the carriage house. Her face is blank; her eyes are wide. The Baron's sleek black Jaguar emerges from its den. It glides along the cobbled driveway on rubber paws. It skulks out of view as if seeking some hidden quarry. "Oh-oh," Kallie gasps as she bends over to retrieve her backpack from the ground. "Gotta go, girl," she quips, dashing along the littered path toward her car. The footing is uneven and her gait unsure, she stumbles, regains her balance and darts onward. Breathless, she arrives at her car. She throws open the door. She jumps in. Fitfully, she searches in her pocket for the keys. "Yes!" she exclaims, finding them. She rams the keys in the ignition, turns them a quarter turn. The little compact chugs out a puff of blue smoke, and clanks as it starts, but it runs. She shifts the car in gear, pulls out circling the cable relay tower, and rattles down the access road. Back and forth she winds along the switchbacks descending the bluff—Gleason road is just ahead, it seems like an insurmountable distance off. And then, "Oh shit!" she screams, jumping on the break pedal with both feet, squealing the car to a stop right at the edge of Gleason road. She can drive no farther; her way is blocked. Someone has stretched a chain across the access road. Kallie bangs her head to her hands on the steering wheel, "No!" she bleats, and bangs again and again, "No, no, no! That weird-o..." And then it strikes her—weird-o. She glances nervously around, and wonders, "Is he hiding in the woods? If I get out, will he grab me?" Kallie cowers for a moment, staring at the outstretched chain. Then she notices a small slip of paper tacked to the post where the chain is hooked. "It's a trick," she thinks, "a trap. He's out there!" She hesitates; the car idles; the air is quiet and still. She stares intently at the paper; goose bumps bristle on her shoulders; the smell of burning oil stings inside her nose. Just then, the Baron's Jaguar creeps quietly from the undergrowth along Gleason Road, and slinks into view at the access road. Black, black as an evil heart on Halloween, it pads its way slowly like a dreaded menace; the motor purrs and growls; two narrow eyes glare through the tinted-glass windows at the trapped quarry. Kallie yowls, "She-it!" and smothers her face in her hands. The Jaguar prowls confidently on, and disappears.

After several seconds pass, Kallie peers between her fingers—the coast is clear. She opens the car door, sneaks out, and timidly, she edges nearer the neatly folded slip of paper. Cautiously, she reaches; her fingers, inept as a baby's, fumble; she removes the pushpin holding the note, unfolds it, and reads the hand penciled words:

> *To whom it may concern:*
> *You are trespassing on private property. If apprehended, you will be handed over to the authorities for prosecution.*
> *Albert Verrhaus, property owner.*

"This was a bad idea, girlfriend," she groans, crumpling the note, and tucking it in her hip pocket, "and how are you going to explain the binoculars to dad?" Trembling, she unhooks the chain blocking her escape, dropping it to the ground; she jogs back to the car, hops in and drives across the barrier onto Gleason Road where she stops, gets out, walks slowly back to replace the chain. "I have to remember about that chain next time I sneak up here," she mutters, haggardly returning to her car, and a lucky escape.

When Kallie arrives at home, she hurries into the house. As she enters, she kicks off her sneakers and rushes to the bathroom with an urgency impelled by nature. After a moment, the toilet flushes, and the sound of running water leaks through the door as Kallie washes her hands. Emerging refreshed, she goes to the phone on the hall table, dials Morgan's number, and while waiting for the call to connect, she composes her thoughts.

A woman's voice answers, "Hello…"

"Hi, Mrs. Jasperson, is Morgan there?"

"Who is this?" Mrs. Jasperson slurs.

"It's Kallie Phillipa, Morgan's friend… Can I talk to her?"

The vinyl window shades, street side, behind Mrs. Jasperson, are drawn. The room is cast in smoky gloom; the only light comes from a shaded table lamp, and the kaleidoscopic glow of a television. Mrs. Jasperson fidgets to light a cigarette before answering Kallie. In the middle of the room, lounging on a legless couch in front of the TV, Morgan gobbles corn flakes from a plastic bowl. Mrs. Jasperson covers the mouthpiece of the phone, drags listlessly on her cigarette, and whispers to Morgan, "It's Kallie. Do you want to get this?" Morgan shakes her head, adamantly gesturing, no. And then she growls sternly, "The little bitch called me a slut. She can go to hell!"

"She says she can't come to the phone now…"

"Oh, okay," Kallie replies, contritely. "Could you tell her I'll call back later?"

"No, don't do that," Mrs. Jasperson drools, puffing indelicately on her cigarette—her diction is garbled; she's been drinking since four o'clock. "Morgan doesn't want to talk to you—and who the hell are you to call my daughter a slut?"

"What? I didn't," gasps Kallie. Stunned by the harsh tone and frankness of Mrs. Jasperson's comment, she stutters, "That's not what I meant, I said I was sorry."

"So you admit it, huh? You lying tramp!"

"No…"

Seething, Mrs. Jasperson assaults Kallie mercilessly, "You didn't get the message did you? Morgan said she ain't going to talk to you—

nobody calls a kid of mine a slut—so, don't ever call back here again. You little bitch. You smart-ass, goodie two shoes."
"I'm sorry…"
"Never!" Mrs. Jasperson rants, slamming down the phone.
Kallie stares at the telephone receiver, bewildered, and whimpers, "Morgan, aren't we friends anymore?"

Shortly before noon, three days later, there is a knock at the Phillipa's front door. Anthony, emerging from his second floor office, yells in response, "Just a second, keep your shirt on." As he descends the stairs, he glances at the screen door. A parcel delivery person is standing outside with a package. "Here I come," Anthony says, reaching the door, and swinging it open, he asks, "Can I help you?"
"I have a package for Anthony Phillipa. Is that you?"
"Yeah, that's me. What you got?"
"Could you sign here?" the delivery person asks as he hands Anthony a pen, and indicates where to sign.
Anthony signs the sheet. The package, about the size of a two slice toaster wrapped in brown paper, is handed to him; he looks at it, shakes it gently and replies, "Thanks a lot." As the delivery person leaves, Anthony walks to the hall table, sets the package down, and glances at the return address: 12848 Gleason Road. "Who do I know that lives up on Gleason Road?" he wonders aloud. Searching in his pocket, he takes out an enamel handled folding knife; cutting the wrapping tape, he carefully opens the box, removes the padding from around the object inside, and stares puzzled, recognizing his binoculars. A hand written note, stuffed beneath them, attracts his attention. He takes it out and reads:

> *Dear Mister Phillipa:*
> *I found these field glasses behind my house recently. Better care should be given them. I would have enjoyed keeping them for myself, but the inscription implies that you are the rightful owner.*
> *Albert Verrhaus*

Anthony lifts up the field glasses, examines them closely, and wails, "Kallie?"

* * *

Victor John Faith

Four: Acceptable Terms

 A year and four months have passed since Anthony's field glasses were returned to him. Kallie is now a senior in high school. Even though she never intended a literal meaning to be taken from her comment, Morgan hasn't forgiven Kallie for calling her a slut—they are no longer friends. During the last summer, Kallie worked at the racetrack for Winston Chase. While there, she learned how to groom and saddle racehorses, walk hots, and she galloped a few of Winston's pensioners at his training farm.
 It is nine o'clock in the morning, one week before Christmas. An early December snowstorm has left the pastures, woodlands and bluffs wearing its chilly wrap—a flocky coat of snow. Hoarfrost encrusts every twig, branch and lofty stick of every tree—an icy gust, blasts snowy flecks, dousing the frigid air with crystalline puffs that drift in a dazzling shiver.
 The Phillipa's house is camouflaged within the winter landscape. Wags and Goldie romp with purpose in the snowbound yard; Wags stops abruptly, squats and does his job leaving a steamy pile—a searing biscuit of poop—before rejoining Goldie in a dash toward the stable. They rush in the open front door and jog down the aisle toward Wicked Punch's stall. A raspy murmur comes from inside, "Easy big boy, we'll be going out in a second. Cashman won't eat all the hay." And then, out of the stall struts Wicked Punch, followed closely behind by Kallie who dangles from his lead rope—one would wonder, who is leading whom.
 It's been eighteen months since Kallie and Reggie rescued the unlucky runt. He was underweight and tiny then, but now, prancing beside Kallie, he is huge. He's grown to nearly sixteen hands in height and filled out proportionately. He's a mass of moving muscle—a sleek bay with black points—he trots, barely advancing his stride, every inch, a stallion to contend with. "Whoa Punchie," Kallie groans as she hobbles to keep up, "give your mom a break…"
 Sometime, during the last year and a half, something has happened to Kallie. She's no taller, even though her woolen stocking

cap adds inches to her height, and although she appears massive, dressed in a snowmobile suit, it's difficult to tell if she's lost or gained weight, but some thing is odd—her steps are tenuous, uneven. She is struggling, ungainly, to stay abreast of her regal horse, and is trailing behind like a dragging train behind a monarch. Her right leg clomps awkwardly to the ground with every step. The dogs lead the way up the aisle to the turnout paddocks behind the stable. Full of energy, Wicked Punch prances; Kallie clods beside him. Arriving at the door, they stop. As Kallie reaches to undo the clasp on Punch's halter, he snorts, paws the pavement eagerly, and then erupting, he charges to freedom. Lunging gaily into the frozen daylight, he bucks, kicks his heels, rips a chattering fart; he gallops, blasting frozen shrapnel from his pounding hoofs—this fierce missile has a mission: a daily romp that builds muscle. Kallie stares transfixed, watching what was once the feeble, orphaned colt. Wags, sitting at Kallie's knee, begs for a rub. Kallie complies, scratching his droopy ears with both hands, and giggles, "Did you see that 'Waggles? That bugger is fast. You know, maybe, some dreams can come true…"

In the Phillipa kitchen, the morning sun is shining through the window above the sink. The stained glass of the upper pane adds cozy warmth to December's anemic light. The aroma of fresh coffee, and fried bacon fills the room with a scent that's stout enough to chew. Reggie is standing at the stove across from the sink; she is buttering crunchy, black toast. Anthony is seated, resting his elbows on the table, hugging a steaming cup of coffee within his clasp hands. A plate of eggs and bacon cools in front of him, another plate cools across the table. Reggie slices the buttered toast, and as she carries it toward the breakfast table, Anthony lowers his coffee and watches her.

"What about some nice earrings?" Reggie asks, placing the toast in the middle of the table, and sitting in her chair. She fluffs her napkin across her lap, and continues, "Kallie doesn't have anything really special to wear; she might like some earrings."

"She has her hoops, those are pretty. I like them. And what about her silver horseshoes?"

"They aren't special, I bought them at a bargain counter."

"Well, they look expensive," he replies, slicing into his eggs. "Besides, you know what she wants for Christmas…"

"After last summer, I don't know if an exercise saddle is a good idea."

"It's what she wants, Reggie." Some egg yoke has dribbled onto Anthony's chin; Reggie gestures to him. Taking her hint, he daubs his chin with his napkin, and then continues talking, "Why don't you get her some earrings, and I'll buy her the saddle? How much can earrings cost—fifty bucks?"

"That's not the point, Anthony," she says, expressing annoyance, and then her tone expresses misgiving, "I don't know if she should try riding again."

Anthony gazes across the table at Reggie; they pause, sharing a secret recollection. "I don't know either, Reggie," he replies sympathetically, "but that's a decision we can't make for her. She's been after me to get her a saddle all year. I can't let her down. Go on pal, you buy her the earrings."

"I was thinking gemstones, Anthony. How fat is your wallet?"

Anthony glances up; his face stretches in surprise. Just then the pounding thump of Kallie stomping her feet on the rear deck interrupts Anthony and Reggie's conversation. The door to the enclosed porch opens, Kallie steps inside followed closely by Wags and Goldie. Reggie gestures to Anthony with her finger pressed to her lips to keep quiet. The door to the kitchen opens, the dogs bound inside, and then, Kallie clomps in. She takes off her stocking cap and tosses it among the boots lined up along the wall next to the door. Then she unzips her snowmobile suit and peels it from her torso, letting it drape from her waist.

"I hope you saved some bacon for me, Dad," she grumbles playfully.

Anthony smiles impishly, and retorts, "You better get your skinny ass to the table, shrimp, or the big dog's going to get it all."

Kallie shuffles to the table and picks up an empty coffee cup; as she does, she leans toward Anthony, curls her upper lip, and through the ample space between her front teeth, she growls aggressively, "Gr-ruff, gr-ruff!" Then, snatching a slice of bacon from his plate, she chides him, "That's what I thought, big doggie. All bark and no bite!" Munching the bacon, Kallie walks to the stove, pours herself a cup of coffee, goes to the refrigerator, yanks open the door and takes out a carton of milk. She pours some into her cup, replaces the carton, and lifting the cup to her nose, she sniffs it deeply. "Ah," she sighs, "a person could live on the smell of a good ol' cup of joe." Lifting her focus from the coffee, she smiles happily, and chirps, "Good morning wonderful parents. Were you talking about a Christmas present for your adorable daughter?"

"No, not a chance!" Anthony replies quickly. "You're not a real daughter, you were adopted—she was, wasn't she darlin'?"

"I think we found her on the street…"

Kallie sneers; her nostrils flair. Ambling to the breakfast table, she taunts her parents, "Yeah, but I'm here, none the less. The only loving child you two old farts have, so it's time to cough up the ching." When she sits down between Reggie and Anthony, she nabs a slice of toast from Anthony's plate, lays a piece of bacon on it, and rocking back on her chair, she devours it with several rapid bites. "Well, talk to me folks," she continues, interrupting her remark with a burp, "what you getting your little bundle of joy?"

Reggie glances at Kallie, and comments glibly, "Maybe we were having a little chat about Christmas, but I don't think your name came up. Did it Anthony?"

"Nope, I don't remember hearing it." As Anthony reaches to the plate in the center of the table for another piece of toast, he asks, "Could you pass me the marmalade darling?" Reggie digs into a faux *Wedgwood* bowl on the table, and searches through several foiled packets. Clumsily, she tosses one across the table to Anthony who grabs it on one bounce. "Thanks," he says, winking at Reggie. "The next time you go to the diner, be sure to cob some more of these, they're great." Anthony opens the packet of marmalade and plops the contents in a massive dollop on his toast. He folds the slice in half and takes a bite. With the dogs curled snugly at their feet, Reggie and Kallie watch silently as Anthony chews—his eyes droop closed with contentment, he smiles blissfully—the marmalade is producing a catatonic effect.

After several prolonged moments of watching Anthony doze and drool, Reggie turns to Kallie, and asks, "Dad and I are going to go to the mall later to do some shopping, do you want to come along?"

"Yeah, sure," she yaps enthusiastically. "I have to get some Christmas cards, and a couple of little gifts for some friends. Just let me take a quick shower first." She looks down at her hobbled leg, and pinching her nose closed, she adds, "This cast is starting to stink again."

"Just a few more weeks and you'll get it off," observes Anthony, returning from slumber.

"I know, Dad, but then, it's another surgery to take the pins out, and God knows how much therapy." Kallie sighs and stares off into space thoughtfully. "And I'll probably have to wear a knee brace forever…"

Reggie reaches to comfort her, but Kallie's mind has wondered off. In a momentary twitch, she remembers an early morning—an overcast, humid summer morning. Mammatus clouds sag from the turbulent sky, but the air is still. "It may storm later," she thinks, "but I can get this ride in." Kallie recalls galloping a tense, gray gelding around the backstretch of Winston's training track. The horse is on the muscle and contentiously snatching the bit; Kallie bridges the reins across its neck; the running martingale adds strength to her effort; the gelding relents and gallops handily on. "Good boy," she whispers, moving comfortably with his elongated stride. She recalls the oncoming breeze, like the roar from a conch held to the ear, rushing through her riding helmet; her gloved hands—clinched fists on the reins—guiding the horse gently in spite of its determined pull, and ahead, the freshly groomed sand track seems to merge, seamlessly, with the sky.

A bay horse gallops lazily between her and the inner rail. "Keep him steady, Kallie," the exercise boy advises as he passes and moves off.

"Thanks, Johnny—will do…." Suddenly, Johnny's horse bounds violently to the right, changes leads and rushes out of control toward the center of the track. "What the hell?" Kallie whispers, and then it happens. Entering the track, just yards ahead, a bull snake uncoils

Too Far A Dream

from weedy cover; it slithers and stretches to a length of six feet. Her horse sees it. It's gripped by fear. It's course wavers. It leaps violently, and plants all four limbs stiffly into the sand in an instantaneous stop. Kallie reels forward onto the gelding's neck; she clings on desperately, cringes, and prays, "Oh God, this isn't good— Oh God!" The horse trembles—the huge snake wiggles at its hooves—it paws its way frantically backward; it brays, panicking; rearing, its forelimbs leave the ground. "Oh shit," Kallie cries, "Don't flip—oh shit!" And then, "Clouds?" she wonders, "Am I flying? Why is my horse floating? How did it get up there?" Kallie slams to the ground; her teeth grind sand. She watches her horse plunging backward; it seems to hover endlessly above her. "No," she pleads, silently remembering a moment that was a lifetime. She admires the tooling on the saddle; she counts the braids in the tumbling gelding's mane; she smells its sweat, and then, she vomits air as the falling horse crashes atop her.

At the breakfast table, Kallie shivers. Anthony presses his hand to her shoulder, but cannot aid her; the nightmare continues. Everything is black now; deprived of touch, taste, smell, vision, Kallie wanders in a groggy world. Faintly, she hears a somber voice explain: *"The knee can't be repaired, there's too much damage, we'll have to replace it with a prosthesis. There's some nerve damage too—we won't know how much until we get in there. We can pin the ankle, it will always be stiff, but she'll be able to walk..."* Far away, she hears sobbing, "Mom? Dad—what's wrong?" she wonders, and then the drowsy blackness brings calm and silence until...

"Kallie, Kallie?" Reggie asks, shaking her. "Are you still with us?"

Kallie shudders, takes a deep breath, and grimacing, replies, "Sorry Mom, I must have zoned out. It's really strange, some times, I remember my wreck like it's happening right now..."

"It'll be with you for a long time, honey. Try not to relive it—it was terrible."

Anthony's eyes have filled with tears, he is trying not to let Kallie know how much her accident devastated him when he suggests, "Go on, shrimp, run upstairs and jump in the shower. Then we'll go and have some fun; I'll buy you a latté at the mall."

"That's funny, Dad. Run and jump—maybe," she says, scooping up two more pieces of bacon and another slice of toast, "but not just yet." As she starts to rise from her chair, the bulk of the union suit tips it backward onto the floor with a crash. Kallie teeters off balance. "Oops," she moans, "that doesn't go on my naughty or nice list, does it?"

"Where is that naughty or nice list, Anthony?"

"I think I sent it off yesterday, but I could send an email to amend it..."

Kallie stuffs the bacon and toast into her mouth. As she bends over to right the chair, Wags and Goldie, who were startled from their nap, rush to lick bacon grease and butter from her cheeks. "Ugh!" she shouts, laughing. The dogs slobber her with ravenous glee, and she squeals, "Down boys, back, back! Help, no more doggie kisses!" She lunges to restrain them and they jostle her affectionately. Finally, they yield long enough for her to put the chair upright, and wipe her face with her shirt sleeve. "I guess I don't need a shower after all," she quips, "the dogs licked me clean!"

Anthony and Reggie are laughing at the dog's antics, when suddenly Anthony grabs his nose in response to some foul smell. "Wow, what the hell is that?" he cries, tears streaming from his eyes.

"What, Dad?"

"Pew, ugh, oh my God!" gasps Reggie.

"What?" Kallie asks blankly, and then it hits her, "Holy cow!" she screams, pinching her nose in a vain effort to block the stench. "Goldie, was that you? Wow, what a fart! What have you been feeding him, Dad—rotten cabbage? Open the door fast, it's Goldie gas."

Anthony jumps to the door and flings it open; he flails the air trying to ventilate the kitchen. Reggie holds her napkin tightly to her nose. Kallie flees, stumbling. Wags crawls shyly under the table, and Goldie sits serenely, pretending to be innocent of the crime.

The *Belleview Crossing* is a typical retail shopping mall. It has four major department stores joined by corridors to a central court.

Too Far A Dream

The central court is the hub of the shopping center. Customers, milling from store to store, inevitably end up resting on the inviting benches, reclining in one of the many 'shaker' style chairs, or taking a break while seated at pedestal café tables. They sip beverages, eat snacks, unlade themselves of their packages, they compare purchases, and chat. From high overhead, sunlight cascades through a glass-domed ceiling and floods the courtyard in a tranquil glow. The space is wide, open and airy. Cedar boughs, decorated with maroon and gold ribbon, sag from the elevated gangways of the second story. A faint melody of festive carols wafts from afar—a tintinnabulum that mocks at jingling cash. Hubbub throbs remotely on the outskirts—the kiosks are busy, the venders frantic. It's Christmas time at the mall.

Anthony, Reggie and Kallie, dressed for the coldest weather, meander into the courtyard. In the balmy tropic enclosed by the overhead dome, they seem comical—down-filled puffy balls of red and blue nylon. Like spherical Christmas ornaments hung from a tree, they sway from side to side as they walk—Kallie waddles. Shoppers, some pushing strollers, some in small gangs, others going solo, dart, shove and dodge as they zigzag through the crushing mêlée—it's a battlefield of desperate shoppers, but the Phillipas are unaffected by the skirmishes that rage around them; they have no mission other than to enjoy a day of leisurely shopping. They stop at the margin of the courtyard, stare at the festive decorations: myriad colored lights flash; white-flocked, stubby pine trees in planters—a forest of them—buffer a seated Santa; huge ribbons, giant bows, enormous pennants, and balsam wreaths dangle everywhere; and the scent of cinnamon and apple potpourri—an aromatic pie for the nose—provides soothing nourishment.

"This is so cool," Anthony giggles, oozing adolescent charm, and rubbing his hands together. "I think we're going to have some real fun spending Daddy's money today. What's the plan, kids—sound good?"

Subduing any betrayal of agreement, Reggie teases, "Anthony, you're like a little boy; you get so excited when you go shopping—behave."

Kallie pokes him with her elbow, and whispers: "Be a good, little boy, or Mommy won't get you a cookie later..."

"That would be the lump of coal in my stocking, wouldn't it?"

"...and Santa Claus might be the only one getting kissed under the mistletoe on Christmas night."

"Santa must have done something really special last year," Anthony replies, winking, "he got two kisses—he would have gotten more, but Mom thought the elves were watching!"

"Poor Santa."

"But this year," he adds, narrowing his eyes fiendishly, "elves or not, Santa's going to have his way with Regina Phillipa. Cookies, milk, the works..."

Kallie winks, concurring with Anthony's plot. In unison, they shout, "Yes!" and exchange 'high-five' salutes.

"Stop it you two." Reggie growls at them. "That lady heard you." She nods to indicate what lady heard. Anthony and Kallie look at an elderly woman in a frumpy, old, tartan plaid coat; her gray hair has a garish, rose tint; and topping her dazzling poll, she wears a hat that would make a fop blush. Anthony snickers. "God," sighs Reggie, gruffly, "you're a mean man! You get a Christmas goodie, and you brag about it all year!" Anthony starts to whistle, *I Saw Mommy Kissing Santa Claus*. "Kallie, ignore your father," she says, scolding her, and then, turning to Anthony, she shakes her finger admonishing him, "No cookie for you little man..." Anthony plants a smooch on Reggie's pointing finger and pleads by singing: *Diamonds Are A Girl's Best Friend*. She crosses her arms, taps her foot on the marble floor, and pretends to stand her ground before saying, "Well, maybe one cookie," then she squints menacingly, and warns him, "but I expect you to be on your best behavior—and you too, Kallie."

"You got it darlin'. Let the Christmas bells ring, Mister P's spending ching!"

"Oh good, they've got them!" Kallie interrupts suddenly. The greeting cards displayed at a nearby kiosk have caught her attention. "You kids go on and play. I'm going to run over there and get some cards."

Too Far A Dream

"Kallie, where will we meet you?" Reggie asks as Kallie hobbles off.

Stopping, and shouting, "Out in front here. You'll recognize me; I'll be the wonderful kid you're buying presents for." And then she's gone.

Anthony cuddles, takes Reggie by the hand, and murmurs affectionately, "Come on darlin', let's head on over to the jewelers. We can kill two birds with a couple of stones."

"We are talking gemstones now, aren't we Tony?" coos Reggie as they disappear into the mad crush of shoppers.

Loitering near the kiosk, Kallie is staring at a reproduction print of the mural she first saw painted on the wall of the grandstands at Dorchester Downs: galloping horses thunder off the print that hangs from the marquee of the kiosk. Below it are arranged stacks of seasonal cards depicting horses. Kallie reaches for a box; grabbing it, she examines it closely. In the foreground of the picture is the painted image of a racehorse; there is no jockey, no bridle, and no race. Beside it, as it strolls round the first turn, walks a foal. In the background are the white spires atop the grandstands of Churchill Downs. The scene is shown in the early light of morning. A fresh blanket of snow covers everything. The caption reads simply: "May your days be bright." Kallie looks at the name of the artist: Charles Foxx. "Do you have another box of these?" she asks the harried vendor. He ignores her. She searches through the pile and finds another box of the same cards, glances at the price on the back, "Eighteen dollars for twelve cards?" she gasps, and then she mutters, "You're not only a good painter, *Charlie*, you're a good thief too." Putting one box of cards back on the kiosk, she reaches into her pocket and digs out several, neatly folded bills. She peels out a twenty, surveys the line of eager customers slyly, then, bumping into a man in line ahead of her, she whines, "Oh, I'm sorry sir. Did I hurt you? I broke my leg and I'm a little clumsy in this cast." She's playing the man for sympathy and hoping for cuts to the head of the line. "I just have this one box of cards for my grandma. She loves horses…" Kallie smiles innocently; the man steps aside and lets her go before him, so do the rest of those lined up in front of him. She

105

hands the twenty to the vendor who rings up the sale, drops the cards into a bag and gives her change. Kallie turns to the man who gave her cuts; mustering every ounce of charm she has in her small frame, she pipes, "Thank you sir, you're very kind. Merry Christmas."

As Kallie moseys away, she makes more of her limp than honesty would allow. Once out of sight of the kiosk, she saunters to the middle of the courtyard and imbibes on the cheery ambiance. She watches the people scurry past her in every direction—all on two good legs—and thinks aloud, "Kallie, you're so lucky. It could have been a lot worse." She wobbles across the courtyard to an unoccupied bench and sits down; off to her left, Santa deals patiently with a boisterous child. Stretching, and crossing her legs, she tucks the cards between her hip and the armrest of the bench; she peels off her down-filled coat and stuffs it behind her back, wrapping the arms around her waist. As her eyes wander among the throngs of shoppers, she wonders, "Where do all of these people come from?" She continues to glance around the crowd, and then her eyes fix upon a solitary man seated in a chair opposite her across the courtyard. "Oh-oh," she thinks, "It's the Baron...."

He's wearing brown riding boots, chocolate colored breeches, a saddle brown turtleneck shirt, and a matching wool vest with a row of gold button closures. Reading glasses hang on his slender nose. From a distance, he seems to be writing, or doodling in a hardbound book that rests on his crossed knees. Unaware that he's being watched, the Baron lays his pencil in the saddle of the book, removes his reading glasses and glances up. His eyes meet Kallie's head on. He doesn't flinch. Kallie trembles. The hot rush of the crowd is frozen. There's a moment of petrified time when the intensity of his gaze could propel a skater. Kallie wonders, "Does he recognize me?" Just then, walking in a dubious rank, three teenagers emerge from the crowd; tough girls, dressed like ruffians approach Kallie from behind. The one on the right, coarse, and expressing a dark humor, has a bare midriff, her navel is pierced with a silver stud, and on her abdomen, just above the zipper of her baggy hip-huggers, she wears a tattoo. Their conversation is brash, loud and peppered with the 'F' word. As they pass Kallie, the one with the tattoo bumps her severely enough to dislodge the Christmas cards tucked in beside her. Startled, Kallie glances at her assailant, and stutters, "Um-ah."

The girl taunts her with a foul curse, "Watch it, you little bitch."

Kallie's jaw falls open; her eyes open wide with shock. "Morgan?" she wonders aloud. "Is that you?"

Morgan glares back at Kallie and makes an obscene gesture with her middle finger—her sinister companions laugh approvingly. "Yeah, girlfriend," she wisecracks, "It's me. Fuck off."

Kallie doesn't respond; she just stares as the three hooligans plunder their way through the crowd, and vanish. Finally, in a rueful whimper, she muses, "Morgan, we were best friends. Why do you hate me?" For a prolonged moment, recalling happier times with Morgan, she glances aimlessly around, and then she looks with purpose. She sees an open seat next to Albert Verrhaus. He's engaged in his book. Kallie has some brave business to transact. She tightens the coat sleeves around her waist, grasps her package in her left hand, trundles across the courtyard, and sits quietly on the edge of the empty seat next to the Baron. The Baron doesn't budge. Kallie places her package behind her back, and inconspicuously as she can, she leans toward the Baron to catch sight of his work. He glances over the corner of his rimless glasses to assess the snoop. His eyes move back to his work. Protectively, he puts the pencil in the saddle of the book and closes it, crossing his hands over the cover. A gold signet ring on his left pinkie finger gleams. Raising his head, he stares indifferently out on the crowd.

"Hello, I'm Kallie May Phillipa," she says, reaching out her hand to the Baron in a shy greeting. "I was wondering what you're drawing? Can I have a peek?" The Baron remains indifferent, like a cast bronze statue—a cold brown figure that lost its warmth in the mold—he is silent, and unmoved. "You've been sitting here a long time," she starts again, trying a new tack. "Are you alone, or maybe you're waiting for your grandkids?" Not a wince from the Baron. Kallie decides that a bold approach is called for. "I know who you are," she says, sitting upright and expressing a confident smile. "You're Albert Verrhaus, the Baron. You have a farm down in the bluffs." The Baron's lips draw tight, and then he blinks. It's not a big one, but it's definitely a flinch. Kallie jumps on the opening by saying: "Nice shack, Baron!"

The Baron turns his head, slowly, cautiously to look at Kallie; he removes his reading glasses with his right hand; he folds them, sliding them into an inner pocket of his vest. He looks directly in Kallie's eyes, and pronouncing each syllable distinctly, he muses aloud, "Kallie May Phill-ip-ah—hum."   He stares off into space and ponders quietly, "It's a Hungarian name, but is it Croat, or Slovak?" Kallie's left without a reply; she doesn't know the answer.   "Phillipik, Phillipich, Phillipa," he continues, sloshing each pronunciation around in his mouth as if he is tasting wine, "Southern Slavic," he concludes finally, "Slovenian I think."

"I think it's French."

Turning to gaze down upon her, he replies drolly, "I doubt it…"

"My dad's name is Anthony, that sure sounds French to me."

"Not originally." The Baron examines her face closely. "If the name is French, there must be a Prussian mercenary somewhere in your family tree. That narrow chin of yours is Hungarian. Oh, and my house is not a shack."

"I was just joking…"

"It wasn't very kind of you. Are you always impolite?"

"Sorry, it was a joke," Kallie whispers as she scrunches back into her chair. "I was just trying to start a conversation."

"You weren't invited to start a conversation," the Baron replies, looking out on the crowd. His attitude remains aloof and distant.

Kallie shifts nervously; she wasn't expecting the Baron's cool reception; she speculates silently, "Yup, he's weird alright, and rude too, no wonder he's always alone." Moments pass.

Finally, the Baron, his eyes fixed on the hustling crowd, asks, "What happened to your leg?"

Kallie's attention is elsewhere, "What?" she responds to his unexpected question.

"Your leg?" he repeats, diverting his focus and nodding at the cast on Kallie's leg.

"It got mashed in an accident. My horse reared up and plopped over on top of me—not a big deal."

A painful shudder causes the Baron to jerk, but he contains it, and says, "I'd say you got lucky, Miss Phillipa. A friend of mine, many years ago, was killed when his horse fell on him."

"Maybe," she replies soberly, "the man upstairs was looking out for me—I don't know."

"Will you be able to ride again?"

"I hope so. The doctor said my knee will be good as new, maybe better—they had to replace it—but my ankle will be stiff." An impish smile curls her lip when she adds, "But he hasn't said that I won't be able to ride."

"Hope for the best, Miss Phillipa."

"Yeah," she sighs, leaning forward, resting her elbows on her knees and rubbing her open palms together. "Sometimes, hope is all we got...." The Baron studies her. Gingerly, she changes the subject to suit her purpose: "Um—you know—I have this thoroughbred colt, his name is Wicked Punch...

"I wasn't aware of that."

"...and I want to race him." The Baron's demeanor softens as Kallie talks. "I have this dream that I'll be his jockey, but I guess I've got to learn how to ride a little better..." She pauses, sits upright, and glances furtively at the Baron slouching deeply into his chair. While he listens to Kallie, he rests his right elbow on the armrest, and strokes his brow with his fingertips. Her words seem to interest him. He glances through his fingers, and their eyes meet. "I'm sort of looking for a teacher," she whispers. There's a flicker of sympathy in the Baron's eyes. His piercing ashen glower fades and he smiles; to hide it, he shifts his hand from his brow and rests his index finger on his lower lip. "Do you take students?" she asks meekly.

The Baron tilts his head in a slight approach toward Kallie, and asks in a steady voice, "What makes you think I can ride well enough to teach?"

"I've seen you..." she replies, advancing her head the same distance as the Baron's nod.

"I don't think that is so, Miss Phillipa, I think you're mistaken..."

"I'm not."

"I'm quite sure you're wrong."

109

"I've seen you ride a lot."

"I haven't performed in public in twenty-five years…" he pauses; the two share an awkward silence, their faces, not a foot distant from each other. Kallie grins without disclosing her mischief. The Baron studies her eyes, her smile, and then he looks down at her hands—a final clue to break the riddle… "The spy," he whispers, "you're the spy on the ridge." He sits upright, clasps his hands behind his head, and repeats, this time with a confident laugh, "You're the SPY." He unclasps his hands, and crosses his arms on his chest. "Did your father ever mention the field glasses you dropped in my yard behind the house?"

"Yeah, I heard about them. It would have been better for me if you'd kept them."

"They are expensive glasses, better care should be taken with them." Kallie glances down, dodging his admonishment. The Baron continues, his voice softer, less harsh and scolding. "If you wanted to see me work my horses, why didn't you just come to the front door and ask permission?"

"Ask permission!" she blurts, jerking her head around. "My mom won't even let me get out of the car at your joint. She says you're very private, that you don't like company." She looks off and mutters quietly, "And everyone else says you're weird…"

"Ah," he sighs, "A reputation can be either a friend, or an enemy…"

"Look," she says, glancing back to regain their eye contact. "I tell you what, you don't have to call me Miss Phillipa. Call me Kallie, and I'll call you Al. Wouldn't that be more friendly?"

"It would, but I much prefer to call you Miss Phillipa."

"Oh-ah…" she stammers.

"And you may not call me Al. You may call me Baron; Herr Verrhaus, or Sir."

"Kind of stuffy, don't you think?"

"Not for a teacher and his student," he says, rigidly. "That's how a lady and a gentleman address one another in polite company."

Kallie nearly bursts at hearing his words: teacher and student. "You'll take me on?" she gasps, "you'll teach me to ride and train?"

"I didn't say that, Miss Phillipa."

"It sure sounded like it to me." She squints her eyes menacingly, and scolds him: "A gentleman shouldn't deceive a lady with his words..."

He's surprised by her touché, but smiles approvingly, and then he gestures at Kallie's cast, mentioning, "Your leg's got to heal."

"Small matter," she retorts. "You can teach me a lot while I'm still laid up. You got any books?"

"I haven't said yes, Miss Phillipa." The Baron leans back in his chair. "You've presented a proposal, but I haven't heard anything about payment, nor have you outlined a regimen for our work."

"You said it again! You said our work."

"But we're not talking about our money. Can you afford to pay me, and are you willing to meet the demands made upon you by your teacher?"

Their conversation is getting serious, and talk about money always makes Kallie nervous. "I've got some money, and my mom pays me for helping out at the clinic..."

"Your mother's a good doctor," the Baron interjects. He's made the connection between Kallie and Reggie. "She's very kind, and very professional."

Kallie's surprised at the Baron's complement, but concurs, "She's pretty great, alright." She pauses momentarily; reaching down, she rubs her thigh fitfully. "Sometimes it falls asleep," she notes, returning to the conversation with an expanded proposal: "I was thinking we could work out a deal. A cash and barter deal?"

The Baron strokes his chin thoughtfully. "What do you propose to exchange in barter?" he asks.

"I could help you out, clean stalls, rub your horses, be your chauffeur—drive you around in your Jag..."

"We'll have to consider that final term carefully," the Baron interrupts touching Kallie on the forearm, "a classic Jaguar is a very special car—very special..."

"Ah-huh," she agrees, her eyes fluttering.

While Kallie and the Baron continue their discussion, Anthony and Reggie roam among the shoppers in the courtyard. They seem to

111

be wandering in no particular direction, they're smiling as they walk, and enjoying a moment of affection—two, middle-age children in love. Anthony carries a large package draped over his left arm; it's wrapped in white and red striped plastic, and judging from the shape it's easy to discern that it's a saddle. Reggie is scrunched tightly against Anthony's hip, she has her left arm around his waist; she swings a small bag in her right hand—Anthony's right arm hangs over her shoulders. They haven't noticed Kallie and the Baron sitting together; as they approach nearer, Kallie calls out, "Hey you two love birds." They recognize the voice, but among the shoppers, they can't place its origin, and scan curiously. Kallie calls again, "Dad, Mom, over here." She waves, extending her arm to full length, and flaps her hand desperately.

They see Kallie, and approach. The Baron stands up, places his sketchbook on the seat of his chair, and while awaiting an introduction, he aids Kallie who struggles to her feet. "Hi-ya, shrimp," Anthony wisecracks when he and Reggie arrive. "I see you managed to stay out of trouble..." Then glancing at the Baron, he wonders, "Or have you?"

Kallie is ready with a retort, but a glint of dazzling light sparkles from Reggie's earlobes. Kallie is stunned; her mouth drops open in astonishment, she gasps, "Holy crap! Look at those diamonds—wow—those are some serious rocks!" She grabs at Reggie, and pulls on her sleeve to bring her closer. "They're huge! You weren't that good a girl this year, Mom."

Reggie is pulled off balance by Kallie's tug, causing Anthony to fall forward into the Baron. "Easy Kallie, down girl." grunts Anthony as he uses the Baron to regain his balance. "Sorry Mister. My daughter grew up on a farm. What she lacks in manners, she makes up for in enthusiasm."

"You must be Mr. Phillipa," the Baron says, reaching out his hand in greeting. Anthony matches his handshake, but before releasing, the Baron turns Anthony's hand over and examines it quickly, and then he observes, "Judging by your knuckles, I'd say you were a boxer. At what weight did you fight?"

"Welterweight," he answers. Then, glancing at Kallie, his expression inquires, "Who is this guy?" His question misses her; she's still transfixed by Reggie's diamonds. He turns back to the Baron, and politely asks, "Have we met? I don't think I know you…"

Kallie gets the message. She looks rapidly at Anthony, and then the Baron, and then back to Anthony trying to remember the correct order for a proper introduction. "Um, Baron Verrhaus, this is my Dad, Anthony Phillipa, and this is my Mom, Regina Phillipa. Dad, Mom, this is the Baron Verrhaus—and I'm Kallie," she adds nervously.

While laughing at Kallie's final introduction, the Baron suggests, "Please call me Albert, Anthony—may I call you Anthony?" He nods, yes. Then he turns his attention to Reggie. "Hello Doctor Phillipa, it's very pleasant to see you again," he says, respectfully shaking her hand. "And, on you, those earrings are quite fetching."

"Hello, Sir," she replies, returning his handshake. "Thank you. I'm a little embarrassed for showing them off, I didn't realize you were here with Kallie."

"She was making conversation…"

"We were talking business," Kallie interjects.

"She offered a proposal," he says, recognizing the shape of the wrapped package on Anthony's arm, "I trust that you won't object if I consider it—she's asked me to be her riding teacher."

Anthony and Reggie are surprised at the suggestion. Reggie glares at Kallie, and then she assures the Baron, "I never let her out of the car when we stop by. How could she know you? When did you meet?"

"Miss Phillipa introduced herself just today, but evidently, we've been watching each other for quite a while."

Reggie's perplexed by his comment, she looks at Kallie, and asks, "Kallie, have you been up to something?"

Kallie shifts uneasily.

"I'm sure she'll explain… Won't you, Miss Phillipa?"

"Does this have anything to do with my binoculars?" Anthony asks, peering inquisitively at Kallie. "You told me last year that you were working on a bird watching project."

113

"I sort of was, Dad," she admits, blushing with guilt. "I didn't lie exactly, I <u>was</u> doing research—just not on birds." She smiles contritely, and tries to change the subject, "Did Mom buy any cookies? What about it, Dad, what say you and me run over to the bakery counter and get a fat old chocolate chip cookie, sound good—yum—and some good ol' coffee? I'll buy."

"You sure know how to play your dad, don't you, shrimp?"

"Daddy," she gushes, "I'm just a little girl. What would I know about playing a man of the world like you?"

"Ha!" he yelps in disbelief. "I think you grew up a long time ago." And then, handing the saddle to her, "Here," he says, "can you carry this bag of laundry for your old dad? I'm getting kind of pooped lugging it around."

"Laundry, huh?" she grunts, taking the saddle. "Odd shape for a sack of laundry."

"What about me," Reggie pleads after them, "and your teacher, can we come too?"

"Sure! The treat is on Kallie—the more, the merrier," Anthony shouts from beyond a wall of holiday shoppers.

"That's not been decided yet, Doctor..." the Baron advises, waylaying her momentarily. "I haven't said I'd accept—I said I would consider instructing your daughter."

Reggie turns to the Baron, and advises him confidently, "I've got to warn you, Sir, she'll wear you down—she's relentless. She won't quit until she wins."

"I think I know that about her," he replies, winking.

Reaching out her arm for him to accompany her, she suggests, "Come on Sir, it's Christmas. We're going to buy you something sweet—we probably owe you more than that. I don't know what Kallie's been up to, but I think she owes you a chocolate chip cookie at the very least."

"I'd love to join you, it's a very kind offer," he replies, suddenly adopting a more formal tone. "But I'd rather that Miss Phillipa's and my relationship not become too familiar—a teacher should always maintain a professional distance between himself and his student. I hope you understand."

"Sure, yes, absolutely."

The Baron reaches down to retrieve his sketch book from the seat of the chair, and then he asks, "Will you make an apology to your husband for me?"

"Of course, don't worry," she replies as he begins to walk away. Then, calling after him, she asks, "Did you have a coat, Sir?"

He stops, stares off into space, and for a moment, he appears confused. "Ah, my coat," he mutters, turning back to Reggie, "Thanks for reminding me. The mall's security police let me check it with them. I wouldn't have gotten far, my car keys are in the pocket." He laughs, and shakes his head. "I'll call soon after the holidays to let Miss Phillipa know what I've decided."

"I think I already know what you've decided," Reggie thinks, watching the Baron leave, but before he disappears into the crowd, she calls out in a cheery voice, "Merry Christmas, Sir."

There is a Christmas Eve tradition at the Phillipa house. Just before going to bed, the entire family—parents, aunts, uncles, nieces, nephews, and the grandparents—gather round the tree and select a single gift to open—a small one, nothing bigger than a shoe box, the big ones are saved for morning. While the children rustle through a pile of dinky packages, searching for one with their name on it, Anthony motions to Kallie that she should join him. During the moments it takes her to trundle to his recliner, Anthony digs in his pocket; withdrawing his hand, he reveals a tiny, velvet-covered box, and announces proudly, "This is for my little pal, Kallie."

Kallie stares at the box; she's suspicious about what it may, or may not contain. But with joyful apprehension, she thinks, "A package like that can hold only one thing—it's too small for my saddle, so it's got to be jewelry..." Anthony smiles, and hands the package to her; it's like a Christmas pageant with Kallie at center stage; her nerves tingle; she's forgotten her lines; she teeters between tears and giggles.

Finally, Anthony whispers, "Open it, Kallie."

She does. There, beneath the open lid, embedded in a midnight blue satin fold, is the glint of diamonds—diamond earrings for Kallie.

115

Her lips quiver. She sniffles to hold back a flood. Her eyes fill with facetted tears. She closes the lid of the box, wipes her nose and eyes on the sleeve of her nightshirt, and then she sits on the arm of Anthony's chair, leans her forehead against his temple and kisses him. With a grateful whimper, she confesses, "I don't know what to say. Thank you Daddy…."

"Say you like them."

"Oh God, I love them—they're beautiful."

"Then tell mom. She wanted you to have them."

Kallie looks lovingly at Reggie; she begins to sob when she says, "Mom, they're beautiful—I love them. Thank you, thank you."

"I was thinking they'd be pretty on you," she replies, "that maybe, I could bribe you into giving up your dream of being a jockey, but I don't think that's going to happen now…." Reaching into her hip pocket, Reggie takes out an envelope, and hands it to Kallie, saying, "Albert Verrhaus dropped this off yesterday. I know what it says. I just want you to be safe, Kallie. I don't want you to be hurt again. Please be careful."

Trembling, Kallie takes the envelope from her. It's made of the highest quality, white cotton rag paper. On its face, hand scrolled in aquamarine ink, is Kallie's name. She turns the envelope over, lifts open the flap, and removes the enclosed letter. A pregnant hush grips the celebrants. Kallie unfolds the letter. Centered at the top of the page, in gold embossed letters is the name and crest of the Baron Verrhaus. The letter quivers in her hand as she reads:

> *Dear Miss Phillipa,*
>
> *I have considered your proposal that I contract my services for your benefit, and undertake to be your riding teacher. The terms and conditions you suggest are acceptable to me. The times and locations at which your instruction should take place must remain at my discretion. However, the duration of our agreement remains at your will.*

I accept your appointment with pride. It is both an honor and a special privilege to serve you.

Thank you Madam.

Kallie trembles as she re-reads the letter.
"Merry Christmas, Kallie."
"You knew about this, Mom, Dad?"
"He stopped by while you were at the library. The three of us had a long talk—you've got your work cut out for you. It won't be easy."
"What are they talking about?" John asks, whispering to Celeste. Celeste shrugs her shoulders, implying that she doesn't know.
"What's going on, Kallie?"
"Nothing Uncle John… I made a friend—it's a long story—and, well, he's going to teach me how to train and ride Wicked Punch. That's all."

* * *

Victor John Faith

Five: On the Mat

Early in January, on a day when the temperature hovered well below zero, Kallie had her cast removed, and shortly after that, she had surgery to remove the stainless steel pins that held her ankle secure while it mended. Now, the fierce winds of March blow. Kallie is attending her twice-weekly visit to the physical therapy clinic. With her hair wet, and wearing a white, terrycloth bathrobe, unfastened at the waist so her flowered swimsuit is visible, she sits placidly on an elevated bench; her right leg dangles in a therapeutic whirlpool bath that churns and bubbles. Isolated, she appears bored, and stares, as if in a trance, at some imagined thing. A parade of background noises: busy, echoing voices, the sounds of splashing water, the remote clank of a heating fan pass by her, unnoticed. Unconsciously, she rubs her knee. On the outside of her leg is a prominent scar; starting above the knee, it descends like an elastic worm, ending well into the middle of her calf—from nose to tail, it's nearly twelve inches long.

An attendant approaches from the echoes. She is a plain, thin woman, five and a half feet tall, with ordinary brown hair, and no make-up to improve her common face. She's dressed in a white sweatshirt, baggy white 'hospital scrubs,' and white loafers. Nothing about her is memorable except her gruff voice—it sounds like a cold car with a low battery refusing to start on a winter morning. "Kallie. Kallie," she growls, arriving at the whirlpool.

The attendant's grating voice jerks Kallie awake; startled, she yelps, "Whew! Sorry, Wendy. I must have dozed off. The warm water puts me to sleep every time I come here."

"Well, out of the pool sleepy-head, it's time to 'pretzelize' your leg—see if we can't get a little more flexion out of that ankle."

"Shoot," Kallie groans as she takes her leg out of the whirlpool and climbs down from the bench. "I hate this part. You weren't an *All-Star* wrestler in a former life were you?"

Wendy snarls like a pro-wrestler. "Just dry your skinny little butt off, and march it over to the mat, we're having a cage match between me and your puny ankle, and the ankle's going down! Gurr-ugh," she roars, striking the 'most muscular' pose.

Kallie sneers at Wendy, and challenges her. "Oh yeah, wimp? You want a part of me? Bring it on, sister..." She struggles to a wide gymnastic mat set off in a near corner, and continues bantering, "You don't want a piece of this action. I'm mean; I'm supreme; I'm a lethal machine!"

Kallie crawls onto the mat and stretches out sitting on her buttocks. Wendy kneels next to her leg, grips Kallie's ankle, and in a gravely taunt, warns her, "Is that so—a lethal machine? Okay. Let's just see if we can't put a little oil in your bearings. Are you ready for this, tough guy—you really ready? 'Cuz walloping Wendy's gonna get cracking."

"You go for it girl..." she hisses, and then she howls, "Oo-ouch, I-eee!" as Wendy presses Kallie's foot forward into a ballet point. "I couldn't do that before I mashed it. What makes you think I can do it now?"

"Doctor's orders, wimp—no pain, no gain..." Wendy releases the pressure and returns Kallie's foot to a normal position, and then, "Ooo-ouch!" Kallie yowls as Wendy applies another foot-lock in what will be a many fall match. "I just love my job," she snarls quietly, inflicting more therapy. And then, mercifully, she grants Kallie a respite. Gently massaging Kallie's throbbing ankle, she asks, "What'd the doctor say when you saw him on Tuesday?"

Forlornly, Kallie answers, "He wasn't real encouraging. He said I could start riding, but..." She takes a deep breath; her expression shows disappointment. "He said I'd probably never have enough flexibility, or enough strength to keep my foot in the stirrup long enough to win a race—he really pissed me off. It broke my heart."

"Doctors are heartless pricks, full of worthless advice."

"Maybe, Wendy, but that has nothing to do with the truth."

"Trust me Kallie, I dated a doctor once," Wendy growls, "he treated me like I was shit. The sex was good, but I always felt like a hose bag when I was with him. He was an asshole in the compassion department."

"I think that's because he's a man, not because he's a doctor.

Wendy laughs, and replies while rubbing Kallie's ankle, "You got some smarts, sister. I should have thought about that before I jumped in the sack with him—they're born assholes, and then grow up to be doctors!"

"Some of them can be nice..." Kallie says with a hint of doubt in her voice.

"Men or doctors?"

"Men. My dad's nice, so is my riding teacher."

"Dad's don't count, honey," Wendy replies sarcastically. "It's in their job description, but even some of them don't show up for work."

"Yeah, I know. I used to have this friend, and her dad baled on her and her mom when she was a kid…."

"You're not friends anymore?" Wendy asks, finishing the massage of Kallie's ankle, and reaching for a towel.

"No…" Kallie sighs, recalling her relationship with Morgan. "We were friends all the way through junior high, and most of high school. We used to have some fun times together, but then she got a boyfriend—he was a prick—and they started having sex—she thought she was pregnant, you know…"

"Poor kid," Wendy groans, wiping her hands on the towel before tossing it aside.

"Anyway, she dropped out of school, and now she's like some drugged out zombie—except, she's mean too, and she might be in a gang. I don't know who she is anymore." Looking off, she adds softly, "Maybe, I never did." Wendy raises from her crouching position, and stands beside Kallie; she reaches out her hand to help Kallie get up. Kallie grasps Wendy's hand, wobbles to her feet, and then, wrapping the bathrobe closed, and tying the draw-cord tight around her waist, she smiles gratefully, and says, "Thanks for the assist, Wendy, and thanks for listening."

Wendy shrugs off Kallie's thank you, saying, "It's my job. I'm just kissing up to keep it."

When they turn to walk toward the women's dressing room, Wendy asks, "You figure you're going to try and get back in the saddle soon?"

"I hope so," Kallie replies. "I've got my first riding lesson Saturday. You should meet my teacher. Everybody else thinks he's weird, but I think he's kind of nice."

"A nice guy," Wendy laughs in disbelief, "and you think that's not weird?"

* * *

Victor John Faith

Six: High Tea

It's Saturday, one-thirty in the afternoon. Today, Kallie will take her first riding lesson with the Baron. She's driving in Reggie's green van onto the long driveway that leads to the main house at the Verrhaus estate. Although the winter's grip on the landscape has broken, dirty snow banks still line the route; they raise and fall beneath the trees lining the drive like frozen crests and troughs in an artic cove. The way is badly marred by frost boils and potholes. The squish and thump made by the wheels of the van as it passes over them is an indicator of just how deeply winter can penetrate the earth—cold doesn't stop at the epidermis, it intrudes to the bone.

Kallie drives the van through the roundabout in front of the house, and then parks within sight of Bucephalus. She glances out her car window at the mounds of burlap that cover the tender roses in their beds. "Will they bloom this year?" she wonders opening the van door to get out. A chilly puddle meets her foot. The air she inhales is cool, and the breeze carries the scent of thawing manure. "Ah," she whispers, "if you love horses, you love that smell." A chickadee flits by—a tiny bird in a beret—Kallie strains to watch it dart for cover in the arborvitae. Gazing upward, letting the sun warm her face, she smiles, lifts her arms above her head, and announces joyfully, "Spring! Thank you, Lord, I thought it would never come." Then, she surveys the Baron's grand, mansion. "Yep, really nice shack, Baron," she mutters softly, marching to the sidewalk, and up the steps to the front door, but before Kallie can knock, the door opens unexpectedly. A woman of late middle-age appears wearing a white, paint stained smock with the sleeves rolled up to the elbows. Her brown hair is streaked with gray and bound up in a blue paisley kerchief. Smudged reading glasses hang from her nose; her eyes have an impish glint. She smiles radiantly, reaching out a plump hand in greeting, and says, "You must be Kallie Phillipa. Albert's been expecting you. Please come in."

Kallie's surprised to be greeted by anyone other than the Baron. "The Baron lives alone," she thinks, "he likes his privacy. Who is this woman?" she wonders as she reaches to accept the handshake, "and why is she so familiar with the Baron?" The woman holds the heavy oak door open; together, they enter the foyer. The woman stops and gestures to a high-backed Edwardian chair placed against the wall next to an ornate coat rack made from elk antlers.

"Have a seat, Miss Phillipa," she says, "I'll let Albert know you've arrived."

The woman turns to leave, and as she walks down a long hall to Kallie's left, she waddles like a common duck, but leaves the regal impression of a swan from royal lineage. The sights that greet her dumbfound Kallie. The hardwood floor beneath her feet is walnut stained, birds-eye-maple. The chair on which she sits is nestled against a wall, wainscoted to five feet in oak paneling. The window next to the elk antler coat rack is made of stained glass and depicts a hunting scene: horses and riders pursue their quarry, a wily red fox that darts behind a hedgerow. In front of her, a formal stairway ascends; its banister and spindles, finely carved and rubbed to a sheen with oil, match the color of the floor and wainscoting. Sixteen carpeted steps rise to a landing; shedding light on the landing is an expansive, three panel stained glass window with more hunt scenes, and then, twelve more stairs turn back and rise to the second floor. The ceilings are high and dark. Coffers segment the spacious lid into a checkerboard of plateaus and defiles—one would need to be a giant to breathe the upper air of this great hall. To Kallie's left, a long corridor leads somewhere; a similar one is on her right. Straight ahead, next to the stairs is an alcove with French doors; through the mullioned sashes, blinding daylight invades. The methodical ticking of a clock echoes through the long, oak paneled corridors; other than this sound, there is only silence, until footsteps, matching the cadence of the clock, cause Kallie to start; she breathes nervously. She glances toward the east wing, and then west to see who approaches. A dark shadow, distant and small at first, grows nearing her; daylight adds form and features; the woman in the smock reappears and instructs with a formalness that contradicts her frumpish attire, "Albert asked me to show you to the dayroom. He has a lesson plan to present. Do you drink tea, Miss Phillipa?"

Kallie's choked up and anxious, but she manages to respond after clearing the frog from her throat, "Tea? Um—tea, yes. Tea is wonderful; I love tea; tea would be nice…"

"This way then," the woman says, leading Kallie through the French doors into the blinding light.

Kallie's bladder is nervous too. She pulls anxiously at the seat of her pants as she follows the woman into the room. "Holy cow…. Oh my God…." she murmurs, entering a huge room with huge leaded glass windows on three sides, and huge, high ceilings and studio tables and easels for painting and paintbrushes and paints and palettes smeared with paint. And canvases, some finished with scenes of horses, some still in progress, there are paintings all over the place. And then there's the sun—the vernal March sun that turns the room into a blinding haze—but Kallie recognizes the artwork, she knows who the artist is that painted these pictures. "Charles Foxx," she gasps.

"Miss Phillipa," the woman says, stopping Kallie in the center of the room, "Albert will be in shortly. I'll serve the tea in here." She turns to leave the room, and glancing back, she adds, "Sit if you like, but please, don't touch anything."

"Sit if you like?" Kallie twitters as the woman leaves. "Sit in a place like this? Sit where, on what, and why would I want to sit with all these pictures around?" Her eyes run from painting to painting. "Wow," she gulps. "Awesome," she sighs. And then she notices, off in a far corner near a side window, the portrait of the Christmas card she bought at the mall. She dashes to it, and squints long and hard at the signature: Charles Foxx. "Holy shit," she blurts out loud, "it's the real thing!"

"Is something the matter, Miss Phillipa?" the Baron asks from behind her.

Kallie spins, surprised and startled. She's been ambushed. She's embarrassed to be caught snooping by the Baron—again. But there he stands. "Um, Sir," she stammers, "No nothing's the matter, nothing, Sir."

The Baron squints suspiciously at her. He's dressed in gray, riding breeches and a newly pressed, white shirt, but he isn't wearing his riding boots. Instead he wears a pair of old leather house slippers that are silent when he steps up to Kallie, and grinning slyly, remarks, "I only ask because I didn't quite hear the comment you just made."

Her tongue is dry, and clicks like a castanet when she answers, "Hole in my mitt. That's what I said. I've got a hole in my mit, and I lost my ring!"

"Yes, that's what I thought I heard you say," he replies restraining a doubtful smile. "Have you seen this work before?"

"Yeah, I collect it," she replies excitedly. Her nerves have been strained, but her wit's still intact. "The first time I ever saw it was at the racetrack. Ever since then, whenever I see a card or a calendar—I can't afford a real print—I buy it. I think this guy, Charlie Foxx is awesome."

"Charlie Foxx?" the Baron chuckles, "then you understand the joke..." Kallie's face goes blank, and the Baron realizes that she doesn't understand. "Ah," he nods sympathetically, "I'll explain. All the pictures are about horses," he begins, "Mostly 'hunt' horses. Do you see the clever, little red fox in this picture?" he asks, pointing to an English foxhunting scene. "The huntsmen call him *Charlie*. If you look closely, you'll see that he's somewhere in all of Foxx's paintings. Sometimes he's hidden, sometimes he's disguised, but he's always there. It's just a little joke the artist is making. I find it amusing."

"That's really cool," Kallie nods, agreeing. And then, noticing foxes everywhere, she laughs, and adds, "Way cool."

"Yes. Quite."

"But Sir, if you don't mind me being nosey, this Foxx guy, do you know him? Does he live here?"

"Yes, you could say I know the artist."

Just then, the middle-age woman returns to the room carrying a square, mahogany service tray by its brass handles. On the tray are a porcelain teapot, three small cups—fine china reserved for refined guests—a tiny urn of cream, and sugar. "Albert," she says, walking to the studio table that dominates the center of the room, "our tea is ready. Miss Phillipa, could you move some of those paints aside so I can put this down?" Kallie looks at the studio table that the woman

125

has indicated with her glance. Gently, she pushes the crumpled paint tubes, brushes and other paraphernalia out of the way. The woman steps beside Kallie, puts the tray down, and suggests. "Albert, some chairs would be nice." The Baron scurries to comply.

"Kind of bossy for a maid…" Kallie thinks as the Baron pulls a chair from alongside the studio table, and two more from behind a stack of blank canvases. He arranges them in a small semi-circle in front of the table while the woman makes her final preparations to serve the tea. The Baron invites Kallie to sit by gesturing with his hand; Kallie sits. The Baron sits next to her. She wonders, "Who will sit in the other chair?"

"Miss Phillipa, do you drink your tea with cream, or sugar?"

Kallie has never had tea before. Tea is just not a beverage that people in her family drink, but she has to decide. "Cream and sugar, about half and half…" she replies, hoping that this time she's avoided an awkward blunder. The woman mixes up Kallie's tea and hands it to her. Kallie smiles politely, and says, "Thank you, madam."

Then the woman prepares two more cups with neither cream nor sugar; one she hands to the Baron, and the other she keeps for herself as she sits down. After a moment, in which both the Baron and the woman lift their cups, and sip as if the tea they drink is a healing liquid, the Baron mentions to the woman, "Miss Phillipa asked me if I was acquainted with the artist, Charles Foxx."

"I think you're very well acquainted with that artist, Albert," she replies with a churlish grin.

"She told me that she's a collector of his work. She's an admirer of his." The Baron sips some tea before continuing, "She mentioned that she'd like to meet him. Do you think it would be an imposition?"

There's a suspenseful pause during which, by the anxious look on Kallie's face, it's clear that she's screaming inside, "Just invite the guy in here already—ring the damn bell and summon him!"

"Not an imposition, but I believe they've already met," the woman replies nonchalantly. "Although, I don't recall that a formal introduction's been made."

"We've met?" Kallie wonders, "When?" And then, she begins to recall clues, "The sketchbook at the mall," she thinks, "and the joke about the fox... Oh my God, it's the Baron!"

"Miss Phillipa," the Baron says, interrupting her speculation, "I'd like to introduce my dear friend and companion, Charlene Fauxhausen." He pauses briefly before the reciprocal while Charlene nods politely, and then he continues, "Charles Foxx, this is Miss Kallie May Phillipa."

"Ah-huh..." Kallie grunts, staring dumbfounded at Charlene.

"You needn't call me Ms. Fauxhausen, just call me Charlene."

"But-but," Kallie babbles, "but you're a woman. I don't understand."

"Charlene's very quiet about her work," the Baron interjects putting an end to Kallie's sputtering. "She uses a pseudonym—she prefers to remain anonymous. In fact, she's so anonymous that almost no one knows she's here. Like I said, Miss Phillipa, the artist enjoys her little joke."

"This is too much!" Kallie gasps, not fully recovered from the shock. And then she asks, "Are you... married?"

"Married?" Charlene replies, bursting into a robust laugh. "No, I wouldn't say that. Our relationship is more of a close business partnership. I paint pictures, and Albert writes verse—so we sell greeting cards. It's what we do for a living."

"You mean you work? Why? Look at this joint you live in—it's a castle—and what about that Jaguar?" Kallie can't believe what she's hearing—the Baron has a partner, and a job.

"We're only comfortable, Miss Phillipa, we're not rich," Charlene replies with a note of teasing in her voice.

By this time, Kallie's gained control of herself, she giggles softly and murmurs, "Holy cow, wait until I tell Mom about this, she isn't going believe it—nobody is."

"Please, Miss Phillipa," the Baron and Charlene blurt in unison, "Don't mention what you know to anyone." Their tone is excited and emphatic.

"It could affect our business," the Baron states firmly.

"And our privacy..." Charlene adds, finishing his sentence.

"Privacy is vital, it must be kept," the Baron repeats, leaning forward in his chair and staring Kallie directly in the eyes. "Tell me, Miss Phillipa, that you will not repeat what you've heard about Charlene, or anything else about the way we live, or what goes on in this house." He speaks his words deliberately, and then he sips his tea urgently to moisten his mouth. "It's very important that a teacher be able to trust his student, and that a student trust her teacher," he continues with chilling gravity. He sits upright, and then his expression softens from one of seriousness to a look of gentle counseling. "At my first riding lesson, when I was just a small boy, my instructor told me, 'Herr Verrhaus, keep your eyes and ears open, but keep your mouth shut.' It's very good advice, Miss Phillipa, and I've practiced that lesson for more than fifty years. If you learn nothing else from me, that will be enough."

Kallie's surprised by the earnestness of their appeal for secrecy, the cheerfulness of her mood has changed to introspection. "Why do I always ruin everything by saying something stupid?" she wonders. She peers down at her tea; the surface of the liquid in her cup—ivory and gold—reflects her embarrassed frown. There is a moment of awful silence, brightened only by the warm spring sun streaming through the windows. Kallie draws a deep breath and lifts her damp eyes to meet the Baron's gentle gaze. "I'm sorry, Sir," she says, her voice shaking, "I promise I won't tell anyone, you can trust me…." She looks at Charlene, whose chubby fingers twitch nervously as she holds her teacup. "Ms. Fauxhausen," Kallie continues stammering with regret, "I really am honored to meet you—you don't know how beautiful I think your pictures are. I just say some stupid things sometimes. Will you forgive me?"

Charlene's tense lips relax into a reassuring smile when she says, "Yes, of course dear, but sometimes a secret may have unintended consequences if it's revealed; we can cause someone a lot of harm without ever meaning too, even if what we say is true." She raises her index finger and places it against her lips to indicate 'secret;' her eyes sparkle in the afternoon sun. "There are some things that people never need to know."

Just then, from outside the dayroom, down one of the long hallways, comes a loud click, and the whir of a grand clock's flutter wheel releasing the chimes. First comes the melody of the quarter hour—the song of the Saint Michael bells. It rolls through the paneled halls and bursts into the dayroom like a chorus of castratos singing praise. Then comes a second louder click as the hour chimes release; they strike a perfect chord, a musical fifth, blaring out time that shakes the house—ONE strike, TWO strikes, followed by an echo that reverberates, almost endlessly, before slinking into silence. Kallie gasps awestruck; the noise is ponderous; she looks at her tea to see if waves have formed from the resonance—the still, amber surface is intact. When she lifts her head to judge the reaction of the Baron and Charlene, "Nothing!" she thinks, "It's like nothing happened!"

"We live with a clock—a very large, old clock," the Baron says calmly. "We hardly notice it, it's like having a kindly old friend in the house."

"Wow!" laughs Kallie, "Kind of a noisy friend though."

"He will grow on you," adds Charlene.

The Baron reaches over to the studio table and gently places his teacup on the corner, "We should discuss your lesson plan," he says to Kallie as he stands, and walks slowly to stop behind Charlene. He places his left hand softly on her shoulder; his gold signet ring reflects a beam of daylight in a dazzling flash. Charlene glances back to see the Baron looking down at her, they communicate, like lovers, or intimate old friends do, without words. Charlene gets up from her chair; holding the tea saucer in her right hand and steadying the cup with her left, she turns to the Baron, and says, "You left your notes in the library. Shall I get them for you, or would you rather have your discussion with Miss Phillipa there?"

"Did I leave my glasses there too?" the Baron asks, pressing his hand against his shirt pocket.

"Right by the inkwell." Charlene pauses, she leans toward the Baron who stands just a foot in front of her. She studies his face for hidden clues—artists are doctors when it comes to examining details. She whispers inquisitively to him, "Albert, your cheeks are a little pale. Did you take your medicine at lunch? I laid the pills next to your plate."

"I think I did," he responds quickly. He stares out the window puzzled, and then recants, "Maybe not..." His gaze returns to Charlene, and he asks, "Would you look under the napkin by the charger? It's only a little late, I can still take it."

Smiling sympathetically, she scolds him, "Albert, you're like a forgetful old dowager, lately. I have to keep my eye on you every minute. I'll have a look." Charlene turns to leave the room, as she moves toward the French doors, the afternoon sun gleams from her white smock and reflects on the polished wood floor—she leaves her impression as a warm ray of light scudding across the varnished boards. When she reaches the door, she lingers, and suggests, "Albert, the library will be more comfortable for both of you. Your textbooks are there, and Miss Phillipa may enjoy seeing your trophies..."

Inferring her meaning, the Baron asks, "Are you telling me that you'd like to get back to your work?"

"No," she answers with a smirk, "I just think your philosophy should be confined to a smaller space."

"Ah-ha," he chuckles, before launching his own rejoinder, "if your cooking were as spiced as your sarcasm, I'd be a fat man, and not the waif that stands here sparing with you. Besides, portly thoughts need room to roll around and get all their appendages in order."

"If a cuttlefish can fit in a conch, Albert, then your library should be large enough for even your big ideas."

The Baron and Kallie watch as Charlene leaves the room, putting an end to the bandying. The Baron abruptly scowls and clasps his hands behind his back; he stares at the floor sulking; he paces ahead three steps, wheels about, paces back four, and stops. After a long and chilly silence, the Baron lifts his eyes to the coffered ceiling, and without taking any notice of Kallie sitting nervously before him, he concedes, "The library it is then."

Kallie fidgets anxiously; she remembers that she had to urinate before she entered the dayroom. Now, after a cup of tea and cream, she's become aware of the painful effect hot liquid can have on a restive bladder. "Sir," she says in a voice swelling with discomfort. "I'm sorry, but I really have to the use the bathroom. Could you tell me where one is?"

The urgency of Kallie's request jars him. Old gentlemen seldom deal well with this situation—directing a young woman to a lavatory. Uneasy, he responds, "It's out the door, to the right and then to the left..." he rubs his forehead realizing that his directions are too terse. "It's on the way to the library," he adds, "we'll pass right by it, I'll show you where it is."

Kallie gets up from her chair, careful not to spill her teacup, or to release her pressing contents. She glances at the corner of the studio table where the service tray and the Baron's cup rest. Without ceremony or hesitation she scrunches to the table and places her cup next to the Baron's. "I'll follow you, Sir," she says. The Baron stiffens and snaps to attention. Like a soldier on parade, he turns on his heels and begins to walk toward the door. Kallie falls in behind and the two file out the door in review order. As they enter the outer hall, the Baron makes an abrupt right turn and marches with his second rank in tow. Ahead, at the end of the corridor, a pair of straight-grained oak pocket doors, loom—one is open—and on the far wall of the room beyond the doors is an immense fireplace with a heraldic coat of arms hung above the mantle. Kallie's interest is seized, and even though she has no understanding of its ornaments, she stops to study it. Embossed upon an ivory shield, a royal blue chevron descends from the Dexter chief to the Sinister base; at the Fess point are crossed sabers; above the sabers at the Honor point, a stylized red and gold eagle with outstretched talons looks to the left; below the sabers, an inverted eagle, identical to the one above, looks right. "Wow," she gulps quietly. The Baron notices that he's lost his recruit and pauses, waiting for her to catch up. Finally, after several moments, Kallie turns to the Baron, and asks, "Is that your shield?"

"Not mine, Miss Phillipa," he answers, looking at it through the open door, "that's the baronial crest of my family."

"That is so cool," she coos. "Do all those things on it mean something?"

"Yes they do," he replies stoically, turning to his left, and lifting his arm to indicate a narrow passageway leaving the corridor. "The lavatory is in there. It used to be the butler's water closet, but we converted it to a full bath when we purchased the property. There's a light switch on the wall to your left." The Baron lowers his arm, and points his finger to a door directly across from the lavatory. "My library is in there, when you've finished, please join me."

"Thank you Sir, I'll be out in a jiff," she says, darting into the bathroom, banging the door closed behind her.

The Baron goes to the door of the library—a heavy, walnut stained oak door—he turns a key in the brass faceplate below a checkered doorknob and enters. The library is not a large room, but the high, coffered ceiling makes it seem spacious. The floor is covered with plush, cut pile, wall-to-wall burgundy carpet, and prominently occupying the room's center is a broad, robustly carved and decorated Baroque style writing table. Expansive bookshelves stretch to the corners of the room, and then turn to surround the perimeter of the library; they're stuffed full of books with colored spines that stand like pickets. Atop the bookshelves, here and there, are tarnished trophy cups, engraved tureens and plaques—the spoils of ancient victories. The library is a cozy space that has the odor of musty paper and leather. The Baron inhales its convivial scent and walks to the front of his desk. He takes the reading glasses he'd left there, and places them in his shirt pocket. Then, taking a sheet of notepaper that he's scribbled on from the blotter, he folds it, and slides it into the hip pocket of his riding breeches. A timid knock on the door causes him to turn.

"I'm ready, Sir," Kallie says, standing in the open doorway. "May I come in?"

"Yes, come in. I was just collecting my notes, but let's not sit down. I've decided that we'll go out to the stable and ride a horse instead. You don't mind, do you, Miss Phillipa?"

"No Sir, she blurts excitedly, "that's what I came here for."

"Good, let's have at it then." He invites her to lead the way by shooing her with his open palms. "I'll get my jacket..." and then he pauses to think.

"Your pills, Sir," Kallie interrupts, "you should probably check with Charlene and make sure you took them."

"Ah yes, yes I should. Thank you for reminding me, but that's not what I had on my mind." He glances at her leg, and raising his right hand to his chest, he lays it flat and slowly brushes invisible wrinkles from his shirt. "I didn't notice when you walked in—I suppose I should have—were you a little off? Were you gimpy?"

Kallie's irritated by the question; she's not reconciled to the weakness her injury's left her with. "I don't think I was," she replies defiantly. "No, absolutely I wasn't. Besides, the doctor gave me the okay to start riding this week."

"Your leg, has it fully healed from your accident?"

"I'm still in physical therapy, but my leg's just as strong as it was before I got hurt." She lifts her right leg, and flexes her quadriceps. Her sinewy muscles pop from below the tight fabric of her blue jeans. "See," she says proudly, "it's the same size as the other one." Then glancing at her outstretched leg, she adds, "Well, just about—maybe it's a little smaller..."

"This is good news then," the Baron says, admiring her skinny limb. "Because today, I'm planning to put you up on *Widow Maker*."

Kallie's mouth flops open; she drops her leg with a thump. "Widow Maker?" she gulps.

"No, no. Don't be worried," the Baron reassures her. "She's a good horse, a big Westphalian. She's just a bit sensitive to the leg aids—that's all." He gives Kallie a menacing wink, and then continues in a cautious tone, "If you touch her with the spur, she'll kick and start to buck. It's not hard to ride her out of it though. You'll be fine."

"Sir," she stammers apprehensively, "ah, Baron, maybe you should put me up on one of your other horses..."

He gestures again for Kallie to lead on. As the two leave the library, he says firmly, "This will give me an opportunity to see how well you ride. Think of this as a riding test, an interview."

As they walk along the corridor toward the hall and foyer, Kallie begins to question the wisdom of the Baron's plan. "I haven't done

133

very well with bucking horses in the past, Sir, and I'm even worse on tests. Why don't you just put me on an old plug, and lecture to me?"

When the Baron and Kallie approach the foyer, a door swings opens near the end of the west wing of the house. Charlene appears, and approaches with a glass of water in her right hand and something else clutched in her left. As the three join in the central hall, she opens her closed fist and reveals the Baron's medication—she says not a word as she hands several pills to him. He tosses the pills in his mouth; takes the glass of water, and gulps a sloshing drink. Handing the glass back to her, he reaches into the front pocket of his breeches and withdraws a handkerchief that he dries his lips with. "Thank you Charlene," he says, replacing the handkerchief in his pocket. "We're going out to the stable. I've decided to evaluate Miss Phillipa's equitation."

"That's a good idea, Albert." She turns to Kallie who trembles beside the Baron, and asks, "Have you had a chance to practice recently?"

"I haven't been on a horse since my accident," Kallie whimpers. Her face is colorless; she's breathing in gasps; her tiny fingers shake.

"Is Albert going to let you ride *Revel*, or *Nimbus*?"

"Widow Maker…" Kallie answers, her voice cracking. "He's putting me on Widow Maker."

Charlene's puzzled by the name, and by Kallie's trepidation. She looks doubtfully at the Baron, and then inquires sternly, "Albert, which of your horses do you call Widow Maker?"

The Baron shifts nervously in his old house slippers; his eyes dart from Charlene to Kallie and then back to Charlene's piercing stare. "It was a joke Charlene," he confesses earnestly. "A little joke, that's all—harmless."

Charlene's cheeks blush, her eyes narrow in admonishment. "You old bastard," she growls, launching a swing and slugging the Baron soundly on the bicep. "Look at Miss Phillipa, Albert, she's trembling. How could you do that to her after you told her she could trust you?" The Baron shrugs his shoulders like a naughty child who's been apprehended. Charlene reaches out to Kallie and takes her hand advising, "You watch out for this old bugger, Kallie. He's an honest

Too Far A Dream

horseman, and a trustworthy friend, but he's an awful prankster, so be careful." Then she takes hold of the Baron by the point of his shirt collar and warns, "And you, Herr Verrhaus, stop being such a rascal and behave yourself!"

"I will," he squeals as Charlene lets go of him. "I was just having some fun."

"Just remember that Miss Phillipa is employing you. That makes her the master, and you the servant."

Kallie lips broaden into a smile at the revelation: that the one who pays the bill is the one who's in charge. She nudges the Baron with a teasing elbow, scolding him playfully, "That was a mean trick, Sir. It's a good thing you didn't pull it before I went to the bathroom. You would have had running water in the library, and it wouldn't be the old plumbing in this shack that caused it."

The Baron's not used to such familiar treatment, and he's unnerved at the glitch in protocol, but Kallie's comment is so spontaneous and genuine that he abandons his stiff façade. He begins to snigger, and then he chuckles, and then he guffaws. His eyes are full with tears; he reaches for his handkerchief, and while blowing his nose, he asks, "Not Widow Maker, Miss Phillipa? Just for the sport of it?"

"Not today, Sir," Kallie responds assertively. "You've probably got a horse named *Easy Chair* somewhere in the barn. I'll give him a ride."

"Alright then," he laughs, putting the hanky back in his pocket while glancing from Kallie to Charlene. "But I think you've gotten off to a bad start by taking the advice of my friend."

"Albert, you're wasting the best part of a very nice day on a silly prank, and I'm sure Miss Phillipa is eager to get started, so you'd better get to work and earn your wage. Your jacket and boots are in the mudroom, your stick is too," she nods her head in the direction of the west wing, "and those boots of yours could use a good polishing. If the Obermeister were alive to see the condition you left them in, he'd let you know how cross he was." The Baron purses his lips; he knows Charlene's comment about the Obermeister is true; it causes him to shudder. While he cowers, and attempts to excuse his neglect,

135

Kallie's goes to the coat rack to put on her jacket. When she rejoins them, the Baron quickly shoos her ahead into the west corridor, but before they get far, Charlene inquires, "Miss Phillipa, did you bring riding boots?"

"Don't need them, I have my half chaps—they work really good."

"He's not going to like the half chaps," she mutters quietly after the two have gone.

To call it a mudroom, is a disservice to the grand house, and the craftsmen who built it. Originally, it must have been an open loggia, and like every other room, it was built on a robust scale. At some past time, someone installed windows between the pillars of ochre limestone that support the tin clad, timber roof, and although altered, it remains an elegant chamber. High and airy, long and narrow, with a checkerboard floor made from black slate, and white marble tiles, one can imagine that here, long ago, trysts were arranged, intrigues planned, romantic pledges made, or broken, and lives alone, or in union were begun. A sudden breeze rattles the glass panes causing an eerie chatter; like ghostly voices engaged in muffled conversation they sigh, hiss and then fade—the sounds of unseen phantoms divulging secrets as whispered hints.

When they enter, the Baron shuffles across the tiles, and sits on a Victorian style cast iron bench, pressed against the rear colonnade; leaning against the bench beside him, a gnarled, buckthorn riding stick with a carved ivory handle and woven silk cracker, rests in conspicuous view. Underneath the bench, his handcrafted boots recline atop an open boot box filled with rusted canisters of polish. "Hum," he sighs, lifting one boot to his lap, and scraping dirt from the welting, "this may take a while."

Kallie, wearing her half chaps, stands, her back to the Baron, staring toward the end of the loggia at a tarnished bronze, birdcage covered in cobwebs and dust. It's a cell with the door ajar; its captive flown away. "That could use a cleaning too," she muses. Outside the windows, a chickadee flits from a nearby juniper and steals a seed from a feeder hanging from the eves. The sudden movement distracts Kallie; she watches as the capped villain ascends and glides in fitted bounds returning to its cote—she's glimpsed a crime beyond her reach, the tiny thief escapes and dines secluded.

The Baron lays aside the fine wire brush he's used to dislodge the mud from the sole of his boots, and then reaching into the boot box, he takes out a tin of brown wax. He pops it open, and using a crumpled scrap of cloth, he scours the edge of the tin for the last remaining daub of polish. "Miss Phillipa," he asks, while applying polish to the toe of his boot, "this colt of yours…"

"Wicked Punch?" she replies, turning to face the Baron.

"…is he the young thoroughbred you plan to race?" Kallie nods, yes. Without looking up from his work to see her nod, the Baron continues, "He's a two year old?"

"He won't be two until May," she answers, taking several steps toward him. "He was born just after the Kentucky Derby." As she walks, the small cleats on the heels of her paddock boots click on the marble tiles. She stops and stands near the Baron, watching him message the wax into his old leather boot. "When I was little," she comments reminiscing, "my dad would let me help him polish his dress shoes—he taught me to spit on them to get a good shine."

"Ah, yes," the Baron sighs, "I think I recall seeing American soldiers doing that." He lifts the boot to examine it closely before putting it down to start working on the other. "My Obermeister would find that very offensive, he thought spitting was vulgar, a gentleman should never spit." He pauses and stares off through the windows, lost, for the moment, in a daydream. He shakes his head as the dream wanes, and then continues speaking, behaving as if his thoughts had never wandered. "At least, not a gentleman who honored his station. He taught me to heat the polish with a candle and then buff it—that way the wax is drawn into the leather. I'd show you how it's done, but we haven't the time now…" Finished, he reaches into the boot kit and withdraws a soft bristle buffer, and then flailing, like a man swatting at irksome flies, he rubs both boots to a luster. "Good!" he exclaims, smiling with satisfaction. And then he adds firmly, "He's two <u>now</u>. You do know that, don't you, Miss Phillipa?" He replaces the brush, sliding it into a lower tray of his boot kit, and then he looks at Kallie to judge her reply. She shifts uncomfortably; his meaning confuses her. "You know that all thoroughbreds have a registered birth date of January first?"

"Sure, I know that," she replies, "but it's just a technicality."

"It's more than a technicality," he says, reaching for his boot hooks. "It's a real disadvantage for him to be born so late in the year. He'll have to race against horses that are older, and have more experience."

"Punch is a pretty big horse, and you should see him run—even my mom is surprised…." She hesitates, and then says in a voice mixed with sympathy and pride, "You know he wasn't supposed to live, but he did. He was a weakling; a runt with crooked legs."

The Baron struggles to pull on his boot. "Have you gentled him yet?" he asks, releasing an exhausted sigh as the stubborn shaft slides over his calf.

Kallie reaches to pick up the Baron's riding stick before sitting next to him on the bench. "Not yet," she answers while examining the buckthorn crop. "His knees have closed up, so I think he could carry a rider, but I've been sort of laid-up. I'm thinking that I should send him to Winston Chase's farm; he's broken tons of young horses…" She pauses, and then in an inquisitive tone, she asks, holding the stick in the air like a conductor lifting a baton, "Was this a gift from someone special?"

The Baron stares, admiring the stick that stands in space before him—he says nothing. Slowly, Kallie lowers it, handing it gently to him. By the way that the Baron closes his fingers around the ivory handle, one would think he was Perceval clutching the Holy Grail. "Yes, yes it was a gift," he replies, fingering it reverently. "A very special gift, but not in the way a gift is usually given," and says no more. Creaking as he rises, he tucks the stick firmly into his left armpit, adjusts his tweed, flat cap, and then, gesturing with his right hand, "Hup, hup!" he orders, shooing Kallie toward the exit from the loggia into the outer garden.

The spring afternoon that greets Kallie as she walks from the mudroom into the Baron's herb garden is not quite the same afternoon she left upon entering the house. It's an unsure description—the day, Saturday, is certain, but the breeze that wafts over the damp and lifeless garden carries the scent of basil, thyme and catnip, and like a soothing narcotic, it skews perception. The day vibrates with excited color. The dull and rusty hues of the dormant soil, glitter; the skeletonized tree limbs, bleached gray by the winter's cold, gleam; shards of ice, pocked and shattered by hurried treading, glisten—from everywhere the spring sun cascades in rainbows, it's a dizzying potion that lulls her restraint. "Sir, may I ask you a personal question?" she asks, suddenly.

The Baron, lagging behind, extends his stride to catch up. Walking beside her, he replies suspiciously, "That depends on how personal the question is, Miss Phillipa."

"You and Charlene, why do you live like this, all alone, keeping so secret?"

The Baron draws his riding stick from his armpit and carries it like a soldier with a saber. Perplexed, he replies, "Honestly, I don't know."

"You don't know what I mean, or you don't know why you live like this?"

"I understand what you're asking, Miss Phillipa, but in all honesty, I haven't an answer to give you, except..." He pauses as they approach the door to the carriage house; he indicates by pointing with his riding stick, that Kallie should enter first. "When a person is young," he continues, "life can seem to go on forever, but as we age, it seems far too short. With our choices, we can be reckless or cautious, either way the results are the same: the consequences of our acts impose limits on us." As Kallie opens and enters the heavy, chevron timbered door, the Baron reaches past her shoulder to the lighting switch—it clicks suddenly as the contacts rotate and engage. "What I'm saying, is that we're 'too soon old, and too late smart.' That's not an apology, and I don't regret anything I've done... I'm just a little sad that Miss Fauxhausen and I have grown old so quickly."

"That really didn't answer my question, Sir..."

"Perhaps not, but that's all I'll say now."

As the light illuminates the interior of the carriage house, Kallie notices the Baron's Jaguar covered with an almost imperceptible layer of dust; the Baron strides toward the car's bonnet, and then reaching into his pocket, he takes out his handkerchief. Pausing, staring admiringly at the chrome hood ornament—a leaping cat lunging from the black lacquered steel—he polishes it with respect, and mutters softly, "Sir William, your cars are legend." He tucks the hanky, unfolded, into his pocket and then, abruptly, continues speaking. "Secrets are only secret if they remain unrevealed; a mystery isn't necessarily an enigma. I think, given time, almost all questions can be answered—not directly, but a good listener can cobble clues and make sense out of hints. Do you know what I mean, Miss Phillipa?" Kallie's face reveals her confusion, but she nods her head, yes to hurry the Baron to make his point. It doesn't work; he continues to ramble as he leads the way toward the entry into the attached stable. "Besides, life would be so dull without riddles. The history of equitation is full of them, and in every age, horsemen create new ones to suit their politics or fashion." He reaches for the stable door latch while holding his riding stick in his left hand at his side; he thrusts his shoulder against the door, jarring it open, and enters the stable—Kallie follows on his heels as they walk along the center aisle between the stalls. The pigeons, high in the rafters above the windowed haymow, familiar with the Baron's afternoon intrusion, do not flutter from their roosts; they coo and preen, like feathered debutantes exchanging gossip. One, colored gray with white bands on its wings, calls in a mocking falsetto, "look-at-the-fool, look-at-the-fool!" The Baron glances up to the tie beam, and there, next to the king post, is the culprit who taunts him. "Franklin," he shouts as if addressing an old friend, "I have a guest, kindly save your insults for later." The pigeon, bobs its head, fluffs its feathers, and beats its wings; it marches left along the tie beam, wheels about and marches back to its post. "Stand at ease my little squab, Charlene will be in later to feed you."

 Kallie listens amazed. "He's named the pigeons!" she gasps softly.

 Just then, the Baron holds out his arm like a cross buck, and stops. He nods his head in a gesture as if to say, look there. Kallie

Too Far A Dream

glances down at the brick alleyway. "Pigeon poop," he cautions, "it's slippery...." And then he strides on.

Kallie side-steps the droppings, and quickening her pace to keep up, she reminds the Baron, "Sir, you were saying something about riddles, and horsemen?"

"So I was," he replies. He halts, stands erect with his stick clutched behind his back, and nods, "Your horse, Miss Phillipa."

Focused on the Baron, Kallie's not been paying attention to her surroundings. The oak boarded box stalls that lined either side of the stable's center aisle near the carriage house have given way to a row of tie-stalls. Great, cast iron newel posts mark the boundary between the aisle and the dormitory; black, iron linked chain, hangs between the posts preventing the tenants from backing off their mangers. In one stall, before the Baron, stands a massive horse. Its tail, banged at the fetlocks, drapes like a skein of ebony thread. Its buttocks, rotund and muscled, bulges. Its coat, like a negligee made from Italian silk, shines. This is a horse bred for noble work. Kallie stands silenced by the sight.

"His name is Nimbus, he's Westphalian," the Baron says, releasing the butt chain and gesturing to Kallie that she should enter the stall. "Go ahead, Miss Phillipa, meet your pony, get acquainted. I'll go and gather his tack."

Kallie is staggered and speechless as she approaches the gigantic horse. Nimbus stands seventeen hands high, he's stoutly built, and projects formidable might. Cautiously, she rubs her hands across his bulging flank as she moves into the narrow stall; Nimbus grunts, and shifts away. "Easy big boy," she whispers, nearing his shoulder, "Pony, my ass." Nimbus turns his head, and surveys Kallie. Brushing his long mane aside, she pats his neck to reassure him; her voice takes on a soothing tone as she asks, "Are you my good boy, Nimbus?" The giant proves gentle. He closes his large black eyes, lowers his head to nuzzle her, and nickers kindly. "You're just a big baby, aren't you?" she sighs, as the confidence she left in the aisle resurges. "A big old baby."

The pigeons coo in chorus, then cease. Somewhere, from a nest overlooking the distant river, ravens call; their dark voices, like

141

warbling tenors, echo through the bluffs and fade on the spring breeze. Chaff, scattered by foraging mice, drifts from the haymow in a listless decent. If Rappunzle's golden hair were unfurled from the mow, it would be a frail pretender to the floating straw. Moments pass in punctuated quiet. And then, Nimbus does what horses do often—he makes dung, and sighs contentment with an exhaustive fart. "That's one huge pile of shit, boy," Kallie comments, "I hope the Baron has a shovel big enough to handle it." She waves her arms to disperse the odor as she leaves the stall; steam raises from the manure; she glances everywhere for a muck rake, shovel or any implement to use as a scoop—nothing is visible. "Sir," she calls out, "is there a muck fork around here?"

The Baron pops his head out of the tack room at the far end of the aisle. "There's a shovel in the end tie stall across the way," he shouts, disappearing back into the tack room.

Kallie stares at the smoldering dung, and mutters, "It had better be a steam-shovel." Nimbus shakes his head. "Sorry boy, no offense." In the end stall, she finds a wheelbarrow and manure fork. Once she's wheeled the barrow across the aisle, she takes up the fork, and begins to load the mess. "Look-at-the-fool, look-at-the-fool," chimes from the rafters. Kallie glances up to see the gray and white pigeon strutting on the tie beam above her. It steps side-to-side dancing miniature pirouettes; first she sees its tail, and then its head, then its tail, and then pigeon excrement—a small, white, palletized turd hurtling from the rafters on a deadly trajectory. "Franklin you dork!" she shouts, jumping aside just in time to dodge the missile. "Cool, cool! Look-at-the-fool." the other pigeons chime in taunting her. Kallie lifts her right hand to Franklin and threatens him by shaking her clinched fist at the very same moment the Baron emerges from the tack room. His eyes are down, and he's distracted. He's examining the bridle that he carries around his arm as he walks. Quickly, Kallie grabs the fork with both hands, and busies herself.

As he draws nearer to her, he asks, "I thought I heard you shouting again, Miss Phillipa. Is something the matter?"

"No—no, Sir, nothing," she replies, stammering. "I was saying that I'm thankful for the fork. You know? I'd hate to have to clean up this mess with my hands." Hurriedly, she scoops the last of the dung into the wheelbarrow while repeating the phrase, "Thanking you fork. Thanking you fork."

The Baron halts before her, and squints suspiciously. "Oh," he replies, listening closely to her chant. "My hearing must be going, because it sounded like you yelled something else." Kallie smiles innocently, and resumes chanting. "Hum... that doesn't sound right," he muses, bending down while removing the saddle and bridle from his arm, and laying them on the floor next to the stall. After returning the wheelbarrow to the stall across the aisle, Kallie rejoins the Baron standing behind Nimbus. "Go ahead," he says, shooing her into the stall, "go in and get your pony. We'll tack him up in the cross-ties."

Kallie nudges her way past Nimbus. She takes hold of his leather halter, disconnects the manger lead, and backs him out into the aisle. "Back! Back!" she commands, mustering all the authority her raspy voice can manage. Nimbus complies willingly, stepping back in dainty movements that contradict what would be expected from such a large beast.

"Good," the Baron growls, standing in the aisle with his arms folded across his chest. "Now billet him."

Kallie quickly attaches the cross-ties to Nimbus' halter, and then looks to the Baron perplexed. The Baron returns her stare with equal confusion. "Sir, do you have a grooming kit?" she asks.

"Grooming kit?" he blurts with embarrassment. "I just had it! It's in the tack room. I'll be right back." He turns and shuffles down the aisle puffing. In a moment he returns carrying a small red tote filled with brushes, a hoof pick and other grooming tools. "Here," he says, handing her the tote, "Carry on."

Kallie grabs a currycomb and briskly rubs Nimbus' coat, first up one side, then the other. "He's almost shed out," she comments, whacking a clump of horse hair from the comb. Then, wedging the currycomb back into the tote, she takes two brushes—one in each hand—and sets to work, buffing the hairy nap, racetrack style, to a uniform sheen.

"Are you showing off, Miss Phillipa?" he asks, jesting. "I think if you can't ride, you can always get a job rubbing horses."

143

She pauses, not sure whether she's been complemented or ridiculed. "Thank you, Sir," she replies, taking the initiative, "A good groom is hard to come by at the track, and when a trainer hires one, he has to pay blood."

When Kallie has finished rubbing Nimbus, she drops the brushes into the tote, and grabs the hoof pick, but before she can put it to use, the Baron stops her. "You needn't pick his feet," he says, "I checked them when I brought him in. Just saddle and bridle him. We'll be working outside in the arena."

"Outside?" she asks, replacing the hoof pick. "I thought you had an indoor."

"An indoor?" he laughs in surprise, "I'm just a Baron, Miss Phillipa, a poor farmer, I'm not a Royal. Charlene and I have a little money in the bank, but we have no crown jewels to mortgage." He chuckles again, whispering to himself, "Indoor, the spy thought I had an indoor." And then he continues in a louder, gruffer tone, "If riding outside was good enough for my Obermeister, then it's good enough for my student."

"I should have worn my long-johns…" Kallie groans softly while lifting the saddle in place on Nimbus' back.

"There you go doing it again Miss Phillipa, but this time I heard you. You won't need any long-johns—believe me. I'll work you until you sweat. And tomorrow, you'll know that you were on a horse."

Kallie smiles at the challenge; her expression betrays her thoughts, "We'll just see about that, Sir!" While reaching for the saddle girth by extending her foot under Nimbus' belly, and catching it with the toe of her boot, she reminds him, "You know Sir, I've had some time off—I'm not asking you to go easy on me, but I might be kind of rusty." She does up the girth, and then, starts bridling Nimbus. "About these riddles," she asks, returning to the topic, "Are you going to let me in on any of them?"

"Ah, the lesson plan," he replies, lowering his head and lifting his cap. "You're too persistent, Miss Phillipa. I had my whole speech worked out—it was very clever—then you got me off track. The riddle part was my introduction." By this time, Kallie's finished tacking the horse. The Baron takes a lead rope from the newel post

… and hands it to her; Kallie attaches it to the dee of the snaffle bit. The Baron retrieves his riding crop from the next tie stall; he examines her work, and approving, motions for her to lead Nimbus to the outdoor arena. "I'll give you the lecture as we walk. Nimbus, h-up!" he shouts. Nimbus starts, and Kallie leads on. "Have you ever heard of Alois Podhajski?" he asks, swinging open the stable doors.

"I think so. Wasn't he in that *Disney* movie about the white stallions?"

"That was Robert Taylor—an actor—he played the part of Podhajski. The late Colonel was someone else entirely."

"I love that movie! Especially the part when the horses jump."

"It's one of my favorites, too. Watch your step…" he says, pointing out where the pavement ends and the gravel walk-way begins. The warm sun has melted the snow from the walk, and although the base is firm, the lingering puddles are a hazard to polished boots. Kallie marches confidently, disregarding the water, but the Baron is more cautious. "They're called *airs above the ground,* the leaps that the lipizzaners do."

"I knew that Sir, I was just testing you."

"Oh," he replies, vexed by her teasing remark. "Anyway, Podhajski said: *Theory without practice is of little value, whereas practice is the proof of theory. It is theoretical knowledge that will show the way to perfection.*" He pauses expecting a comment, or at least some quizzical reply, but none is forthcoming. "Are you listening to me, Miss Phillipa?"

"Yes Sir, I heard every word."

As the Baron, Kallie and Nimbus reach the end of the outdoor arena where a mounting block stands ready, he continues quoting Podhajsky, emphasizing every word as if reciting an address: *"Theory is the knowledge, practice the ability.* And, *Knowledge must always take precedence over action.* You'll hear me repeat those words many times. I believe them, and they are the basis for my teaching."

Kallie halts Nimbus next to the mounting block as the Baron finishes speaking, "Will I have to memorize the whole thing, Sir?" she asks, pulling the irons to the ends of the stirrup leathers.

"Yes," he replies as she draws up, and tightens the girth. "And a lot more too. Now, Miss Phillipa, if you please, mount up."

She hesitates, and quickly checks the fit of the bridle, "Better to be safe than sorry, Sir," she says, closing the snap on her helmet strap while stepping onto the mounting block. And then she leaps aboard Nimbus in a single, easy move. "I picked that up at the racetrack."

"You can mount, Miss Phillipa," he notes calmly, "but can you ride?"

Kallie opens the right rein, bringing Nimbus about, and at a slow walk she enters the arena. The Baron follows close behind. While he walks, he slides the butt of his riding stick under his belt behind his back; fastens the collar button of his waist length, brown leather jacket, and adjusts his riding gloves. Nimbus sloshes along in the moist, sandy surface of the arena.

"The footing is actually quite good," he comments, kicking the toe of his boot into the sand, "I would have thought it to be more heavy after the warm weather we've had."

"It seems to be good along the rail," Kallie reports. "Do you want me to stay on the left rein and go large, or should I half the school?"

"Yes, go large. At a walk," he replies, fixing his gaze suspiciously upon her. "Are you playing with me, Miss Phillipa—have you studied dressage, are you familiar with the school figures?"

"I may have read a book or two—maybe even that one by Podhajsky…"

Surprised, the Baron half-halts a stride, stuffs his hands into his jacket pockets, and shakes his head while muttering, "Oh good, a sneak who's also an expert."

"Thank you Sir, I heard that," Kallie shouts from horseback.

"I meant for you to hear that…"

"I thought you did, Sir."

"I did Miss," he snaps curtly.

"So you said, Sir."

"Should we carry on, Miss Phillipa, or shall we carry-on?"

"Carry-on, Sir!"

"Then so we shall!" he barks, "Continue at a walk."

"At a walk it is, Sir!"

"That's good then, we understand each other." The Baron huffs at the dispatch of the words he and his student have just exchanged. He reaches behind his back and yanks his riding stick from his belt and, slaps it soundly on his boot with a cracking report. He clears his throat in preparation for resuming his lecture, and then starts to talk in slowly measured speech. "What I'll teach you Miss Phillipa, is the theory of riding—the theory of <u>all</u> riding—no magic, no tricks, no hocus pocus. And then it's up to you to practice."

"That's what I want, Sir!" Kallie exclaims, turning to address the Baron. Unknowingly, she's closed her legs more than is wise on a well-trained horse. Nimbus follows her cue, and, as if on autopilot, he departs into a bounding trot. "Whoa boy," she yelps, giving a tug on the reins. He returns instantly to a graceful walk. "That was close…" she mumbles, catching her breath. Then, she addresses the Baron, "That's what I want, Sir—no hocus pocus. I want the meat and potatoes, the nuts and bolts. None of the regular bullshit…" The Baron plants his feet in an abrupt halt, and stares in shock at hearing her cursing. "I'm so sorry, Sir," Kallie pleads, trying to sooth the transgression. "I didn't mean to use that word—I know it's not ladylike—I won't swear around you again. I promise."

A forgiving smile creeps over the Baron's lips. "I do go out in public, Miss Phillipa," he assures her. "I hear words much worse than that from girls younger than you at the mall. Tough girls who swear only to show off, or to impress their friends by using foul language."

"I'm not one of them." Kallie protests.

"I know you're not. You cursed honestly. I don't have a problem with that. An honest expression of emotion is refreshing. It just caught me off guard when you said bullshit—there's no need to apologize, your emotion was aptly expressed by the word." He pauses a moment, and then tips his cap at her, saying "I can assure you, Miss Phillipa, what I teach you will contain no bullshit, and having said that, let me also assure you that my methods are very simple." He starts to walk, almost with a swagger, as he moves into the subject of his lecture—a subject few horsemen have studied so closely, or lived so intensely. "I'll walk along side, you listen to what I have to say, and then we'll see how you do on your own. Oh, and Miss Phillipa, there's nothing wrong with acting like a lady either." And then, as an aside to himself, he whispers, "But that might take years of practice."

The comment escapes Kallie as she and Nimbus walk along the rail. The large, dark bay gelding moves with the bold assurance of a skilled athlete. Each of his strides is measured, his footfall is cadenced and regular, the undulations of his muscles—relaxed, but powerful—are almost musical, melodious, and work in concert to impel the great beast forward. Kallie is just along for the ride—Nimbus husbands her kindly.

"There are only two things you must understand if you are to ride a horse," the Baron says, walking briskly alongside. His tone carries conviction and certainty. "The knowledge of two fundamental forces of nature—forces that govern the universe—is all that is required to maintain control, and direct the energy of a horse. Those forces are inertia, and gravity. Sir Isaac Newton described the inertial tendency of an object moving in space in his first law of motion. Are you able to recall what Newton said, Miss Phillipa?"

She appears stumped, and hems and haws indecisively, trying to remember the exact wording. "I did pretty well in science, Sir, but if I don't get it just right, it's because I'm nervous, but here goes: *Once an object is set in motion, it will tend to stay in motion on a straight line, until it encounters another object or force.* Is that about right?"

"Yes, good!" he replies, tapping his stick along the calf of his boot in applause. "Think of Nimbus as an object moving through space under the influence of inertia. He will continue to move…"

"In a straight line?"

"Yes, in a straight line until acted upon by another object or force. Correct? So, what is that other object or force?"

"Me?" she answers meekly.

"You. Yes, Miss Phillipa, you are the other force. By using the aids, you can add to, or annul the momentum of the moving object, and thus assist it, retard it, or deflect it." He looks up at Kallie; his expectant stare demands a response. "Theoretically, very simple. No?"

"I get that, Sir. It's kind of like when I header a soccer ball past the goalie."

Too Far A Dream

"Just like that, but much more subtly. Architecturally, a horse is a very unstable structure. When moving at walk, it has three hooves on the ground. The base of support, from side to side, and this depends on the horse's confirmation, is only about ten to twelve inches wide. At trot, if it's a schooled trot, the base of support is about four and a half inches wide. Relative to the height of the object, the base of support is very narrow. Now remember that the mass of the horse is cantilevered above the base..."

"Cantilevered, Sir?"

"...Its belly is wider than its feet—the flanks of the horse protrude beyond the base of support." He holds his riding stick vertical as he walks beside her, takes off his cap, and hangs it on the end of his stick. "See how my cap is hanging to one side of the crop? My cap is cantilevered. Without a counter weight, it would be impossible to balance this object on its base. That's what makes a moving horse relatively unstable, and very amenable to the influence—the force—of the aids. But there is something else that assists the horse in keeping its balance, and it's often confused with inertia, and that's momentum. Let me give you an example." The Baron replaces his cap, walks to the center of the arena, and motions for Kallie to follow him. She opens the left rein and Nimbus turns toward center. "Do a ten meter circle on the left rein, then change within the circle to the right, and then halt."

Nimbus marches quietly at walk, executing the serpentine change within the circle under imperceptible cues. This is not Kallie's doing. Nimbus is well schooled, and responds to the simple act of Kallie turning her head to look where she's going, and the shift in her weight as the change of direction occurs. Now walking on the right rein, she gives a light tug on the reins, Nimbus halts leaving his back hollow and his stance askew.

"We'll talk about that halt another day, Miss Phillipa," he says, shaking his head admonishingly as he steps in beside her. "You've ridden a bicycle, haven't you?"

"Yeah. Some of my friends and I used to mountain bike in the bluffs—it was a blast. You should have seen some of the wrecks! I always thought it was a lot like riding a horse."

"It sounds like fun," he replies, smiling in amusement, "and in some regard it is like riding a horse, but this is the point I want to make."

"Oh, sorry Sir, I didn't mean to get you off track."

"You didn't…"

"Okay then."

"It's very difficult to balance on a bicycle when standing still, but once moving, it gets easier as we speed up—that's the effect momentum has. Momentum is a product of mass and velocity. As the velocity of an object increases, so does its relative mass, and it will take more force to disturb its inertial tendency causing a deflection of its trajectory. That's how an unstable object, like a horse, is able to balance on a narrow base. Standing still, the horse just widens its base by spreading its limbs and standing squarely on all fours; at trot, it would be a very precarious balancing act were it not for the combined effect of momentum and inertia."

"I am so glad I didn't take a nap during physics…" Kallie groans.

"That brings us to the second fundamental force, gravity. We aren't talking about objects moving freely in space, we're talking about objects moving under the influence of gravity. If I apply a force to an object, under the influence of gravity, and move its mass beyond its base of support, what happens?"

"Duh!" Kallie gasps mordantly. "It would fall down."

"Good! Now you know everything you need to ride a horse, except for a few little things." He tucks his riding stick into his left armpit, and stepping along side Nimbus, he places his hand on the horse's shoulder. "Let me show you how this works. Close your legs a little, and square him up." Kallie squeezes with her calves, and Nimbus squares up. The Baron gives a stout push with his arm; Nimbus braces against it, and does not budge. "Did you see what happened?" Kallie shakes her head, no. "That's right, nothing happened. I applied a force, and according to theory, Nimbus should have fallen over, but he didn't. Why?" Kallie grunts the first sounds of a reply when the Baron interrupts, "That was a rhetorical question; you don't have to answer."

"Oh, okay."

Too Far A Dream

"Nimbus applied a counteracting force by shifting his weight within his base of support—he didn't <u>want</u> to fall down. And that's the key to the aids: A horse, or anything else—you and me—will always defend itself. He will do what he needs to do to prevent his falling. Now let's try our experiment again. Ask him to walk forward by closing your right leg." Kallie gives a quick nudge, and Nimbus walks. "Ask for more, we need a good working walk." She nudges again. "Good," the Baron says, "that's the walk we need." He moves to Nimbus' shoulder, and just as the horse lifts its right forelimb, the Baron pushes on the base of its neck. Nimbus immediately crosses his legs, and steps to the left. "There!" he shouts, "that's the effect of gravity, and the same thing will happen if I apply a similar force to the flank of the horse—he'll step sideways with his haunch."

"That's pretty simple, Sir."

"Yes, so it is, Miss Phillipa, but don't be mislead. It's much easier to move a horse sideways, than to move it forward, and forward must always come first. There is nothing more difficult, than to train a horse to move resolutely forward in response to the slightest application of the driving aid."

"I've heard that, Sir. *Ride your horse forward, straight, and calm.*"

"That's how some teachers put it these days," he replies, curling his lip sarcastically. "But forward, straight, and <u>calm</u> is not correct, and it's not what is exactly needed."

"I'm confused Sir. Almost everyone says it that way, at least everyone that I've read."

The Baron halts and pivots slowly as Kallie continues to walk Nimbus on the ten meter circle. "Those people are talking about riding sport horses, not horses that have to work for a living—certainly not a military horse, a police horse, or a racehorse. Calm horses are for frightened and inadequate riders. The calmest horse is probably sleeping."

"Podhajski said it, and he was in the army…"

"Podhajski was an aristocrat!" he retorts brusquely. "He rode for the Royal Court, his rank was ceremonial… and he was wrong about this."

"You're an aristocrat. Aren't you Sir?"

Stung by the comment, he admits self-consciously, "I have a title, yes. But I'm right, and he is not! The exact quotation is: …*ride your horse calmly forward, and straighten it.* Now, that may sound like the same thing, but here is the difference. The rider must be calm, not the horse—I think someone added an unnecessary comma to the Count d'Aure's statement." He pauses, and smiles with secret satisfaction. "Do you see the distinction?" he asks. "A calm horse is not necessarily one that is confirmed on the aids; he might just be lazy, inattentive, or worse, dead to the leg. Calmness has nothing to do with it. A calm horse is always behind the aids, slow to act, and a labor to ride. I want my horses hot off the aids—I drive, they go forward. Now, this instant!" He slaps his riding stick on the calf of his boot and shouts, "Sit deep, and close your legs, Miss Phillipa!"

Without hesitation, and with no consideration of the consequences, she does as commanded. "I-eee!" she screeches as Nimbus bounds forward into a lofty passage on the quarter-line—his diagonal pairs of limbs hanging at the height of their swing arc for what seems to be an inordinately long pause before grounding. "What the hell have I done?" she yelps from the edge of panic.

"Good! That's what I want—a horse hot off the leg."

"Holy shit! Make him stop, Sir," she cries, flopping awkwardly in the saddle.

The Baron laughs robustly, and claps his hands in delight, shouting, "Now, Miss Phillipa, sit more deeply, massage rhythmically with your calves, and hold your hands in position."

Nimbus makes an effortless transition to piaffer—the passage, in position. Kallie squeals in joy and terror. "Holy crap! I've never done this before. This is so cool!"

"Lighten your seat, release your leg slightly, and give with the hand—be ready." Kallie executes each command instantly, but in sequence. Nimbus, like a sprung spitball, vaults to trot. "Post! Get off of his back, rise to the trot, and go large!" Nimbus roars toward the track along the rail. Kallie, bouncing tentatively at first, begins to feel the rhythm of the warmblood's gigantic stride, and then, as if struck by one of those transient inspirations, she relaxes and finds her balance—grace and elegance overcome the pair, they move as fluidly as a spring rain flows across ice. "Half-halt in the corner," the Baron shouts, "leg first, and then the hand... Quick, one more on the outside!" As the two round the corner onto the short side of the arena, Nimbus is noticeably more collected. His haunches are lowered and driving powerfully forward; he lifts his shoulders and raises his neck as his face approaches the vertical; he advances slowly in a measured and cadenced, collected trot—every inch of flesh engaged in locomotion—the proud, courageous trot of a warrior's mount. "Very pretty, Miss Phillipa. Nice work."

For the next thirty minutes, Kallie, and Nimbus play—the Baron giving kind instruction. They do passage into walk pirouettes; trot half-pass, and bold, exhilarating extended strides at canter lengthening. Finally, the Baron notices his shadow—long and narrow—and he glances at his wristwatch, "Miss Phillipa," he calls out, "it's time to cool him down. You've shown me enough to judge your ability."

"Thank you, Sir, I really don't want to quit..." She takes her feet out of the irons, and stretches her right leg. Groaning, she adds, "...but I think my leg is going to fall off."

"It will take a long time for you to recover from your accident, I never have recovered from some of my riding injuries..." The Baron ambles to the opening of the arena, and waits as Kallie and Nimbus make their way to the exit. "That's the odd thing about growing older, all the little knocks and bruises that seemed so insignificant when they happened, come back and hurt worse on their second visit." He reaches behind his back and tucks his riding stick under his belt. Kallie and Nimbus draw to a halt beside the mounting block where the Baron waits; she swings her right leg over the horse's back and dismounts with a splash as her feet strike the soft ground.

"Good boy, Nimbus," she gushes, patting him on the flank. "You're such a good boy." She lifts the saddle flap, and gently

153

loosens the girth. "Do you want me to cool him out with a walk around the arena?"

"Not necessary, just walk him back to the stable, we'll put a blanket on him and cool him in the aisle."

Kallie slides the irons up the stirrup leathers and ties them securely home. "Last year, at the track, I saw a gallop girl get conked on the head by one of these when someone's horse got away—she dropped like a sack of potatoes, got a concussion and about ten stitches. It wasn't pretty. She bled all over." She shrugs her shoulders in a gesture of foreboding. "I'd hate to see that happen again."

"That's very good advice, Miss Phillipa, accidents don't injure people, carelessness does."

Leaving the reins draped across the horse's neck, she grasps the chinstrap of the bridle; takes the lead rope from the ground alongside the mounting block and connects it to the dee of the bit, "Hup, hup Nimbus!" she barks, leading him to the gravel path that winds back to the stable. The March afternoon sun, although two hours above the horizon, is loosing its battle with the vigilant winter chill. Wisps of steam rise from Nimbus' back; the great horse shakes his head and neck fanning the fog into clear air. As the Baron walks silently alongside Kallie, he shivers. "So what do you think, Sir?" she asks, skipping to disguise her lameness. "Do I have what it takes to be a jockey?"

"Yes, I think you do, but... probably not yet."

Kallie's shoulders sag with disappointment, "But you said I ride really nicely."

"Yes, you do, you have a lot of natural ability, and you move well with the horse, but that's not enough. Everything we do when we ride a horse is un-natural..." he glances at Kallie to see her brow knit with confusion; he continues, hoping to help her understand. "I know that sounds odd, but there are many things that humans were never intended to do, like paint pictures, write books, or go into outer space. We can do these things, but we have to train ourselves to do them. It's the same with riding. We have to train our bodies to move in ways, and act with a precision that nature never required from us—it just isn't a job nature intended us to do. Riding a horse isn't natural for the human, nor is it natural for the horse to be ridden. These two items make the task very difficult to master. You show promise, hard work and practice will improve it, and you'll have to make some sacrifices. Remember, that talent must be tempered by training."

"My mind is pretty well made up on this, Sir. I'm going to do what ever it takes. I'm going to race in the derby." She pauses to face the Baron; Nimbus stops; the Baron stops, the three stand face, to face, to face. "A good teacher can help even a poor student… Are you a good teacher, Sir?"

The Baron hesitates before replying, "Honestly, Miss Phillipa?" He stares deeply into her eyes while exhaling softly, "Do you want my honest opinion?" And then he growls with absolute certainty, "Albert, the Baron Verrhaus is the very best."

"Good!" she growls back. "That's what I thought, then do your best with me—I won't disappoint you, Sir."

The Baron smiles apprehensively, he understands well the challenge placed before him. "Nor will I disappoint you, Miss Phillipa," he replies warmly, and then, removing his riding glove, he offers her his right hand to seal the pact. Kallie returns the gesture, and they shake hands consummating their oath.

Nothing more is said between the teacher and the student on their return walk to the stable—promises of this sort are taken seriously by old gentlemen, especially when the prospect of failure is real, and the consequence is heartbreak. Not all roads are smooth, nor do they all lead to a chosen destination; some are gouged with ruts, bridged with corduroy, and lead to nowhere. Albert, the Baron Verrhaus has known both: success and oblivion… "Will my promise spare her pain, or cause it?" he wonders as he, Kallie and Nimbus enter the stable.

"Look-at-the-fools, look-at-the-fools!" cry the pigeons, launching into disarrayed flight among the high rafters. The exposed timbers and posts overhead, impede the flock, and split their ranks. The late afternoon sun, cascading through the haymow windows, flashes from their clapping wings as they tumble and dive in frenzied delight raising dust, and dislodging cobwebs. From the far shadows, down the long aisle near the carriage house comes a sound: "Coo, coo," and the pigeons, like wasps drawn to nectar in August, plummet akimbo

155

to the call. Franklin alights first, followed by his feathered kinsmen. He struts regally—a royal squab among his squires—the plumed dauphin is here to dine. "Your dinner, Majesty..." comes a voice hidden in the shade. "Will you dine with your Court, or with your Queen, Sire?" Franklin launches onto wing as Charlene emerges from the shadows and stands among the pigeons foraging on the cracked corn she scatters across the herringbone brick. He soars above the tie beams, dodges between the king posts, acrobatically displaying his airy prowess before folding his wings in a kamikaze dive that ends in a flutter—he comes to rest on Charlene's shoulder. "Some corn for the Prince?" she asks, placing a kernel between her plump lips. The pampered bird bobs its head forward and backward. Finally it succumbs, and plucks the meal from her lips.

"Charlene!" the Baron shouts, horrified, "That pigeon pecks at horse manure all day. You feed him like that, and then you want to kiss me goodnight!"

"Just a little peck, Albert..."

Kallie laughs in amazement at what she's witnessed. "That is <u>so</u> funny!" she says, fighting to catch her breath.

"It's disgusting, Miss Phillipa! I assure you, pigeons make a delicious entrée, but they're dirty, awful pets."

"You wouldn't eat Franklin," Kallie gasps in shock. "He's got a name... You wouldn't eat a little bird with a name?"

"Maybe not—not Franklin anyway. But I would like to avoid kissing anything that eats dung. I don't think my palate could ever adjust to the taste."

"Me too, Sir," she whispers aside to him, and then she reconsiders, "Oh wait, I kiss my dogs. Um, maybe I should cool out Nimbus and let you solve this problem on your own."

"Trust me, Miss Phillipa, in forty years I've never found a solution. I don't think I'll find one today. That woman has a mind of her own."

Kallie ties Nimbus off to a newel post, and removes his saddle while saying, "All the same Sir, it's worth a try." And then she adds sarcastically, "Good luck." She lays the saddle down, pulls at the lead rope releasing the knot, and as she walks up the aisle leading the horse, she giggles to herself, "We wouldn't be women if we couldn't think for ourselves."

"You needn't be so snide, Miss Phillipa. I think you're intentionally cruel sometimes."

"Not me, Sir."

"Yes, you are," he adds gruffly, tagging along behind. "And stop snickering—a horseman does not snicker." As the two walk quietly up the aisle toward the carriage house, the pigeons sit fast at their meal. When they arrive where Charlene stands, Kallie reverses direction and leads Nimbus back toward the stable exit continuing his cool-down. The Baron enters the tack room, emerging, momentarily, with a gray and red, striped quarter sheet. "Miss Phillipa," he says as she approaches on her return, "throw this over his haunches." He hands her the blanket; Kallie complies and continues on her walk. The Baron retreats to the end of the aisle, and, as he leans against the stucco wall that separates the stable from the carriage house, Franklin takes wing in brief flight, alighting on the Baron's shoulder. "You're far too bold little squab," he notes mischievously, "and too trusting as well." Franklin coos adoringly. The Baron examines him with a squint of his eyes. "Creamed peas and some crusty bread would make fine companions for you," he says, reaching his hand to his shoulder, and clutching Franklin, gently holding him at arms length for a better view. "Some raisin and walnut stuffing, that would be good too..."

"Don't even think of it, Albert," Charlene interrupts, whispering a threat. "Now let him go."

The Baron releases Franklin who flies to join the other pigeons eating at Charlene's feet. "How did the lesson go, Bertie?" she asks, reaching into the pocket of her smock for another handful of corn.

"Quite well," he answers, expressing satisfaction, and folding his arms across his chest. "She is very able, a little crude with the aids, I think, but she has a basic understanding of the theory." He laughs. "If she is as capable as she is cocky, she could be very good."

Just then, Kallie and Nimbus walk by, having completed a circuit of the aisle. The Baron pushes off from the wall and approaches them. "Miss Phillipa, I'll walk with you a while. I'd like to discuss something." As he steps by Charlene, the pigeons scatter, only to return to her feet once he's past.

"Yes Sir," Kallie responds, pausing for him to join her.

"As you were," he says, shooing her on. "We'll talk while you cool out your pony."

"Albert," Charlene calls to them as they begin a circuit of the center aisle, "I'm going back to the house to start dinner—Oh, and you had a call from your publisher. He'd like you to call him back, so don't dally out here too long."

"Yes, yes, I won't. Did Brian say what he wanted?"

"He needs you to proof the typesetting on Monday."

As Charlene leaves the stable, the heavy, door closes with a slam upon her passing; Nimbus ignores the abrupt noise and walks calmly on. The Baron reaches in his front pocket, takes out his crumpled handkerchief and blows his nose. "My sinuses' act up every spring, it must be the mold from the rotted leaves," he says, replacing the hanky.

"August is the worst for me—ragweed."

"Pollen doesn't seem to affect me as much as mold and dander."

"They have a shot for allergies now, clears you right up."

"I know," replies the Baron, reaching behind his back to retrieve his crop, "but the drugs react with the medication I'm on. They cause my blood pressure to elevate."

Kallie looks at him with concern, his cheeks are dull and colorless, "Are you alright, Sir?" she asks. He ignores her question, so she asks again. "Sir, do you feel okay?"

"I'm really quite well for a man my age—my health is good, and I have no trouble sleeping."

Innocently, she inquires, "How old are you?"

Twirling his riding stick in his fingers, he replies, "I'm young enough to get out of bed and dance with my horses." He does a little jig, skipping from foot to foot. "See?" he asks with a broad smile, "Could a really old man do that?"

"Not too bad, Sir—my dad can't even dance that good."

"But tell me, Miss Phillipa," he continues, his voice changing to a serious tone, "I don't mean to pry, it's just that I have to ask because you've involved me. You have this dream, and quite possibly, you have the talent to make it come true..."

"Sir?" she ponders hesitantly.

The Baron pauses in the open doorway of the stable, and stares at the sparse snow dotting his meadows. Kallie and Nimbus make a small circle, coming about to stand at his side. Sheltered from the cool breeze, the late afternoon sun shining into the stable aisle warms the still air, the Baron smiles, and comments optimistically, "I think the spring is my favorite time of year—even though it's difficult for me to breathe—there's such anticipation in the season. I'll be able to prune my roses soon." He glances at Kallie, and asks with undisguised pride in his voice, "Do you like roses, Miss Phillipa?" She nods her head, yes. "This is a harsh climate for them though, my roses always suffer." Drifting off in thought, he looks down at the mud that's accumulated along the welting of his boots; probing at it with the tip of his stick, he dislodges a small clod. "Sacrifice," he announces suddenly, "choice and consequence."

"What do you mean, Sir?" Kallie asks, startled by the rapid change of subject.

"Men have been using horses in war, and employing them as beasts of burden for nearly three thousand years. It's a very old, and honorable tradition that you want to be a part of, Miss Phillipa. It's a terrifying responsibility to live up to—the horse is a noble creature, but only if we as riders and trainers conduct ourselves with equal nobility. You'll be required to make some hard choices if you intend to be a good rider, and to make these choices without the benefit of having a clear view of the consequences." He gazes off at the distant sky, distracted momentarily by a red-tail hawk soaring above the high trees that line the bluffs. "And you'll have to make sacrifices—nothing must come between you and your dream."

"Why are you telling me this, Sir?" she asks, betraying her irritation. "I've already thought about all this stuff. We shook on it—I made a promise."

"You're young, and a person's interests change."

"Yours didn't."

"You don't know what dreams I had when I was your age." He breathes a sigh—hollow and deep—that reveals resignation. "Often, the plans we have when we start out in life are changed by events over which we have no control, and where we end up is very different from what we imagined. We can never judge, just by looking at them, whether or not the scars a person carries are self-inflicted."

Kallie is jarred by his comment, but she replies confidently, "That sounds really depressing, Sir. Sure, plans can change, but that doesn't mean that we should be disappointed, that we should quit dreaming, or give up. Sometimes, things work out for the best—I mean look at you and Charlene, you guys have everything." She pauses thoughtfully before continuing, the sound of doubt creeps into her voice, "Well, sometimes they do, work out. You know?"

The naiveté of her comment shows as pain on his face. "Yes.... You're right, of course. We mustn't quit dreaming, Miss Phillipa. Someday, if we truly believe in ourselves, we may indeed become what we pretend to be. I don't mean my remarks to be depressing, I'm just saying this because Charlene and I don't really have any family—not that we're lonely; Miss Fauxhausen and I are very happy with our lives—we made choices when we were young, choices that have caused us to be alone; we don't regret what we've done, but I'm nearing the end of my career, and I don't intend to have another student after you. I want to believe that what I have to teach you will go from me, and then someday, pass to your student. That's the tradition, a teacher's legacy. It started long before my Obermeister; he shared his knowledge with me; I carried it on, and soon, it will continue through you. You will succeed, Miss Phillipa, wherever your dream may lead you." Kallie remains quiet. A moment passes, shared in silence. "Miss Phillipa," he continues, speaking softly, "please, don't send your horse to someone else for gentling—the job is yours alone to do. Both you and Wicked Punch have much to learn, and between us, we have a promise. Bring your horse to me. This is where your dream should start."

* * *

Seven: Sweet Iron

On the first day of April, a Tuesday, Wicked Punch was moved to the Verrhaus estate on Gleason Road. Fresh off winter pasture, he still wore a coarse coat, and took to his new residence like Dickens' 'Pauper' exchanging places with the 'Prince.' He paced nervously throughout his first night. His quarters, a palatial box stall with an automatic water dispenser, may have seemed too opulent to a horse of common breeding—the foal of a doomed mare, and a sire without winning blood—but introduced to the noble company billeted in the Baron's stable, the young race prospect soon settled in and assumed a more regal bearing. He shed his heavy coat to reveal that underneath he was a proud thoroughbred dressed in bay, trimmed with black points. Fledermaus, Nimbus, and the Baron's pensioned hunt horse, Revel—seasoned campaigners, battle tested and left unscathed—comprised the cadre of brave knights that would tutor, and initiate him in regimental life. High aloft, Franklin and his feathered brigade kept nightly watch—no villain would enter these premises without risking a poopy bombardment.

Every morning, the Baron would arise at five-thirty, dress in his riding kit, have a quick coffee and a Danish with marmalade, and then go out to the stable to begin his work. By six-thirty Kallie would arrive with her fortifying cup of joe in hand. Together, they'd feed, and ready the Baron's horses for their daily turn-out. But Wicked Punch was assigned a special duty. While the other horses were lead from the stable to the grazing meadows, he waited patiently—his work would begin soon, the life of a racehorse follows a routine.

Gentling a young stud colt can be both difficult, and dangerous. When introduced to the surcingle, cavesson and the longe line, Wicked Punch bucked, wheeled, and plunged; like a fractious child attempting to avoid a bath, he bolted, straining the muscles and the patience of his handler. But the methods the Baron employed are tested and true; given time, and unyielding kindness supplemented by strict discipline and calm precision, Wicked Punch's instinctive defiance relented. Gradually, he learned to work forward on the circle guided by the longe line, and urged on by the whip. He didn't learn quickly—he wasn't an apt student—but he learned well. Kallie apprenticed at the Baron's side. She studied his methods, and slowly acquired the skills necessary to use the tools that classical horsemen employed.

After three weeks of legging-up on the longe line, the snaffle bridle and bit were added—cold steel, in a mouth unaccustomed to it, begins what often is a contentious marriage. In the hands of a careless butcher, the snaffle bit can be a cleaver, but in the hands of a master, the hard iron melts into a soothing balm. Albert, the Baron Verrhaus is a master. He sweetened the bit with sugar before placing it in Wicked Punch's mouth; softly, he used it to massage the tongue and bars where the bit would rest, and then he put the cavesson on the horse, and longed him. Within days, Wicked Punch willingly accepted, and champed the bit. "This is the most important lesson you will ever teach a young horse," he advised his student. "Nothing can ever restore a ruined mouth. Take time making the mouth supple and yielding to the bit, and your horse will trust your hand."

Near the end of the fourth week, he taught Kallie to work her horse in driving reins. "Now your horse must learn about contact," he said, beginning his lecture by attaching long, leather reins to the snaffle. "There are three ways European horsemen use the driving reins to work the horse forward into contact with the bit. Here is where the final duty of the horse will dictate the means we employ. The English will run the reins through the stirrups of a saddle. While it works well enough for training a hunter, the irons bounce on the reins conveying sudden jerks to the bit—it leads to a hard mouth. The Austro-Hungarians—the Germans—will use the surcingle with side reins, but leave the driving reins free. They do this because they still teach the airs above the ground, and it's necessary to have the reins free when the horse leaps. The French will use a surcingle, and thread the reins through the upper turrets. I prefer the French approach because it places the bit and rein in a position that will mimic the hand position of a jockey." When he'd finished tacking Wicked Punch for driving, he placed himself at the rear of the horse, took up the reins and a driving whip, and then, instructed Kallie to

Too Far A Dream

slide a leather lead rope under the chinstrap of the bit and hold the two loose ends together. "Lead him on," he said from his position behind the horse. "Stay calm, and walk slowly. If he tries to run off, or go up, release the strap. I've got hold of him." But nothing happened; the Baron's advice was unnecessary for this horse—this time. It would be the last step before backing Wicked Punch. The first thirty days of training had passed.

* * *

Victor John Faith

Eight: Trickles

It's five-thirty a.m. The sky at dawn on the thirty-first day is marbled with wisps of high cirrus clouds set between shafts of crimson daylight. A cold May breeze rustles across the grassy meadows from the northwest. It's only twenty-eight degrees above zero when the Baron skulks out of his single bed to glance at the thermometer outside his window—it will be warmer as the spring sun approaches zenith, but now, an anemic dawn, and the chilly air excite a shiver. The room is wrapped in quiet, except for the sound of the Baron's grand clock that beats its tick and tock downstairs. In another bed, separated from the Baron's by a small nightstand, Charlene sleeps. He's careful not to wake her as he steps into his leather slippers, and leaves the room making his way to the bathroom across the hall. The toilet flushes. The sound of water running in a washbasin trickles softly. The alarm clock on the nightstand buzzes to life. Startled, Charlene bounds from under the covers to sit upright. The Baron dashes through the door, "Oh sorry, so sorry," he yelps, rushing to silence the alarm. "I don't think I set that before bed."

"I set it," Charlene replies, yawning and stretching.

"You could have mentioned that last night," the Baron scowls, "The damn thing almost caused me to arrest."

While he stands beside her bed, and struggles with the clock, she smiles fondly at him. "Bertie," she snickers, pointing at the open fly of his gray, silk pajamas, "It looks like you left the bull outside the barn."

He glances down to see his privates exposed. "Oops!" he laughs, taking action to restore his modesty, "it's an old bull, and I don't think he can do much harm anymore."

"I don't know Albert," she says, winking. "It didn't look harmless just now…"

"You should rub your eyes, and make sure you weren't dreaming."

"No, I prefer to remember it the way I saw it. A dream would be less charming."

With the embarrassment of a little boy who's just been told that he's cute, he smiles shyly and replies, "What you think you saw, old woman, was the remnant of a romantic fantasy. Like the old saying goes: *If wishes were horses…*"

"…Young girls would ride?"

"No," he answers, restraining a laugh. "That's not how the saying goes."

"It used to…"

Flustered, he scrambles to change the subject. "Why did you set the clock?"

"One of my clients from out east wired me some money for a game."

He knows what she means by *game*, she means poker, but he's surprised, and asks, "Today?"

She nods her head, yes, while the Baron shuffles to his dresser and takes a pair of white cotton, crew socks from the top drawer. "And tomorrow, too," she adds, adjusting the blouse of her pajamas, and sliding, with a groan, out of bed. As she goes to retrieve her housecoat lying across a steamer trunk at the foot of her bed, she continues talking. "I'll probably be at the club for a couple of days. There's a player coming in from Palm Springs, and two from Las Vegas, so you're going to have to deal with making your own meals." She draws the belt of her housecoat around her waist and ties it. "If it warms up this evening, you could grill a steak. I saw a bag of charcoal in the mudroom behind *Gilbert's* cage. It's from last year, but it should still be good."

By this time, the Baron is tucking his white shirt into his riding breeches. For a brief moment he stops and looks quietly out the window. "I saw him yesterday," he says as if whispering a solemn prayer to a sleepy congregation, "He was at the bird feeder…"

"Who?"

"Gilbert."

"Bertie, that squirrel ran away more than five years ago. It couldn't have been him. They don't live that long."

"But he didn't flee when I called his name. He looked right at me. I'm really quite sure it was Gilbert. *Gilbert, the dancing squirrel...*" the Baron sings softly. Then, as he starts to do a little tap dance, the crusty soles of his slippers click like a cat's toenails on the hardwood floor. *"Gilbert, the dancing squirrel."* he sings again. *"Give the girl squirrels a whirl..."*

"Albert," Charlene teases, watching him dance like a marionette, "we're going to get you a puppy. I think you need a little lap dog—a kissy little lap dog."

"No... Gilbert was amusing, but I don't have the patience to mind a puppy—they're too much like people." He stuffs the crew socks into the front pocket of his breeches, and then asks, "Will you be down for coffee?"

"If you promise to brew it strong."

"Sure."

"No Albert, I mean really strong."

"Thick as tar..." he grumps as he leaves the room.

It's seven-fifteen a.m. In the Baron's stable, Kallie is mucking the tie stalls; she puffs a cloud of chilly breath as she lifts a heaping forkful of manure into the wheelbarrow. Cleaning these stalls is not a difficult chore. Tethered to their mangers, the geldings drop their dung in a single heap in the gutter; there's no need to search the straw bedding for hidden turds. Inside the tack room, the Baron is humming a Rossini overture. Kallie rests the muck fork atop the manure in the wheelbarrow and listens, "Rossini," she whispers, "It's always Rossini," and resumes her work. Just then, the Baron emerges from the tack room; cuddled within his arms is a miniscule saddle, and a racing bridle. He struts, still humming, to where Kallie labors.

"You were late this morning, Sir," she says in a tone that is very matter of fact, "So I fed and turned the horses out without you." She gives a final fluff to the straw bedding. "Revel was stocked up again. If you want, I can come by after school and take him for a jog—just some light exercise..."

"What about your homework?"

"Gees Sir," she groans, jabbing the manure fork into the wheelbarrow. "It's the last month of my senior year; I finished up all my credits in February. I can goof off until graduation if I want."

The Baron lays the saddle and bridle next to the stall that Kallie's just finished cleaning. "You aren't expecting me to pay you for the ride, are you?" he asks, as Kallie wheels the barrow out the stable entry.

"Pay me? Ha!" she shouts. "That would be the day…"

"Ha!" he shouts back. "When you pay me for the lessons, I'll pay you for the ride."

"Ha!" she snipes from outside the stable.

"Ha yourself, Miss Phillipa!"

"Ha, ha-ha, ha-ha!" echoes from the distant manure pile.

The Baron stares at the open stable door; he shakes his head and whispers in disbelief, "And I should get a puppy? I take enough abuse from my student…"

"Were you saying something, Sir?" Kallie asks, suddenly re-entering the stable.

"Did I say something? I don't recall saying anything. You must have heard the pigeons cooing."

"Ah yes, the pigeons."

The Baron examines the stall that Kallie's just finished cleaning. "Did you lime the wet spot when you mucked?" he asks. She shakes her head in a gesture meaning, no. "Here then," he says, handing her a gray, felt saddle pad. "Lay this down in the center of Nimbus' stall, and then step on it a few times."

She takes the saddle pad; looking at him skeptically, she inquires, "And why should I do that to a new saddle pad?"

"Nimbus and Punch are stabled next to each other. Horses in a herd, even a small herd, form relationships. If you'd spent more time observing the horses, and less time sassing me, you'd have noticed that," he adds sarcastically. "Now, Nimbus is a bold and aggressive horse—he's the leader. Fledermaus is big, but he's shy; he stays back and differs to Nimbus. And Revel, well Revel was second in command even though he's old, but now there's a new horse in the heard, and he's taken the second place from Revel."

"And this has <u>what</u> to do with tossing the pad in Nimbus' stall?"

"Odor."

"Odor?"

"Trust me. Do as I say." Kallie's doubtful, but complies. After tossing the saddle pad into the stall, she treads on it lightly. "Step on it," the Baron commands, so she picks up her pace. "No, not faster. Put your heels down and get some weight on it—stomp on it."

"Good enough, Sir?" she asks, trampling the pad into the straw.

"That should be fine, Miss Phillipa. We just need to pick up the scent of Nimbus' urine." Kallie lifts the damp saddle pad from the straw and hands it back to him. "Good," he comments, examining it. "That should make your job a little easier. Now rub it up and down the front of your sweater and breeches."

"Like heck!" she gasps. "I'm not going to wipe horse pee all over myself, these are brand new jeans."

He glares at her with stern and certain eyes, and growls, "You will, Miss Phillipa. You can launder your clothes tonight, they'll be fine, but you know from your own experience how long it takes to heal a broken bone." He thrusts the pad at her. She darts aside. He squints menacingly, and holds the pad at arm's length. She takes hold of it and begins to rub it across her chest and thighs.

"This is so humiliating," she whines. The Baron chuckles quietly. "Oh, this stinks, this really stinks. I'm going to get booted from school."

"You said you didn't care about school…"

"I don't, but I have friends—you know?"

"They'll accept you."

"Yeah, from a distance."

"It's an honest aroma that quite becomes you, Miss Phillipa, you smell like a horse, and not just any horse, you smell like Nimbus." He laughs, as she smells her hands, and then he continues, "Wicked Punch respects Nimbus. So—when you get to mounting him later today, he'll respect you, too." He sniffs the air as he takes the pad from her, and then as an afterthought he adds, "And tomorrow, before you come over, take a good shower with some unscented soap, but don't put on any deodorant or perfume."

"Okay, but this is so unfair," she moans, brushing her hands down her chest in disgust.

"I thought you liked the smell of horses."

Too Far A Dream

"I do... but I don't like walking around wearing their poop!"

"Stop complaining," he scolds, "we have a lot to accomplish this morning. Bring your pony out and tack him up for longing."

Kallie scuffles the few steps to Punch's stall. She takes the lead rope and halter that hang from a brass towel rack affixed to the heavy, oak door, and then grunting, she slides open the door, and enters the stall. The young racehorse lifts his cleanly chiseled, narrow head from the manger, turns and gazes calmly at her. His dark eyes, nearly hidden by long eyelashes, sparkle as she enters; he nickers in recognition when she asks, "Hi-ya, big boy. Happy to see me?" He tosses his head up and down as if to reply, yes, and then his nostrils flare exposing their crimson interior as he snorts confused. He arches his long neck, and curls his upper lip as she draws near—the scent is familiar, but out of place. He's curious. He knows Kallie's shape and voice, but her perfume is confounding. He sniffs her apprehensively, curling his lip a second time before the Baron's tonic takes effect—he lowers his head in submission to the scent, and allows her to nuzzle him. "That's my good boy," she whispers, placing the halter on him and connecting the lead rope. "Today's a big day for you. Today I'm going to get on you and ride." Wicked Punch swishes his tail nervously when Kallie leads him from the stall and stands him in the cross-ties—he senses that something is different about the mood, there's an anxious tension in the air, and unfamiliar equipment is present. He rocks side-to-side. Kallie grabs a currycomb and scours the dust from his coat. Next, she takes the brushes and rubs the nap back in place. Last, she picks his hoofs. She does it all with quick precision, and without a sound. The Baron, standing by in Nimbus' stall, studies her movements like a surgeon observing a resident, ready to step in should the unexpected happen.

"Very good, Miss Phillipa," the Baron comments when she's finished. "Now the snaffle bridle and the cavesson."

Kallie reaches for the bridle, and sliding it over her left arm, she hangs the cavesson on her right shoulder. She approaches Wicked Punch and unfastens his halter, re-attaching it around his neck. "Easy big boy," she says, taking the crown piece of the bridle in her right hand and the bit in her left. The bay colt complies, lowering his head

169

to accept the bit. In one quick move, Kallie slides the crown piece and reins over his ears, "Piece of cake, huh Punchie?" And then she places the cavesson over the bridle, and affixes the cross-ties to the side dees.

"Be sure that the cavesson isn't interfering with the reins, Miss Phillipa."

She knows that the upcoming work will require the reins to be free, and checks them carefully—her safety could be compromised were everything not perfect. "They're clear, Sir."

The Baron walks from the stall to join Kallie. "Good," he says, smiling. "Proceed to do them up for longing." She does as told, twisting the reins, and sliding the throat-lash between them. "Now step to a safe distance, please, Miss Phillipa," he says, directing her into Nimbus' stall. Calmly, he takes up the gray saddle pad and carries it under his arm to the front of the horse. "Whoa," he whispers, "easy fellow." Slowly, he presents the pad to Wicked Punch for examination. The anxious horse snorts at the unfamiliar sight; his eyes bulge; his nostrils flare; he shakes his head and peddles backward in the cross-ties. "Whoa," the Baron repeats in a soothing tone. The sixteen hand thoroughbred stands his ground, straining against the ties. "Easy, easy," he repeats softly, blowing a whiff of Nimbus' scent toward the alarmed colt's nose. After another moment of resistance, Punch yields, and steps forward, hesitantly at first, to smell the pad. "There, that wasn't so bad as you thought, was it fellow?" the Baron asks quietly while stroking the horse's outstretched neck. "We'll let him get a good smell of it before we move on, Miss Phillipa." Kallie watches as the Baron allows Wicked Punch to nibble the pad.

"Why are you letting him chew on it, Sir?"

"Scent and taste are related senses. I want to be sure he recognizes the smell. It will make him more submissive when we saddle him."

"I'm glad you didn't make me taste it."

After a moment, Wicked Punch has calmed and released the tension on the cross-ties. "There," the Baron sighs, glancing toward

Kallie. "Now come here and take the pad so he can make the connection with you."

She moves closer to the horse while saying, "Easy big boy, easy boy." Punch sniffs her; he exhales and breathes deeply. Next he sniffs the pad, then her, the pad, her... "This is so cool," she giggles quietly.

"Toss it on his back the same as you would the surcingle," advises the Baron, standing beside her and comforting the horse. "But don't make a big deal of it—he's broke to the feel of something on his back." Kallie flips the pad on Punch's back, and adjusts it to the shape of the withers. "Do the same with the saddle." She reaches down to retrieve the tiny exercise saddle from the edge of the aisle, and tosses it up. The horse's back sags suddenly as the saddle makes contact. "There, there fellow," whispers the Baron. "Do up the girth, but don't tighten it yet—he's sucking air." Kallie knows that this means the horse has puffed up against the girth, and when he exhales, the girth will need to be secured. She moves the saddle to its place behind the withers, and does up the billets and buckles.

"That went pretty well. Don't you think so, Sir?" she asks, stepping back relaxed. But before the Baron can reply, Wicked Punch fires a cow kick catching Kallie soundly on the thigh. The blow sends her toppling to the ground. "I-eee!" she yelps, leaping to her feet. "E-ouch! Where the heck did that come from?" She cocks her arm instinctively threatening to slug him.

"No, don't hit him, it's too late. He won't be able to make the association between his act and your punishment. You have to be faster."

Kallie drops her arm, steps away from the horse, and then rubs her thigh. "I'm okay, Sir, thanks for asking."

"You needn't be cross with me, Miss Phillipa. You were slow to act, and you were out of position."

"I didn't even see it coming," she groans, still rubbing her thigh. "That was stupid Kallie..." she mumbles, "really a dumb move."

"Are you alright?"

"Pretty sure. He got me on my good leg."

"Sure?" he quizzes doubtfully, staring at her.

"Yeah."

"Well, good enough then, let's carry on. Right?" He attaches the longe line to the center dee of the cavesson, disconnects the cross-ties, and leads Wicked Punch into the breaking day.

Kallie, wincing in pain, hobbles along behind, and grouses, "So much for your idea about wetting the pad. All it did is piss him off!"

"Yes, well, he kicks at Nimbus, too."

"You could have mentioned that."

"You shouldn't have trusted him." He glances back to check on Kallie who's limping three paces behind. "Two centuries ago, Edward L. Anderson wrote a little book about training horses for use by cavalry…"

"You're going to lecture to me now, aren't you, Sir?"

"If you catch up, I'll give you the benefit of what I've learned, yes." She jogs into position on his left. Wicked Punch, prancing nervously, is on his right as they walk along the gravel path toward the arena.

"Okay Sir, lecture away."

"Thank you, Miss Phillipa," he replies, and then his tone turns serious. "In his chapter on *Vices, Tricks, and Faults*, Anderson notes very personally that, and these are his words: *I am far from saying that all horses are naturally vicious; but I do say that the horse does not voluntarily obey the demands of its master, and that he who depends upon its willing obedience is in a precarious position…*"

"That sounds awfully cold."

"Perhaps, but it's smart and safe." As they approach the entry to the arena, he clears his throat, and continues speaking, "Anderson goes on to say: *Restraint and control must be irksome to all animals, and it is natural that the high-spirited horse, to avoid the tyranny of man, should attempt to escape restraint and control.* What Anderson meant is, that we must never trust a horse to do as we expect. You learned that just now, and I was reminded of it—again." They enter the arena. As they walk toward center, he gazes at the puffy clouds overhead, smiles, and when they halt at X, he adds, "The 'man upstairs' never intended that horses should be enslaved by men."

"We've been doing it for a long time, Sir…"

"Yes, so don't be surprised when they kick out."
"No Sir..."
The Baron motions to Kallie that she should step back. "I'll longe him for a while in the side reins. You go and stretch out your leg on the grass, and think about what I've just told you." Their eyes connect as he reaches to attach the side reins; his betray misgiving. She purses her lips, her eyes narrow, mirroring his anxiety—she knows the implication of his words, and the seriousness with which he spoke them. She also knows that backing a young colt for the first time can result in the horse being of service to man, or a danger to him—both outcomes are tragic: the horse looses its freedom, or man looses a friend.

Kallie slinks over to the grassy margin of the arena and sprawls on the ground with a thud. She massages the welt swelling on her thigh. The Baron and Wicked Punch begin their work on the longe. It goes well enough at first. Wicked Punch, with thirty days of training, is familiar with the routine, but bearing a saddle is new— he's tentative and the Baron can sense his brewing restiveness. Holding the longe line in his left hand, he tucks the longe whip into his right armpit. Punch kicks out once and farts. Methodically, the Baron reaches with his right hand, grasps the longe line, and bringing it across his body to his right hip, he steadies himself in anticipation. Wicked Punch lowers his head as if to sniff the ground. As he advances around the circle, long and low, his black mane splashes over his ears. His coarse, stubby tail swishes when he farts a second time. The Baron takes a step forward with his left leg and plants his heel firmly in the dirt. Up snaps Punch's head lifting his front hooves from the ground. He squeals like a raptor descending on a rodent. He bounds forward bucking. The footing beneath his driving hooves explodes—shards of clay splatter the blue sky. The Baron is ready and stands his place. Kallie jumps to her feet, and stares transfixed. Wicked Punch bolts. Round and round the Baron he races swirling like a bay tornado—a dark wind without reason. The Baron is braced and patient, he knows the storm must fade. But then the unexpected happens. Wicked Punch rounds his back, leaps and kicks out bucking, and when reunited with the ground he plants his hooves in an instant halt. "He's not done yet," advises the Baron. Punch rocks back on his haunches, squeals and rears. Up he goes, and higher still, his front hooves flailing the air like a mad drummer. The Baron is kind, but he knows what he must do, he doesn't dally; he doesn't hesitate, he gives a stout tug on the line—the horse teeters. He pulls again, and the horse falls off his feet—his support gone, he topples, sprawling on his side. Seconds collide in an instant—everything, at once, is done. The horse rests motionless. Kallie shrieks. The Baron coils the line as he goes for his prey. With speed so swift that neither eyes can see nor words describe, he pounces, kneeling across the downed horse's neck. Wicked Punch thrashes in an attempt rise, but the Baron holds him down.

"Oh God!" Kallie cries, "You're going to kill him."

The Baron, breathless, and with irritation unfamiliar in his character, yells back, "He's fine damn it. I just threw him. Get over here and watch what I'm doing."

She knows now that he intended to pull the horse over, and she obeys, dashing to stand behind him. "What can I do?" she whispers.

"Nothing," he whispers back. "Just be near him; let him see you; make him know that his freedom depends on you." She moves within his eyesight. Wicked Punch, like a penitent before a priest, whines mournfully. The Baron glances up at her from his position on the horse's neck. "We got lucky," he says quietly. "Had you mounted straight away, it might be you here on the ground." Wicked Punch makes a feeble attempt to throw the Baron from his neck, but ever the gentle man, the Baron holds firm. With a soothing voice, he consoles the subdued horse, and kindly strokes its cheek and neck. "I don't like using strong tactics to defeat an animal, harsh treatment can be risky. It must be saved as a last resort, and then, be used only in the most able hands."

Kallie concurs, her voice stern, and grim, "Since he's put on weight and gotten fit, he's been an asshole..."

"If, only once, the horse discovers that it can overpower its master, we've lost—it will never again be safe to use." Punch's breathing has changed from short, frantic gasps to deep, regular breaths. "He's submitted," the Baron whispers, "I'm going to let him up. Make eye contact with him as he regains his footing, but stand off to the outside in case he bolts again. And Miss Phillipa, when he's up, step in and rub your hand firmly up and down his mane—it's what the dominant horse would do. If he turns his head to look at you, push it away instantly, and rub again. Do not let him initiate contact. The greater horse always rubs on the lesser; that's the way nature intends it to be, and we must conform."

Kallie moves to the outside of the circle, far enough away to be out of reach of the horse's hooves should he thrash as he rises. The Baron checks to make sure the cavesson and longe line are fixed safely; he pats Wicked Punch lightly on the shoulder as he lifts his knee from the horse's neck. "Easy fellow, steady," he says quietly, as he steps away. Punch exhales deeply and groans. He lifts his head and neck. With his limbs folded beneath him, he rolls from his side onto his belly; he kicks out one fore limb, and then the other, and with a second groan, he strains, lifting himself to his feet. Kallie dashes to his side and begins rubbing vigorously up and down his neck. "Are you alright, big boy?" she quizzes anxiously. Wicked Punch farts his reply. "That's what I thought," she laughs, continuing to rub his neck. "You're short of words, but long on wind."

"That will do, Miss Phillipa," the Baron calls from inside the circle, "we've got to get him moving." Kallie turns and jogs to the grassy margin of the arena. "Hup, hup fellow—WALK!" he barks, swishing the longe whip. Wicked Punch, tentatively at first, complies. "He's fine, Miss Phillipa. We only injured his defiance, not his pride—he'll still have heart enough to run."

"If he keeps his feet on the ground..."

"True, so true. They can fly, but they can't run well in the air—TROT!" Wicked Punch executes the transition from walk to a lofty, forward trot. "Miss Phillipa, do up your riding vest, and make sure your helmet is secure..."

"Yes Sir," she replies nervously. She knows what's coming; the plans haven't been altered by the outburst of the horse. Her heart starts to thump. Her tongue sticks to the roof of her mouth. Her stomach revolts, and her throat feels like it's filling with vomit. *"Get a grip, Kallie!"* her inner voice scolds, *"You've wanted to do this forever—now grow up.*" She fumbles as she closes the snaps of her vest, "Crap, I should have spent the money and got one with a zipper." Her lips are blue, and her breaths irregular as she walks toward the Baron.

"Whoa fellow, whoa," the Baron orders while jerking on the longe line. Wicked Punch transitions from trot to walk, and then halts.

Kallie joins him in the center of the arena. "Are you nervous, Sir?" she asks, hoping for some reassurance.

"I've done this before, Miss Phillipa. I'm not nervous. But you, now you should be nervous. This is the first time you've broken a horse."

"I'm not nervous—not a bit…"

The Baron squints his eyes, and notices Kallie's cheeks trembling. "We've talked about this many times, Miss Phillipa," he advises her tenderly, "I've told you what to do—do that, and you needn't worry."

"I'm not worried, Sir. But thanks for the advice." She reaches into her back pocket, takes out a pair of calfskin riding gloves and pulls them over her twitching hands. "Is it really cold this morning?" she asks. "My lips feel numb."

"They're blue…" he answers, nodding to her that she should approach the horse.

"It felt chilly, must be colder than I thought."

"Unusual for this time of year."

Kallie leaves the Baron standing in the center of the circle and strikes out toward Wicked Punch; she takes several steps, and then pauses, turning back to him to ask, "Are you sure we should do this when it's so cold? Maybe we should wait a day or two until it warms up—he might be less frisky then." He smiles sympathetically, but doesn't answer. "Just a thought, Sir—never mind." She takes a deep gulp of cold air and resumes her march. Like a soldier charging a forlorn hope, she knows there's no turning back, no retreat, only victory or everlasting peace—both impose an unearthly calm. When she reaches Wicked Punch, she pats him gently on the neck, and in a voice more raspy than usual, she pleads, "Be a good boy for me, won't you, Punchie?" Cautiously, she sets about her task. She frees the reins from the throat lash. Next, she moves to the saddle, checks that it's centered behind the withers, and tightens the girth. Finally, she lowers the nearside stirrup to its full length. "Breathe Kallie," she whispers, "remember to breathe." With both hands, she grasps the stirrup leather at its connection to the saddle, and applies her weight—Wicked Punch leans toward her to steady himself, but doesn't fret—she releases, and after a moment she repeats the action. "He seems willing to accept my weight, Sir...." The Baron remains silent; he is studying every twitch, every reflex, and every gesture that the horse makes. "I'm going to put my foot in the iron...."

A simple, "Yes," is his reply—direct, and without equivocation.

Kallie takes hold of the stirrup, and slides her left foot into it. Grasping the pommel with her left hand, and taking a little hop step, she grabs the cantle with her right and hoists herself up to stand in the stirrup. She pants; Wicked Punch rests easy.

"Good. Now lie across the saddle, and hold onto the off side girth. If he threatens anything, drop the iron and slide off. I've got control of him here."

When she leans over her horse, she shudders as a vision of her accident flashes through her thoughts: the horse rearing up; endless seconds of weightless flight in free-fall; a thump as the ground strikes her back; the sound of snapping bones, splintered beneath a crashing horse. "Why am I doing this?" she wonders aloud. "I should have just paid Winston..." The horse stands firm.

"Again, Miss Phillipa, and this time, be more casual—pat him, and let him know you're there." She does as told. The horse stands firm. "Very good. I'm going to move in and walk him now. Stay as you are." The Baron coils the longe line in neat loops as he walks toward Kallie and Wicked Punch. "Easy fellow," he says on his approach. "Stay calm, Miss Phillipa, the worst is behind us now." Kallie knows better—she's on her belly, lying across the saddle; her left foot is in the iron, her other leg, clinched like a pretzel, crosses behind it at the ankle—the horse could explode at any moment, and send her flying off. "Are you quite comfortable?" he asks, holding taut the shortened longe line. Her reply is in the form of an anguished groan. "We'll take it slow…. Walk on, fellow." Kallie tenses as the horse takes its first hesitant steps at walk. When the Baron quickens the pace to a working walk, the muscles in her calf begin to convulse. "Oh God, oh God, oh God…" she mutters softly.

"Steady on, fellow."

"Please Sir, not too fast."

"Steady on…"

They make one complete circuit of the arena. "You're doing fine, Miss Phillipa, stay relaxed." As they embark on a second tour, her abdomen aches from the relentless pounding of the gait; her shoulders burn, as she stretches to maintain hold of the girth; her buttocks, strangled by a wedgie brought on by the jarring steps, go numb. "And Miss Phillipa, try to remember to breathe."

"Oh yeah, that's it! Breathe Kallie—breathe girlfriend," and as she does, a sudden, calming feeling of warmth drains down her legs. "I-eee!" she screeches feebly.

"Are you alright, Miss Phillipa, is everything going fine?"

"Even better than you know, Sir…" she whimpers helplessly. Like an anxious terrier with a bladder control problem, she drips an embarrassing trail of 'happy tears.' "Oh shoot, shoot, shoot!" she moans to herself, "Why now? Mom can hold it for hours. Next time Kallie, pee <u>before</u> you get on the horse."

"Good then, let's proceed."

Kallie can sense the warm liquid cooling. "Oh God, please tell me there's not steam coming from my butt."

"Slide your right leg over his back, and try to sit erect." She hesitates. "Quickly, Miss Phillipa!"

Two thoughts race through her mind, one she verbalizes: "In a second, Sir." The other she keeps to herself: "Oh God, I'm going to piddle on his saddle."

"Whenever you're ready then."

She waits another moment, and then squeezing her abdominal muscles as tightly as she can, she takes a gasp of air, and lifts her leg over Wicked Punch. The horse walks steadily on. "I'm up Sir," she giggles uncontrollably—as much from ecstasy as from embarrassment.

Too Far A Dream

The Baron turns to face Kallie and Wicked Punch, and walking sideways and backward away from the pair, he uncoils the longe line. "Keep him walking on the circle, take up the reins in your left hand, but don't apply any contact. And with your right hand, grab a hank of mane."

With the sound of sudden panic in her voice, she asks, "We're not going to trot, are we, Sir?" As a precaution, she hastily knots her fingers in Wicked Punch's black mane.

"Not today," he says calmly. And then as an aside, he adds, "At least, I hope not today."

Punch swishes his tail, and passes a squeaking fart. "I think I feel him bunching up. I think he's going to buck!"

"Stay relaxed, and ride through it—pretend you're a cowboy on a rodeo bronc."

"Easy for you to say, you're not on his back!" And then, just as Kallie finishes speaking, Punch starts off at a bounding trot.

"Follow him, Miss Phillipa, help him to move freely by rising the trot." The longe line draws taught as the horse moves around the circle. "Steady on fellow..." the Baron calls out, nervously gasping for breath. The horse perks his ears, and assumes a regal posture—his head on the vertical, leading his swelling chest. Puffed up and full of pride, he strides forward, his muscles rippling; droplets of sweat bristle on his neck; his quarters undulate like a tsunami at sea; he is, every powerful inch, a thoroughbred. Once around the circle they go without mishap, a second time, and then a third. For ten long, magic filled minutes Wicked Punch and Kallie trot before the unthinkable happens: the horse squeals, blows from its swollen nostrils, drops its head and walks.

"Easy fellow, easy. Walk," the Baron says quietly. "Walk on..." he repeats as he coils up the line while approaching. "Whoa fellow. Rub his neck, Miss Phillipa." Wicked Punch comes to a halt with his black mane a mess of matted burls from Kallie's excessive rubbing. "Good form, Miss Phillipa, very good form indeed. Take a deep breath, you may dismount your pony now."

"I don't think I dare, Sir."

"No, no, you may. I've got hold of him." Kallie's stuck to the saddle, but the Baron is confused as to why. "Are your legs a little wobbly? Do you need a hand getting down?"

"No, no," she blurts, "that's alright, Sir. I can manage." She swings her right leg from the offside of the horse, kicks her left foot free from the stirrup, and drops to the ground. He was right. Her legs are wobbly; they collapse under her sending her sprawling in the dirt. Wicked Punch turns his head and stares at her—if horses could laugh, this one would. The Baron watches as she sits upright. Her jeans are wet and discolored from the zipper to the pockets. He notices. His eyes grow wide with surprise. Kallie knows that he knows. "So I peed myself!" she flares in embarrassment, struggling to get to her feet. "It happens sometimes. I've got a weak bladder—some women do. You men are so lucky you don't have this problem." He's left without words, he tries to speak, to say something reassuring, but he only stammers. "It's so aggravating," she continues venting, "It never happened before my accident." Feverishly, she brushes the sand from her damp buttocks, and lap, and then her frustration subsides. In a rueful tone she whimpers as she glances down to examine her jeans, "I just get nervous now, and it happens."

This is not a situation most men would deal well with, but the Baron is from another age. He's refined, a gentleman, and empathetic. "I'll take care of the horse," he says calmly and quietly. "I know that Charlene has a hair dryer in her bathroom. I know she'll let you use it."

"Thank you, Sir."

"Go on, hurry. It couldn't have been comfortable riding like that."

"Yes Sir," she says, turning and breaking into a jog toward the manor house.

"And Miss Phillipa," he adds, stopping her in her tracks, "men piss their pants too, and for the same reason you did. Courage is mere bravado if not tempered by humility."

"That's very good. Who said that?"

"I did, just now."

"Well Sir, that's one I will remember...."

The Baron watches as Kallie scampers along the gravel path leading to the house. Her left thigh is swollen, inflated from the kick; her right toe is lagging, and drags behind, scuffling. When she disappears into the logia, he turns to Wicked Punch and rubs his mane saying, "That was a clever quote wasn't it, fellow? I'm going to have to write it down."

The next morning, The Baron, Kallie, and Wicked Punch follow the same routine, but with a different result: the horse acts up, and Kallie gets thrown. It's not unusual for a young horse to throw its rider during the breaking process, and Wicked Punch turns out to be a usual horse. The following morning, the first Saturday in May, he dumps Kallie twice. That afternoon, Anthony and Reggie, John, Celeste, and their three children, the dogs Goldie and Waggs, and Kallie repeat their long-standing tradition of watching the Kentucky Derby on TV. John mixes the mint juleps, adding an extra splash of bourbon to each glass "for color," and he looses money on the race again. Sunday morning, Kallie mounts and promptly hits the dirt one more time. And then, that's the end of it; Wicked Punch relents and settles into his new work of galloping under a rider.

* * *

Victor John Faith

Nine: On the List

The racetrack opened two weeks ago, and Kallie's eighteenth birthday party, complete with a cake in the shape of a horse, was celebrated at a reserved, cloth-covered table high in the rafters of the clubhouse suite. "The best party ever!" she exclaimed as the first horse in the first race of the first day of the new season went to post. Her whole family attended, and many of her friends. Uncle John celebrated from the mutuel windows; her Grandpa Stuart hung out at the bar and flirted with a middle-aged barmaid; Anthony and Reggie watched the races from their chairs at the table and ate buffalo wings; Celeste tended to the Phillipa children who played on the jungle-gym; Winston Chase, betting slips in hand, paced anxiously before the television monitors. Juan and Lupé, dressed for the occasion in their finest clothes—they'd washed their newest jeans, and pressed their most festive shirts—but still, they appeared nervously out of place, and hovered nearby sipping beer from plastic cups. The Baron sent a hand painted birthday card autographed by Charles Foxx, and his regrets.

Last Sunday, June first, Kallie attended a baccalaureate ceremony at the Belleview High School, and then in the gymnasium on Tuesday, after a benediction by an Episcopal pastor, a long-winded, sleep inducing speech by a 'past-his-prime celebrity', and some self-serving remarks by the president of the school board, at exactly nine fourteen in the evening, she received her high school diploma.

It's now four fifty-nine Thursday morning. The alarm clock beside Kallie's bed is set for five, but before it can startle the house with its rude clanging, she opens her eyes, reaches her hand calmly, and disarms it. The clock is no longer necessary, Kallie's eighteen, a high school graduate, and she's emancipated. But something else has changed too. Her small room, across the hall from Anthony's office, is tidy. The pile of dirty clothes, heaped in the corner, is gone; there are no dust bunnies under the bed; the beanbag chair is missing, and the magazines that were strewn around the floor are neatly filed in a bookshelf. Kallie sits upright in her bed, yawns and stretches, and then an expression of anguish shows on her face. "Ooo-ouch!" she yelps, and bounding from her bed, she races down the hall into the bathroom. A moment later, the toilet flushes, and Kallie emerges relieved.

Across the bluffs, in the Baron's stable, Fledermaus, Nimbus, Revel and Wicked Punch begin to stir. In the rafters overhead, Franklin and his cooing comrades take to their morning flight. In the master bedroom of the manor house, Charlene sleeps next to the Baron's empty bed. He awoke early, quietly left the house, and now wanders among the rose bushes skirting the roundabout.

In east Belleview, on a weary street lined with row houses adjacent to the rail yards, a rusted, old sub-compact rattles to a smoking stop. An exhausted young woman in a waitress' uniform staggers from the car and plods her way up the several crumbled cement stairs that lead to a two-story clapboard duplex. There is no grass, there is no yard, and there's no front porch, only a cement slab before the battered entrance to the building. From a broken window in an upstairs unit, a shredded, green curtain flutters in the early breeze—the other windows are covered with plywood. The woman pauses on the slab, her dark, shoulder length hair is mussed; the blouse of her uniform is un-tucked from her skirt, and she carries a bib apron, pantyhose, and a yellowed brassiere in her hand. When she reaches to unlock the door, she teeters and drops her keys—they clink as they strike the slab—and then steadying herself against the door, she grumbles the 'F' word repeatedly as she retrieves them. Making a second, haphazard attempt, she fumbles with the lock, it resists, but finally the deadbolt releases and the door gives way. The tired woman enters an unlighted hallway—a darkened stairwell ascends to the boarded-up unit on the upper floor—she closes and locks the outer door, oblivious to the litter and debris scattered throughout the hall. The door to her apartment is to the right of the stairs; the last person to enter or leave has left it ajar; she gives it a depleted shove. "Home..." she sighs, and stumbles in. Scribbled on a slice of masking

183

tape affixed below a buzzer on the doorjamb is the woman's name, it reads: Morgan Jasperson.

On a mattress, off-center of the room that Morgan enters, a young man and woman are sleeping. The woman, lying on her back with her arms folded across her breasts, is dressed only in panties; the man, on his belly next to her, is naked—an unzipped sleeping bag is scrunched between them. One tattered couch against the far wall with an oval coffee table in front of it, a mismatching armchair and side table in a corner by a window are the only furniture—too young to be antique, too old to be stylish, all the furnishings appear to have been castoff rubbish salvaged from a street corner. As Morgan passes in between the coffee table and sleeping couple on the floor, she tosses her pantyhose and brassiere at the couch—they fall in a heap against the armrest—and then she walks to the armchair near the window, spills the contents of her apron on the side table, and collapses fatigued into the chair. The early morning sun, breaking over the bluffs on the eastern side of the river, cascades through the dirty window and lights Morgan's face, but the dawn's crimson hue fails to make her pale cheeks glow. She shuffles among the wadded up bills and mound of coins from her emptied apron and makes a preliminary count. "Tips sucked last night," she groans disheartened, and gazing out the window, she wonders, "How am I going to pay the landlord?" Soon, she's nodding off. When she awakens later that afternoon, the sleeping man and woman will have gone, and Morgan's skimpy tips will have gone with them.

Back at the Phillipa house, Kallie, dressed in a long red T-shirt and crew socks, is leaning on the kitchen counter staring anxiously at the coffeemaker that gurgles and chugs, spitting out its rejuvenating tonic. Wags and Goldie pad in; Goldie sits and sniffs the air, Wags licks Kallie's calf. "Do you boys want to go out?" she asks, stirred from her concentration on the steaming coffee. Both dogs make a dash for the back door, and she follows them. "Want to go out for a poop and pee?" She opens the door letting them run free to do their jobs, and then shuffles back into the kitchen.

Anthony enters, dressed for work in khaki trousers, a blue oxford, short-sleeved shirt, and penny loafers. He watches as Kallie takes two coffee cups from the cupboard above the coffeemaker. Lifting his nose to sample the aroma, he inhales, and sighs, "Ah, fresh joe. Do you have a cup for your old man?"

"Do you want some eggs and toast with it, Dad?"

Anthony glances at his wristwatch, and then at the kitchen clock, "No thanks, shrimp," he answers, "I'll stop by the diner in town." Kallie pours two cups, and carries them to the table, handing one to Anthony. He slurps, and gasps, "Holy cow. This isn't joe, this is joe-jitsu. Wow!"

"Good stuff—huh? I like it strong."

"Strong?" he gurgles, "I could pave the driveway with it." Then, pulling a chair from the table, he asks, "Are you running behind this morning? You're normally dressed and out of the house by now."

"Nope. I'm taking the day off—I sort of earned it. I'll stop by the Baron's this afternoon for a lesson, but this morning, I'm going to the track and apply for a jockey's license."

"Are you sure you're ready, Kallie?"

She takes a sip of her coffee while standing at the table, "If not today Dad, then when?" she replies with a confident smile.

"I just thought you'd wait a while, until your horse was at Dorchester Downs at least."

"I've got to gallop him, and we'll have to send him in for his official works, and gate approval. I want to make sure I've got all the paperwork done," she says, walking to the stove, and placing a skillet on the burner. "He's still three months away from racing, but I have to be ready now. With my luck, anything could go wrong."

"What do you need from me? Do I have to sign something? When do I turn his papers in?"

Kallie drops a pad of butter in the skillet and ignites the burner. "I don't know. I'll talk to the Baron and Winston. I don't think the racing secretary needs the papers until he works—I'll check." She goes to the refrigerator, removes a carton of eggs, takes out five, cracks them into a bowl, and scrambles them. "Are you sure you don't want any?" she asks, gesturing with the bowl. "I can scramble a few more."

"You're having five eggs by yourself?"

"And maybe some toast, too. I'm hungry…"

Anthony shakes his head in amazement, and asks, "How the heck do you stay so skinny?"

"My metabolism's high," she replies, laughing. "And stress—I'm under a lot of pressure."

"Eating like that will catch up to you when you reach my age."

"Right Dad," she teases, "you're so buff."

"Tell that to mom when she comes in, would you?"

"Yeah. Sure. Like you love birds need any help. I'm glad my bedroom is way down the hall, otherwise I wouldn't get any sleep." Anthony blushes at her comment and tries to cover by taking a loud slurp of his coffee. As she pours the eggs into the skillet, they sizzle and pop when they hit the heated butter. "Oops," she says, leaning to look at the height of the flame, "Got the pan a little too hot…"

"Is Winston going to let you work for him again this year?"

"Yeah. I'll walk some hots and groom for him, but when I get my bug license, I can gallop at the track in the mornings—make some extra cash. Maybe, I'll even get a race or two. A lot of trainers like getting the five pound allowance for riding a bug. I'll work on Winston, see if I can't get him to name me up."

Anthony rests his cup on the table, and then confused, he asks, "Where does that come from, *bug*?"

"From the asterisk they print by an apprentice's name. Makes sense, huh? Are you sure you don't want any eggs?" In response, he raises his hand in a gesture as if to say, no thanks. Kallie scoops the eggs onto her plate and joins him at the table. Just then, there's a dull thud, and a scratching sound that comes from outside the back door. "The dogs want in…" she mumbles, stuffing her mouth full of eggs.

"Eat, eat your breakfast, I'll get them. We wouldn't want you to starve…" He gets up from his chair, and opens the back door; the dogs bound in, ears flopping and their tails swishing. "Do you guys want a dog biscuit?" he asks, scratching Wags on the neck. They dash to the cupboard. Anthony laughs, and notes, "It's amazing how dogs can act dumb when they're being scolded, but understand every variation of the word treat." Then, walking to the cupboard, he takes two, jumbo biscuits from a box. "Sit boys, sit," he says before handing them the treats. "Good boys. Now go lay down and be quite." Wags and Goldie curl up under the table at Kallie's feet, but they're not quite—the noise they make while crunching on their dog biscuits echoes throughout the room. Anthony returns to the table and grabs his coffee cup; Kallie's nearly finished eating her mound of scrambled eggs; he watches as she scours the plate for the last tiny morsel.

"That kicked my butt," she announces while pushing her plate toward the center of the table, and then wiping her mouth on the sleeve of the T-shirt, she burps. "I won't have to eat again until noon. Excuse the belch."

"It's a good thing that I taught you to eat like a lady, and to use a napkin…"

"I said excuse me…"

"You're excused, but I'm having doubts about taking you to the Gasthaus for dinner on Saturday. Between you and mom, the two of you could belch out a polka." Kallie chuckles impishly and starts to suck air. "Don't even try it, shrimp," he warns, but before he can finish, she lets fly a prolonged, window-rattling burp. "Very nice Kallie," he groans sarcastically. "You act more like your mother every day. You're both so crude."

"You married her Dad—must have been for her other qualities," she winks suggestively, "if you know what I mean." Anthony blushes—he knows exactly what she means, and stutters flustered. "You naughty boy," she taunts while getting up from the table to carry her plate to the sink, "And Dad, you should oil those bedsprings. With all that squeaking last night, it sounded like you were killing mice. Squeak, squeak, squeak."

"Well, then don't listen outside the door—nosy."

"Well, I almost called the cops. It sounded like bloody murder!"

"So we made a little noise…"

"A little noise? Ha!"

"Don't you have to get to the track?"

"I've got time Romeo, keep your pants and shirt on."

"That's it!" he shouts laughing, making a rush at Kallie. "I don't take sass from any woman." Anthony catches her, pinning her against the refrigerator. "You got time for some nuggies, woman?"

"I-eee!" she cries as Anthony rubs his knuckles on her head. "Help, help! Goldie! Wags!" The dogs enter the fray, barking. "Murder!" Kallie squeals. "Romeo's trying to kill me!"

"Yeah, beg for mercy you skinny, little smartass."

And then, as if someone fired a cannon in a cathedral, "What the hell is going on?" booms Reggie from the entry of the kitchen. Anthony, Kallie and the dogs stand ridged as gothic statues. "It's barely five freaking o'clock, and you two are at it. Anthony, let her go."

Instantly, he releases Kallie from his playful hug, and stammers meekly, "Ah, hi-ya darlin'. Did you sleep well? Gosh you look pretty this morning."

"That's bullshit, you lying sack," she sneers, attempting to disguise a smile.

Wags and Goldie slink to safety under the table, and cower.

"Morning Mom."

"Don't good morning me, Kallie."

"Maybe I should go and get dressed," Kallie peeps, dodging past Reggie in the entry, and then stopping, she whispers back to Anthony from behind her mother, "I think she's a little crabby today, Dad. Must not have gotten enough sleep."

After Kallie's gone, Anthony walks to Reggie and embraces her affectionately. "I meant it, you do look real pretty this morning darling," he says, resting his hands on her buttocks.

Sarcastically, she coos, "You're such a bullshiter, Romeo."

Three hours later, Kallie, driving Reggie's truck and towing a trailer, is stuck in a line of stalled traffic waiting to enter the backside security gate at Dorchester Downs. Ahead of her at the gatehouse, idles an old pick-up truck. Two men and a woman lean, arms outstretched, against its hood as a security guard pats up and down their torsos. Another guard is checking, what must be their papers, before directing them back into the truck. As Kallie hangs her head out the window to get a better view of the action, she hears one of the guards say to the driver of the stopped pick-up, "The commission ordered the sweep, don't blame me." For the next ten minutes it's stop and go as the security guards pass some vehicles through the gate, and order others stopped and searched. Finally, the only car between Kallie and the gate clears security, and now it's her turn to stand inspection. She pulls up to the waiting security guards, and as they step up to her truck, she smiles with all the charm she can muster. "Morning, gentlemen," she says, her low raspy voice dripping seductiveness. "I have to go and see the stewards."

"Good morning ma'am," they say in unison. Both guards are of average height, and both are dressed identically—navy blue slacks, black military issue shoes, crisply pressed white shirts, and dark blue neckties. "The commission's ordered a sweep," they reply, matter-of-factly. Kallie tries to remain calm, but then she notices that draped on the lanyards around their necks are credentials that read: *Racing Commission, Security*.

"Could you please turn off the ignition and step out of the vehicle ma'am?" the guard on the right asks politely.

Kallie glances at his nametag, it reads: R. Andrews. "Yes sir," she replies shifting the truck into park and turning the ignition off. "What's this about?"

"Could you step out of the vehicle?" asks the other officer.

As she climbs out of the truck, she reads the other security officer's name: S. Barnes. "I just have to see the stewards. What's…"

"Step away from the truck ma'am," security guard Andrews interrupts, "lean against the wall next to the window with your arms up, and your legs spread; stare at your toes and don't talk until we've inspected your vehicle."

Kallie's not used to being given orders, but the guard's frankness is intimidating and she complies without argument. Andrews reaches inside the gatehouse, takes out a long-handled, inspection mirror, and hands it to security guard Barnes. While Barnes uses the mirror to check the entire undercarriage of Kallie's truck and horse trailer, Andrews rifles through the cab of the truck. Kallie feels her bladder

189

growing anxious; she raises her eyes to summon strength, and then, there, within the gatehouse, just inches away from her on the other side of the window, with his amplified eyes and a yellow-toothed smile, is the Hawk. She shudders like Hamlet before an apparition of the dead King, and pleads silently, "Oh God, Kallie, please don't piddle now." Barnes returns to the gatehouse and stores the inspection mirror inside. "Anything?" he asks Andrews who's still poking around in the passenger compartment.

"Nothing yet. Is the exterior clean?"

"Yeah. Should I frisk her?"

Andrews grunts, "Affirmative."

Barnes steps beside Kallie to pat her down, but before he starts, he asks, "Ma'am, do you have any sharp objects in your pockets, like a knife or needle that could injure me?"

With her voice shaking, she answers, "No sir, nothing."

Barnes crouches down and begins to feel around her ankles; he lifts up the cuffs of her jeans and checks her socks, and then with both hands around one of her legs, he moves upward to her thigh. Kallie responds instinctively, and with good reason—she squeezes her buttocks together, and holds her breath.

Barnes sees her tense up. "You can relax ma'am," he says to reassure her, "unless you're trying to hide something." Kallie's too shaken to respond with anything other than an apprehensive groan. After he's checked the other leg, Barnes runs his hands up and down her arms and torso. "She's clean," he says to Andrews who's emerged from the truck cab. "Did you find anything in there?"

"Nothing. Did you check her license?"

"My driver's license?" Kallie asks from her spread-eagle position.

"Your racing commission license," Andrews responds.

"I don't have one. That's why I'm going to see the stewards. They have to give me approval before I can apply."

Barnes and Andrews look at each other as if dumbfounded by the revelation; the Hawk leers at Kallie from his inner office; a moment of silence passes, and then exasperated, Barnes groans, "Sorry

Too Far A Dream

ma'am, but you need to have a valid license to enter the grounds, we can't let you in without one. You can drop your arms now."

Kallie's emergency is growing more critical with each minute that passes, panic is in her voice when she asks, "What can I do, I really have to see the stewards...."

"Do you know someone on the grounds with a valid license?"

"Winston Chase..."

"Can you call him, and have him send someone up here to sign you in?"

"He's at his training farm this morning, but his barn foreman is here."

Andrews has inferred the meaning behind Kallie's nervous dance, and smiles at her sympathetically, "What's his name?" he asks. "I'll have him paged over the PA."

"Juan Espinosa."

He turns to Barnes and says, "Have Jim page Espinosa, could you Stan?" Barnes nods, yes, and enters the gatehouse. A moment later the Hawk's voice booms over the public address system: "Juan Espinosa, you have a visitor at the stable gate. Juan Espinosa, please report to the stable gate." An expression of relief surges across Kallie's face, and then Andrews says, pointing to an open parking area outside the gate, "You'll have to back out of line ma'am, and park over there."

"Can't I just make a U-turn and go out so I don't have to back up the trailer?"

"Sorry, I can't let you do that." He motions to the other vehicles lined up behind Kallie's truck and trailer that they should back up. "And ma'am, if you need to use a restroom, there's one right over there in the other gatehouse." Without a word of argument, and with no hesitation, Kallie dashes the few steps across the entry road to the restroom, and disappears inside. "After you've moved the truck..." he yells too late. "Poor kid, probably wants to gallop horses."

By the time Kallie comes out of the bathroom, Andrews has moved her truck and parked it out of the way. Both he and Barnes are busy inspecting another vehicle. As she passes by them, Andrews glances up and hollers, "Catch kid," and tosses her the truck keys. "And kid, sorry about the search—orders, you know."

"Thanks," she answers, making a leaping grab for the airborne keys. "You saved my life."

"Probably," he teases playfully as he continues with his business, "Try not to loose it galloping horses."

"I'll try not to, sir. Thanks again..."

"And kid, my name's Robert, but everybody calls me Andy..."

"I'm Kallie Phillipa," she grins with a smile that reveals the space between her incisors, "But everybody calls me Kallie"

She's made a new friend, but before she can seal the friendship with a handshake, a Hispanic man's voice calls her name and distracts her. "Kallie? Hola!"

She turns to the sound, and sees Juan, carrying a lead rope, shuffling toward the gatehouse. "Juan! Que passa, hombre?" she shouts as he approaches. "Can you sign me in? I've got to get the stewards approval to get my license."

"Si, non problemo," he replies, greeting her. "You be a jockey, no?"

"If things work out—si."

Juan steps into the gatehouse and signs the clipboard that the Hawk hands to him. He then returns with a blue slip of paper in the shape of a bookmark with the words 'visitor pass' printed on it. "Nothing to it," he says handing the pass to her. "You want I come with you?"

"No, that's okay. I'll stop by the barn when I'm done. I'll buy you lunch at the kitchen."

"Si, bien," he says holding his clinched fist out to her. Kallie closes her fist and lightly raps the top of Juan's. "We cool little sister. Later," he says laughing, and then leaves to return to his chores.

With a shy wave to Andy to show off her visitor's pass, Kallie marches toward the one story, cement block, administration building that houses the kitchen, the racing secretary's offices, and the backside office of the stewards.

It's nearly ten o'clock, and the grounds are abuzz with activity; people wearing muddy shoes and dusty clothes scamper everywhere.

A hundred voices, human and horse, speak nonsense in unison—their meaning is lost in the din of a multilingual hubbub. Hanging on makeshift clotheslines outside the rows of stables, colorful leg wraps and matching saddle towels flail in the morning breeze. A syncopated line of trotting horses, under the prodding of their riders, makes hasty way to the in-gate before the security guards close it to training. Other horses, lathered and dripping sweat, walk, buck and dance, as they leave the track to return to their stables after completing their exercise laps. A gallop girl, wearing a red and white riding bonnet, blue jeans and half-chaps, wheels by on a bicycle. When she reaches the administration building, she skids the bike to a sudden stop, drops it in the grass, bounds up the stairs, shouts "Hola!" as she ricochets into a wizened cowboy in the doorway, and runs breathlessly inside.

Kallie strides in on the girl's heels. "Someone should teach your friend there some manners. She almost spilled my coffee…" the cowboy grunts as Kallie passes.

She pauses, surveying the tilt of his enormous wide-brimmed hat, his weathered skin, and steel gray eyes. "Sorry sir, she must be in a hurry."

"That's no excuse for being rude ma'am," he drawls before turning away. As he shuffles off, the spurs on his boots clink against the cement sidewalk like quarters pitched into a coffee can.

"Yeah. You have a nice day too, Tex," she offers under her breath. And then it hits her: the intoxicating odors of smokey bacon, fried pork sausage, steamy powder-milk biscuits, damp leather and fresh manure whisked together in the air to create an odd scented banquet suited only to a horseman's appetite. Kallie inhales; struggling to prevent her words from leaking out as a shriek; she tilts back her head, and with closed eyes, whispers, "God, I love this place." During the moments she lingers under the aroma's spell, half dreaming, half awake, dozens of horsemen file beneath the vaulted ceiling of the administration building's atrium; they're propelled by an urgency that only the final call for entries could incite. They scurry into the racing secretary's office—silent, serious, and somber as mourners at a wake—determined to keep their entries secret.

Victor John Faith

"Attention horsemen," blares from the public address speakers, shaking Kallie from delirium. "Here's the rundown for Sunday's races: The first race has six; the second has five; the third has eight..." She follows the hoard that crushes through the secretary's door—tall, and short men; fat, and thin; young, and old; jockeys, agents, owners, some rag-tag, and others smartly starched—all on a common mission, they jib around, grouse, or joke, jest, laugh, and wait their turn to name their entry, or to be named 'up'. Kallie slides behind the throng, making her way along a narrow, white walled corridor; past the track vet's office, past several desks crammed tightly in a cubby-hole—a name plate on one reads: Fran Croaton, Paddock Judge, on another the name plate reads: John Shenman, Identifier. Beyond the desks is a single door that opens into a windowed room—only the windows are visible to her as Kallie approaches. As she reaches the door, a polished brass marquee with black lettering announces whose office this is: Racing Commission, Track Stewards. She takes one step in. In three of the four corners of the room, two against the windows, and one facing them, are broad wooden desks. Square desks with overhanging tops. Cheap desks—the track's owners know not to waste money on furniture that's only used for a few months each year. In stark exception to the desks, are the chairs behind them—over-stuffed, executive style, high-backed, leather upholstered chairs—the stewards demand comfort as well as respect. A grim looking, skinny old man is seated in one. The windows are behind him. His head is down, and he's signing papers with a gold-plated fountain pen. His straight white hair, combed back and severe, shines in the glaring sun like a porcelain helmet. His stiffly pressed white shirt glows translucent as if made from onion skin, and a red, silk necktie below his pointed chin hangs like a blood-stained gorget—this man is a figure to dread, a desiccated corps that's animated. Kallie knocks timidly on the door. The man ignores her. She knocks again. He doesn't budge.

"Sir? Sir, are you a track steward?"

The man stops signing papers, his hand rests motionless. "No," he reports curtly, "I'm the chief, steward." And then, without looking up to see whom he addresses, he snaps, "Do you have business with the commission?"

"Um, maybe," she stammers, "No, not with the commission, with the stewards."

He glances up to see Kallie cowering just inside the door. "Are you here to answer a summons, or to settle a fine?"

"No, no, nothing that serious," she laughs anxiously, trying to brighten the mood.

He glares at her. His faded blue eyes narrow to slits. He's got the advantage with his back to the sun, Kallie is fully lit, and he studies her from tiny head to tiny toe. "A kid," he thinks, but his condescension speaks louder than his thought. "Don't waste the commission's time," he snarls. "What do you want?"

"I need you to sign my license application."

He lays his pen on the desk, and holds out his hand, waiting as she digs in her jeans pocket to find the paper. "Well?" he growls watching her fidget.

"Here," she says, handing over a single, folded page. "I just need your signature for the authorization."

As the steward takes the application from her, she notices the engraved name badge clipped to the pocket of his shirt: Maxwell Heppner, Chief Steward. She trembles recalling her first meeting with this man. She left a bad impression. Two years ago, she nearly knocked him to the floor outside the racing commission office under the grandstands. She was rude—he was cross, and let her know. She remembers him. She wonders, "Does he remember me?"

He peruses the application, first one side, and then the other. Finally, he places it before him on the desk. He leans back in his chair, clasps his hands behind his head, and glares at her. "Kallie May Phillipa," he sneers. "So you want to be a jockey?"

"Yes sir, I do."

"Dangerous job...."

"I know that, sir."

"You're a girl, and kind of puny."

"It's not against the rules for a woman to be a jockey," she replies confidently.

Her response irks him, and he lets her know by curling the corners of his mouth in an abbreviated frown. "Can you prove that you're sixteen by providing a birth certificate?" he asks.

"I'm eighteen."

"You don't look it," he snaps, "and that's not what I asked. So, just answer the question. Can you provide a birth certificate?"

"Uh-huh. I can do that."

"Have you been licensed as a jockey at another track in North America?"

"No sir."

"Have you ever been licensed to gallop horses at an officially recognized meeting in North America?"

"No sir, but I've galloped horses at a training farm." Kallie can feel her stomach twisting in knots.

"Not the same thing," he snarls sarcastically. "Have you ever broken a horse from the starting gate, under the supervision of the starter?"

"Um, no, sir."

"Have you ever been banned from racing in any country under the jurisdiction of the Jockey Club?"

"No... sir."

"Have you ever been convicted of a felony?"

Kallie's lips are beginning to tremble; her insides are churning; she can feel tears filling her eyes. "Never sir," she sniffles.

"And, Kallie May Phillipa, you say that you want to be a jockey?"

"Uh-huh," she mumbles, and then gathering her wits and every bit of courage she has, she blurts, "I mean yes! Yes, I want to be a jockey. It's all that I've ever wanted to be, and I'm going to be the best."

"I don't think so," Heppner replies coldly. "You're too puny. You've had no experience, and I don't see that the outrider's approved you. You'd be a danger to the other horsemen." He leans forward, takes her application from his desk, and thrusts it at her. "Go away Kallie May Phillipa. The track is no place for little girls." He doesn't even pause to judge the impact of his insults; instead, he looks down and resumes his work.

At first she's stung by Heppner's demeaning comments, but the hurt is instantly replaced with rage. "No, I won't," she says firmly.

There's a moment of silence so ghastly that the dead would retreat in fear from it. "What did you say?" he asks, lifting his eyes in an incendiary stare.

"I said I wouldn't go. You're a public servant; you work for the racing commission, and they serve at the will of the public. You're rude, and I won't go until you apologize."

"Is that so?" he asks in a tone of voice that bristles with indignation.

"You owe me an apology…"

"Is that so?" he rails, slamming the palm of his hand on the desk. "An apology? You want me to apologize for looking out for the safety of the people who work here? You want me to apologize for protecting the traditions of racing? You want me to apologize for doing my job?" And then he huffs, "NO! But I will do something much better." Heppner's face is as red as his tie when he shuffles through his shirt pocket to find a bound notebook that's so miniscule it appears ridiculous. He flips it open, scribbles something tiny, and jams it back in his pocket. "There!" he snarls, "Now leave Phillipa, or I'll have security escort you out of here."

Kallie wants to stand her ground, but her knees are chattering, and the mixed emotions of rage and fear cause her to stammer. "Okay, I'll go, but I will get a license. I will be back."

Heppner reaches for the telephone, and lifting the receiver, he starts to dial. Kallie waivers, her courage succumbs to her fear and she bolts from the office. On unsteady legs, she wobbles out through the corridor; bumping through the horsemen huddled in the racing secretary's office, she staggers into the atrium; she pauses, and in a panic, she searches among the many doors for one. "Where the heck is a bathroom?" she whimpers inaudibly. She spies it. It's there, fifteen feet to her left. She dashes for it. She grabs the stainless steel door handle and pulls. The door flings open. Into the bathroom she flies. Before she even finds a vacant stall her jeans are unfastened and the zipper's down—she finds one. In she plunges dropping her trousers, and sits. And then she sobs. She weeps and curses, "Asshole, asshole, asshole! The pompous, no-good-for-nothing asshole."

"Are you okay in there?" asks a husky voice from the next stall.

As if she'd been struck by shock, she stops wailing. "Oh shit," she murmurs, and leans over to peek under the partition into the next stall. There she sees boots and half chaps facing the commode. "Oh God," she prays silently, "please tell me that I'm not in the men's can."

"You alright, honey?" the voice asks again.

Kallie sits upright, and cupping her hands atop her head, she stares at the ceiling, and groans exasperated, "Oh no…"

"No?" the voice comes again.

"No, I'm alright…"

"It just sounded like you were bawling, honey."

The toilet flushes; the feet turn and leave the stall. Kallie grabs a hunk of toilet paper, rolls it into a ball and wipes her eyes. She repeats the process with the paper, except that the second ball is put to another use, and then she drops it into the toilet. As quietly as she can, she stands, and zipping up her jeans, she sneaks to the stall door to peep through a space between the door and the partition. Someone is standing at the washbasin, they're scrubbing their hands. Someone, about five and a half feet tall, wearing black denim pants, half chaps, and boots. Someone, with skinny legs, wearing a hooded sweatshirt, and a riding helmet bends over the sink and vomits.

"Ah," comes a husky sigh. "That should get me down to a hundred and nine pounds." Someone is a jockey.

Kallie observes the jockey lift their head from the sink. Above the washbasin, she sees the jockey's reflection in the mirror, the jockey has blonde bangs and wears makeup, "It's a girl," she giggles, relieved, "Oh, thank you, Lord."

Hearing the giggle, the girl jockey glances suspiciously toward Kallie's stall. "Got a problem in there?"

"No, no problem," she answers, emerging from the stall. "I'm just happy to see you, that's all. Did you just hurl?"

"Yeah, I got to make weight for this afternoon's races." Kallie watches as the jockey takes a paper towel, dampens it, and scours her face. "Drank too much beer last night—I shouldn't do that, it makes me want to eat."

"The beer made you hurl?"

"No, it was the double hamburger I ate for breakfast—shit, was it good!"

Kallie laughs in agreement, "I love burgers. The most perfect food known to man."

The girl jockey joins in the laugh, and then holds out her hand to shake, "I'm *Bernadette Keats*. What's your name?"

Kallie hesitates—the jockey wipes her hands in the towel. "Kallie Phillipa," she answers, grasping Bernadette's hand.

"Everybody around here calls me *Bernie*," the jockey adds while she and Kallie shake.

"Nice to meet you Bernie, everybody calls me Kallie."

Bernie tugs on Kallie's hand, pulling her closer so she can whisper, "Don't tell my agent about the burger. He'll fine me. Okay?"

"Okay, Bernie."

"What were you bawling about in the crapper? You got trouble with your man?"

"Yes, and no. He's not my man, but I got trouble with him."

Bernie's curious, but confused as she drops the paper towel into the waste bin. "Tell me. What's up?"

"I went to see the stewards about getting my bug license approved." Kallie pauses to watch as Bernie pinches her cheeks, bringing color back to them after throwing up. "Are you still a bug?" she asks.

"Lost my bug two years ago…"

"You've been around then, tell me, are all stewards assholes?"

"Most of them that I know. Who'd you see?"

"Max Heppner…"

"Not *Max the Ax*?" she shrieks. "Jesus freaking Christ, Kallie. Oh shit. You got trouble now. The asshole put you through the ringer, didn't he?"

Kallie's eyes begin to tear up again, "He wouldn't sign my application; he said I was too puny—rude prick. I told him he'd have to apologize for that, and then he threw me out of his office—threatened to call security, and have me booted off the grounds."

Bernie's face is expressionless and white as Heppner's starched shirt while she listens to Kallie. "That's bad, that's really bad…" she groans, expressing her trepidation. "Just pray you don't get on his list."

"Why?"

"If you get on Heppner's list, you might as well leave town. He'll make your life a living hell. No one will come near you—guilt by association they call it."

"Oh-oh…" Kallie gulps, staring down at her toes.

"Oh-oh? No! He didn't. Tell me no."

"He took out this teeny-weeny book…"

"Holy freaking shit!" she brays, taking a step away from Kallie.

"He scribbled something in it…"

"Was it in his shirt pocket?"

Kallie steps toward Bernie for reassurance, "Yeah…"

"No, no. No you don't girl," she begs, holding her hand out to restrain her. "Stay away from me, Kallie. I've got to make my living back here." Fear is evident in her voice when she shouts, "You're a dead woman—you're on his freaking list." Bernie makes a lunge for the door, shoving her way past Kallie. "Don't ever talk to me again—never!" she pleads, escaping from the restroom. Kallie follows near behind her. Once in the atrium, Bernie wheels to face Kallie, and gestures again with her open hand. Just then, Max Heppner walks from the racing secretary's office, and heads on a direct course toward Bernie. She turns to see him just in time. "Well good morning Chief Steward Heppner," she gushes, "That's a very handsome tie you're wearing today. Is it Italian silk?"

Max Heppner stops and stares down at her—his chilly, blue eyes, like spheres made from glacial ice, bear fiercely on her. His mouth is a tight, un-waivering line of doom. "Don't kiss up to me, Keats, it won't help. You're going to screw up one of these days—count on it. Until then, Keats, be smart and stay out of my way."

Bernie stands motionless and silent as the chief steward moves on. He glances into the Horseman's Office, and then disappears into the kitchen. Kallie makes a move toward her, but Bernie holds up her hand, and glares menacingly before dashing for cover in the smoking lounge.

It might be only in Kallie's imagination, but from that moment on, it will seem to her that everyone on the backside tries to avoid her. She stands isolated, in the center of the atrium, like a waif who suffers from plague—she doesn't have the plague, it's worse: *she's on the list.*

* * *

Ten: Schemes and Lies

At about the same time that Kallie's being berated by Chief Steward Heppner, Anthony is driving his sport utility truck along Gleason Road toward the Verrhaus estate. When he reaches 12848, he turns into the driveway, passes between the limestone pillars that mark the entrance, and continues along the narrow, tree-lined, cobbled stone drive to the manor house. "Nice shack..." he muses softly, pulling into the roundabout, and catching his first sight of the mansion, he adds, "...no wonder Kallie's spending so much time here." The Baron's roses are just starting to bloom—a symphony of colors: yellow, white, pink, and shades of red, all are music to the eye. And the air, scented like young debutantes at a cotillion, is evocative, enticing memories of summer days and nights spent in charming company. In the center of the roundabout, Bucephalus reigns defiant above his watery reflection. Anthony stops his SUV, and gawks transfixed. "Wow," he sighs, getting out. The only sounds he hears are the splash of water in the fountain, and the sprightly melody of song sparrows flitting within the arborvitae. "Yes, I could live here," he whispers, observing every visible inch of the estate's buildings and grounds—the massive old mansion; the carriage house and stable; the cut green lawn; the manicured hedges; the overhanging trees, and the shafts of sunlight that seem to fall, as if guided by an intentional hand, on the barbed roses.

"Can I help you?" an unexpected voice asks from behind him.

Anthony turns to the sound; he's startled to see a woman, dressed in a painter's smock, squeezing out from within the arborvitae hedge. "Um," he stutters, not recognizing her, "I don't know. I'm looking for Albert Verrhaus. He does live here, doesn't he?"

"Why yes, he does. He's just on the other side of the hedge doing some trimming." The woman wipes her hands on the front of her smock as she approaches, and then reaches a hand to greet Anthony. "I'm Charlene Fauxhausen," she says, introducing herself. "I'm Albert's companion. Are you Anthony Phillipa?"

Anthony clasps her hand, "Yes I am," he answers, perplexed that this unfamiliar woman should know him. "Have we met?"

"Never," she says, pointing to a sign painted on the back door of Anthony's vehicle: *Anthony Phillipa Real Estate*. "You probably didn't steal that man's truck, so you must be Kallie's father." She eyes him skeptically, and then laughs, "But I could be wrong, you could be a scoundrel, it wouldn't be the first time I made that mistake."

"No, I'm Kallie's father, I just look like a scoundrel…"

"Good," she says, releasing Anthony's hand. "It's nice to finally meet you. Albert mentioned that he found your binoculars in our backyard—said he captured them from a spy, I still don't know what he meant by that—but it was a long time ago. I'm surprised you haven't stopped by before—with Kallie or something. Your wife is here at least two or three times month…"

Anthony nods his head, and blushes with embarrassment, "I probably should have come sooner, but Kallie warned me to stay away. She said that the Baron preferred his privacy, my wife agreed, but neither mentioned that he was married."

"We're not married. Albert and I are close friends."

"Oh…" he says, implying a delicate apology. "I didn't mean to assume…"

"That's alright, Anthony, no one knows. And I'm the private one, in fact, not many people know I live here—I'm like the housekeeper who cleans while you're gone, you see the results, but you never see the lady with the broom."

"They said that he's always very busy…."

"Busy?" Charlene giggles, "He's retired, how busy could he be? Kallie, no doubt mentioned that he's a little eccentric…"

"She never did use that word, exactly."

"Rumor has it that he is, you know."

"I think she referred to him as cool—not meaning that he's aloof—but cool in a *cool* way." Anthony, without intending to, but out of mindless habit, glances at his wristwatch.

"Oh I'm sorry, Anthony," she says, noticing him fidget, "I didn't mean to chatter on and take so much of your time. You came to see Albert, let me call him for you."

"No, no," he replies, in a vain attempt to deflect his rude gesture. "I didn't mean... It's a habit, that's all."

"Albert! Albert, Kallie's father is here to see you. Albert?"

The Baron, appearing unusually robust, tanned and fit, pushes his way through the arborvitae near the spot where Charlene came through. He's wearing a white dress shirt with the sleeves rolled up, and the cuffs of his tan slacks are bloused inside his high, lace-up work boots. When he strides up to Anthony, he smiles broadly, and greets him in a tone of voice reserved for honoring the most respected guests, "Hello Anthony. You're looking quite well."

Anthony extends his hand to shake, "So how are you, Albert? You've gained a few pounds since Christmas. Have you been going to a gym?"

"A gym?" blurts Charlene in laughter.

"Don't be cruel, Miss Fauxhausen. It was an innocent complement. Anthony intended to flatter me."

"Even so Albert, you've got to admit, that would be the day..."

His broad smile shrinks to a playful smirk as he chides her directly, "I don't need a gymnasium, I stay fit just by tending to the Baroness's commands."

"If I commanded you to *go jump in a lake*, would you?"

"If the Baroness so wished, how could I refuse her?"

"Ha!" Charlene wails again, slapping her thigh in laughter. "Excuse me Anthony," she says, barely containing herself, "but this old man will say anything to shift the blame. If he looks healthy at all, it's because he's had to work for his living by trying to keep up with your daughter."

"I hold my own," the Baron rebuts smartly.

"She runs you ragged..."

"You're wrong about this."

"...She does."

"No," he corrects her slowly, "she's just an eager pupil, a joy and a challenge."

"Admit it Albert, you come in from her lessons looking like a whipped hound."

He purses his lips and scowls an admission, "A little weary perhaps, but it's been good for me. There! Now, shouldn't you go back and tend to the hedge?"

"No, no, no Albert, one should never punish their confessor…"

Charlene's comment causes a break in the banter long enough for Anthony to interrupt. "Well, whatever the reason, you look great, Albert."

"Thank you, Anthony, I think so too."

Charlene, now standing beside the Baron, rubs his back affectionately and adds, "Yes he does. Kallie's what it took to get the old Baron off his rump."

The Baron glows from Charlene's loving touch, and quips, "Only a woman would notice that a man's backside is more fit." And then he changes the subject, asking, "But Anthony, why have you made a trip way out here? I don't expect your daughter until later this afternoon. Do you have a message from her? May we offer you tea, or a beverage?"

"Thank you," he replies gesturing, no, with his hand. "I've been drinking coffee all morning. But if you don't mind, could I use your bathroom?"

Both the Baron and Charlene smile at Anthony's request, "Ah," they think, "the mystery of Kallie's weak bladder is solved." As if cued, "Yes of course," they say together. "Come up to the house."

As the three make their way along the brief stretch of sidewalk, Anthony turns to the Baron and mentions, "Kallie was disappointed that you weren't able to make it to her birthday party."

"I know," he replies, taking a hanky from his hip pocket and blowing his nose. "But I think I redeemed myself with an apology, and a small gift."

"Yes, she has the card framed on her wall. Is Charles Foxx a friend of yours?"

"It was my fault Anthony," Charlene interrupts before the Baron can respond. "I was away on business, so Albert had to see to things around here."

"We figured there was a reason that you couldn't come."

"Watch your step, Anthony," she advises as they mount the low stoop in front of the main door. "There's a loose paver…"

Anthony stops, glances down, and nudges the tile with his toe. "A little 'thin-set' will fix that. I could have one of my men come out and make the repair."

"It's such a little thing, Albert will get to it someday."

"The chore list never ends," sighs the Baron.

"No," Anthony insists with the sound of gravity in his voice, "someone could stumble on it. It'll be a favor, but you both have to promise that you'll repay me." The Baron and Charlene are caught off guard by the proposal, they're apprehensive, but smile consent. "Great!" shouts Anthony, "then here's the payment clause. You have to promise that you'll have dinner with us at the Gasthaus this Saturday night. We're celebrating Kallie's graduation—we're going to spend some of the money her mom and I put aside for her college tuition. Just the five of us, is it a deal?"

The Baron looks to Charlene, his eyes ask a silent question.

"I have nothing planned, Albert. I think we should go."

"Wonderful," Anthony says, grabbing Charlene's hand to shake on the deal. "Kallie will be so excited—maybe she'll even wear a dress." And then, assuming a more dignified pose, he reaches for the Baron's hand, "It's too small a thank you for everything that you've done for Kallie—you're a good teacher for her."

The Baron smiles impishly, and asks, "Do they still send around that Bavarian shot-board, and sell beer in the boot?"

"They have a nice pilsner I think you'll like."

"Six-thirty, Seven?"

"Seven for cocktails, eight for chow, and then we'll polka all night."

Charlene giggles, "He's certainly fit enough to polka, Anthony." And then turning to the Baron she asks, "But tell me, Bertie, do you remember how?"

Saturday evening at six forty-five, Anthony, Reggie and Kallie drive along Commerce Avenue through the Belleview warehouse redevelopment district near the rail yards, and into the parking lot of the Gasthaus Jägermeister. The Gasthaus is located in what used to be, the tasting house for the Steinkeller Brewery, a complex of nineteenth century, red sandstone block buildings that wear neglect in plain view. Closed and abandoned years ago, the victim of a shift in taste from robust lager to lighter flavored ale, the brewery now awaits renovation, or the wrecking ball. As they approach the main entrance to the Gasthaus while looking for a place to park, Anthony points to the Baron's Jaguar parked in a *reserved* space next to the door. "Well, they're on time," he says, "and it looks like the Baron has connections."

"Tony, why don't you let Kallie and me off here while you park? We need some time to check our make-up."

"Sure," he says, glancing around at the full parking lot, "It looks like I may have to park in back—the food here is great." He stops at the main entrance, and Reggie and Kallie get out. "Don't slam the doors," he shouts, but too late, both doors bang shut. "Thanks," he calls back to them as he drives off, "that's really good for the equipment."

"Sorry Dad…"

"Sorry Tony…"

Although Reggie is an attractive woman, most people who meet her would describe her as pretty, but rugged. Yes, she's often rough in her manner, and casual with her attire, but tonight she is impeccable in both her demeanor and dress. Stunning is not too strong a word to use. Her blonde hair is swept back in a French braid, and a long curl dangles from each of her temples; accenting her neck, a narrow, flat-linked gold chain suspends a gleaming diamond solitaire. She's adorned in an ankle length, spaghetti strapped, open backed and sleeveless, ivory colored silk gown that's split along the sides to her mid thigh—a simple piece of fine cloth that adds grace to her slender body. When she moves, all who see her will gasp and wonder, "Who is this princess? Has she come from the splendid Court of Kublai Khan?" And Kallie, always comfortable in a T-shirt, and blue jeans scented with leather, is scrubbed and preened. Recognizably a woman, wearing a sleeveless, pastel flowered sundress that drapes below her knees, she'll turn heads and cause men, both young and old, to gawk and drool. The beauty of the pair would inspire vigilance in any husband, or father; Anthony's guard will be up tonight.

Reggie and Kallie enter the Gasthaus unescorted. The door arrests the glaring evening sun outside; within, the light is dim and cozy—glowing hues, cast by chandeliers fashioned from stags' antlers, reflect from amber colored, walnut paneling. From beyond their view, in a secluded, private party room, come the sounds of a concertina, and someone attempting to yodel above the jeering laughter of their comrades. As Reggie and Kallie approach a chubby, middle-aged hostess taking reservations, eagerly waiting diners, standing elbow-to-elbow, give way like peasants before royalty. Reggie commands the moment; regally, she struts to the hostess' station and announces, "The Phillipa party of five is here. We have a table reserved for seven o'clock."

People usually dress for dinner at the Gasthaus, but they don't DRESS. The hostess, impressed by the sight of Reggie and Kallie, hesitates from surprise before glancing in her reservation pad, and down a long list of names. "Phillipa, party of five?" she asks. And then, smiling respectfully, she says, "Yes, Ms. Phillipa, your table is ready. Your guests have been seated already. If you'll follow me, I'll show you the way."

Reggie beams at the hostess, and replies, "Thank you, but my husband is parking the car. Could you direct my daughter and me to the restroom? We need to wash our hands."

"They're to the right, around the corner, next to the coat check," she says, nodding to her right. "The ladies says *Fräulein* on the door."

At first, Reggie starts off to her own right, but then notices that she's headed to the hostess' left. "I always make that mistake," she gripes, "It's a fifty-fifty chance, and I end up going the wrong way every time."

A moment later, Anthony opens the door, and bumps his way through the crowd just in time to see Reggie and Kallie disappear around the corner. "Hi, *Gretchen*, is our table ready?" he asks the hostess.

Gretchen looks up from her pad, and blushes—from her expression, it's evident that Anthony is a frequent customer. "It's all set Mr. Phillipa. Your wife and daughter just went to the lady's room. We seated your friends about five minutes ago." When Anthony scrunches behind the hostess' station and wraps Gretchen in a bear hug; she squeals joyfully as her heels lift from the floor. "You're going to be trouble, aren't you Mr. P?" she teases.

"That depends on whether or not you dance with me."

"A polka? Are you planning on closing the place down tonight?"

"I've been known to go a full fifteen rounds," he brags, lowering her back to the floor.

Anthony's hug has left Gretchen's ample breasts oozing from her jumper; hastily she adjusts the bib of her apron to restore her modesty—now she's really blushing. "I don't think it would take that long," she whispers, "I'd punish you enough in the first round."

"You know, I believe that about you, Gretchen," he whispers, his dark eyes sparkling mischievously. Then, casually, he reaches into his pants pocket, withdraws a folded wad of bills, peels one off, and hidden from the on-looking eyes, he hands it to her. "Who's cooking tonight?" he asks.

"Frank..." she says, glancing at the bill—she chokes, it's a hundred.

"He's a good cook." Anthony smiles confidently. "Give Frank twenty; twenty each to the bartender and the accordion player, and keep the rest for yourself. I want tonight to be special."

Gretchen beams, slipping the money in her apron pocket, "Anything you want Mr. P..."

From amongst the crowd, a disgruntled patron, long on the list to be seated, grumbles obnoxiously to his wife, "Did you see that? The rich son-of-a-bitch just bought himself a table." And then he makes his feelings known to everyone. "Hey lady, are we ever going to get a table? We've been here long enough to cook the damn meal ourselves!"

The hair on Anthony's knuckles tingles, and he turns to eye the big mouth, but Gretchen intervenes before he can respond. "Ignore him Mr. Phillipa, he's my problem, and if he gets rude again, I'll have

Donny boot him out. We don't need a turd like that stinking up the place."

"I doubt if the asshole could even boil water…"

Gretchen pats her hand against Anthony's chest and chuckles impishly, "If he's hungry now, just wait. His party was going to be seated next, but not anymore."

"Oh you're pretty—and mean …"

"I can be. By the way, Mr. P," she teases seductively, "did I mention that you look very handsome in a suit? I don't think I've ever seen you wearing one."

"Well darlin' you should see me without one," he boasts, puffing up his chest.

"Okay Romeo, you can quit flirting now…" comes an unexpected voice from behind him.

Anthony jerks around to see Kallie with her arms folded across her chest, and tapping her foot in a scolding fashion. "Um-Kallie," he cowers. "Honey, how long have you been there?"

"Long enough to see you in action—you letch."

"Where's Mom?"

"She's coming. So you better shape up."

Just then, Reggie returns from the ladies room. "Anthony?" she asks, eyeing him suspiciously. "Have you been misbehaving?"

"He's a man. What do you expect, Mom?"

With the Phillipas reunited, Gretchen asks, "Would you like me to show you to your table, Ms. Phillipa?"

"Please, Gretchen. It looks like it could be a long night."

"This way then," she says, taking several menus from the hostess' station, and leading the party toward the dining room.

The main dining room of the Gasthaus is one of those kitschy spaces where *over the top* is a refined, and ongoing pursuit. The walnut paneled walls are covered with an odd collection of German, Bavarian, and Austrian memorabilia—it's not eclectic, because no obvious effort has been spent on selecting FINE art. Provincial flags stream from stag antler chandeliers; crudely rendered oil portraits of men wearing lederhosen glare from gilded frames; a sinister cast of ruggedly hewn würzelmen stare out from the shadows; escutcheons with heraldic animals, and emblems of feudal chivalry congest the hodgepodge; faded picture post cards fill in the blanks, and then there are coo-coo clocks. Alpine coo-coo clocks. The owner of this place must be in love with coo-coo clocks—they're everywhere. Ticking, clanging, coughing coo-coo clocks hang in profusion.

At the first sight of the mad assortment of junk, Kallie halts transfixed, "Whoa…" she utters, gawking. "Dad, is the owner of this joint nuts, or what?"

"It's not the burger hut, is it Kallie?" he teases, bumping into her. "Ah, you want to keep moving, shrimp?"

"Why haven't you taken me here before? This is great."

"We have," he answers as they weave in between the tables crowded with diners. "The würzelmen scared the crap out of you. You bawled and bawled. We had to leave early."

"I don't remember that."

Anthony puts his arm around her shoulder, and whispers, "You were three years old…"

"Oh."

"…you had nightmares for a month."

By this time, Gretchen has led the Phillipas beyond the main dining area, and they squeeze through a narrow passageway into a cramped, but inviting, private party room. It's decorated as outrageously as the rest of the restaurant except that, on the far wall, looms a soot-scared, stone fireplace that's large enough to burn a cord of wood. Six, sturdy oak tables—rubbed and worn—jut from the sidewalls; people eating, drinking and laughing fill each to capacity. One long table, large enough to accommodate a household of patrons, occupies the center of the room right in front of the fireplace. Seated at the end nearest the fireplace are the Baron Verrhaus, and Charlene Fauxhausen. When the Baron sees Anthony, Reggie and Kallie enter the room, he rises to his feet, steps away from his chair, and stands proudly as a palace guard waiting for a company of crowned heads.

Gretchen chaperones them to the table. "Will this be okay, Mr. Phillipa?" she asks while setting out the menus, and nodding to the Baron. "Herr Verrhaus insisted on this one."

211

"It's a wonderful table," Reggie gushes, reaching to greet the Baron and Charlene.

"Perfect Gretchen," Anthony adds, pulling a chair out so Kallie can sit next to her teacher. "The best in the house."

"I'll send your server in to take your orders for cocktails..." and then, aside to Anthony, she whispers, "Tonight, the liver dumpling soup is to die for. Can you smell it?"

He lifts his nose and sniffs the air. "You know I'm going to have some, Gretchen," he drools, "so tell Frank to keep it hot."

"I will," she assures him, leaving them to arrange their seating.

Kallie makes a move to grab the chair that Anthony's pulled out for her, and prepares to sit, but then she remembers her manners. Before anyone can notice her faux pas, she takes the Baron's hand, and says with all the grace and refinement she can muster, "You look very handsome, Sir. I'm so glad you could come." She repeats the greeting—substituting *fetching* for handsome, and *Ms. Fauxhausen* for Sir—while reaching across the table to shake Charlene's hand.

"Kallie," Charlene reciprocates, "that's a very pretty dress. Never have I seen you looking more lovely."

There's an evident glow of pride in his cheeks when the Baron adds, "Nor have I, Miss Phillipa. A grain of sand, slowly polished, has become a stunning jewel."

"We had a fight about the dress," quips Reggie.

But the Baron interrupts her, motioning to Kallie, he says firmly, "You mustn't sit there, Miss Phillipa. You're the honored guest." Stepping to the chair at the head of the table, he directs her, "Sit here, at the head of the table. Your mother should sit in that chair, next to me, and your father will take the one next to Ms. Fauxhausen."

Kallie's surprised that he would bark orders to her at her party, and she's uncomfortable with being the center of attention. "Really, Sir, this one's okay," she protests shyly.

"Tradition, and respect," the Baron growls solemnly as he holds the chair ready for her to occupy. "You must accept the respect given you by your company, and allow us to honor you with a toast—that's the tradition, and this <u>must</u> be your seat."

There's no arguing with the Baron on matters of tradition, and Kallie knows it. "Yes Sir," she replies meekly, and follows his orders. So does Anthony. Quickly, he shoves Kallie's vacant chair under Reggie, and dashes to his assigned seat next to Charlene.

The Baron slides Kallie's designated chair under her as she sits. "Fine," he says, taking his seat next to Reggie. "This is as it should be. Would anyone care for a drink? I'm going to have some beer. Some pilsner, I think."

"You bet!" answers Anthony, rubbing his hands together. "I'm as parched as a mummy." Reggie scolds him with a stare. "What? What did I do?" he protests, "Kallie can drive us home… We can enjoy ourselves—darlin'."

"Just don't be falling asleep on the way home *darlin'*," she growls. Then, politely, she asks, "What are you going to have, Ms. Fauxhausen?"

"Call me Charlene, Reggie—please…"

"Charlene, are you going to join the boys?"

"I'd like to, but Albert gave me the keys to his car. He hasn't done that in ten years—he won't even let me drive it from the carriage house to the front porch, he's so protective of it." And then, she commits the sin of sins, she adds, "I don't know why, after all, it's just a car."

The slam of the Baron's jaw hitting his chest is loud enough to hear. "What?" he blubbers, disbelieving the flip comment. "Just a car?" he wails indignantly. "It's a classic automobile, the last of Sir William's great cats. The finest automobile ever made!"

The look that Charlene gives the Baron in preparation for her retort is as dry as Anthony's parched mummy. Silence reigns just a moment; all eyes are fixed on the Baron. Charlene's lips curl mischievously. "Got you, didn't I, Albert?"

"Huh?" he huffs, realizing that he's the butt of her joke. "That was truly mean, Miss Fauxhausen, and I think you said it in a mean spirit."

Kallie starts to giggle; Reggie joins in. Anthony's unsure as to which side he should take, and glances nervously from Charlene to the Baron, then back to Charlene.

"Albert. Sweet Albert," she teases, "You and that old car are just too easy a target."
"I love that car..."
"You must, you spend a lot of time tinkering with it."
"It's temperamental..."
Anthony's made up his mind and chuckles. Reggie's giggle has changed to yowl, and when she inhales, her sinuses rattle, and she follows that with a honking guffaw so raucous, that only barnyard geese would find it charming—but that's how Reggie laughs, and the whole party joins her. The nub, "Albert. Sweet Albert," is repeated several times before the last giggle fades and the party quiets down to comfortable chatter. Soon afterward, a barmaid takes their drink orders, and disappears through a swinging service door that's disguised to blend with the paneling on the wall next to the fireplace. A few moments later, she returns carrying a tray propped on her shoulder. With the skill acquired by steady practice, she takes a folded tripod with her free hand, opens it beside the table and lowers the tray to rest on it. "Is the pilsner for you Herr Baron?" she asks, handing a tall, narrow glass of beer to him.
"With a twist of lemon?"
"Yes Sir," she replies, offering a saucer of lemon wedges. "The one liter boot of lager, I assume, is yours, Mr. Phillipa?" she asks with a hint of teasing in her voice. Anthony nods, yes. "A bottle of draft for Ms. Phillipa," she continues while distributing the remaining drinks, "Charged water for the Baroness, and for Miss Phillipa, a cola. Just let me know when you're ready for refills, or for your server to take your dinner order."
"Thanks *Amy*," Anthony replies while grasping the boot with both hands. "Fifteen or twenty minutes should be good..." As Amy disappears through the hidden door, the scents of countless sour-roasted German delights drift throughout the room, and every hungry stomach growls. Holding on to his beer, Anthony rises to his feet. "A toast," he proclaims, lifting the boot. The Baron, Charlene and Reggie all stand to join Anthony; the other diners in the room hush in anticipation; Kallie, not knowing the protocol, starts to get up, but

Anthony stops her saying, "Kallie, you stay put for now, in a second you can get up and make a speech."

"Speech?" she gulps.

He winks kindly, giving her the reassurance that only a loving father can, and whispers, "Don't worry."

"Okay, Dad."

"I'm not very good at this," he starts, "but here goes. I'd really like to say something smart and clever, but I'm not smart, and I never learned to be clever. What I did learn, growing up, is how to fight, and sometimes, that meant walking away—even from a fight I knew I could win. It wasn't cowardly. It didn't mean I was chicken. It only meant that I was very careful. I learned that when I got in the ring, win or loose, I should leave having gained more than I lost." Anthony's voice cracks with a sound of youthful idealism, tempered by the disappointment and regret that age brings. His nose is moist with emotion; he sniffles, and continues his toast, saying, "I didn't win every fight, in fact, I lost more times than I wanted, but I know now, that we learn more from loosing than from winning. A reputation is built by accumulating victories—sadly, even easy wins can make a person famous—and fame is the first thing we loose when we're beaten. What we gain from defeat is wisdom. That's what builds our character, and that's what helps a true champion to survive." He pauses, sniffs quietly, and blinks in a failing attempt to disguise the dampness in his eyes. "Kallie," he says, his voice quivering, "I hope you never loose, but when you do, be wise. And when you win be kind."

For the briefest moment, there's a poignant silence, even the coo-coo clocks seem to skip a tick. The Baron lifts his glass, and with admiration and reverence in his voice, he toasts softly, "To Miss Phillipa."

"To Kallie," Reggie and Charlene concur as everyone clinks glasses.

Kallie was uncomfortable being the object of attention before the toast, now she's trembling. "Do I have to make a speech now?" she whimpers. "Because if I do, I'm just going to bawl. Can't I just say thank you?" she pleads, "Please?"

The Baron smiles across the table to Anthony, "I don't know about you, Anthony," he chuckles, "but to me, that sounded like an acceptance speech…"

"A fine speech. I've heard dozens just like it. Ladies?" he asks as they nod their approval. "Good then. Let's drink."

The toasters retake their seats, sip their beverages and the entire party engages, for a short time, in light conversation. When he's finished drinking about half of his pilsner, the Baron tilts back in his chair, folds his hands in his lap, and turns to Kallie; the others notice that his mood has shifted, that he's less lighthearted—they give him pause to speak. "Miss Phillipa," he asks, pondering, "what are we going to do about your situation with the chief steward?"

Kallie, who's been leaning with her elbows on the table, sits upright and weighs her response carefully. "Well Sir, I really don't mean any disrespect, but it's my problem, not yours. Heppner is a bully, and he thinks he can push me around. Right now, I'm not sure what I'll do, but I'm not going to let him keep me from riding."

"He has pushed you around, and he can keep you from riding at the track—forever if he wants to."

The muscles of Kallie's jaw quicken as she grinds her teeth; she rests her elbows on the armrests of her chair, and clasps her hands together resting her chin on them. "I've read the rules, Sir, I could appeal to the racing commission."

"They won't hear your argument…"

"Why not?"

The Baron, with the same calm that an executioner shows before dropping the ax, replies, "Because Heppner upheld both the letter, and the spirit of the law—he didn't violate your rights, neither was he capricious nor arbitrary."

"Yes he did, and he was…"

"No, Miss Phillipa, you have a dream, you don't have the right to be a jockey—you've got to prove that you're capable."

Her jaw's active; she chews the grizzle of his words. "That's crap!" she scowls, her breath coming in shallow puffs. "Don't I have any rights? He can't keep me from riding my own horse."

"You don't own the horse, you signed it over to Anthony so you could become a jockey. You've studied the rules..." The Baron pauses to take a sip of his beer—a lingering, thirst quenching, excruciatingly long sip—and then, he utters a magic word. "But..."

"But? But what?" she quizzes anxiously.

Albert Verrhaus loves this. He's hooked her, and now he's ready to reel her in. He raises his napkin to his lips pretending to cover a burp. Finally, he continues, "You've studied the rules, BUT you don't know how the game is played." A cunning smile forms on his lips. "There may be a solution."

"What? Tell me, tell me," Kallie pleads, twitching on the edge of her chair.

"You're not going to suggest that Kallie do anything wrong, are you?"

"No Anthony, nothing wrong."

"Oh. Oh, okay."

"Albert," Charlene asks, doubtful of his honesty, "what shady trick are you up to?"

"Nothing illegal dear, we'll just slide Miss Phillipa in through a loophole."

Kallie beams with renewed hope. In her experience with him, the Baron's never given her advice that failed—he's teased and tricked her, but never has he misled her. "I don't think that Max the Ax is going to like this," she says, smiling impudently.

"Max Heppner isn't involved, that's why this will work. We sneak in behind his back. We'll go through the <u>front</u> door—right to the racing commission."

Just then, the Baron's attention is diverted from Kallie, to Amy emerging from the hidden door. As she approaches the Phillipa table, the Baron quickly tips up his glass, and sloshes down the last few drops of beer. "Will you be wanting another, Herr Baron?" she asks before he can return the glass to the table, and then looking over Anthony's shoulder at his half full boot, she teases, "A little slow tonight, aren't you, Anthony?"

"Gretchen told me to take it easy so I could dance with her later..."

217

"Well," she clucks, "if the gals are lining up to have a go at you, put me on the list too."

"Absolutely!" he blurts without stopping to consider his response, and then he hears the faint rumble of Reggie's fingers drumming on the tabletop. "Oops," he whispers aside, "looks like headquarters may have different plans…"

Amy's not convinced that Reggie's irritation is counterfeit; quickly she redirects her attention to the Baron. "Same again Sir, or would you like to try something else?"

"No thanks," he replies, "The pilsner is quite good. I'll stay with that."

"Is everyone else alright, another cola—anything?" She waits, but no one volunteers an answer. "Okay then, I'll get the pilsner, and send your server out to get your dinner order." When she turns to leave, Amy glances back, and gives Anthony a discreet wink.

"I saw that, Dad. You're disgusting. You flirt with anyone in a dress."

Anthony crosses his arms on his chest, and answers smugly, "I flirt with women in pants too—your mom wears pants."

"It's too late to suck up now, Anthony…" Reggie comments, still drumming her fingers.

"Look out Romeo," Kallie warns, shaking her finger, "she's got your number." She narrows her eyes, and asks sarcastically, "Now, do you mind if the Baron and I continue our conversation?"

"Not me, shrimp, yak up a storm. I'm just as interested as you are to hear what he has to say."

"Good," she chirps, and then grumbles quietly, but loud enough to be heard, "Letch."

"What I was saying, Miss Phillipa, is that you don't need a jockey's license now. Ship your horse to Mr. Chase's training farm; we can finish most of his training there. You don't need to be licensed if you're not at the track, besides, the secretary probably wouldn't authorize you a stall at the track anyway. You can ride your horse at the farm and get the experience you need."

Kallie's interest is piqued. "What about his works, and gate approval?" she asks.

"Transfer the foal certificate and Jockey Club registration back to your name; turn the papers in to the secretary, and then go the commission office and apply for an owner's license.

"But what about Heppner?" she quizzes skeptically.

The Baron rocks forward, folds his arms on the table, and replies confidently, "That's the loophole. The rules state that any owner of a horse, that's registered by the Jockey Club and eligible to race at a particular race meeting, and who's papers are on file with the racing secretary, must be licensed by the commission. Did you understand that? The law <u>requires</u> that all owners be licensed."

"And so?"

"So," the Baron continues with impish glee in his voice. "As a licensed owner, you have an absolute right to train your horse as you see fit—that means ride, and everything else—and the stewards can't interfere. Max Heppner is powerless, unless you violate some other rule, then he'll fine you, or give you days."

"You mean I don't have to take a test to get a license?"

"Not to ride and train your own horse…"

"One problem," Kallie interrupts, "I want to be a jockey, not a trainer, and a jockey can't own a horse."

The Baron smiles at her naiveté; leans back in his chair; rests his elbows on the armrests; puts his hands together as if praying, and presses his fingers to his lips. "Have you looked at the back of a race horse's foal certificate—a good horse?" he quizzes tactfully. "There might be ten or twenty transfers of ownership recorded. You can transfer ownership every day if you want, there's no restriction against it. Here's what you do…"

Now everyone at the table is paying attention. Kallie's smirking as if she's about to get even with Heppner; Anthony is grinning as if he's about to sneak in and close a lucrative real estate deal; Reggie's face is blank because she can't believe that Kallie's teacher is advising her to undermine the spirit of the law, and Charlene, well, she and the Baron are in business together, and she knows that if there's something that needs to be done, he'll find the best way to do it.

"First," he continues, folding his arms across his chest. "Get the license so you can get past security, and then go to the track every morning after you gallop Wicked Punch. Go up to the viewing box on the backside and hang out next to the outriders—their station is right next to the box. Make friends with them; get to know them by their first names; let them know you're an owner, and that you're going to ship some of your horses in for schooling. On the track, the outriders are the eyes and ears of the stewards, and the stewards listen to them."

"This is so cool," Kallie gloats in a hushed breath.

His tone of voice is uncharacteristically devious when the Baron resumes talking. "Whenever you ship in to gallop, tell the outriders that you're on a baby and that he's a little green—that's the worst kind of horse. Use a different color saddle towel on him each time, and call him a different name. They'll keep their eyes on you because they don't want anyone to get hurt, and think that you can ride a lot of tough horses."

"This is really sneaky," Anthony giggles. "You should come and work for me, I could use you to get by some of the city councils I have to deal with."

The Baron's flattered by Anthony's comment, but instead of continuing, he presses his finger against his lips in a gesture meaning, hush.

"You can keep talking, Herr Baron," Amy says, stepping to the table with his drink order. "I'm sworn to secrecy—I won't squeal, not even if I'm tortured."

"They have ways to make you talk, Fräulein," he cautions her, squinting his eyes. "And the plot we're hatching is quite diabolical. We can't risk an innocent life on it."

"Innocent? Ha! You don't know me very well, do you?"

"I prefer to assume the best of one so charming as you, Fräulein."

Amy's surprised by the warmth and sincerity of the Baron's reply. "That's the nicest thing I've heard tonight," she says, setting the pilsner on the table in front of him. "This beer's on me. Thank you, Herr Baron."

When Amy's safely beyond hearing, he resumes disclosing his plan. "Now here's the tricky part. Some morning, when the gap is closed, and everyone is in the kitchen having coffee, find out where the outriders sit, and ask if you can join them."

"Do you think they'll let me?"

"You'll have proven yourself," he replies, unfolding his arms. "You'll be a horseman, the same as them—they'll have seen you work." He pauses, takes a sip of beer, pats his lips with his napkin, and goes on talking. "Make some light conversation about how much you love riding, that you love speed, and the challenge of competition. Tell them that—and direct your conversation to the head outrider—that you think training is, well, boring, and that you're thinking of selling your horses, and applying for your bug. Then you ask him if he'll recommend you to the stewards."

Anthony has a doubtful expression on his face, and asks, "Albert, do you really think it will work? From what I've heard, this Max Heppner is pretty smart."

"So far Anthony, what I've suggested is fairly simple. Your daughter is clever, I know that from experience, but can she be charming?" The Baron stares at Kallie as if to require a reply. Instantly, the gleeful smile disappears from her face. "You don't have an option here, Miss Phillipa," he advises sternly. "If this is going to work, you've got to play the game—you're going to have to be polite to the stewards."

"Does this mean that I have to suck up to Heppner?"

"No. Stay away from Heppner. Don't ever let him see you, but watch him closely." And then as a reminder, he asks, "You remember how to spy, don't you?" Kallie acknowledges him with an embarrassed nod that says, yes. "I thought so," he chuckles, and continues hatching his scheme. "There are three stewards. The chief steward, and two state stewards. Any one of them can sign your application—the most important thing is the outrider's recommendation. Wait for Heppner to leave the office, and then go in and have one of the other stewards sign." He pauses; his eyes narrow, and when he finally speaks, his voice takes on a tone so serious, one would assume he was advocating something seditious. "Miss Phillipa, be charming, humble, and most of all, be respectful. The power of the

221

stewards is almost absolute, and at the racetrack, they expect to be revered as gods."

Kallie shudders at the thought of having to grovel before her nemesis, but the Baron's convinced her. "I can do that," she agrees with a sigh of acquiescence.

"I don't know if I like this," Reggie interjects, adding her misgivings. "It sounds dishonest. I think this is the wrong lesson for a teacher to be giving."

"It's deceptive Regina, but not dishonest," he replies with reassuring calm. "People with power can sometimes become jaded, and as a result, they behave cruelly. Kallie can't defeat Heppner directly because the authority of his position would be challenged, but she also can't allow this man's prejudice to prevent her from pursuing her career." The Baron rocks back in his chair, stares confidently at Kallie, and proclaims, "And Miss Phillipa, if you play the game well, and avoid trouble, given time, even Max Heppner will grow to respect you, just as I have."

Kallie's encouraged by his words, but fidgets nervously; she shifts from side to side in her chair, and grimaces with discomfort. Everyone at the table notices, and knows the cause. "I can do this, Sir," she says, betraying urgency, "You can trust me." She lowers her voice to a whisper, and groans, "But right now, I really have to whiz." Propelled with the dispatch that only such a mission can require, she gets to her feet with appropriate decorum, and scurries to the ladies room with the deftness of a field mouse pursued by an owl.

While Kallie is conducting her private business elsewhere, the company at the table settles into a discussion about the merits of the Baron's plan. They sip their drinks, anticipate the scheme's pitfalls, and improvise remedies. The murmur of conversations at adjacent tables fills the room. The hidden door opens, and like a wall cloud before a thunderstorm, the enormous scent of delicious German food rolls out—sauerkraut; onion broth; fresh mushrooms sautéed in lard; roast beef, lamb, and fried rabbit in sizzling brown gravy—the heavy blanket of aromatic turbulence buffets the hungry party, and in its wake is redemption: a maiden with an order pad. She approaches the table like a sprightly virgin—youthful and innocent. Her dark, shoulder length hair is done up in neat pigtails fastened by ribbon; she wears a white blouse with ruffled sleeves and an open collar, a puffy skirt, a festively embroidered bib apron, and when she arrives, with pen and pad at the ready, she wears a fragile smile.

"Hello," she says, introducing herself. "My name is Morgan, and I'll be serving you tonight."

"Morgan?" Anthony wheels his head, and gasps in surprise. "Miss Morgan Marie Jasperson? Little Morgan?"

"Hello Mr. Phillipa. Hi Reggie," she replies shyly. "Is Kallie with you tonight?"

"Well get out of town!" he shouts, jumping to his feet to greet her. "Gosh you've grown—you're a woman now."

"Anthony, you'll embarrass her…"

"Yeah, she's here," he bubbles, oblivious to Reggie's scolding. "She's in the bathroom, she'll be right back. I haven't seen you…" he pauses to remember, "Oh gosh, since the Kentucky Derby. What was that, two years ago? Boy, we miss you—remember the fun we used to have?" And then he adopts a gentlemanly tone, and recites, "Miss Morgan Marie Jasperson I presume. Remember that Morgan?"

Morgan giggles, and then replies like a southern bell, "I have a recollection of our meeting, but you're wrong to make any presumption about me, sir."

Anthony yelps joyfully, he wants to smother his 'Miss Morgan Marie Jasperson' in a hug, but his desire is stymied—she's out of reach across the table. Instead, he pelts her with questions. "How have you been? What are you up to? Why don't you ever come around anymore?"

"Um," she fumbles, cloaking anguish behind a forged smile. "I've been really busy since I left school, and moved out on my own. I've thought about calling…" She wonders as she answers, glancing first at Reggie, and then at the guests, and then back to Anthony, "Don't they know? Didn't Kallie tell them?"

"That's okay, Morgan," Anthony reassures her. "We know, it's tough living alone."

"No, no. That's not it," she protests, concocting a charade. "I'm doing fantastic, the tips are great here…" but before she can go on, Anthony interrupts.

"Kallie!" he calls, seeing her meandering on her return from the bathroom. "Look who's our waitress. It's Morgan."

Kallie stops short of the table, and examines the young lady. At first she doesn't recognize her old friend, and when she does, she's uncertain how she should respond after so long a period of ill feelings. "Hi Morgan," she says after a moment of silence. "It's nice to see you again." Her movements are unsteady on her approach to Morgan, and her limp, even though she tries to hide it, is noticeable.

Morgan's reply is warm, but not affectionate as the two young women make a cool embrace, "Hey girl," she says quietly, "looks like you got a bum leg there. Didn't I see you in some kind of cast last Christmas?"

Morgan's breath smells like she's just smoked a cigarette, or maybe, something else. Kallie draws away, but doesn't end the hug, and then she answers, "I had an accident at the farm a year ago. I'm better now, all healed up, but my ankle and knee still give me trouble sometimes."

"Whoa," Morgan groans with an odd mix of sympathy and satisfaction, "that's real bad luck."

The intended irony stings Kallie. "Old wounds take time to heal," she thinks as they make a chilly break, but before she goes to retake her seat at the head of the table, she pauses to look closely at her childhood companion. Morgan's left cheek has an abnormal puffiness, and a discoloration that even the heavy make-up that she wears can't hide. The signs are obvious—someone's slugged her recently. Kallie's not surprised. While the two haven't been in contact, she's heard rumors that Morgan is running with a tough crowd: a late night crowd, a party crowd, a loose, promiscuous crowd. Secretly, she's distressed that the gossip is true—Morgan's bruised face is more than a hint—but Kallie's careful that her question isn't too probing when she asks, "Morgan, are you alright?"

"She was just telling us, Kallie," Anthony interrupts. He's fond of this young woman—paternally fond, like a parent who believes that his child is pure—and he's eager to learn what's happened to her since they were last together. "Here Kallie," he says, gesturing that she should take her seat, "sit down and let Morgan bring us up to date." As Kallie sits down, Anthony pleads, "Come on Morgan, you were telling us about your job, let's hear it all. Come over here and tell us."

"Well, everything is really great," she starts, puffing up with counterfeit pride. "You know I moved out of my mom's place last summer?"

Both Anthony and Reggie glance an inquiry at Kallie that asks, "Why didn't you tell us?" She shrugs a shamed reply that means, "I didn't want you to worry."

"Anyway," Morgan continues, beaming falsely, "I got this fantastic apartment—it's so nice, with a gorgeous view of the bluffs—it's down by the river, just a few blocks from here, so I can walk to work, but most of the time, I drive my car. It's a great car…" She pauses to clear her throat, and then flips through her book so she can start to take their dinner orders. "It's really economical, Mr. Phillipa," she resumes, standing next to Anthony, "You'd like it, even though it's not new. I could have afforded a new one, but I'm trying to save money to finish my GED—that's a big goal of mine. And I got this great job here," she jingles the change in the pocket of her apron, "You wouldn't believe how much I make in tips. My paycheck alone pays the rent, and I put the tips in the bank."

Morgan's story is a happy one, and convincing enough, but Reggie remembers her difficult experience as a single woman supporting herself through college, and Morgan's joy seems less than genuine. "Do you live alone, Morgan," she asks, trying not to be intrusive, "or do you have a roommate?"

"I've got some roommates, a guy and another couple. They're really fun, they help out with the rent, and we even have breakfast together sometimes."

Anthony is glowing with pride, glad of her success, ignorant of the truth. "You keep working on that GED, Morgan. If you work hard, you might get into a college when you finish it up."

"Yeah," she replies boasting, "That's my plan. Maybe I'll be a doctor or something, if I don't get married. I don't know—I'd kind of like to have some kids."

Kallie panics in silence, "A baby? Please Morgan don't." And then, she expresses her feelings aloud. "If you want, I can drop by some afternoon, maybe we could go get some coffee, and talk about old times."

Morgan knows that Kallie really means to say, "A baby is a mistake," and blocks her with a casual dismissal, "That would be cool, girlfriend, but my roomies work nights, so we couldn't hang out at my apartment. We could meet somewhere—I'll call you…."

"You won't call," Kallie stews, rebutting Morgan's suggestion silently, "Why are you lying? We were best friends; we shared everything, I can help you." But before she can speak the words, Morgan starts her steady job.

"Have you had enough time to look at the menu?" she asks courteously, "If you're hungry for appetizers, try the sauerkraut balls, they're fantastic."

* * *

Eleven: The Baited Trap

The two-year-old season is difficult for a young race prospect, and it's disappointing for its owners—promise seldom leads to success—but somehow, year after year, stale hope rallies, and horsemen dream of greatness. It's a silly dream.

The plan that the Baron hatched at the Gasthaus has caused Kallie to attack her dream with determination. On Sunday, June eighth, Kallie moves her horse from the Baron's estate to Winston Chase's training farm. On Tuesday, she gets her owner's license. During the next thirty days at the training farm, she gallops Wicked Punch at six o'clock every morning—every morning, sun or shower—and then she rides another five horses for Winston. By nine o'clock, she's done with her chores; by nine twenty, she's standing in the viewing box at Dorchester Downs talking to the outriders, and exchanging stories with the other trainers, owners, and anyone else who'll talk or listen. Her new friends give her a nickname—every jockey has a nickname—they call her: *Kallie the PIP*, (short for pipsqueak) and she likes it. She studies the Rules of Racing like most people study a bible, and commits chapter and verse to memory. She files Punch's Jockey Club papers with the racing secretary, and she avoids the view of Chief Steward, Max Heppner.

By Thursday, July tenth, everything is ready. Wicked Punch has been in training for ninety days; it's time to bring him to the track and prepare for his official works. Now, the game begins. It's ten-thirty. The in-gate is about to close. Kallie is leaning on the railing of the viewing box sipping her coffee. She watches as a pack of unruly thoroughbreds makes a dash for the gap—delinquent stragglers who take their exercise late, and spunk at hard labor. Above her, a hazy blue sky, like a sheet of empyrean sapphire, extends from zenith to horizon; her mind wonders, dawdles within the vastness. "God, I love this place," she thinks, letting her thoughts drift. Nothing can scuttle so fine a day, nothing except the clouds stacked in the distance, craggy, cumulus clouds, sheared at their height to form anvils. Silently, she thinks, "There'll be thunderstorms when it heats up this afternoon." Suddenly, an agitated voice jars her back to earthly business.

"Bernie!" the outrider shouts to a jockey on a bucking two-year-old that's just entered the track, "get that baby moving." Kallie turns her attention to the in-gate where Bernadette Keats struggles with her horse. It paws at the track's sandy surface; it snorts, and then it kicks out behind, slashing the air and sending clods of dirt flying. "Shit-shit-shit," Bernadette squeals as the baby rears, but she's glued to the saddle, and hangs on. Teetering on hind limbs, the rank two-year-old pirouettes, and when it comes down on all fours, it tries to escape by plunging toward the in-gate. Bernie gains control of the horse, and gets it pointed in the right direction, but then it renews its shenanigans. It turns, and charges the inner rail where it makes an attempt to unseat her by scraping against a cross member.

"Gees," the outrider scowls disgustedly, "looks like I'm going to have to save Keats' ass..." and then he and his horse launch like a missile from a trebuchet. "Get that piece of crap off the rail, Keats. Keats," he hollers, "I've got horses working yet."

Kallie glances up the track to the three-quarter pole; she sees a horse and rider galloping out of the first turn; the jockey crouches low on the horse; the two gain speed as they enter the backstretch; by the sixteenth pole they move to the groove along the inner rail. "Shoot," she gulps, "they're working five eighths…" She peers across the track to the outrider. Keats' horse has planted its rump against the inner rail, and it's refusing to move. She glances back to the five eighths just in time to see the jockey raise his stick and send the horse. "Jake!" she yells, "you got a runner coming!"

The outrider responds to Kallie's warning—he knows what he has to do. Agilely, he slips a leather lead through the dee-ring of the stalled horse's racing snaffle; the roweled spurs on his cowboy boots flash in the morning sun as he kicks his horse into gear. "Haw, haw," he shouts. His leather chaps flap like ostrich wings, and he flails with his split reins. "Use your damn stick, Keats—haw, haw!"

"Whap, whap, SMACK!" goes her long, feathered crop, and then she screams, "Get, get up. Get!"

Too Far A Dream

The baby bounds from the rail like it just farted jet fuel. "Keep him going Bernie," the outrider yells, leading the pair to the center of the track, and just in time. The working horse, now at top speed, blasts by on the inner rail with a force so hot it could blister skin.

"That would have been a good wreck...." a cool, dry voice says from behind Kallie. "Too bad, I'd like to have seen it. Keats can't ride for shit anyway."

She spins her head, and without identifying the source of the snide comment, she growls an angry response, "Bernie wouldn't have been the only one hurt, you asshole."

A wispy man, only an inch taller than her, bristles at her hostile remark. "Yeah, like I care?" he snarls dismissively. "The bitch would be out of the way—one less jock I have to beat."

Kallie can't believe the callousness of this person. She measures him from his slick dark hair, to his sinister brown eyes, to his size six feet. The little man is no threat to her—she could deck him with a feeble cough—emboldened, she issues an insult, "Who are you shrimp, some bug-boy who can't get his first win?"

Incensed, he recoils, miffed. His nostrils flare; his scrawny arms twitch; his eyelids flutter with disbelief. "What?" he gasps, taking an aggressive step toward her. "Who the hell do you think you are, calling me a shrimp?"

Kallie pushes off from the railing of the viewing stand, and elongates herself to appear as tall as she can; she turns to face the diminutive provocateur. "I'm Kallie Phillipa. I'm an owner, and a trainer, and this must be a bug that I'm talking to." She lowers her voice half an octave and growls, "Back off, bug boy."

The stunted adversary hesitates, and then he blinks. "Ah, the PIP," he scoffs backing down. "Kallie the PIP. I've heard about you. Rumor has it that you're on Heppner's shit list—not a good place for a little girl to be."

Kallie's bruised, but she recovers. "Could be worse for a little boy..."

"I've been there before," he sneers. "I can afford it. Can you PIP?" Kallie flinches. "That's what I thought—no balls." Kallie wants to slug him. Pumped with bravado, he nimbly retrieves a business card from his shirt pocket. "Here," he says, thrusting it at her. "If you ever need a jock to get one of your loosing nags a win, call my agent."

Kallie takes the card and reads it: *Earl Donnbury, Jockey*. And a motto: *No harm, no foul.* She stuffs the card into the back pocket of her jeans, and with a cocky smile she grumps, "Never heard of you Earl, but I'll keep the card—they're out of toilet paper in the women's bathroom…"

With a frozen glare, he puckers his lips, and while pointing his finger at his rump, he whispers. "You can kiss it, PIP…"

"There's not enough there for a real kiss. Would you settle for a peck?"

Earl Donnbury is known for his tenacious riding and rabid temper, not his wit. He hates to be bested at anything—especially by a woman—but his only remaining response would be obscene, and he knows better than to use it. At the racetrack, an altercation that involves profanity can result in a fine. The stewards protect the noble tradition of racing. Neither gentlemen, nor ladies, swear in public. Instead of risking a fine, and further humiliation, he steps back, and slinks away to the far end of the viewing stand—far away from Kallie the PIP.

She turns back to watch the action on the track just in time to see *Jake Witzman*, the outrider, galloping his horse back to its station next to the viewing stand. "Hey Jake," she shouts, "that was a close call. Good work."

"Thanks for the 'heads up' PIP," he replies, catching his breath while backing his horse under the covered chute beyond the outer rail. "I heard that horse coming down the groove, but I figured he'd pull up." He reaches above his ear, withdraws the cigarette that he stores under his helmet, and lights it taking an exaggerated drag. "Those two-year-olds can be a pain in the ass—they're so stupid. And poor Keats, that's all she gets to ride—got lucky today, the baby saved her life. Came pretty close to loosing it though…"

Now is not a good time for Kallie to mention that she plans to bring her two-year-old to the track tomorrow, so she sticks with the present topic by asking, "Why can't Bernie get any good rides?"

"She can't keep the weight off," he replies, flicking the ash from his cigarette. "She isn't half bad as a jock—she's got some guts. But when she eats, she gets a big ass."

"Yeah, women get big butts, and men get beer bellies…"

Jake laughs, and then starts to cough. "Smoke must have gone down the wrong pipe," he says, wheezing and slapping his chest.

Kallie studies Jake as he hacks. "Is he forty-five or fifty? A pack a day or two?" she wonders. He gurgles hoarsely, and spits out a huge projectile of phlegm. "Nice, Jake, feel better?" she asks, matter of factly.

"Sorry. Had to dig deep for that one," he apologizes, wiping his mouth with his shirtsleeve. "Did I just see you talking to *Earl the Squirrel*?"

"Earl Donnbury? Is that what they call him, the Squirrel?"

"Yeah. He's the leading jockey on the grounds, but he's nuts."

"He gave me his card."

"Did he say he'd ride for you?"

"Not exactly."

Jake crushes the roach of his cigarette on the horn of his roping saddle. "You should talk to his agent. See if you can name him up when you got a horse ready. The kid can do magic—great hands—beautiful to watch."

The moment is here. "I might do that, Jake," she muses aloud, and than she inserts her intended topic. "I've got to start schooling some of my young horses out here soon. They've got ninety days at the training farm, and it's time to bring them in and let them get used to things around the track. Are you on tomorrow, or is Hicks working the backside?"

"Me," he replies, crossing his leg over the saddle horn. "Bill is working at the starting gate."

"Cool," Kallie whispers. Jake hears the comment, but misses the meaning: *I'm in*! "Hey Jake," she asks, implying both confidence and caution, "If I bring one of my horses in tomorrow, will you keep an eye on me? He's a pretty tough cookie, and I don't want anyone to get hurt."

231

"Sure PIP," he says with a relaxed grunt. "That's what I'm here for."

"Good. I'm not worried, but knowing that you're looking out for me helps—a lot. Thanks Jake."

The next morning dawns overcast. A passing thunderstorm during the night dropped a half an inch of rain, it left puddles in potholes, and refreshed parched lawns. After she's finished her chores, and galloped six of Winston's horses, Kallie leads Wicked Punch from his box stall at the training farm, and loads him in her waiting trailer. "Big day for you, boy," she whispers soothingly, patting his rump. As she closes the tailgate of the trailer, she asks, "Do you know what's up? Do you know that you're going to the track?" As if to answer, Wicked Punch makes a high-pitched squeal, farts a noxious blast, and kicks the tailgate. The concussion of the strike causes Kallie to jump back. "I'll take that as a yes," she clucks gleefully. Then, scampering across the shed row, from the loading area to the tack room in the barn, she performs a mental checklist: "Bridle, running martingale, saddle towels—the new ones—and a felt pad, my flat saddle, helmet, chaps, vest. Let's see, am I forgetting anything? Nope, they're all loaded." As she dashes into the tack room to grab her coffee mug, she stops abruptly, glances at an official looking document taped to the chalk board on the wall next to the telephone, and utters an exasperated groan. "Ugh, the health certificate! I almost forgot it. Next time Kallie, write this stuff down," she scolds herself. She snatches the document from the wall, takes her mug, and flies out the door. Like a bunny with a club foot—brisk but not nimble—she bounds across the shed row to the trailer. "You okay in there?" she asks, jumping in place to catch sight of Wicked Punch munching contentedly at the manger. "Good," she answers, making the short dash to the cab of the truck. In she leaps, and then carefully, she drives away.

It's an easy, fifteen-minute commute from the training farm to the racetrack. The traffic is light, and Kallie has no need to hurry. She moseys down the highway at fifty-five miles per hour with her arm hanging out the truck window. An irritated driver honks, and makes

Too Far A Dream

an obscene gesture at her as he whizzes by, but she doesn't even notice him. She's busy considering each step in her plan. Her eyes are focused on the spotted surface of the freeway, and she's talking to herself, "The in-gate is closed between nine and nine-twenty so the tractors can groom the track. I'll get there just about when it opens for training. Park by Winston's stable—there's that tree stump by the curb—get the boy ready, and then ride Kallie, ride like you got pepper up your ass." She laughs excitedly, and squirms nervously as she signals her exit from the freeway onto the off-ramp. Straight ahead, beyond two more intersections, she sees the gleaming, burnished copper spires of Dorchester Downs, towering above the high and wide glass façade of the grandstands. "Kallie the PIP is coming," she shouts to no one but herself. "Lock up your money, hide your valuables—nothing is safe when the PIP's in town." She chuckles with anticipation. "This is going to be so cool. Kallie the PIP, and her Wicked Punch." She yelps gleefully, driving onto the access road leading to the backside security gates, "This is just too great!"

Unlike the day when she first visited with Max Heppner, the race meet is well under way, and the racing commission has instructed security to stand down. Now, instead of stopping every vehicle at the gate, a quick flash of a license, gets the bearer a lax wave through—unless the driver is pulling a trailer. Kallie stops at the gate. The security guard, Robert Andrews, her friend, gets up from his stool against the gatehouse and steps to Kallie's truck window. "Hey Andy. What's up?" she asks, cheerfully.

"Not much PIP, just trying to stay cool, and hoping it doesn't rain again," he answers while she holds her license out for him to inspect. "You can put it away, Kallie, I've been looking at it every morning for a month now." He glances back at her trailer, and asks, "You bringing a horse in?"

Just then, Wicked Punch lets fly with one of his familiar kicks. "Wham!" the tailgate booms. "Yeah, a two-year-old of mine that I'm bringing in for some schooling. I call him Punchie."

"From the sound of that kick, I'd say you got an ornery one on your hands. Do you have his papers, and health certificate?"

233

"His papers are on file in the secretary's office," she answers proudly, and then she reaches behind the sun visor of the truck to retrieve the health certificate. "Twenty-one day certificate, and a current coggins," she says, handing the papers to Andy.

"Let me check the roster, see if he's on the list. What's his name, Punchie?"

Kallie giggles at his honest mistake. "No Andy, that's his nickname. His registered name is Wicked Punch."

"Oh," he grunts, flipping through several alphabetized pages. "Wicked Punch. Yep, here it is. Is the escape door unlocked so I can get a look at him?"

"Have at it Andy, but watch out. He's kind of nippy."

Andy grimaces, shakes his head from side to side, and pleads softly as he approaches the trailer, "Please God, don't let the little sucker bite me, please." Cautiously he opens the escape door, and when he peers in, "WHAM!" Wicked Punch kicks the tailgate again. Like he just got a karate chop on the back of his neck, Andy's head snaps back instantly. "Yup, must be him," he blurts, relieved that he didn't see a mouthful of teeth. He slams the door, and jogs to the truck cab to return the papers to Kallie. "Here you go PIP, and good luck with Punchie—I think ya could use it."

Andy jumps onto the curb, out of the way, and Kallie stows the papers behind the visor, but something seems amiss, she has an odd feeling that someone is watching her. She looks right—no one. She looks left—no one, just Andy. No, not Andy, but there, in the gatehouse office, fixed on her from behind telescopic spectacles, are the eyes of the Hawk. She matches the refracted stare; seconds pass—tense, tedious seconds—and then the magnified eyes blink. Kallie's lips stretch into a proud smile. "Got you, Jim," she thinks, shifting her truck into gear. "I got my license, I know the rules, I'm legal, and if you want a piece of the PIP, you're going to have to work to get it."

Any victory can buoy a person's confidence, and this one, little or not, sets Kallie afloat. As she drives through the gate to enter the backside, she waves an elated high five at Andy; then, driving onto Bold Ruler Boulevard, she glances back at the Hawk in the gatehouse office, and gives him a diminished salute.

At barn number C-6, Winston Chase's stable hands are buzzing around like wasps lured to a can of soda pop. In a stall, two down from the tack room, Kathy and Janet (interns from the technical college) pick manure from the bedding and toss it onto a muck sheet that's spread on the walking path outside the door. Tied to a hitching post in front of the tack room, stands a tall, dapple-gray horse—it's soaking wet and sudsy, white froth drips from its belly. Nearby, rest a wash bucket, and a green, rubber garden hose. As Juan emerges from the tack room carrying a sweat scrapper, Lupé comes around the corner of the barn leading a prancing roan gelding that's saddled and ready to be ridden. Juan and Lupé exchange a few words in Spanish, and then Lupé leads the ready gelding on another spin around the covered shed row. Juan shoves the sweat scrapper in the back pocket of his worn blue jeans, ambles to pick up the garden hose, and turning on the water, he drenches the back of the tethered gray. The running water splashes everywhere rinsing away the soapy foam.

While Juan washes the tall horse, a male jockey, wearing fringed, black leather chaps decorated with silver studs, a black riding vest and black helmet, peddles his bicycle to the tack room, and stops. He folds his arms across his chest, and balancing the bicycle between his legs, he shouts to Juan, "Juan! You got that speckled red horse ready?"

Startled, Juan stands erect, and then turns to answer, "Sí, Mister Rousham. Is coming with Lupé."

The jockey, Derek Rousham, lifts the heel of his boot, lowers the kickstand and dismounts his bike. "Better hurry, I have four more to work before the track closes."

No sooner does Juan repeat "Sí, sí," then Lupé appears from around the corner leading the roan horse. Without either of them stalling a step, Derek falls in behind Lupé, and they walk together with the horse. Deftly, Lupe releases the lead rope from the bit. Derek grabs the reins and the pommel with his left hand, and the cantle with his right. Lupé hesitates for one step; Derek draws next to him, and while hopping on his right leg with his other bent at the knee, Lupé grabs Derek's lifted leg and tosses him into the saddle.

"Juan? Same as yesterday, two miles?" Derek shouts, riding off with the horse.

"Sí, Mister Rousham. Fácil dos milla."

Just then, comes the sound of thunder, a rattling, pounding thunder—the kind of thunder that a cross horse makes by slamming its training plates against a tailgate. Worried, Kathy and Janet come out from the stall they're working in, and stare at the far end of the shed row. Juan, puzzled, turns off the hose nozzle, and watches curiously for the source of the clangor. Casually, Winston Chase emerges from the tack room with a bead of snuff juice leaking from between his lips, and announces confidently, "Sounds like Kallie's pulling in with her horse." And sure enough, Winston is right. Kallie's truck and banging trailer appear in the parking area at the end of the shed row, and inch to a thumping stop.

"¡Hola! Juan, Lupe. ¿Qué pasa hombres?" she yells, jumping from the cab of the truck. And then running to the rear of the trailer, she flips open the door latch, swings open the door, and laughing, she shouts, "Enojado caballo. I think he's pissed off. The Hawk gave him a dirty look..." Kallie glances at her wristwatch. "Nine fifteen," she whispers, "Got no time to waste." She darts inside the trailer, releases the ties from Punch's leather halter, clips on a lead rope, and quickly backs him out. For a moment, he has all four hooves on the ground, but not for long. Up he goes on his hind limbs—Kallie stays relaxed, "Easy big boy," she whispers to calm the muscled thoroughbred. He listens, and comes down as light as a puff.

"Maybe you should think twice about this, Kallie," Winston hollers from the tack room. "He seems kind of fresh. This ain't the training farm—they won't put up with any shit out here."

Kallie ties Wicked Punch to the side of the trailer. "Thanks Winman, but I got to do this," she hollers back. "It's too late to chicken out now, besides, they have an ambulance on the grounds."

"If you get hurt, I don't know you."

"You're cool. I'm not a squealer, I'll die before I give you up to the Hawk."

Winston glances around nervously; he scurries to the wooden hitching post and raps it with his knuckles. "Don't be saying things

Too Far A Dream

like that, it's bad luck. You ain't going to die. Don't be making trouble for yourself you don't need. Oh gees," he groans, looking at his knuckles, "that hurt like hell." For being a tough, old, wizened cowboy, Winston is as tender as a first kiss—in both heart, and body. He whimpers while holding his dinged fingers to his lips, "Ooo, ouch!" And then noticing that the eyes of his staff are on him, he regathers his manliness and growls, "Kathy, go and help Kallie, and the rest of you, get back to work, we got hots to walk."

Kathy hands her pitchfork to Janet, and jogs up the shed row to Kallie. The rest of the idle crew re-busies themselves with their work. "Hi, Kallie," she murmurs as she reaches the trailer. "Are you really going to gallop your horse here? God, you got guts."

"Guts, maybe. Brains, definitely not." Kallie bends down to get her saddle and bridle out of the tack compartment below the manger of the trailer. When she stands up with her arm covered in riding equipment, she reaches out with a free hand to low five Kathy, but Kathy winces. "Blisters?" Kallie quizzes. "You should wear gloves."

"No, it's not blisters. I grew up on a dairy farm; I've been using a pitchfork for years. But," she chokes up, and struggles to clear her throat as she continues, "there was a real bad accident this morning. Some hot-walker got his hand tangled in a lead rope; the horse spooked, ran over him, and dragged him about a block. I don't know his name, but one of the trainers coming back from the kitchen said he was hurt bad…"

"It happens," Kallie responds calmly. "Don't worry girl, everybody takes the same chances. Its part of the J-O-B."

Alarmed, Kathy replies, "Not my job. I'm a summer intern, I'm just here for the credits."

Kallie drops her saddle and other paraphernalia on the ground, but the heap is well organized—at the track, even disorder is sensibly arranged. She grabs a brush from a tote box inside the tack compartment, and pitching it to Kathy, she asks, "Has Winston let you rub any horses yet?"

Kathy fumbles the reception, and the brush bounces from her formless chest, to her thigh, and into the sand. As she crouches to pick it up, she answers, "He still has me mucking stalls—says that

237

there's gold under the manure, and if I work hard enough, I'll find it. He thinks he's funny—like he expects me to laugh. I tell him, that when I'm out of vet school, that's when I'll find the gold, and it's not under any damn horse manure." When she begins to brush Wicked Punch, he squeals once, and kicks out. "Sorry fella'..." she says, continuing to rub him, but much more carefully.

Kallie is listening inattentively as she works at readying to saddle her horse. She holds the felt saddle pad up-side-down under her chin so that the fenders are at her waist; with her hands free, she takes a navy blue saddle towel and slides four inches of it in between the pad and her waist, and letting the rest of the towel hang loose along her thighs, she grabs the fenders and the corners of the towel. She releases the pad from her chin, and it summersaults onto the waiting towel. "Perfect every time," she says privately, and then, she notices that Kathy's not finished rubbing Wicked Punch. Expressing more irritation than she intends, she asks, "Are we going to groom, or ride?"

Kathy's peeved. She stops to knock a wad of horsehair from the brush bristles, and looking at Kallie, she replies tersely, "I'm not fast Kallie, but I'm thorough."

"That's okay Kathy, I didn't mean it that way," Kallie assures her apologetically, and then she explains, "It's just that out here, we have to be quick. Horses get real pissy when they stand around, and we don't want anyone to get hurt. Here, could you hold this?" she asks, handing the ready saddle pad to Kathy. "I'll finish rubbing him out."

"Fine," she gripes, exchanging the brush for the pad. "I like cows more than horses anyway. At least they don't bite or kick..."

This is a wrong thing to say to a horseman, but Kallie ignores the snide comment, and quickly completes the grooming process. She hands the brush back to Kathy, takes the pad, flips it onto Punch's back—his ears perk in response—and she adjusts it to conform to his withers. "Saddle," she barks like a marine. Kathy, laggardly picks the gallop saddle from the ground, and plops it in Kallie's hands. "Thanks Kathy," she quips sarcastically, throwing it in place atop the horse. When she's done up the girth, she demands, "Bridle." Kathy, finally getting the message, acts with greater vigor.

Too Far A Dream

"Here," she responds, passing the bridle to Kallie.

Kallie releases the halter, slides it around the horse's neck, and refastens it. With swift, able movements, she throws the reins over Punch's head, and bridles him. "Just about ready," she announces, dashing to the tack compartment to get her helmet and riding vest—she puts them on. Then, out of view of everyone, she takes a small make-up compact from inside her vest, opens it, and dabs a large smear of white greasepaint in the center of Wicked Punch's forehead. "There," she says, putting the compact away. She takes hold of the reins, undoes the halter allowing it to dangle from the rope, and leads her disguised horse into the alleyway in between the shed rows. "Thanks again, Kathy," she shouts when she reaches a large tree stump next to the gutter of the alleyway. "Well, here goes nothing," she says to herself, "nothing but the PIP." She stands Wicked Punch in the deep gutter—it lowers his height by about six inches—she hops onto the tree stump, and then, in a single agile bound, she leaps aboard. "Good boy," she whispers, giving him a soothing pat on the neck as she clucks him forward. Slowly, down the alleyway, they amble toward the racetrack.

From the door of the tack room, Winston watches as the two pass by. He takes the tin of snuff from his shirt pocket, digs out a large dip of gritty tobacco, stuffs it in his lower lip, and mumbles, "Come back in one piece, Kallie..."

The walk from Winston's shed row to the racetrack is quiet and uneventful. Wicked Punch behaves like he's out for a morning stroll through an abbey—his head bowed, eyes half closed in meditation—the babel and racket coming from the stables along the route go unnoticed as he plods by. Kallie, on the other hand, rides with keen attention—someone ahead spills a muck sack into a dumpster, and she flinches; a monstrous ventilation fan roars, cranking gusts of air into a stuffy barn, and she cringes. "Sudden movements, loud noise," she thinks, "can spook a green horse." But they don't frighten hers. She and Wicked Punch leave the stable area and tread along the sandy bridle path that abuts the backside parking lot. Ahead, behind a tall, whitewashed fence, is the track. The wide gates are swung open. A horse, trotting double quick, clops by, and then disappears as it enters

239

the track. "This is it, Kallie," she giggles anxiously as the two amble to the elevated running surface of the track. "Remember to stay calm…" Kallie and Wicked Punch pass through the in-gate, and take their first tentative steps on the groomed cushion of the racetrack—like a pillow-top mattress, it sinks and recoils under hoof. They stop and stand. "Be a good boy," she whispers, nervously scrubbing his mane. She looks left at the timer's hut, and then up the long straightaway of the backstretch coming out from the first turn. Horses and riders gallop into view. She looks ahead across the expansive infield between her and the grandstands. In the distance, tiny horses and riders work down the lane to the finish line. She looks right, down the straightaway where only elbows and hind ends race from view around the far turn. She looks at the viewing stand—it's packed with people, watching—and then she sees the outrider and his pony at the ready. "Jake," she shouts, urging Punch to walk. "Jake, it's the PIP. Got a minute?"

Jake Witzman moseys his horse from the outrider's chute to rendezvous with Kallie. "Yeah, PIP. What do you need?"

"I just wanted to let you know that it's the first time on the track for this baby."

Jake surveys Wicked Punch. "Big boy, isn't he?" he observes with a lighted cigarette between his lips.

"Now he is. He was born a runt, but he grew more than we expected…"

"The one leg's a little crooked."

"Damn Jake," she chuckles in amazement, "how'd you see that? You're the first person in a long time that's noticed it. It's not a problem, solid as a rock. Comes from his daddy's side. This other baby I'll be bringing up later has the same thing."

"Uh-huh," he grunts, examining the horse more closely. "Plenty of muscle…. Kind of funny markings though, I don't think I've seen a star like that before."

"Yeah, right in the middle of a hair whirl," she replies, hoping he hasn't noticed that the star is really greasepaint.

"Is that his name?" he asks, nodding an indication at the blue saddle towel. The embroidered name on the towel reads: *Shady*

Too Far A Dream

Character. Kallie nods, yes. Jake gives her an apprehensive wink, and then with a hint of caution in his voice, he advises, "Well, let's hope he doesn't turn out to be a criminal. I'd hate to have to dig you out of the dirt. Be careful, PIP."

"I always am, Jake," she says as they turn their horses in opposite directions—Jake, to return to the chute next to the viewing stand, and Kallie, to back track to the quarter pole.

Kallie's used to galloping her horse at the training farm; she knows his tricks and foibles, but she's not accustomed to the hullabaloo on a crowded racetrack. When she asks Wicked Punch to trot, she bridges the dimpled, rubber reins across his neck, and as the pair back track along the outer rail toward the quarter pole midway through the first turn, Wicked Punch settles into an easy, forward stride—Kallie settles in too. At one with his motion, she rises the trot.

The overcast sky dulls the contrast between light and dark, and obscures the gentle undulations of the running surface. Their brisk movement makes the warm, still air seem like a favorable wind. The squeaking saddle leathers, and rhythmically drumming hooves create a noise that's orchestral; like tribal music from exotic provinces, it's a bewitching sound. They reach the quarter pole, make a half turn, and face the inner rail. They halt, and wait. Moments pass slowly, but soon, the way is clear to go. Kallie gulps a breath. She clucks her tongue, and Wicked Punch trots; she turns him into the center of the track, clucks again, and he canters. She stands, knees flexing with the stride, in a half-seat position—weightless, and with him, she glides like a skier on muscle bound snow. Coming out of the first turn onto the backstretch, she clucks a third time, and Wicked Punch gallops. Under calm control, they pass the half-mile post in front of the viewing stand—Jake studies them closely—and they gallop on. Halfway through the far turn, Kallie clucks a last time. Wicked Punch's stride is long, and his pace quickens. Still air can whistle in the ears, and cause tears to run from the eyes if one rides fast enough. Kallie hears the wind, and feels the water on her cheeks. She crouches lower. Her heart raps in her chest. Faster they go. She gasps for air. They go even faster. They enter the stretch, where a mad dash can cash a check. Wicked Punch drives against the bit—his tug on the

241

reins is almost equal to Kallie's weight—he has depthless strength to spend, and without restraint, he will. With a sixteenth to go before the finish line, the saddle towel waves as if whipped by a storm. The whistle in her ears becomes a whine, and tears squirt from her eyes. "Just want to take the edge off you, boy," she whispers, with her nose pressed behind his ears. Then, driving her heels forward she rises higher in the saddle, leans back bracing against the bit, and pulls her eager horse back to a hand gallop. The grandstands gleam on her right as she stands in the irons, and when she gallops across the finish line with one hand on the reins, and the other held high in salute, she yells to a crowd that isn't there, "The PIP is here. Yes! And her horse that races dreams."

The rest of the way around, she gallops Wicked Punch out—an easy go, under light contact. She passes the in-gate and the viewing stands letting him canter another quarter mile. Then trotting, she turns him around, and they head for the exit gate where she turns Punch to face the inner rail—this is a usual practice at the racetrack, and it helps to calm the horses.

"Hey, PIP! Hold up a minute, will you kid?" Jake calls while trotting up beside her, and then he squints his eyes and scolds her. "You kind of let the boy go down the stretch. In the future, if you plan to work 'em, check in with the clocker first. Okay?"

Kallie wasn't expecting this. "Honest Jake, I didn't plan it. I was only going to send him a little," she replies with a raspy stutter in her voice. "He sort of got away from me, that's all. I won't let it happen again. Really."

"Yeah," he says, softening his tone. "He's a pretty tough bugger, and if he weren't a baby I'd think you were pulling my leg, but next time it happens, I'm going to have to report you for working without authorization…"

"Sure Jake, sorry. Don't hold it against me. I guess I just like to go fast."

"Everybody does, PIP," he grunts, reaching behind his ear for a smoke, but there's none there. He fidgets nervously, and continues, "I'll let you skate this time, but that means you owe me. Just remember, this is <u>my</u> track, and what I say goes." He smiles impishly,

Too Far A Dream

and then, a churlish grin invades his leathery cheeks. "Hey PIP," he adds, hinting, "I seem to be out of smokes. Do ya know what that means?"

Kallie doesn't need to answer; a groan is good enough. The message couldn't be clearer if Jake had signaled it with semaphores. "At least that means he'll be paying attention when I come up again," she thinks as she turns Wicked Punch toward the exit and escape.

On the way back to Winston's shed row she jogs, and gives herself a needed scolding. "Damn it, Kallie! When are you going to learn? Now you owe Jake a pack of smokes—that's worth half an hours work—damn it, damn it, damn it." She trots to the tack room at C-6 and shouts, "Hey Winman, the PIP lived, but I need a big favor..."

"What?" he responds, coming out from the tack room. "You come with good news and bad in the same breath? What do you need?"

"I got to get my hands on a pack of cigarettes—I have to pay off a debt."

"Sorry, PIP, but I don't smoke."

"¡Kallie, aquí!" Juan shouts from the stall he's working in. "Los tengo algo de." And then, with an overhand pitch, he tosses a full soft-pack of unfiltered cigarettes to her.

She grabs them out of the air, and shouts back, "Un millón de gracias Juan. You just saved my butt."

"No es poca cosa," he replies, returning to his work.

As Kallie rides Wicked Punch to the truck and trailer, she slides the smokes inside her vest. When they reach the parking area, she dismounts, and then, darting as quickly as a humming bird in flight, she slips the leather halter—still attached to the lead rope—over her horse's racing bridle; she grabs a rag from her tote, flits into the trailer, and soaks it in the water bucket, whizzes to Wicked Punch, and scrubs off the phony star. Next, she undoes the saddle girth, removes the saddle and pad—plopping them both on the ground—then she takes a clean, red saddle towel with an embroidered name that reads, *Wicked Punch*, and preparing the pad in the same manner as she did previously, she re-saddles her horse. "There, just about

243

ready," she says, stepping back to check that all is safely fitted. "Now the polo wraps." Scudding again to the tack compartment, she snatches two pairs of soft velour, scarlet leg wraps, and in sequence, as she flickers around the horse—she dresses his shins in red. "Perfect!" she declares, admiring her work. And then, freeing Punch from the halter, the two jog back to the tree stump where Kallie remounts to continue her charade.

Jake has no clue that Kallie's on the same horse when she trots up to him with the cigarettes. "Debt paid in full?" she asks, handing him the smokes.

"Yeah, PIP, we're cool," he answers, winking like a lenient sovereign. And then, looking Wicked Punch over, he observes, "Damn, if I didn't know better, I'd swear that was the same horse. They almost look like twins. Half brothers are they?"

"Same sire, different dames," is her abbreviated reply as she departs at canter for an easy lap around the racetrack.

The next morning Kallie follows the exact routine she set the day before, with one exception: she promised Jake that she wouldn't work her horses as briskly down the lane, and she won't.

First, she rides the horse that wears the navy blue towel, *Shady Character*.

"He's got some talent, PIP," Jake shouts to her as they hand gallop past the viewing stand.

"Thanks Jake," she shouts back.

Next, she rides the horse that wears the scarlet polo wraps and red towel, *Wicked Punch*.

"This one seems to have more brains than that Shady Character of yours," he yells as they canter by the viewing stand.

"Thanks Jake," she yells back.

Finally, she plays a trump. She rides a horse with a white snip in between its nostrils. It wears Kelly green polo wraps, and a matching towel with the embroidered name: *Twodollarbilly*.

"Good looking baby there, PIP," he hollers as they lope by the viewing stand.

"Thanks Jake," she hollers back.

Too Far A Dream

Like a play that's aptly directed and acted, the ruse is flawless.

While Kallie lopes Wicked Punch, the Hawk, in full police dress, drives to the viewing stand, parks his golf cart behind the outrider's chute, and hikes the single flight of stairs to the elevated platform. He pulls a crumpled paper napkin—it's seen frequent and varied use—from the hip pocket of his slacks and scours rigorously on the lenses of his eyeglasses. "Ah," he sighs approvingly, when he holds the stout spectacles at arm's length to examine them, and then, putting them on, he hooks the springy bows behind his ears. "Hey Witzman," he inquires on approaching the railing next to the outrider. "Ya seen that Phillipa girl out here yet?"

Jake, smoking a cigarette, and with one leg crossed over the saddle horn of his roping saddle, moves his horse out and stands it broadside along the outer rail in front of the Hawk. "Who?" he asks.

"Phillipa, Kallie Phillipa."

"Oh," he chuckles. "You mean the PIP."

"Who?"

"Everybody out here started calling her the PIP, because she's a pipsqueak."

"Kinda' suits her," he smirks. "Ya seen her today?"

"Yeah Jim-bo," he replies, casually puffing on his cigarette. "She's just going around on her third, now."

"Third, third what?" he asks, expressing confusion and suspicion.

"Horse," he hacks. "What do you think, that we ride motorcycles out here?"

The Hawk grimaces—he and Jake Witzman are not good friends. They work together, and get along, but their relationship is less than cordial. "She only has one on file," he retorts, snarling.

"I don't think that's right Jim-bo. She's been up on three."

"Ya sure?"

"Yep, right as rain."

"The… little… sneak!" he growls, and then he gloats menacingly while hustling back to his golf cart, "Got her—the little sneak is mine."

When Kallie finishes loping Twodollarbilly, she stands him facing the inner rail to mark a recess from the day's training. "This is

245

just the coolest," she whispers, "Another few weeks of this and then I'll work him. God, I can hardly wait." On her way back to Winston's shed row, she fights to suppress her virulent excitement—she'd love to pester everyone, and spread the germ of her scheme, but wisdom is beginning to rule her judgment. Hushed, she rides with contagious joy.

The stable hands at C-6 shuffle placidly as Kallie trots her horse by. At 10:30, their morning chores are nearly done, and the fatigue they earned between five o'clock and now, weighs on their slumped shoulders. Kallie's chores aren't finished yet. She still has a horse to bathe and cool out, and then she has to ship him back to the training farm, clean her tack, and finally, later this afternoon, she will ride a lesson with the Baron. It's a long day of hard work—all part of her J-O-B.

She halts her horse beside her trailer. After dismounting, she takes the halter and lead rope, and in one seamless movement, she removes his bridle, slipping it over her shoulder, and replaces it with the halter. Next she takes the tiny galloping saddle from his back, and hangs it in the tack compartment along with the bridle. Last, she unravels the green polo wraps from his shins, rolling them into tight wads, and tosses them into the tote box. "Bath time," she coos, leading her undisguised Wicked Punch to the hitching post in front of Winston's tack room. "Juan, are you done with the hose?" she asks. "I got to hose a hot."

"Sí Kallie, por de pronto," he replies from out of sight within the tack room.

She ties the lead rope to the hitching post, but no sooner does she squat to pick up the hose, then a voice booms over the backside public address system.

"Attention horsemen…" it says. Her usual response to these broadcasts is to give them detached attention—the rundown on the day's entries, what extra races are filling—today is no exception. She turns on the hose and begins to fill a wash bucket, but then, the next words over the loudspeaker cause her to start. "Attention horsemen. Will Kallie May Phillipa please come to the steward's office? Kallie

Phillipa, report to the stewards." There's an audible click as the microphone shuts off, and then there's a moment of cowering silence.

Kallie stands petrified; water splashes aimlessly from the hose. Punch drops his bay head, and shudders. A bantam cock, in a neighboring shed row, crows an alert. The squeak of wooden chair legs scraping against concrete jars Kallie as Winston Chase pushes away from his makeshift desk. "Was that you? Did they call your name?" he asks, appearing in the doorway. His voice indicates that he knows the seriousness of a summons to the steward's office. "What do they want with you, PIP?"

"I really don't have a clue," she says, shrugging her shoulders in reply.

"They don't just call ya in for nothing…"

"I haven't done anything wrong, I'm legal. Maybe you're wrong Winman, maybe they just want to chat."

"Ooo Kallie," he groans, "you know that ain't the case."

"Could be."

"I don't think so," he replies shaking his head doubtfully as Kallie puts down the hose, picks up the wash bucket, and starts to bathe Punch. "You better get up there, Kallie. It's not a good idea to keep them waiting."

"When I finish my chores here, Winston…"

"Juan!" he barks, "Get off your butt and take care of this hot. And Kallie, get your ass up to the office."

Juan scurries from the shelter of the tack room and comes to Kallie's assistance. "Honest, Juan, it's no big deal," she whines, handing over the wash bucket. "I'm not in any trouble."

As his foreman takes over her chores, Winston barks again, "Right now, PIP."

"Okay, okay. I'm going." A month ago, a summons by the stewards would have brought quaking knees to Kallie—Winston wasn't called, and his knees are chattering—but today she's sanguine. She's legal—license in hand. She's confident. She knows the rules, and she has a plan. "What do they want?" she wonders as she saunters to the steward's office. "The papers are on file; health certificate and current coggins—okay. Maybe Jake reported me for working down

247

the lane," she muses. "No, not Jake. Stay cool, Kallie, and be nice." In the kitchen, to her left as she enters the atrium of the administration building, jockeys, their agents, trainers, and hangers-on play cards, and slurp coffee. The sound of bells and clattering flippers comes from a pinball machine in the horseman's lounge. Ahead, in the Horsemen's Benevolent Protective Association office a middle-aged woman hands something to someone who may be a bloodstock agent. To her right are the offices of the racing secretary, and the stewards. She turns right and strides in.

"Can I help you, little missy?" a condescending man, with multiple pink chins that tremble like turkey waddles, asks from behind the counter.

"I'm here to see the stewards," she replies coldly. "I know the way. I've been here before."

"Sure, sweetie," he grunts, leaning on the counter top—his breasts, huge as fat hams hanging in a smoke house, slough inside his sweaty shirt. "I just thought you might be lost."

"Nope, not," she retorts. She passes the track vets office, and turns right. "How'd he ever get to be the racing secretary?" she wonders as she makes her way down the narrow hallway leading to the stewards office. "Be nice, you have to work with all of them, Kallie," she reminds herself silently taking the last few steps toward the polished brass marquee. The door is open. The chief steward is seated at his desk. The sun glares over his shoulders. Her eyes are fixed on only him. She raps on the doorjamb, and announces herself. "Kallie Phillipa reporting to the stewards as requested, sir."

Max the Ax mumbles something inaudible; he's occupied signing a mound of papers.

"What?" she asks.

"Come in, Miss Phillipa," a frail looking steward seated to the right of Max Heppner replies. "The chief steward has some questions for you."

Kallie walks over to greet the man who's just spoken to her—the name plaque on his desk reads: *Edward Cantrell*. He's scrunched low in his chair, his tie is crooked, and his sandy blond hair is mussed. She reaches out her hand to shake, but he doesn't get up, and then she notices his wheel chair. His feeble right arm is strapped to the armrest. His gnarled right hand clasps a joystick. As innocently as she can, she withdraws her hand, and ponders, "Was it Uncle John, or Dad? Who was it that told me about Eddie Cantrell? I can't remember. Is this him; Eddie Cantrell—the jockey?" And then she asks, staring admiringly at the shrunken man, "You won the Kentucky Derby once, didn't you Mr. Cantrell? My dad, or my uncle told me about you. They said you had the best hands in the business, that you could take a horse from last to first by wiggling your fingers."

"I won the Preakness too…" he replies with a grateful smile.

"Phillipa," a gruff voice interrupts, "Mr. Cantrell is a state steward. Your business is with the chief steward."

Kallie spins around like she's just been blindsided by a roundhouse punch. "Yes sir," she stammers, facing him. "I was just meeting your staff while you finished your work."

"Not my staff," he growls, correcting her. "We're all equal here, but this *is* my investigation."

"Investigation," she wonders, "What's he investigating?"

Max Heppner glances at the far wall behind Kallie. Nonchalantly, she turns to see what he's looking at. Seated on a metal folding chair, hidden behind the door, is the Hawk. The chief steward diverts his attention from him, fixes his eyes on Kallie, and inquires, "What are you doing here, Kallie May Phillipa?"

Standing with the Hawk to her rear, and Max the Ax to her front, her predicament is less than cozy, but she's not unnerved when she answers, "I'm responding to a summons. And sir, you can call me, Miss Phillipa."

"I mean, Miss Phillipa, what are you up to?"

Mustering all the tact she can, she replies sincerely, "With all due respect sir, I guess I must not be understanding you. I'm just here at the track doing my job."

"And what job is that?"

"Training my horse."

The Hawk leans forward—his skinny buttocks resting on the edge of the chair, he rubs his cupped hands together.

"Training your horse, is that so?" the chief steward quizzes sarcastically. "May I see your license?"

As Kallie reaches into her back pocket to retrieve her license, she notices the Hawk smiling—it's the kind of self-satisfied smile one wears when they pass gas undetected. "Here it is," she says, surrendering it.

When he takes the license from her, the chief steward holds it up in the glaring daylight and examines it. He inspects it for any flaw, turning it front to back, and top to bottom. He checks the laminated edges; he scrapes his finger nail on the validation sticker; he looks at the barcode; he squints at the photograph of Kallie, and then he lays it on the desk before him. "Training your horse, that's interesting," he says while rocking back in his stuffed chair.

"Yes sir."

"This is a *Class C, Owner's License*. It's not a trainer's license. Are you sure you want to tell me that you're training?"

"Yes sir."

"Do you understand that you're admitting to me that you're guilty of a rules violation?"

"No sir."

"No, you don't understand?" he huffs.

Kallie, calm and composed, replies, "Yes, sir, I do understand what you said, and no sir, I'm not guilty of a rules violation."

"Huh!" the Hawk scowls, springing to his feet. "The outrider saw you on a horse."

"Is that so, Miss Phillipa?" the chief steward snarls, continuing to grill her. "Is that true?"

"Yes sir."

"That compounds the offense. Galloping a horse requires another license that you don't have." He adjusts his accusatory tone, his voice becomes stern, "Training and galloping, serious charges, Miss Phillipa. And what about worker's compensation insurance, do you carry any?"

"No sir."

"Another violation!" the chief steward scoffs in disbelief. "What else are you guilty of, do you really think that you can run around here and make a mockery of our traditions, ignore our rules, violate our laws?" And then, solemn as a 'hanging judge,' he pronounces, "No, Miss Phillipa, not at this racetrack."

The Hawk fidgets gleefully. As if he's in a line of clog dancers at a hootenanny, he taps with his toes while shuffling his feet. Kallie glances back at him—from the look on his face it's clear to her that he smells a happy victory. His jittery movements seem to shout "Throw the book at her, give her some days." She looks across the room to Eddie Cantrell—his eyes are down, and he's perusing a book. She returns her focus to the chief steward; calmly, she stares into his chilly eyes. All is quiet. The stare continues—neither Kallie, nor Max Heppner blink. *"Be respectful, Kallie,"* her inner voice says, and then she blinks deliberately.

"Well, Miss Phillipa?" he asks, seizing the advantage.

"Sir," she replies, "may I answer the allegations?"

"I wish you would."

Two years of reading the Rules of Racing, months spent memorizing chapter and verse, every sentence parsed, and now she needs the words to come to mind. She pauses, weighing the charges. "Be honest, direct, and Kallie, be nice," she thinks. And then, like a prologue spoken by the chorus in a Greek tragedy, she prepares her audience for a tail of woe—a tail that turns, and strikes an offending villain. "You're right, sir," she begins, her words carefully chosen; her answer precise. "I own a state-bred horse, it's been registered with the United States Jockey Club, its foal certificate is on file with the racing secretary, and it's eligible to compete at this race meet. According to Statute number 240, Chapter 7877.0130, subpart 1, I'm required to have a class C owner's license, and I do. The racing commission issued the license to me after they investigated the truthfulness of the statements I made on my application, but the application asks only the name of the horses I own; it doesn't require that I name a trainer."

"I am familiar with the rules, Miss Phillipa, you don't have to quote them to me, but if you want to use the statutes, don't omit the parts you don't like. As regards 7877, the part you left out goes on to say: *and under the care of a trainer licensed by the commission."*

251

"I was curious about that too, sir," she responds with an impish smile, "because that wasn't in an earlier edition of the rules. So I called one of the racing commissioners to ask him about it, and he told me to talk to their lawyer."

The chief steward pounces with a growl. "The commission doesn't have their own lawyer…"

"Actually sir, they do, it's the State Attorney General."

He's vexed by her response. "She wouldn't know that if she were bluffing," he muses. He narrows his eyes in an attempt to intimidate her, and asks, "You spoke with the Attorney General?"

"Well, yes sir, I did—um, not the Attorney General himself, but his assistant that advises the racing commission—and he told me that it was never the intention of the legislature to prevent an owner from training, entering, or racing their own horse, and to make that a requirement would impose a hardship—you see? Some people can't afford to spend fifteen hundred dollars a month for a public trainer, especially if they can do the job cheaper by themselves, and sometimes, they can do it better, too."

"If you can't afford to pay, Miss Phillipa, you can't afford to play."

Kallie's gaining confidence. "That's not what the Attorney General said. He told me to look up Chapter 7899—that has to do with the granting of a variance. Well I did, and then I called him back. He said that if the rules impose an unreasonable hardship, and that means if someone is denied their rights to participate in racing only on the basis of their income, then it would represent both a hardship, and discrimination, and that person could apply to the commission for an exception."

"What?" he scoffs, thrusting his arms upward in disbelief. "Are you saying that the Attorney General advised you to apply for an exception to the rules? Are you claiming that you're aggrieved, and that you want a variance?"

No sir, I'm just telling you what I was told. I don't need a variance, I'm legal now."

By this time, the Hawk is starting to perspire, fog is forming on the thick lenses of his eyeglasses, the armpits of his shirt are soaked with sweat—this isn't the way he thought the investigation would go. On the other hand, Eddie Cantrell has stopped reading the book on his lap—The Rules of Racing—he sits upright in his wheelchair, he's listening intently, and his narrow cheeks are stretched by an ample grin. The chief steward lowers his arms, and clasps his hands atop his head; agitated, he rocks back and fourth in his leather chair. "Just how do you figure that you're legal?" he asks—he's still sure of himself, but he's curious too.

"I'm an owner licensed by the commission; I have a legal right to enter my horse in any race—if he's eligible for it. I'm responsible for all my bills, my horse's care and safety, and I am responsible for his medications. And, if there's a violation, I'm the one who pays the fine, or takes the days." With all the talking that she's been doing, Kallie's tongue is getting parched, and so are her lips—small drops of white spittle are starting to form at the corners of her mouth. She tries to continue speaking, but her desiccated larynx only croaks.

Taking pity on her, Eddie Cantrell barks, "Jim, get Miss Phillipa a glass of water, would you please?"

The Hawk grunts his dissatisfaction with the order, but he complies. It's not a big job, his chair is situated right next to the water cooler. He fills a paper cup, makes the few steps to Kallie, and offers her the drink.

Kallie slurps the contents in one gulp, and when returning the cup to the Hawk, she says, "Thanks, Mr. Peterson, that was really nice of you." She returns her attention to the chief steward, and continues, "Because this track couldn't operate without us, owners are granted privileges, and one of them is that we can train our own horse, or even our entire homebred stable—if we have one—any way we want."

"Not here you can't, the trainer of the horse must be listed in the daily program. You need a trainer, Miss Phillipa."

"Not if I operate as a private stable, and don't have stalls on the grounds—I train at an off-track facility; I don't stable at Dorchester Downs. Besides, I've looked at a lot of programs over the last couple of years, and in the entries, under owner, it says something like John Doe, and under trainer it says, owner."

The chief steward coughs and sputters, "Well, those are exceptions, those people have been around a long time. They're established."

"Do they have rights that I don't have?"

Her question is replied to with dead silence. Eddie Cantrell turns his wheelchair to face the chief steward, and shakes his head slowly, side to side to indicate, NO! The Hawk sits down on the metal folding chair, and with his elbows on his knees, he rests his head in his hands. Max Heppner, his hands still clasp atop his head, jigs in his chair. Finally, he answers Kallie. "No, they don't have any special rights," and then he recants his earlier position, "And yes, owners do enjoy certain privileges. They can train their own horses, but we try to discourage the practice—ninety percent of them aren't qualified to even pet one. I can only advise you, Miss Phillipa, you should have a trainer."

"You mean someone for the program…"

"Yes, and to saddle the horse in the paddock."

"Like a *program trainer*, sir?" The chief steward balks nervously, but Kallie continues before he can respond. "But if I'm training my own horse, and pretend that someone else is the trainer, wouldn't that be fraud?" She's got him right where she needs him; like a spaniel poised on a sitting pheasant, she waits for his next move.

Acquiescing, he cautions her. "Be careful, Miss Phillipa, you've made your case quite well so far, just don't get too cocky. You didn't answer the issue of worker's compensation yet."

Kallie has this one covered too. "Well sir," she says, "as the owner and the operator of my own business, the law doesn't require that I carry worker's compensation on myself, but if I ever hire a groom, I'll file the required paperwork with the commission."

Max Heppner glares at the Hawk. Kallie's answered all of the charges honestly and correctly, he's satisfied with her explanations, but he's cross that the head of security has wasted time on a sloppy investigation. He's ready to yield to Kallie, but he can't let her win outright. That would compromise his authority, so he scolds her, "You won't get stalls here. I'll accept that you can train from off the grounds, but you need a lot more experience before you can call yourself a horseman." Then he squints his eyes at her in a threat, and warns, "I'm going to keep a very close watch on you, Miss Phillipa, and if I find out that you're working with other people's horses, I'll suspend your privileges."

Kallie gasps silently.

The Hawk springs from his chair so quickly that his spectacles fly up and knock him in the forehead. "That's it," he shouts, giddy that he's been reprieved. "She is! Jake Witzman told me that he saw her on three horses this morning. She must be training publicly; she only has one horse. Either that, or she's working illegally as a gallop girl."

The slack that the chief steward was granting her suddenly turns taut. "Is this so, Miss Phillipa, are you galloping other horses?"

Kallie emits an embarrassed chuckle. "So that's what this is all about." she thinks.

"This is no laughing matter, Miss Phillipa," the chief steward upbraids her.

"No sir, it isn't," she responds, composing herself, "but it's just kind of funny how these things get started…"

"What things?"

"Misunderstandings, sir."

"Go on…"

Kallie pauses before continuing. Cautiously, she looks around the room and out the open doorway down the hall—several horsemen are gathered around the paddock judge's desk—she looks back at the chief steward, and asks, "Sir, may I close the door? You never know who's listening." Intrigued, he nods, yes. Kallie tip-toes to the door, smiles at the people talking with the paddock judge, nudges free the door stop—quietly it swings shut—and then she returns to face the chief steward. "Before I answer your question sir, can I ask you something about your investigation?"

"I don't know, it depends on what the question is…"

"Well," she begins. Her demeanor has changed; like a trial lawyer in a custom made pleading suit, she stands straight-backed, erect, and serious. "I'm not here answering these questions because of an official summons, am I?"

255

Max Heppner lowers his hands from his head to his lap, and then twiddles his thumbs. "No," he answers suspiciously. "An official summons would be in writing, and you'd have three days to answer, and you could be represented by counsel."

"So this is an investigation?"

His voice ascends the scale of notes as he answers, "Yes."

"Is our conversation private? If I tell you something, will it be repeated to anybody outside this room?"

"This isn't a legal proceeding, Miss Phillipa, there is no right of privilege, and what you say won't be heard with prejudice, or be covered by any part of the data practices act." The chief steward quits twiddling his thumbs, and for the first time a whisper of compassion is present in his voice when he asks, "Are you considering whether or not you should admit to a violation, or maybe, implicate another person in an illegal act?"

"No sir, it's just that I'm in business, I plan on making my living working with horses, and I want to know if the rules protect confidential information."

Max Heppner hesitates, and then glances to the state steward for an answer. Eddie Cantrell considers the question and stares off contemplatively. There's a large quartz clock that hangs on the wall behind where the Hawk sits; the tick of the magnetically driven second hand is loud as a base drum corps on review—it beats out several measures before the state steward speaks. "Chapter 7877.0155 clearly doesn't provide confidentiality," he replies, still mulling the issue in his mind. "Neither does 7879. I don't think that any conversation you may have with the stewards is protected by privilege—certainly, our rulings are public. What about you Jim, are you obligated by law to keep any information confidential?"

He's on the spot. The Hawk is a security guard, not a lawyer, and he stutters nervously, "Um, um," he mumbles, "not that I can think of—nothing, nothing at all. Nope, nothing."

"What do you have to tell the chief steward, Miss Phillipa?" Eddie Cantrell asks.

"It has to do with the way I train, I want to keep it secret. If the other horsemen find out what I'm doing, then I loose my competitive advantage…"

"Oh," Eddie replies with an understanding smile, "I get it. You're in business and your methods give you an advantage in the market—methods may be considered intellectual property—and you want to keep those methods secret because they're proprietary. If what you propose to tell us is considered a *trade secret*, you're safe. Trade secrets are protected." He directs his remarks to both the chief steward, and the Hawk when he continues. "While there's nothing in the rules that pertains directly to this kind of conversation Max, there are federal prohibitions against releasing trade secret information. She can seek civil remedies should anyone violate her rights." He looks back to Kallie, smiles reassuringly, and adds, "If you disclose anything that may be considered a trade secret, we would be precluded by law from disclosing it to anyone else. Does that satisfy you?"

"I think so…"

"What are you talking about, Eddie?" the chief steward cries exasperated.

"Just helping out, Max," he replies. "Go ahead, Miss Phillipa, tell us what you have to say."

"You can call me Kallie, Mr. Cantrell."

"Thank you, Kallie, now go ahead and talk freely."

"Jake didn't see me up on three horses…"

The Hawk grunts incredulously, and mutters, "Now she's calling the outrider a liar."

"…he saw me on the same horse three times."

"That's a load of crap!" the Hawk bawls.

"What? Why?" the chief steward babbles. "I don't get this, you'd better explain. What's going on, Miss Phillipa?"

"This is going to sound a little crazy, but what I've been doing is, I bring my horse up once for some wind sprints, and then I go back to the barn, change his saddle towel so he looks like a different horse, come up again and do some distance work, then back to the barn for another quick change, and come up again for some training

257

exercises—like lead changes—you see? What I'm doing is called *interval training*, sir. My teacher used interval training when he was in the military. Maybe you've heard about him, Albert Verrhaus, he's a Baron."

The chief steward shrugs his shoulders to imply that he hasn't, and replies, "A Baron? No, the name isn't familiar."

Kallie's disappointed, but not surprised. "After all," she thinks, "he's a private man." And then, she continues, "Anyway, he trained his steeplechase horses that way, and he cleaned up—you should see his trophy collection. I take lessons from him. He taught me all the theory; how to work a horse for long slow intervals, and then, how to add fast sprints—they use it in Europe a lot, some really big name owners and trainers swear by it."

"I've heard about interval training, Miss Phillipa. It may be unorthodox, but it's no trade secret."

"Well, it is if you understood how I do it, and what I do at the training farm. That's the secret part." She gives the chief steward a playful wink, and adds, "That's why it doesn't matter to me that I'm not stabled at the track. I might be young, and sure, I'm a pipsqueak, but I'm not stupid. I'm not going to let the guys around here know what I'm up to. I just have to bring my horse in for some schooling, get his required works, and then wave to the losers from the winner's circle."

"That's it. I've heard it all now!" Max shouts. "Can you believe this? She's serious!" he huffs, turning to Eddie Cantrell.

"I rode for a guy from Ireland who trained his route horses that way. I won two graded stakes races on one of them. The horse was solid as a rock—raced until it was twelve."

"You're not buying her story are ya?" the Hawk interjects, pleading. "Max, Eddie?"

Peeved, the chief steward holds up his hand in a gesture meaning, enough. "Jim," he moans, "her methods are unconventional, but they're not illegal. I have my doubts about them working—Eddie thinks they do, and I'm not going to argue with a jockey about this. What I do know is, if the horsemen around here find out what she's up to, they'll laugh her off the grounds, and then they'll laugh at us

Too Far A Dream

for letting her do it; so keep this to yourself. Got it? And you," he growls, returning to Kallie, "keep quiet, and consider yourself very lucky, because if there's a next time, trust me, it may turn out a lot worse for you—bravado will only carry you so far."

Kallie realizes from the firmness of his tone that the chief steward means what he says. She's met her nemesis, and triumphed, but she also knows that some victories involve the intervention of luck, and that good fortune played on her side—this time. "I really appreciate your advice, sir," she responds with a relieved sigh. "I promise, you won't regret it. Is there anything else—can I leave now?"

The chief steward looks at Eddie Cantrell. "Eddie," he asks, "do you have anything?"

"Good luck, Kallie," he says, with a kind nod of his head.

"Thanks Mr. Cantrell."

"Jim?" The Hawk grumbles something incoherent. "Okay, Miss Phillipa, you may leave now."

"Not another word Kallie," she cautions herself silently as she turns to leave. And then she wonders as she scurries, in a panic, down the narrow hallway, "Am I going to make it to the bathroom before I pee myself?"

After she's left the room, Max Heppner clasps his hands together, rests his elbows on the desktop, and glares at the Hawk. "What the hell was that all about, Jim?" he scowls. "Maybe you don't like the kid, maybe you think she's a smartass—she is, and I don't like her either, but don't haul her in here again unless you have the facts. She's clever, she knows her stuff, she's a fighter, and she made us all look bad…"

"Tenacious as a pit bull," Eddie adds.

"Disguised as a pipsqueak."

"She's taller than me, Max," Eddie says, laughing, "and I think she's tougher than you."

The chief steward smiles, and comments drolly, "And she has bigger balls than both of us."

"Guys, guys, she's just a fucking kid!"

The chief steward's grin vanishes. "You better watch your step, Peterson," he warns as the Hawk cowers. "That <u>kid</u> is bright, and

259

she'll have you for lunch. Now get out of my office, and go back to work—and Jim, don't ever use the 'F' word around me again. Is that clear? Never! Do you understand me?"

The Hawk stammers, "Yes. Sorry. I won't." Then skulking from the office, he mutters out of hearing range of the stewards, "I'm going to get you, PIP—I'm getting even. Count on it."

As the door to the office closes, Max Heppner gets up from his chair, goes to the door, swings it open, and wedges the door-stop under it to prop it open. When he returns to his desk, Eddie Cantrell observes quietly, "You know what, Max? I think you and Jim are wrong about Kallie. She has a lot of talent, and I think she's going to be okay, maybe even good. I like her."

"Me too."

"What?"

"Me too, I like her too," the chief steward whispers in confidence.

"But you said..."

"She needs some guidance, Eddie. You know, the tough cop routine. I might take her on as a project—enforce some discipline. She needs it."

"Perfect job for you Max," he chuckles.

And then, as if revealing a guarded secret, he whispers again, "I lied to her."

Eddie lifts his eyebrows in a manner as if to ask, "About what?"

"I do know who her riding teacher is," he responds with a note of jealousy evident in his voice. "And she's right about the trophies." Then, meant as an aside, he continues, "He has two that belonged to me... He was a good horseman, but he's not a Baron—he just pretends he is. He's a strange man, you know? Eccentric."

"I've known guys like that."

"It must be thirty, no, forty years now..." Eddie watches, as the chief steward seems to drift off in private thought. During the lost moment, he rocks back in his chair, frowns, and muses aloud, "So that's what's happened to you, Albert." And then with a sigh so deep it could fill a void, he wonders, "And how is our little cousin, is she still painting?"

* * *

Twelve: Jump Up and Fly Away

The next week passes without any more trouble blocking Kallie's way. She settles into her deceptive routine of riding Wicked Punch, and her two phantom horses—they behave, cause no ruckus, and engage in no shenanigans. Jake Witzman watches her. When the horsemen on the elevated viewing stand ask, "Who's the shrimp?" he laughs, puffs on his cigarette, and tells them, "That's the PIP. Her stable's three beers short of a six-pack, but she's tough as a pickled turkey gizzard." The Hawk watches her too. He hides under the viewing stand, spies on her with magnified sight, and awaits a slip. "I'm going to get you PIP…." he chants over and over and over. When Kallie leaves the out-gate to return to Winston's shed row, he follows her. He lurks behind the manure bin across the alley; he skulks among the virginia creeper that clings to the security fence next to her truck; he slinks in between the stacks of baled hay, and studies her every move. "I'm going to get you PIP…." he chants over and over and over. But not yet.

On Tuesday, July twenty-second, at eight forty-five in the morning, Kallie pulls into her parking place next to the vine covered security fence surrounding the backside. The morning sun on this mid-summer day shines through an unclouded sky. Flying low over the shed rows, the Canada geese that nested this spring in the reeds lining the edges of Dorchester Downs' infield ponds, have their fledglings out for their first flights. Their wedge askew, they report like barking dogs in feathers, and test their wings on propitious drafts. Kallie pauses, waylaid by awe, as the huge birds clear her view—gone perhaps to distant sloughs to preen and nap. She watches the empty sky for a moment more, and betrays in a whisper that she knows, intimately, the dangers of her upcoming task. "That's got to be scary," she says, adding a sudden quiver for emphasis. "They don't even think about it, they just jump up and fly away—they never think about falling."

This morning, her routine is less nonchalant than it has been in recent days. Paying careful attention, she unloads Wicked Punch from the trailer—his robust flesh ripples; his fine summer coat, like fluid chocolate, glistens dark bay. With cautious precision, she runs red, elastic support wraps around his cannons—polo wraps are for exercise, supports are for work. His stout legs, with the exception of a crooked knee, are unmarred, steady, and well stayed. She throws up the saddle, pad, and scarlet towel; she draws up the girth, and billets it securely—the broad ribs of Punch's swollen chest, strain against the leather girdle. With a strange mix of nervousness and aplomb, she slides the racing bridle over his perked and twitching ears; she fastens the noseband, buckles the throat lash, and then checks that all is fit and safe. Arrian, in preparation for battle, attended to his horse like this. Soldiers and jockeys alike, trust their lives to the sturdiness of their tack—worn leather will do more harm than an opponent's best effort.

Kallie returns to her truck and takes out her armor: her helmet, riding vest, half-chaps, and a pair of form-fitting, calf skin gloves. She dresses beside the trailer. Pulling a red, paisley print kerchief from her hip pocket, she covers her head, and ties up her hair; she squeezes into her helmet, and secures the chinstrap. Punch watches her—for him, today is just another day. Her riding vest goes on next—her aegis—followed by her half-chaps, and then her gloves. Last, she reaches into the tack compartment of the trailer. Punch watches her. She takes out her riding stick: a whip of forty inches, a tapering shaft of leather-wound fiberglass. On the business end, four rows of rawhide *feathers* are laced within the winding before the paddle—it's a jockey's saber. To a horse that's meek, it's an implement of dread; to the bold, it's an emblem at the vanguard. Everything is ready. Kallie checks the time: 9:05. "Ten minutes to wait…" she sighs, "and then, we jump up and fly away."

While Kallie waits for the in-gate to reopen, Albert, the Baron Verrhaus drives his sleek Jaguar through the security gate, rolls slowly into the parking lot adjacent to the backside kitchen, and parks. As the tinted-glass, power windows close, the darkly colored cords of Wagner's opera *The Ring*, drift out, and disappear. The driver's door swings open. His saddle brown riding boots emerge first, followed by the man dressed in a pale blue, single-point oxford shirt, and khaki breeches cinched at the waist by a cordovan belt. His polished silver spurs prick the eye with reflected daylight when he turns and bends to retrieve something from the car—a riding crop. He closes the door and locks it. He glances at his jeweled wristwatch; it reads: 9:10. "It won't be long now," he whispers as he marches to join the growing crowd on the viewing stand.

From behind the tall, white-washed fence surrounding the track, black clouds of diesel soot blast from the upright exhaust pipes of the ground crew's tractors, like chimneys on factory row, they testify to labor.

The Baron climbs the single flight of stairs to the viewing stand. When he passes in between two wooden benches arranged in the center of the elevated platform, he takes a moment to recover his breath before stepping up to the railing overlooking the racetrack. He watches as the grounds crew, far across the track, grooming finished and harrows in tow, disappear behind the starting gate in the chute at the top of the stretch. A flock of geese glide a circular path above the infield ponds, and then twisting and flopping in near inverted flight, they spill air from their wings, and plummet akimbo in dizzying acrobatics before alighting on the water. "I just don't get out here often enough…" he muses silently. "I've forgotten how beautiful this place is."

"Hello, Albert," a man's voice, half an octave below middle C, intrudes.

Startled, he turns abruptly to respond, but instead, upon seeing the man, he pauses—he's unfamiliar, at least the Baron recalls no recent meeting, but something, something about this man jogs a memory. And then, as if meeting one whom he left long ago as forgotten, he replies calmly, "Hello, Maxwell."

Neither man volunteers to embrace, nor do they shake hands. They stand with two feet, and forty years of distance between them. Max Heppner, with his glazed porcelain hair, starched white shirt, and crimson necktie, and Albert Verrhaus in his boots, breeches and regal bearing—each studies the other with a retrospective glare. This is one of those moments when a distracting noise would be a welcome interruption, but none is forthcoming. Finally, beginning uneasily, Max Heppner says, "You've grown older, Albert."

"One does, Maxwell, but the years have been more kind to you."

Max Heppner bristles at the complement, he doubts it's sincerity, but puts it aside when he replies, "We all wondered what had become of you. Not a word for all those years, and then here you are."

"I made a new life for myself, Max."

"It looks like you carried the old one with you," he observes, nodding at the Baron's attire. "You're still playing the role of an aristocrat, aren't you? Albert, the Baron Verrhaus, with your custom made boots, and your shirts tailored in Paris. At home, they'd laugh at you, and call you a fraud."

"Perhaps, but here, I'm happy."

"I bet you are," Max scowls.

"And you're still bitter," the Baron adds while unconsciously tapping the calf of his boot with his riding crop.

Max reacts to the sound and glances down at the gnarled buckthorn crop. If malice could drain from an angry man's heart, the platform at Max Heppner's feet would be soaked with it. His voice shaking, he utters ruefully, "The stick, you have the stick." The Baron quits his tapping, and lifts the crop by its carved ivory handle. "May I look at it?" Max, almost pleading, inquires. The Baron, slowly hands him the object of desire, laying it reverently within Max Heppner's outstretched, palms—like the sacred Eucharist in the grasp of a believer, Max bows his head and stares in wonderment. The appearance of the stick is bedazzling: an ivory handle etched with cross-hatching stained by years of sweat; a flared butt engraved in fine dentils; where the handle connects to the varnished buckthorn, a cap of checkered gold draws the eye to windings of silver and gold metallic threads, that crisscross the shaft to its very end, where twenty-four inches of woven silk thong twirl back to a keeper at the handle, and two, very tiny, gold appliqués that read: *Maxwell Heppner, Capt. – 4th Reg. Hussars. 1897-1948*, the second reads: *Albert, the Baron Verrhaus, 1931-*. With his eyes flooded in tears of envy and regret, Max utters, "This stick should have come to me, it was father's, I was the eldest of his sons."

"You weren't a soldier—father and I were."

Max, his voice quivering, snaps back, "A stepson! He wasn't your father... His stick doesn't belong with you."

"He married the Baroness Verrhaus—my mother," the Baron retorts with condescension as he lifts the stick from Max Heppner's hands. "He was Herr Obermeister, and served in the Life Guard. His stick belongs in a titled hand."

"You disgraced the family," Max growls angrily. "You gave up the title when you ran off with Charlene—she is our cousin for Christ's sake! You ruined everything."

"You loved her too, Maxwell, and had she chosen you, you would have done the same."

"Bastard!"

"I lost so much less than I got..." the Baron whispers as he turns away from Max Heppner who continues to chide him.

"You pompous aristocrat!"

The Baron turns back, and replies calmly, "Forty years is a long time for your wound to fester, Maxwell. When I've finished with my student here, I'll be out of your life again. So, in the meantime, can we at least, be polite to one another?"

A snide smile creeps across Max Heppner's lips as he answers, "I've met Kallie—I don't know how you continue to attract pretty young women—she's tough, and smart, and she'll shame you with her success. I'll see to it."

"Then we want the same thing, don't we stepbrother..."

With that final comment, the Baron turns his back on Max Heppner, and returns his attention to the track. Max Heppner, the angry stepbrother—wounded, but yet defiant—skulks away.

Kallie glances at her wristwatch, and announces with an eager smile, "9:15, time to go." When she pushes off from the trailer, she stuffs the handle of her riding crop down the seat of her pants so that the clapper juts above her head. She removes the leather halter from Wicked Punch letting it swing with a thud against the trailer, and then, taking the chinstrap, she leads him to the stump next to the curb in front of Winston's shed row. "Three holes should do it…" she says to herself as she shortens the stirrup leathers; she grabs the billets of the girth and draws them up snug, "Good. Now Kallie, jump up and fly away." In one movement, she mounts the block, in a second, she bounds into the saddle—Punch holds steady. Allowing her legs to dangle free of the stirrups, she gathers the reins halfway to the buckle, then making a loop, she wraps three turns of surplus around the gathered end, and slides the buckle through the loop making a tight knot. "Good to go, *we're locked and cocked and ready to rock!*" she whispers gleefully as she nudges her colt forward into a walk. "Take your time, Kallie," she continues whispering, "you've got five minutes before the gap opens—remember to breathe."

Winston Chase is sitting in a chair propped against the open doorway of his tack room as Kallie and Punch walk by; he looks up from the daily racing program that he's reading and gives her a tobacco stained grin. "Big day for ya, huh PIP? Gonna send the boy out for some air?"

"Yeah Winman. We're going for the bullet," she answers with a grin as wide as his.

"Yeah, well, ya don't get paid for fast works, ya get paid for fast races…"

Kallie laughs at the wisdom of Winston's remark, and gives him a jab, "When did you last cash a paycheck, Winman? One day you eat wieners, and for the rest of the week you eat wiener-water soup."

"That's a mean thing to say PIP," he retorts, chuckling. "And ya know it ain't so—I cash a winner once in a while."

"Sure, Winman. Wish the PIP luck!"

Winston waits until Kallie's gone about twenty yards down the alleyway on her way to the track, and then in his loudest voice, he shouts so everyone within a furlong can hear: "GOOD LUCK PIP, and REMEMBER TO HOLD ON!"

"Good advice," she thinks, taking a left turn onto the bridle path that leads to Nearco Lane, then once she's well beyond Winston's shouting range, his last words recur, "Remember to hold on." She and Punch walk on in silence, and she reviews her plan. "Back track to the seven furlong pole; move to the rail at the five-eighths, at the half, it's *peddle to the metal*. I wonder… should I show him the stick to perk him up?" Kallie's lost in thought and unaware that a gallop boy on a fly-speck, gray gelding is approaching the bridle path from her right, but the sound of him singing jogs her.

"*I got a happy feelin', a feeling about you; you're a magic racehorse, with lightning studded shoes.* Hi-ya PIP, what's new?" the rider asks as he moseys up beside her. "Mind a little company?"

"Leo!" Kallie answers in surprise. "How've you been, man? No, no, company is good. I'm going to work my baby for the first time—he's not nervous, but I am. Are you still working for Chad Simmons? You look good. I thought you just ponied horses. Is that one of Chad's—nice—is it a baby? Am I talking too much?" Just then, Wicked Punch rips a grumbling fart, a fart so loud it could be heard above the roar of a passing train.

Leo, his eyes wide with amazement and focused on Punch's swishing tail, laughs almost uncontrollably, and replies while waving his hand to disperse the odor, "I think maybe you got your answer. Gassy bugger ain't he? Whew!"

"Sorry Leo," she apologizes, pinching her nose closed. "Manners are the part of training he was absent for."

"Reminds me of my ex-wife, she could fart like that…"

"My dog Waggs can hang a stinker too—brings tears to your eyes." With the in-gate coming into view, but still two hundred yards in the distance, and still closed, both Kallie and Leo slide their feet into their irons. "Better safe than sorry," she offers, and then renews her questioning as they continue to walk. "You didn't tell me, is that one of Chad's horses?"

"Nope, he's mine. Chad just program trains him." Leo's full of pride and bluster, and brags on, "He's an allowance winner—picked him up for five hundred bucks after he bowed a tendon." Kallie looks cautiously down, and scans the horse's forelimbs. Leo notices her worried glance, and says to reassure her, "That was a year-and-a-half ago. He's all healed up. I've hit the board twice with him already this year. His name is *Wallysfirstdance*—he's a Kentucky bred, seven years old."

"How old is that in dog years?" Kallie asks, teasing him.
Leo adjusts the visor of his chase helmet, and purses his lips as he attempts to calculate the sum. "Hum," he muses before answering, "About the same age as me, I figure."

"I didn't know gallop boys lived that long…"

"Make fun if you like, PIP, but us two senior citizens will blow by you like a Montana whirlwind. Care to find out?"

Seduced by her own bravado, Kallie asks, "What?" And then she taunts him, "What you got to show me, grandpa?"

"How far you working?"

"Half mile."

"I was gonna breeze five furlongs, but I can do a half. Want to work together, you know, go in tandem?"

"Shit no!" Kallie shouts, faced with the challenge. "It's his first work…"

"It'll be good for him," Leo coos, baiting her. "I'll take the outside and keep your boy on the rail. Down the stretch it'll give him something to run after."

"Ha! Run after? My ass! You have no idea how I've been training him. This is my derby horse."

Leo winks impishly at her, and cupping his hand next to his mouth, he says, "The secret's out, PIP, we all know what you're up to. Chad's been watching you 'cuz that one horse of yours, Shady Character might be worth claiming. He says he talked to the outrider, and Jake told him that you're doing some kind of interval training on all your horses."

"Ha!" Kallie clucks relieved that her real plan is still hidden. "If he tries to claim one, he better be ready to take all three—they're bonded."

"Ya know that most of the guys back here don't believe in that interval stuff. Myself, I'll wait to see how this boy works. Think he's fast enough to keep up with us?"

"Yeah…"

"Good! Here's the plan. We back track to…"

Before Leo can finish, Kallie interrupts him, "Hold it Leo, hold it. I didn't say I'd do it. I know he's got to go in company, but he's just a baby. I don't want to wreck him. He's got talent, and I've got my own plans for him."

"Hey PIP, you're not a jock with a chicken heart, are ya?"

Leo has her riled. "I have plenty of guts," she retorts, glaring at him. "That's not the problem."

"Sure, PIP, whatever you say," and then he starts to cluck like a chicken.

"Don't push your luck, old man…"

By this time the two riders have nearly reached the in-gate—the white-washed gates are still closed—and while Kallie stands Wicked Punch at halt waiting for the gates to open, Leo walks Wallysfirstdance in small circles around her. She takes the moment to think about the challenge. "Having Leo's horse on the outside could help us to set a steady pace, and keep Punchie from blowing the turn; he might have more confidence with another horse next to him—we could beat them easy, no sweat." Silently, Kallie ponders. Then, as if by instinct, she glances at the viewing stand where, towering a story and a quarter above her, she sees the Baron. He raises the butt of his riding stick and touches it to his forehead in salute—she smiles back and offers a nervous wave of acknowledgement. "Would he do it?" she wonders, looking across a seemingly un-traversable distance into his pale, but earnest blue eyes for an answer. *"There is a difference between bravado and courage, Miss Phillipa,"* comes the cool reminder of an early lesson. Finally, the gates swing open; the knot in her stomach vanishes; she yanks her stick from behind her back, and holding it like a ready saber, she waves confidently to the Baron, and shouts, "Thank you, Sir. Today we fly away!" She hesitates a moment more for Leo to draw along side of her. "Another time Leo, not today," she says before tapping Punch on the shoulder and dashing through gap to the clocker's shack. Excitedly, anxiously, nervously she barks to the timekeeper: "WICKED PUNCH WORKING A HALF FOR PHILLIPA!"

The man in the shack scribbles the words, depresses the talk button on his walkie-talkie, and says "Wicked Punch, in the red towel and wraps, going a half for Phillipa." And a moment later he adds

"Wallysfirstdance, black towel, gray bonnet, going five-eighths for Leo Sands."

Far across the infield, in the pressroom five levels up in the grandstands, three men sit. With binoculars focused on the incoming horses, and their hands poised to start precision timepieces, they wait. "I'll take Sands," one says. "Okay, I got Phillipa," the second replies. The third breathes easy, lays his binoculars aside, and slurps from a cup of coffee.

"First in, first out—let's do this," Kallie whispers, back tracking along the outer rail to the seven-eighths pole. The sand and loam track that stretches before her is freshly groomed, not another hoof has disturbed it. Like newly seeded corn rows seen from an extreme height, the neat hummocks and groves left by the harrows will soon be pummeled under a rain of racing plates. At an easy trot she passes the five-eighths pole. As she goes by the three-quarter pole, Wicked Punch slows momentarily, humps his back, announces himself with a high-pitched squeal, kicks out behind, and farts. "Good sign," Kallie comments standing high in the irons to avoid the fracas. "You know what's up, don't you?" Just before the black-and-white seven-eighths pole she brings Punch down to a walk, turns him to face the inner rail, and halts.

A half-mile up the track, leaning against the guard rail of the backside viewing stand, the Baron watches. He holds a tiny pair of binoculars to his eyes. He breathes deeply, and trembles. "Be careful Miss Phillipa," he prays.

Sitting on the saddle with her knees almost in her stomach, Kallie lowers her racing goggles from the crown of her helmet, and covers her eyes. She grabs the billets of the girth to check that they're secure. She bridges the reins, brings Punch a quarter turn right, and clucks—he moves off willingly. At first they trot, and then they lope, and then they canter. As she enters the backstretch, she takes Wicked Punch from the center of the track, toward the inner rail. When they pass the eleven-sixteenths mark, she rubs the crest of his neck and urges him on, "Steady boy," she whispers. By the five-eighths pole they're throttled up, but still short of wide open. Ten feet of daylight separate them from the rail. At the nine-sixteenths, Kallie crouches lower—her belly on Punch's withers, her chest against his neck, his black mane clinched in her teeth—she peeks between his ears, and brings her stick within his view. The big bay grumbles at the sight and launches forward. Ten yards ahead, three strides, three splits of a second is the half-mile marker. She turns his nose inward. With six feet between them and the rail, Kallie cocks her arm lifting her stick—the wind jostles its feathers—she swings, the clock starts, and as the stick slaps its target...

"RAIL, RAIL!" cries a charging voice from behind.

"WHAP!" the report of her paddle echoes like gunfire. The onrushing horse and rider have just enough room to squirt by on the inside.

"RAIL!" the voice screeches past her ear.

It's too late to check her horse—they're racing now, like it or not. "You piece of shit, Leo!" Kallie screams from two lengths behind Wallysfirstdance. Leo can't hear her—she doesn't care. From three lengths behind, she shouts, "You asshole!" and then Wicked Punch yields another length—Wallysfirstdance had a head start. Kallie brings her stick forward and jiggles it by Punch's nose; he kicks in and hugs the rail four lengths behind, but he gives up no more ground. Pellets of fresh dirt clog the air. This is how a pincushion in a busy tailors shop must feel—pricking clods, as sharp as needles, jab the trailing horse and rider. Chunks of earth scatter from the leading hooves, and ricochet from cheeks, chins, and shoulders. Hail, made from mud bounces helter-skelter everywhere. Second place is no pleasant place to be. Wicked Punch lays back his ears—aggressive horses do this before they attack—his stride lengthens, his pace quickens. "Oh-oh..." Kallie groans as they scorch by the three-eighths pole. "Oh no," she groans again, feeling Wicked Punch seize the bit—she's on a *pissed off* cannon ball with hooves; a rocket with attitude; a bay bomb with a sizzling fuse that's going to explode, and it does.

Riding a racehorse that's on the muscle and running wide open is euphoric. Sights are skewed. Colors meld in random flashes of light. Sound is hushed. The spirit transcends the flesh, and the quick is reposed. Fast moments are odd things—speed stretches them—the faster one goes, the slower time flies, and for Kallie, time is standing still. This is why an athlete trains: the mind must retire for the body to act—instinct is not ruled by thought, thought is too slow. Kallie will recall none of what she does now.

She starts to breathe, steady, soothing breaths. Her racing heart grows quiet. Her herky-jerky movements transform to gestures of fluidic grace. Like a Hindu siddha, she is formless and free—she moves without disturbance, results precede her asking, she and Wicked Punch blend. To an outsider, the power and mystery of the pair would bring an epiphany—to the pair, *it's just a day at the office*. They round the stretch turn. The horse ahead is failing. Three-sixteenths to go, and Kallie takes Punch to the outside. Eight jumbo strides later they're trailing by a head; two more strides and they've drawn even. In perfect unison with her horse, matching stride for stride with Wallysfirstdance—there is no discord, no disharmony, it's a rare alignment of stars, and man, and beast—she thinks, "Yes, yes, this is nature's way; we must conform." Kallie cocks her head and whispers, "Kiss my little ass, Leo," and then she's back to work. She does not touch Punch with the stick—she doesn't have to. A sixteenth, and some extra ground to cover before the finish line, and the pair draw clear. One length, three lengths, seven lengths…

In the grandstands, five levels overhead, the timekeeper watching Kallie and Wicked Punch mutters, "Holy crap, I had them at twenty-one and change at the quarter, and they haven't faded…"

"They're smoking," replies the one watching Leo Sands.

The third puts down his coffee and stares. As the lead widens, he asks, "What's the name of that horse?"

"Wicked Punch. The trainer's Phillipa."

"The PIP?"

"The PIP."

With seventy yards to go, Kallie and Wicked Punch put Wallysfirstdance away, eighteen lengths and still going, nineteen, twenty, twenty-one lengths. The only thing that stops them from adding more is the finish line. Four seconds and a fifth later, Leo and Wallysfirstdance fly through the beam to record their time—a second place finish. Leo stands up in the irons and easies his horse. Kallie lets her horse gallop for another quarter, but Wicked Punch is cross and has more fight to give. "Enough already," Kallie scolds him rising up in the irons to take a firmer hold. Like a boxer that's utterly devastated an opponent, he's ready to take on the cheering crowd, and charges on another eighth. "Oh shit. Shit-shit-shit-shit-shit!"

"Um, sir..." the Baron says, leaning over the guard rail of the viewing stand to get the outrider's attention. Jake Witzman is lighting a cigarette and doesn't hear him.

"His name is Jake," a man standing next to the Baron mentions.

"Jake, Miss Phillipa may need your help."

Jake glances up the track to the six furlong turn, he sees Kallie standing upright in the irons and tugging to pull Wicked Punch up; he nudges his horse out of the chute, puffs on his cigarette, and waits. "Nah," he replies finally. "She's got a good hold on him. She's okay."

The Baron, his breathing irregular, grabs at his chest, "What?" he gasps, and then he realizes that he's placed his field glasses in the pocket of his breeches; hurriedly, he takes them out and fixes his sight on Kallie—her face is the color of crushed ice, and rigid as stone, but Wicked Punch is easing.

"The PIP's a good rider, buddy," Jake Witzman says, turning his horse to face the Baron. "Nothing to worry about. Did you get a time on that baby of hers? It looked pretty fast to me."

The Baron watches as Kallie and Punch, now at a hand gallop, pass the viewing stand. "Beautiful, Miss Phillipa," he shouts as loud as he can, "Wonderful ride," and then he answers Jake, "No, I didn't have a clock on them..."

"I gotta find out," Jake replies, tossing his half-smoked butt aside; then he wheels his pony and lopes to the timer's hut by the in-gate. Within a few beats of an anxious heart he returns. "Forty-four and two," he announces giving the Baron a chapped smile.

"Fast... that's really fast."

"A couple ticks off the track record—damn that's some fast little horse she has there."

"He's fast, but maybe too fast," the Baron utters apprehensively. "A hard run like that is a sure way to buck his shins."

Kallie's nearly to the quarter pole before she's able to bring Wicked Punch back to a trot; she turns him around and back tracks along the outer rail to the exit gate. Standing in the irons, and leaning over him with her bridged reins across his neck for support, she trembles—the surreal experience of racing gone, consciousness returns, and it's unpleasant. Her knuckles are white, and she's powerless to release her grip on the reins. Her lips are blue. Her thighs shake like aspen limbs in a winter storm. Her right ankle, cramped and locked in position, aches unbearably, and then there's a cool sensation so familiar to her—she's wet her pants. She sits down to hide her soaked trousers and wonders, "Why the heck does that always happen?"

The Baron descends from the viewing stand, walks to the bridle path, and waits for Kallie to leave the track. He giggles softly, "That was fast," and then he grouses, "Too fast for a baby—they could have been hurt. Should I scold her?" he ponders. "No, the other rider urged them on. Punch is a bold horse, and she probably couldn't rate him—it was a wonderful ride though, a wonderful ride."

Kallie and Wicked Punch appear at the exit gate, and stand facing the inner rail—the brief recess that's part of their routine. When they turn to leave, the Baron sees two comical faces masked in mud. He can only just glimpse what appear to be Kallie's blue eyes fluttering behind her spattered racing goggles. Everything else is mud. Wicked Punch is mud from poll to hoof. They're not so much flesh and bone as whimsy made from clay. He smiles, watching, as they shed clumps of dirt. Then, for the briefest moment, a youthful recollection abducts his thoughts, and he whispers to no one, "I remember well how that feels. Was I ever that young? My God, those were splendid days." Young enough to dream, but too old to race—he calls out to her, "Miss Phillipa!" Still as a statue, Kallie seems frozen in the saddle; he calls again, "Miss Phillipa, shall I help?" Kallie's eyes are focused elsewhere, and she remains silent. "Miss Phillipa, shall I take your horse?" She replies with stern and steady reticence. "Miss Phillipa, are you quite alright?" he asks, joining her.

The muscles of her jaw twitch, but her teeth are clinched when she replies softly, "Hush…" and then she nods to indicate that he should walk along side.

He takes the hint, but struggles to keep up; even at a walk, the horse has a long stride. "Is something the matter?"

"Sort of…" she whispers.

"Are you injured? Is it your knee, your ankle? Do you have a cramp?"

Kallie crouches over Punch's neck, and confides, "My fingers are numb. I can't let go."

As she sits upright again, the Baron reaches for the chinstrap of the bridle, leads Punch into the grass along the edge of the bridle path, and halts him. "Relax, Miss Phillipa," he says sympathetically while jiggling the reins free of her grip. "Now, shake out your hands and see if you can't loosen them up." Kallie shakes her fingers feebly above her lap. "Is that better?"

"Yeah," she sighs in relief, lifting the racing goggles from her eyes, and looking down to the Baron.

He sees that tears are beginning to wash the sand and mud from Kallie's cheeks. "Tears?" he wonders, "From joy, relief, fear, pain?" He's uncertain, but he reaches out to her, and asks, "Would you like to dismount?"

"I can't move," she groans.

With his concern for his student growing, he grabs Kallie's boot to remove it from the stirrup. "Here," he says, giving her ankle a tug, but Kallie resists, and keeps the iron locked snuggly home.

"Sir, please. You don't understand," she whispers frantically. "I don't want to move. I peed my pants…"

"Oh," he responds, not fully understanding, and then it strikes him, the cause of her rigid bearing. "Oh, oh…"

"I don't know when. I didn't even know I did it until I got Punchie stopped. Do you think anyone in the viewing stand saw— couldn't you tell?"

"Um…"

"I'm so embarrassed. Why does this always happen?"

"Ah…"

275

"Kallie the PIP—ha!" she scowls. "If any of the guys find out, they'll call me Kallie PEE!" The Baron's relieved that Kallie's accident wasn't a serious one; he doesn't intend to further upset his student, but he's amused by her predicament, and laughs. "What are you laughing at?" she snaps. "It's not funny—this is serious. I can't control it. I feel so stupid—cripes!"

The Baron gently lifts her foot out of the iron, and while messaging her calf, he jests to help lighten her mood, "I'm glad you didn't ask to use one of my saddles..."

Kallie giggles, replying, "I'd clean it."

"I know you would, Miss Phillipa," he says, allowing her leg to hang free, and then he asks, "Does that feel better?" She nods, yes. "Good. Drop the other one, and I'll lead your horse back to the stable. Stay seated, Miss Phillipa, no one else need know about this."

As the Baron starts to lead Wicked Punch off at a walk, Leo Sands jogs up from behind. "Hey PIP," he shouts as he passes, "if I could catch it, I would kiss it. You got a hell-of-a-horse there."

Turning abruptly to Leo, she asks, "What?"

"Your little ass. I'd kiss your little ass," he shouts riding away toward the shed rows.

Puzzled, she yells, "What are you talking about?"

"Never mind, PIP. I know ya didn't mean it."

"That guy is so strange," she mutters. And then she winces in pain. "Ouch! Damn that hurts. Have you ever had a wet wedgie, Sir?" she asks, grabbing at the crotch of her jeans.

He's too much of a gentleman to answer her directly—he knows what she's asking, but he gives her a dodging reply. "I've ridden in the rain, Miss Phillipa," he answers, smiling. "So I can say that I've experienced some of the discomfort you're feeling. Is that what you mean?"

"I guess so, Sir..."

"A wet saddle can give you an awful rash—talcum powder helps..."

The rest of the way back to the shed row, the Baron, Kallie, and Wicked Punch walk in silence. Soon, Kallie's lost in thought attempting to recall the work she and her horse have just performed.

Horses and riders, going to, and returning from the track, pass by her unnoticed. Only sketchy glimpses, and abbreviated sounds recur to her—the details of the timed work are absent. When the three reach the stable, all of Winston's help are busy at their chores and unaware that there's a hot horse to bathe—this is a good thing. The Baron leads Punch to the wash stall in front of the tack room, and stands him in such a position that when Kallie dismounts, the horse will shield her from everyone's view. "Jump down, and unsaddle him," he instructs while bending over to pick up the water hose. Kallie no sooner complies, than the Baron, seeing that she's lifted the saddle out of the way, opens the nozzle of the hose, and douses her jeans with water.

"I-eee!" she shrieks, jumping back in surprise. "Why'd you do that?"

The Baron redirects the spray to Punch's cannons, and winking, he whispers, "Your secret is safe, Miss Phillipa. I only hope you have some dry breeches in your tack compartment."

She holds the saddle out at arm's length so she can get a clear view of her soaked pants. "That was a pretty accurate shot, Sir, thanks."

"My pleasure, Miss Phillipa."

"Can you hold him while I get his halter from the truck?" The Baron nods, yes, and Kallie dashes to store her saddle, and retrieve the halter.

In her absence, Winston Chase emerges from the tack room; he's uncertain who it is that tends to Kallie's horse, but if attire and demeanor are clues, it can only be one person: Albert, the Baron Verrhaus. He's heard about the Baron—Kallie's conversation nearly always contains some reference to him—but he's never met him. It's odd that a man of Winston's age and experience should be shy, or intimidated by another's reputation, but he is, and he approaches meekly. "Ah-um, ah, ah," he stutters. And standing as straight as he can to show his respect, he reaches out his hand in greeting. "Are you Kallie's teacher? Are you the Baron Verrhaus?"

"I am," he replies, returning Winston's greeting by shaking hands. "And you must be Mister Chase, *the Winman*. I read about you in the sports pages occasionally, you're quite a good trainer as I understand."

The complement disarms Winston; he grins broadly displaying a full mouth of tobacco stained teeth, then he shakes the Baron's hand more vigorously, and says, "It's an awful pleasure to meet ya, Baron."

The enthusiasm with which Winston is shaking hands causes the spray from the water hose to go awry; the Baron escapes from Winston's clasp and turns it off before either of them, unintentionally, joins in Kallie's wet charade. "Miss Phillipa speaks very well of you Mister Chase," he comments, laying the hose aside. "She respects you greatly, and I trust her judgment, so please, call me Albert."

Winston is stunned. Here is a man who struggled up the rungs from *muck-sack*, to groom, to trainer, and now he's on a first name basis with a titled aristocrat. Winston is nervous, he's elated, he needs a chew—he needs it, now. By habit as entrenched as instinct, he reaches into his shirt pocket and withdraws his can of snuff; the shiny lid reflects a flash of sunlight when he opens it. "Ah," he sighs packing a two-finger dip in his cheek, but before he can return the container to his pocket, the Baron stops him.

"Is that snuff?"

"Ah—yup," Winston answers cautiously.

"When I was in the cavalry, that was the only tobacco we could use while mounted. I haven't had any since my discharge. May I?" Winston timidly passes the container of snuff to the Baron and watches him open the lid; he lifts the can of finely ground tobacco to his nose and sniffs. "Ah, that brings back some fond memories," he says with a sigh. Then he takes a small pinch, and packs it in his lower lip. "I'll regret doing this, Mister Chase," he adds, handing the can back to Winston, "But, thank you."

Sharing a pinch of snuff is a ritual that's imbued in symbolism; it implies trust, respect, and a fellowship that only tobacco addicts understand. Albert, the Baron, and Winston, the Winman have exposed a common vice that seals their bond.

"Hey Winman," Kallie interrupts returning from her truck. "Do you guys know each other?"

"We've just met," Winston replies, hiding the snuff container in his shirt pocket. Both he and the Baron watch as Kallie holds the leather halter around Punch's neck with her right hand; reaches for the bridle crownpiece with her left, and pulling it forward over the horse's ears, slides the bridle off allowing it to rest on her forearm. Then, in two easy movements she slips the halter over Punch's head and buckles it. Winston smiles proudly and announces, "I taught her how to do that when she started working for me last year. She's a damn good hand."

"Miss Phillipa has shown me many things she's learned from you, Mister Chase."

Kallie reaches down, picks the hose up from the ground, and starts to bathe her sweaty colt. "Better stand back, gentlemen, I'd hate for you to get soaked in the process."

They step out of the way, and from a safe distance, Winston notices Kallie's soaked trousers, and asks, "What's that PIP? It looks like you wet your pants?"

Kallie laughs to cover up her embarrassment, and replies, "Gee Winman, I guess it does. The Baron got a little careless with the water when he was cooling Punch's legs—I hope he was a better shot with a rifle. When I'm done here, I gotta run over to the thrift store and see if I can't get some dry ones."

"I don't think they make them that small," Winston whispers aside to the Baron.

"I heard that…" Kallie scowls, turning off the hose. Then she picks up a sudsy sponge, and lathers Punch's near side.

"You should eat more meat, girl, you're just skin and bone."

"That's all I ever eat, Winman—it doesn't help. My metabolism is too high."

"You work too hard," the Baron interjects.

"Nah. You call this work?"

"When was your last day off?"

"Not since I came back to work for you, Winman. That was what, in April?" she replies walking around to scrub the horse's off side. Then cupping her hand to her cheek, she remarks quietly to the

Baron, "He should know better than to work me so hard, I'm just a little girl…"

"Toughest one around, and ornery too."

"I can attest to that," the Baron agrees.

"You men always stick together, don't you?"

"It's the only way we know to survive, Miss Phillipa."

By this time, Wicked Punch is covered in suds from head to haunch—Kallie is sudsy from head to toe. She picks up the hose and begins to shower him off. Like froth, on a glacial stream cascading down an alpine valley, tufts of foam are lofted by the roiling current. "There," she says, when she's finished rinsing, "A quick once over with the scraper and we're finished!" She handles the sweat scraper like a rapier, if the horse was an opposing foilsman, the seconds wouldn't see the parries, and couldn't count the touches—instantly the excess water is shed from the horse. "About that day off, Winman…" Kallie teases, stuffing the blade into a belt loop, "I thought you wanted to say something."

"Um, yeah. I was thinking about saying something…"

"And?"

"Well, first ya gotta tell me how your horse went."

"He worked pretty well," Kallie replies coyly as she bends over to retrieve the hose.

"Come on, PIP. Tell the Winman."

While still holding the lead rope, she sprays some water on her face to wash away the mud and soap. "Forty-four and change," she mumbles above the splashing.

"What?"

"I think she said forty-four and change," the Baron answers. "It was a bullet work."

Winston's eyes swell to twice their size, and he gasps in disbelief, "No! How much change?"

"Two," Kallie says, turning off the hose, and standing upright with a huge grin.

"Damn. Holy-moly, that's fast. That's got to be the fastest today. A bullet work!"

Too Far A Dream

"Now what were you saying about a day off? I'm kind of tired after burning up the track."

"Shoot, you burned the hind end off a mule…"

The Baron looks askance at Winston, and asks with a smile, "The what?"

"The hind end off a mule," he replies laughing. "She went faster than a burrito fart. Forty-four and two, that's great!"

"Ah Winman, the day off?"

"You got it! Hang that pot of gold on the walker and go on home."

"With pay?"

All of a sudden the excitement Winston was showing vanishes. He hems, and haws—money is at stake—he wrinkles his brow, squints at Kallie, and then, after spitting a small gob of tobacco juice on the ground, he grumbles, "Okay."

"He's just an old sweetie isn't he, Sir?"

The Baron smiles, then answers, "I think you could coax money out of Ebenezer Scrooge, Miss Phillipa. Let's just hope you're able to do as well when it comes to passing the entry box at the derby."

Kallie's not sure what the Baron means, but she doesn't ask him to explain. Instead, her attention is drawn to his teeth. "Sir," she inquires suspiciously, "are you chewing tobacco?"

The Baron's lips slam shut, and he gives a muffled reply, "No, Miss."

"I believe you are…"

"Don't tell Charlene," he pleads.

"Will you let me out of my chores this afternoon?"

Winston nudges the Baron with his elbow and chides him. "Ornery, I warned ya she was ornery."

"And I told you I'd regret having the tobacco. I blame this on you, Mister Chase."

Winston chuckles. A moment ago the Baron almost begged for a pinch of snuff, and now he's suffering the consequences. "A gentleman doesn't blame anyone else for his mistakes, Albert…" he advises.

281

"Harrumph" the Baron growls. Then he turns to Kallie, and grouses, "Alright then, I'll see to your chores, but I'll be expecting you tomorrow afternoon—like clockwork, Miss Phillipa."

"Yahoo!"

"I tell ya what, PIP," says Winston, taking the lead rope from her. "Why don't ya unhitch your trailer and take off now. I'll hang Punch on the walker and stick him in one of those empty stalls down on the end of my shed. He'll be fine. No one will ever find out."

"Really Winman?"

"Sure PIP, I'll make sure that Juan feeds and waters him. Go on now and get outa here."

Kallie, excited, and without thinking, shouts, "Thanks Winman," and slugs him on the bicep—he winces. The Baron acts more quickly and steps away before she can lay a blow on him, too. "Oops," she murmurs, retiring her fist. Then, nodding respectfully, she whispers, "Thanks a lot, Sir. See you tomorrow." With that, she turns, and jogs along the alleyway to her truck and trailer.

"She still has a limp doesn't she?" observes the Baron.

"But it don't seem to hold her back none."

The two men watch as Kallie unhitches the trailer—they envy her youthfulness, they cherish her teasing affection, and together, they all share a zeal for horses.

* * *

Thirteen: Red Juice

Shortly after six in the evening the day that Wicked Punch got the bullet work, Anthony and Reggie arrive at Longview from their separate jobs. It's not often that they get home at the same time, but today is not an ordinary day. Weary and hungry, they enter the front hallway, Reggie checks the telephone message machine, and Anthony slides off his loafers. "Should I start the grill darlin'?" he asks while Reggie scribbles on a notepad. "I took out some pork chops this morning. Grilled chops and corn on the cob sound good to you?"

"Yum, you bet."

"Chops 'n corny-cobs it is then," he replies, stepping behind Reggie to embrace her in an affectionate hug, and then he asks, "Say darlin', do you want to go up stairs and fool around with a rough-neck cowboy? Kallie won't be home for another hour."

"Anthony," Reggie giggles as she jostles to break free of his embrace, "I've been standing in horse shit all day. I stink like hell, and besides, you've got to start the chops." Anthony tightens his grip as Reggie makes another attempt to escape, but she stops when she feels him kissing her neck—he knows her weakness—and her resistance fades. "Ah," she murmurs, "you sure know how to make a girl tingle." And then fawning, she oozes, "I've got time for a quick shower with a naughty cowboy. Can you join me?"

"We could take a long shower darlin'," he whispers while unfastening the buttons of her blue denim shirt. Suddenly, glancing over Reggie's shoulder, Anthony exclaims, "What the heck?" Turning, Reggie gasps. They stare astonished, through the open doorway to the dining room and see the table set with plates, napkins, silver cutlery, and wine goblets. Even more astonishing is the aroma wafting from the kitchen: the scent of seared meat lingers in the air, and spices stewing in tomato sauce. How could they have missed it? *Red juice.* Pork chops stewed in tomato sauce, and served on a fluffy bed of mashed spuds. It's Kallie's favorite meal, and the only one, other than eggs, that she can cook. It's Anthony's favorite meal too, he hesitates a moment sniffing, and wonders, "Has an angel has come to make dinner?" Then, as his erogenous urge dulls, he mutters, "Oh-oh darlin', better button up, looks like we got company."

Reggie hurriedly fastens the buttons of her shirt, and calls to the kitchen, "Kallie? Kallie honey, is that you? What are you doing home so early?"

"I got the afternoon off," Kallie shouts from the kitchen. "Are you guys hungry? I'm cooking supper."

"Starved," Reggie answers enthusiastically. And then in a hushed tone, she whispers to Anthony, "Sorry cowboy."

Anthony's face shows disappointment, his romantic plan interrupted, he tries to salvage his fading libido by kissing Reggie passionately before she jogs up the stairs to the shower, alone.

"What kind of wine do you guys want, chianti, or burgundy?" Kallie asks, leaning through the kitchen entry into the hall. She's surprised to see Anthony standing alone, staring up at the vacant stairs. "Where'd mom go, wasn't she with you?"

Anthony doesn't answer immediately; he continues to gaze up the stairs—a door slams; the sound of water splashing in a shower trickles through the hall—he pauses a moment longer, finally, he lowers his gaze, and answers, "Yeah, but she wanted to get cleaned up. She's in the shower... And Kallie, I think that chianti is a burgundy."

"Oh. Oh yeah, I knew that, Dad."

"Sure you did, shrimp."

"I meant Italian, or French, you know Chianti, or Burgundy."

Anthony chuckles at her doubtful comment, and replies, "Nice save pal, but I'm not buying it. What you got cooking?"

"Red juice and spuds. Sound good?"

"Not what I had in mind just now," Anthony sighs. "But it is my favorite."

"Mine too. I put the chops in a couple of hours ago, so the meat will be falling off the bone. Are you going to want a salad, or do you want something else on the side?"

"A salad will be great, with cherry tomatoes and blue cheese."

"You got it, big guy," she chirps disappearing into the kitchen as Anthony makes his way into the half bath at the end of the hall.

"About a half an hour before the chow's ready, Dad. Why don't you open the wine, and relax? I've got everything under control in here." Anthony is washing his hands, and can't hear her over the sound of the running water. "Dad?" she asks, "Did you hear me? Dad?"

Later during dinner, among the clatter of busy table knives and forks, Kallie chatters endlessly about her morning at the track. What she can't remember about Punch's work, she makes up. She talks about Leo's challenge, and how far behind he was left at the finish line; she imitates Winston Chase shouting, *holy-moly that's fast. You burned the hind end off a mule*; she describes the Baron's panic when she caught him chewing tobacco, but the details of her experience— the ride itself—she omits. She also doesn't mention that she wet her pants.

While listening attentively, Anthony devours the tender chops and whipped potatoes; his cheeks are red, flushed with pride and two glasses of wine, when he gushes, "I'm so proud of you, Kallie. Crazy dreams can come true. I always believed you have what it takes to be a jockey. You're the toughest little bugger I know, and the most stubborn too—I never doubted you, PIP."

The comment brings a mist to both Kallie and Reggie's eyes. "That's so sweet, Daddy," Kallie says, picking up her napkin, and while pretending to wipe her mouth she daubs a tear before it can betray her.

"I'm proud of you too, Kallie," Reggie joins in. "It takes a lot of courage to do what you've done."

The loving moment lingers until Kallie, worried that her embarrassment will show, quizzes impishly, "Does this mean that I get out of doing the dishes?"

"I'll just stick them in the dishwasher," Reggie volunteers. Then with a motherly smile, she turns to Kallie and suggests, "Why don't you and Daddy go out on the porch swing and let your stomachs settle—it won't take me long in here, I'll come out later."

"No Mom, not with Dad…"

"What? Why not?" Anthony interrupts—he's been disappointed once this evening, he doesn't want it to happen a second time.

"I kind of want to talk to mom," she stammers. "I've got to discuss some private stuff. You know, Dad? Girl talk."

"But we're pals, aren't we? You can talk to me…"

The dining room brightens with Kallie's glowing affection as she replies tenderly, "We're the best pals, Dad, but I need a woman's advice. It's not the kind of thing I could talk to a man about. You understand, don't you pal?"

Anthony is crestfallen. There are things in Kallie's life that won't be shared with him—he's not a woman, and his daughter is no longer a little girl. This is a hard moment for any father to face, but Anthony recovers gracefully and answers, "Sure Kallie. I've taken a few punches to the head, but I understand. Girls got to stick together."

Kallie gets up from her chair, walks to the head of table where Anthony sits, and then kissing his cheek, she coos, "I love you, pal." He inflates like a delicate soufflé in a warm oven, and then instantly slumps when she asks, "Can you take care of the dishes?"

"Um, uh-ha, okay," he grumps. "If you let me come out and join you gals when I'm done."

Reggie nods a silent, yes, as she stands up from her chair. Anthony winks his acceptance. Then, she pulls the unused napkin from the waistband of her jeans, lays it beside her plate, and wipes her lips with the sleeve of her shirt. "That was a very nice supper Kallie, excellent grub." She covers a burp with her hand while ambling toward the main hallway that leads to the front porch. "It really filled the old pie hole. I'll be outside…"

"Hold up, Mom, here I come," she yelps. Reggie waits by the doorway for Kallie to join her. And when they leave together, like little girls on their way to the playground, they hold hands.

Anthony remains seated; he sips the last intoxicating drops of chianti from his goblet, burps contentedly, and sighs, "Ah, that was mighty delicious…"

The evening sun is an hour above the horizon. It's not low enough for the sky to erupt in incendiary color, but not high enough to prevent the daylight blue from failing. A temperate zephyr, expressed from the river bottoms, puffs through the white-fenced meadows shaking dusty pollen from the timothy grass and clover—

the scent of honey and fresh cut lawn perfumes the air. The porch swing lists and yaws in the mild breeze, and overhead, the oak leaves rattle like muted castanets.

"What's on your mind, Kallie?" Reggie asks as they mosey onto the front porch. "I get the feeling that you have something serious to discuss."

"Mom, can we talk about something very personal?"

Reggie steadies the swing so Kallie can sit. "Do you have boyfriend? Do you want to ask if I think it's okay for you to have sex?"

Kallie studies the question before answering; its bluntness is perplexing. "No, it's nothing like that, Mom…" she replies, plunking into the swing. "It's worse."

Reggie scrunches in next to her. "Worse?" she wonders, restraining her trepidation. "What could be worse?" Her next thought is, "Drugs? I've heard rumors about jockeys using them… Jimmy Evans got ruled off last year after testing positive for cocaine use. I could have missed a sign—maybe that's why Morgan and Kallie aren't friends. It's got to be drugs. No. This is stupid Reggie, it can't be drugs, just ask her what's going on." Reggie reaches her arm around Kallie's shoulders and embraces her in a comforting hug. "Honey, what's bothering you?" she asks apprehensively.

"Um, well, um," she answers, her words coming in fits, "this isn't easy. It's kind of embarrassing. I'm worried, I think I have a problem."

The hesitation with which Kallie speaks, causes a mask of seriousness to cover Reggie's face—stiff as papier-mâché, her expression is fixed and grave. "You're feeling okay aren't you, honey? You haven't been feeling any unusual pains, like cramps, or found a lump or swelling? What is it?"

Kallie clinches her mother's hand, and starts again, "I really can't explain it… I don't know… You know, Mom?" She stares directly in Reggie's eyes—Reggie meets her nervous gaze—and then Kallie continues, "I don't remember it ever happening before my accident, but now, whenever I get stressed out or excited…"

Reggie hugs her tightly and pleads, "What, honey?"

"It's like I'm weak or something. I just can't hold it. It's like I've got no control…"

"Hold what? Do feel a tingling in your back? Do your fingers go numb?"

Kallie snaps her head back in surprise at Reggie's question. "Oh my God," she thinks to herself, "she doesn't understand; she thinks I'm getting spastic. Oh my God!" She looks in Reggie's panicked eyes, and blurts rapidly, "No Mom, not that, I feel fine. I can't hold it. My bladder. I pee my pants. It happened today when I was riding. It happens a lot."

"Ah, ah," Reggie sputters.

"I can't control it. I don't know what to do. Can you help Mom?"

Reggie replies with confusion and shock, "Um, I don't, I don't know…"

"Does it ever happen to you, you know, when you get nervous?"

Reggie is beginning to regain her composure when she answers, "No…. No…. Never."

"Oh God, Mom," she groans desperately, "I feel like such a looser." The tone of her raspy voice grows emphatic as she rails, "The Baron had to squirt me with a hose today so none of the guys would see that I peed all over myself. I can't be a jockey pissing my pants all the time." Kallie sits upright freeing herself from Reggie's hug, and shouts, "Shit! Oh shit-shit-shit!"

Kallie's rage is earnest, but Reggie has to fight to prevent an ill-timed chuckle—it's the little tragedies that are so ironic, and vexing; sometimes a laugh is the only remedy. With a restrained smile, and all the reassurance she can muster, she whispers, "Your grandma used to wet her pants. We used to joke that her bladder was weak as a butterfly's fart. Lots of women have that problem. It's not a big deal."

"It is if you're a jockey…" Kallie moans.

"It is if you're a jockey," Reggie concedes with a sigh.

"I can't wear a diaper."

"Maybe there are exercises, maybe the doctor can help you…"

Just then, Anthony swings open the screen door. Both Kallie and Reggie gasp at the intrusion and bark in unison, "Not now, Dad!"

"Oops," he whimpers, scampering to safety behind the screen. Then, pressing his lips against the woven mesh, he grovels, "Sorry ladies. Just call me if you need me. I'll be watching TV."

Once Anthony is gone, the placid evening engulfs mother and daughter as they fall into a momentary silence. They rock back and forth on the porch swing—propelled by the light breeze, restrained by gravity. The muffled sound of a television laugh-track comes from within the house, and in the upper sky, a nighthawk screeches, plunging on a moth.

"It wasn't what I expected..." Kallie says suddenly, breaking the silence.

"What wasn't?"

"Working Punchie," she replies, her voice trailing off, and betraying disappointment. "I wasn't afraid, I think. I don't remember feeling anything—nothing. I thought it would be exciting, you know, riding that fast, but it just seemed like, so what, big deal, is it worth it?" Kallie gazes off at the distant bluffs glowing crimson in the setting sun; her mood is melancholy as the wife of an absent mariner, contemplating the cruel ocean. Reggie is kind, and gives her space to ponder. When her thoughts return, Kallie continues, "I've been there, Mom. I've gone as fast on a racehorse as you can go, and I know it's crazy, it's nuts." Reggie feels the porch swing vibrate as Kallie shivers. "I got lucky last year when that horse flipped on me; Eddie Cantrell is in a wheel chair—I got real lucky—I can still ride, Eddie's a cripple."

"It's a very dangerous profession..."

"It's a lot more than that, Mom," Kallie replies with an emphatic, but steady voice. "Look at Bernie Keats; to make the weight, she hurls all the time. She binges, and then runs to the can and throws up. She's freaking bulimic, and so is Derek Rousham! And Earl Donnbury, sure he's a good jockey, but he has the attitude of a serial killer. And then, there are the drugs and the booze—Mom, it's not just dangerous, it's insane!"

"There are risks with everything, Kallie. To be the best, you have to be willing to do whatever it takes."

Kallie stares off again. And then, with an apprehensive sigh, she whispers, "I don't think I want to… I don't think it's worth it… It's just a dream…."

*   *   *

Fourteen: The Dodgers Artful

The next morning, Kallie no sooner pulls her truck into her parking place at the track, than Winston Chase is hot footing it toward her. Gasping and wheezing, he shouts, "PIP, hey-ya PIP. We've got trouble."

She steps from the truck to confront him, and asks, "What's up Winman? What kind of trouble?"

"With the Hawk," he answers winded and short of breath. "Last night he pulled up while Juan was watering; he cornered him and wanted to know whose horse was in the end stall, but Juan played dumb—said he didn't know." Kallie knits her brow as she listens to Winston's report. "Then he asked if Juan didn't know whose horse it was, why was he watering it? The Hawk was really pissed off, he said he was going to get to bottom of it." Winston rifles through his shirt pocket to retrieve his snuff can, and after packing a bulging dip into his cheek, he whispers cautiously, "I think the guy really has it in for ya. Juan said he kept talking to himself—he was muttering *I'm going to get ya PIP. I'm going to get you,* like he was crazy or something. I know he's gonna to be back."

"Did he say he'd be back this morning?"

"He's probably been here already. Has Punch been tattooed yet?"

"I've been putting it off," Kallie replies, snickering. "I didn't want to get three different tattoos for the same horse."

Winston exhales an exhausted sigh, "Whew. No way he can identify him, but ya gotta get him out of here. I know what Jim can be like when thinks somebody's breaking the rules, and if he figures I'm in on it, he's gonna make me suffer."

"That skinny, four-eyed-asshole," Kallie scowls. "He isn't going to make it rough on anybody." She smirks fiendishly, and snarling through her clinched teeth, she promises, "I'll take care of this, Winman. The Hawk isn't going to take it out on you because you did a favor for the PIP." She holds her arm upright and gestures with her index, and middle finger. "Two can play this game. Do you see that?" She threatens defiantly, showing Winston her index finger. "Here's me," she scowls. And as she lowers her index finger, she displays her middle finger in an obscene gesture. "And here's for the Hawk."

Winston's jaw gapes at the vulgar sign. "Don't be doing that," he cautions her. "He might be hiding around here. Giving him the finger will get ya a two hundred dollar fine."

"Fine! Freaking fine," she bellows rabidly. "Let them fine me. I'll show that asshole that nobody can catch the PIP." She pounds her heels into the limestone gravel of the parking lot, and stomping to her trailer to get her saddle, she mutters, "Try and get me, Hawk, try and get me…"

As fast as a bounding horse over a hurdle, Kallie's up and away. Today she's not fooling around; she rides only one of her horses: Wicked Punch. They back track around the track once—light exercise to stretch tight muscles, and loosen any cramps that may be lingering after yesterday's work. When she returns to Winston's shed row, the Hawk is waiting in plain view. The white shirted, blue slacked scarecrow in spectacles leans rigidly against his golf cart—he's an apparition of dread, everyone's worst fear. Kallie's been tested by this scoundrel, and she's bold by having bested him. "Good morning, Jim," she chirps from atop her horse as she rides to the wash stall.

The Hawk pushes off from his golf cart. "Don't take a smart tone with me, Phillipa," he hisses at her. "I know what you're up to—I've got you."

Winston Chase cowers in his tack room; peeking in between the door hinges, he watches as Kallie leaps from her horse to confront the Hawk. "What have you got, Jim?"

"You—PIP," he replies with a bellicose sneer. "Someone snuck an unapproved horse into that end stall and kept it there overnight." He glares at Kallie with his magnified eyes, and presses his interrogation. "You stabled that horse on the grounds last night, didn't you?" Kallie looks in the direction that the Hawk is pointing, but remains silent. "That's a violation of the rules, Phillipa. What do you have to say?"

"My horse is hot, do you mind if I cool him out?"

"Don't try to dodge the question, kid…."

Kallie bristles at the demeaning comment; she clinches her fists; her biceps snap taut, but wisdom overcomes her instinct, and rather than popping him one—her first impulse—she curves her lips in an amiable smile, and replies, "I think you've made a mistake, Mr. Peterson. Punchie spent last night at the farm. It must have been someone else's horse."

"No ya don't. Don't try pulling that crap on me, I got a good look at the horse, and he looked just like this one here."

Kallie smirks, and answers dismissively, "He's bay with black points—looks like ninety percent of the horses out here. Did someone tell you it was my horse?"

"No," the Hawk replies fidgeting.

"Did you check the lip tattoo against the papers on file with the secretary?"

His ire rising, he sizzles, "No."

"So you really have no proof that it was my horse; you just have my word that he wasn't here."

"But your trailer was," the Hawk growls smugly, folding his arms across his chest. "How'd ya ship the horse out? Tell me that, kid. Let's see if ya can lie your way out of that."

"Oh-oh," Kallie ponders, but she doesn't balk. Fabricating as quickly as an angler caught with a fish out of season, she recovers. "The Baron was here looking for a good dressage prospect. Some trainer, the Baron didn't say who, had a seventeen hander, and told the Baron to take it home and try it out." Now Kallie is getting warmed up—the second lie is always easier than the first. "Well," she continues, "the horse was acting up and wouldn't load, so he asked if I'd ship my horse with him to keep it calm—so I did."

The Hawk is doubtful. He really should know better, but the story seems genuine. He makes one last attempt to trip Kallie by asking, "Why didn't ya use your trailer?"

"Too short—it's only six-six. They needed a seven footer…"

He takes off his glasses, and cleans the fat lenses with a tissue from his pants pocket. Putting them back on, he squints suspiciously at Kallie, and warns her. "You're going to screw up, Phillipa. It always happens. And when ya do, I'll be there—count on it."

"I won't screw up, Mr. Peterson," she replies earnestly. And as the Hawk turns away heading to his golf cart, Kallie whispers aside, "At least you'll never catch me at it—asshole."

The rest of the day progresses normally, except for one thing. When she's finished bathing Wicked Punch, she hangs him on the walker, and then, instead of running to the kitchen for a cup of joe, she meanders up and down the shed rows on a mission of purpose. "So, asshole," she fumes defiantly, "you want to play cat and mouse? You think you can catch me breaking the rules? Well the PIP might be little, but don't let my size fool you. I'll show you that I'm not afraid of a fight, you skinny turd." As she scouts, she counts the empty stalls—in every barn she counts at least two. Some barns are more than half vacant. In D-4, across the alley, and down the shed row from Winston's stable, two stalls are empty. "Perfect!" she whispers glancing inside. "Right in the middle of the barn." She looks to the right and sees contented horses standing with their inquisitive heads poking out over the dutch doors, and then she looks to the left, same thing. "If you want to hide," she thinks, "Join a crowd," and then she moves on. But just in case her nemesis is out of sight, quartering her trail, she wanders a while longer—she doubles back; slinks through impassable passages; slithers between straw bales; lurks with stealthy vigilance. Finally, confident that the Hawk is on a cold scent, she winds her way back to her truck to await an opportunity—an opportunity to foil a villain.

An hour ticks away; Kallie passes it lounging in the cab of her truck. Ten minutes more crawl by, and then, the racing secretary's voice crackles over the public address speakers as he calls the entries for Friday's races: "Attention horsemen. Here's a rundown. The first, second and third races are good with ten. The fourth is off, and we'll be taking sub-race two..."

"Another two-year-old maiden race," she gripes softly, looking at the condition book. "I would have entered Punchie in that race if he were ready. Well—couple more weeks...."

"The fifth is short one horse, the sixth, seventh and eighth will go. The ninth is off, and we'll use sub one." The squeal of the microphone keying off echoes through the backside, and then it's keyed on again. A feminine voice announces: "Attention. Would the chief of security please report to the stable gate?" Then comes the squeal, the echo, and finally silence.

"Yes!" Kallie yelps, bounding into action. "He's out of the way." As quick as a fly outpacing a fly swatter, she zips to the hot-walker, attaches a lead rope to Punch's halter, and the two buzz together to the empty stalls in D-4. "In you go, Punchie," she says as they dash into one of the stalls. "You're going to motel it tonight." She glances out over the stall door—the coast is clear. She slips out, latches the door closed, and darts away unobserved.

The next morning, after her chores are done and she's galloped Wicked Punch, Kallie goes to the administration building to file a stall application with the racing secretary. "Sir? Excuse me," she shouts, stepping to the long counter that separates the rabble from the racing officials. A slightly built man, who's been crouching behind the counter, stands up; his arms are loaded with copies of freshly printed condition books.

"What do you need, sweetie?" he asks, plunking the books on the counter before her.

She surveys the man silently, "Young, curly hair, brown eyes; he didn't shave this morning, but he has a cute smile." And then she answers, "I have a stall application for the racing secretary. Would you tell him that Kallie May Phillipa is here?"

Now it's his turn to survey Kallie, "Young, but legal, her boobs are small, but she has a nice ass, and a pretty smile." And then, heaping more maturity into his voice than could be supported by his appearance, he replies, "I can take the application, Miss Phillipa. My name is Chuck Wallace; I'm an entry clerk. It is <u>Miss</u> Phillipa, isn't it?"

"No…"

"You're married?"

Confused, Kallie answers, "No."

"Got a boyfriend?"

"No."

"So you're single, and no boyfriend…"

"Um, yes."

"Great," Chuck replies seductively. "I got a little confused when you said that you weren't <u>Miss</u> Phillipa. I thought you might be married."

"No, no, that's not what I meant." She's embarrassed and flustered; she knows she's being flirted with—she likes it, but a man taking a sexual interest in her is something she is not used to, and it rattles her. She smiles politely, and continues with a blush in her cheeks, "What I want is…"

Chuck responds with an equivalent glow, and drips a hinting "Yes?"

"What I want is for the secretary to time-stamp my application. I've got to have a record of when it was turned in."

"Not a problem, Kallie," he replies, winking. He turns around and signals to a jumbo hulk of a man leaning on a desk in the rear of the room. The nameplate on the desk reads: Willis Richard Dudley, Racing Secretary. The huge man nods an acknowledgment to Chuck Wallace, and begins his lumbering journey to the counter, but before he arrives, Chuck turns quickly to Kallie, and asks nervously, "Kallie, don't take this the wrong way, but I think you're pretty. Can I call you, sometime? Would you like to go out, have a coffee or something?"

The only way Kallie knows to respond is to stutter, "Um, ah, um maybe, ah okay."

"What ya got for me, Chuckles?" the giant interrupts as he plods to the counter.

"Miss Phillipa needs her stall application time-stamped, Willie."

Willie's voice rumbles up from a belly as big as a sack of feed oats when he says, "The hell ya say. Nobody else asks for that."

"I need a record of when it was turned in. You know? So I have a record."

The counter almost groans when Willie folds his arms and leans on it. "You're that PIP girl, ain't ya?" he asks.

"Yes sir, I am."

"Heard about ya, PIP…"

"Good stuff, I hope," she replies, placing a completed stall application on the counter before him.

Too Far A Dream

Willie glances down at the form, but doesn't budge. Instead, he turns to the entry clerk, and mutters, "Stamp it, Chuckles." Chuck Wallace scurries to an entry booth and inserts the form in a time-clock—the mechanism clunks—then he returns and shows the time-stamp to both Kallie and Willie. "That what ya want, PIP?"

Kallie nods, yes, and replies, "Thanks, Mr. Dudley."

Willie ignores her courteous remark; he just glares down at Kallie. Without taking his eyes off her, he grunts at Chuck Wallace, "Now go file it with the rest of 'em, Chuckles."

Chuck Wallace takes two steps backward out of Willie's sight, and silently mouths the words, "I'll call you."

Kallie is excited by Chuck's offer, but she hides it. She's just about to turn and leave, when Willie snarls at her, "Ya ain't gettn' no stall, PIP."

"What?" she asks abruptly. "There are empty stalls all over the grounds."

"Not for you there ain't…"

"Well, my application is on file."

"I said, ya ain't gettn' no stall! The horsemen out here had to earn their licenses. They put in their time. You got in because of a loophole, and I don't like that, PIP—it's like ya cheated. Ya ain't proved yourself to nobody."

Kallie's not surprised by the racing secretary's attitude; she's come to realize that prejudice is part of a game that she's determined to win. Politely, she smiles, and replies, "We'll see."

When she returns to D-4, she tosses the bedding in the empty stall next to Wicked Punch, and moves him into it. Then she cleans the stall he's just spent the night in. When she's done, she sneaks away. A day later, she moves Punch to a stall in B-2, and the next, he's in C-1. Every day, he hides in a different stall. And so, with the Hawk never far behind, the game of *catch me if you can*, continues. The artful dodgers remain one step, and a day ahead of capture.

On Friday of the following week, Kallie works Wicked Punch again. They go five-eighths in fifty-nine and four-fifths—one tick short of the day's fastest work. A six-year old, graded stakes winner

297

from Kentucky shipped in during the week and got the bullet work. Had the two met in a match race, the homebred two-year old, would have been defeated by less than a length.

"That horse of yours has some class, PIP," Jake Witzman shouts to Kallie as he lopes up to chat before she leaves the out-gate. "*Alydarling* was only a fifth faster. He's earned more than four hundred thousand, and your baby almost put him away—hell-of-a-horse you got there, PIP. He's fast, real fast." He takes a long drag on his cigarette, hacks aside, and then adds, "Ya know PIP, you ought to consider applying for your bug license. Forget about all this training bullshit—I think you'd make a good jock. I'll give ya a recommendation to the stewards if you want… Think about it."

Glued deep in the saddle, Kallie smiles meekly, salutes Jake with her trembling riding stick as she exits the track, and then she shouts back to him, "Thanks Jake, I really needed to hear that right now. I'll let you know." But time is running out. "August fifth," she muses as she and Punch make their way along the crushed limestone bridle path. "Just a little over a month left before the track closes, and we still need one more work and a gate approval. That only leaves enough time for two races—he's got to break his maiden this year; he's just got to." Her mood turns grim, and the chill of honest fear—fear gained from experience—causes her to shiver before her thoughts wander on. "I don't want to work him from the gate; well, I want to, but I've never done it before; I don't know if I have the guts. I can show him the gates, and school him, but—oh shit—I don't want to get launched, anything can happen there. It's not worth it to me. I want him to get the best shot possible; shit, he's my derby horse; it wouldn't be fair for me to do it." Kallie reaches down, strokes his mane pensively, and wonders, "Should I ask a jock to do it? Maybe Earl the Squirrel would break him for me." She sighs a relieved breath, and then her inner voice attacks. "*Why is this happening to you, Kallie? What are you, a chicken shit? What will the Baron think; what will he say? Jake just offered to sign your ticket—you could get your bug—that doesn't happen every day. And dad, it will break his heart.* Shut up already. *God, Kallie, you've got a big mouth. For two years, all you've talked about is being a big-shot jockey—you want to ride in the derby—and now, when it comes to running with the big dogs, you pee like a puppy."*

Two years of instruction under the most able teacher, more time than that spent in reading and studying equestrian theory, almost a hundred and twenty consecutive days of training a racehorse, and it comes down to a momentary dispute that must be litigated in her soul—bravado and courage contend.

"I love riding so much—*Yeah, so much that every time you get excited, you pee your pants. It's disgusting.* I'll get over it—*If you have a diaper under you.* It's not the speed, that doesn't scare me; that's nothing, it's just nothing, nothing; it's like there's nothing there. I expected to feel something—the biggest rush—but I don't remember, it's like I go blank. Like when I crashed; when it was happening, it was like I wasn't even there—*You were in the zone Kallie; that's where champions play. Dad told you that.* I know, I know..."

As Kallie and Wicked Punch leave Nearco Lane, and enter the alleyway that leads to Winston's shed row, tears drip from her eyes; like droplets of morning dew that appear from out of nowhere and drench the summer grass, tears—soaking tears—drench her cheeks. Kallie weeps unobserved, and pleads silently, "Why, why the hell am I bawling? I've got a great horse—a really great horse. Sure, I got problems with the guys in the office, but they can't stop me from racing. I've got my license. I can ride, I can train, and I love it—God, it's so much fun. And babies, teaching a baby to do this work, that's where the rush is. Jockeys just ride a horse for a couple of minutes; for them it's just another ride, just a job—they don't do shit—and look at them, they're nuts, or assholes, and most of them are both. But a trainer, a trainer lives and dies with his horses. They panic when a baby's off its feed, or gets the snots. I've watched old guys puke when their horse snaps a leg and has to be put down—cripes—they turn into crybabies. And the jockey, he just walks away like its nothing—*It's part of the J-O-B, Kallie, you've got to ignore the risks.* Well, I can't do it, and I can't be that cold. I don't ever want to be that cold—*Then you can't be a jockey.* Oh God..."

299

Victor John Faith

The morning following his second official work, with the sun an anemic glow just below the horizon, Wicked Punch rests quietly in a usurped stall. Kallie arrives at the track early, very early, even before she goes to Winston's training farm to do her chores; she creeps through the waxing light to check Punch's condition. With the tenderness of a mother smoothing talc on a baby's behind, she rubs her palms up and down his shins; they show no signs of heat—heat would be an indication that trouble is brewing—and then, leading him in hand, she jogs him up and down the shed row to check for any sign of lameness; he shows none, but he doesn't go out to gallop. Instead, the he gets a day off—this is normal after a hard work—but Kallie doesn't, she's off to the farm to start her chores. As she dashes down the secret shed row from Punch's lair; she's quick and cautious, but not enough. Two strides before turning the corner to anonymity, a golf cart, bearing the Hawk rolls out from under cover. He spies Kallie's fleeing heels as they round a corner, and he identifies the fugitive who wears them.

"Ah-huh," he chuckles with sinister glee, "It just takes time, PIP. I told you I'd be there when you screwed up. Now I know what you're up to." Like a jailer counting heads, he surveys every occupied stall. Twenty stalls, twenty horses: one dapple-gray; one chestnut, and the rest, bay with black points. He consults his stall assignment list: a small booklet secured to a clipboard on the steering column. "D-3, east side," he whispers as the sun, now a crimson arch, sends its first rays of light scattering across the shed roofs. "Twenty stalls, nineteen assignments. Number twelve should be empty. Now whose horse do you think is in that stall, PIP?" The Hawk, wet with anticipation, stops his vehicle in front of number twelve, and hisses ominously, "Punch-ie, hey big boy. Punch-ie...." The horse inside the stall responds with a squeal and a fart before betraying himself with an appearance at the door. The Hawk coaxes on, "Punch-ie, do ya want a carrot?" Carrot is a word that Wicked Punch knows well, and so do most other horses. Eighteen bay heads with black manes and muzzles, one chestnut head, and one dapple-gray, emerge from the stalls to greet the Hawk, and the crime is solved. Punch nibbles innocently at the incriminating tidbit that Jim Peterson—the cunning Hawk—offers him. "Got ya, PIP," he giggles as Punch nuzzles him for another treat, but the Hawk doesn't offer more. Instead, he complies by scratching Punch's ears. "There, there," he whispers while performing the uncommonly kind act, and then he asks, "Do you like your Uncle Jimmy; do you like me scratching your ears?" He replies with a nicker, and presses the treat issue by inflicting a begging nudge. "No more treats big boy, we don't want ya to get fat…" He rubs more vigorously, and Wicked Punch sags like sweet chocolate in a loving hand. "Is your mommy a bad, bad girl? I think so. Uncle Jimmy is going to teach mommy a lesson. What do ya think, big boy; is that okay?" The Hawk's soothing talons are seductive, and the horse that farts fire is corrupted.

As Wicked Punch nickers contentment, the Hawk is distracted by the sound of approaching footsteps; he turns to glance along the shed row, and sees a heavy bodied woman of average height walking toward him. "Good morning, Jim," the woman says with a voice that's friendly and warm. "You're here early. Is something wrong; have you lost something?"

The Hawk knows this woman; other than Kallie, she's the only female trainer at the track. He has had dealings with her before, and they have all been pleasant. "Maybe, Kate," he replies with a smile that indicates he hopes for a closer friendship. "I was just looking at the stall assignments, and this stall is supposed to be empty…."

"It was last night when I left." Kate Finnegan says, shuffling to inspect the horse occupying stall number twelve. "Not one of mine—nice looking though, I wouldn't mind training on him." She moves away from the stall, yawns widely, and stretches by extending her thick arms high above her wavy hair while arching her back. The Hawk watches; at the extent of her reach, her sweatshirt lifts above the waistband of her jeans revealing a smooth, round tummy. To Jim Peterson, Kate Finnegan is as pretty as a woman can get. Her plump figure would make a flattering portrait within any gilded, baroque picture frame; he nearly swoons at seeing her full, exposed midriff, but out of shyness, he conceals his fondness for her. "Ah, oh…" she sighs when her back yields a stubborn pop, and then she returns to the subject, and asks, "Do you know who the horse belongs to? Did you check its tattoo?"

Still bewitched by the sight of Kate's naked tummy, the Hawk's answer is waylaid by a silent dream: *"Oh Kate, if I were younger, and better looking... Would you have me, could you love me?"*

"Jim?" she asks, intruding on his daydream.

Fantasy is as near to true love as the Hawk has ever come, and like a man who awakens from a whimsical slumber, he replies numbly, "Kate?"

"Did you check its tattoo?"

"Oh, um," he stutters, "I didn't have to, I know who owns him—the PIP."

"That pretty little girl who works for Winston?"

"That's the one. She was keeping this horse at his farm, and shipping it in every day to gallop. It looks like she got tired of hauling in and out, and decided to move in permanently."

"Clever girl..."

"Not that clever," he scowls. "I almost caught her at it last week, but she denied everything—she's a good liar too—almost convinced me. And since then, she's been changing stalls every day, dodging me every time I get close—little sneak. But now I got her; I'm calling her in. We'll see if a fine will teach her some respect."

Kate Finnegan knows that Jim Peterson is a bully, especially toward someone whom he judges to be a runt or weakling, and this is what she and most others find disagreeable about the Hawk. And although she thinks of him as being petty about enforcing the rules, and vindictive when challenged, she has also seen him secluded, late at night in his guard shack reading Hemmingway, and verse by Robert Frost, and that intrigues her. To this chubby woman of middle age, once divorced, and now a widow, Jim is an enigma. She's noticed how kindly he behaves toward the horses—scratching their ears, and giving comfort, and he always has a carrot concealed somewhere—but how callous and mean he is with people. It puzzles her, and Kate believes that a man who loves horses is redeemable, if he's prodded to improve.

Too Far A Dream

Kate turns and confronts him. Like a nun, berating a boy who's been caught misbehaving, she shakes her finger and scolds him. "Why are you always picking on people, Jim? Nobody respects you for it; nobody thinks more highly of you; it doesn't get you anywhere. Why don't you just talk to the girl? It won't hurt you to do that, see if something can be worked out that is good for both of you. You don't have to turn her in… and a fine? Well, that's just plain mean, it stinks, and I don't like it. For cripes sake, think about it, you don't get people to respect you by beating them up—especially a little girl—show some tolerance, a little kindness, or Jim, I can guarantee that you're going to be a very lonely old man." And then, turning her back to him, she stomps away.

The sudden flogging stuns the Hawk; inexperience with women has caused him to misjudge the effect his bluster would have. Instead of making him seem powerful and cunning, attributes he judged that Kate would find attractive, it just made him seem shabby and vile. He's dejected; the lovely Kate is hustling away from him; his cupboard of repentant words is bare, and he whines remorsefully, "Kate. Kate… Kate?" But his pleading is wasted, his regret, too late—too late for amends, but not redemption. Silently he considers her advice, and struggles with his conscience. "I can't just let her off… Sure she's a kid, but she's a trainer too, and she broke the rules. There are consequences for that. The whole game falls apart if people don't obey the rules. The rules protect everybody out here; they protect the horses, and they protect the traditions of racing. She's got to know that." He reaches into his pants pocket, and withdraws the tissue he uses to clean his glasses—his conflicted emotions tell on his face, and damp eyes have fogged the lenses of his spectacles. "I'm not a bad guy for doing my job—I'm not an asshole—maybe I am kind of tough, but I'm not mean. And so what if the guys out here make fun of me—I don't care—people have always made fun of me, I'm used to it." His brow knits as his private turmoil continues. "They should try doing this job, it's not easy, you don't make a lot of friends at it—friends expect favors, breaks, and that can't happen—ever. Maybe I do get lonely sometimes, sure, but it's a good job, I like it, and what I do is respectable and important. Kate knows that; the PIP has to know it too. I got to call her in—but not today. I got to sort this out." With his shoulders rounded and his head drooping, the Hawk slinks to the golf cart; groaning, he slouches behind the steering wheel, and ponders, "Maybe I should talk to her. She has to come back to feed and water her horse tonight, that might be a good time to clue her in that she's playing with trouble. But she is so stubborn. She'll never listen!" Immersed so deeply in his thoughts, he fails to notice that life is stirring in the shed row, but he's startled back to reality when he summarizes his thoughts by shouting aloud, "Shit!"

"They do that on their own, Jim," Kate Finnegan offers in casual reply as she waddles past pushing a wheelbarrow heaped with oats. And eighteen hungry bay heads, one chestnut, and one gray, respond with a ravenous stare.

When Kallie sneaks to Punch's stall later that evening, she finds an official looking notice taped to the stall door. In boldfaced type— large, black type—the heading announces: **SUMMONS**. Frozen rigid in horror, like a dissenting witness at a lynching, she gawks at the hanging text, and groans, "You knew it would happen Kallie; getting caught is part of the game." Under normal circumstances, she could crack a walnut in her little fist, but now, taking the summons in hand, her grip is frail. Trembling, she rips the seal; unfolds the notice and reads:

> Kallie May Phillipa:
> You are hereby ordered to appear before the racing secretary at ten o'clock, on the morning of August 7.
> Purpose: To answer allegations that you are occupying the private property of Dorchester Downs without proper authorization.
> Signed,
> James Peterson, Chief of Security.

From overhead, the amber sky drips a buttery glow on the tin-roofed sheds. The breath of evening, balmy, scented with oats and molasses, barely moves the dusty cobwebs hanging from the rafters. A weary groom, leading a beaten filly back from the seventh race, ambles by; the shuffle from the filly's hooves against the gravel surface, like the sound of aged ballerinas in toe-shoes, echoes softly and fades. Distracted, and detached from the scene, Kallie, ponders the unwelcome correspondence. "Every day it's another fight to prove myself," she sighs. Then, resting with her back against the shed wall, she slides into a resigned crouch on her heels. *"Pick a fight you can win before you put on the gloves,"* her inner voice advises. Kallie stares pensively at caramel-colored sun as it melts into the suburban prairie. "I'm ready to deal with this," she whispers looking back at the typewritten page she holds. "I started this fight…" And then, crushing the summons into a tight wad, she resolves defiantly, "and it's a fight I'm going to win."

At six-thirty in the morning on August 7th, Willie Dudley bulges from the entry of the racing officials' office, and plods his way toward a cluttered bulletin board in the outer lobby. As he approaches it, a jockey smaller than Willie's thigh, steps out of the way excusing himself.

"Sorry Willie, didn't hear you coming."

"What? Didn't ya feel the floor shaking, Mickey?" Mickey is unsure of Willie's mood, and rather than risk offending him, the tiny jockey remains silent. The big man grunts as he lifts his massive arm to post Kallie's summons on the board—even in the cool of morning, sweat marks his short-sleeved shirt. "When I walk around here, everything shakes. I'm four hundred and eighty-two pounds of manly flesh. I can blow down a mountain with a fart."

Now, sure of his mood, Mickey replies snickering, "I bet you could Willie—no chunks, just wind. And lots of thunder too."

"Women love that about me," he laughs holding his rolling belly with both hands. "Lots of me to love. By the way, how's that little sister of yours? Does she still wanna ride the white stallion?"

"Yeah," Mickey chuckles accepting the wisecrack. "But she said that it's hard to find a saddle big enough to fit a stud like you."

Mickey trembles under the weight as the giant wraps his huge arm around the jockey's shoulders. "You tell her to keep on looking, but if she can't find one, she can ride me bareback."

At nine fifty-five, Kallie opens the outer door of the administration building and enters the atrium. In the track cafeteria to her left, prep cooks and servers scurry removing the breakfast smorgasbord, replacing it with lunch—it's a hub-bub of scuttling workers carrying stainless steel chafing dishes, pots and pans to and from the kitchen. On her right, an agent scolds a jockey. Clad in leather chaps and a tie-dyed T-shirt, the colorful jock stares remorsefully at his feet as the agent brays, "You got suspended for twenty one days? Who'll pay the fine, how will we eat?" Undeterred by the discussion, Kallie marches to the double doors of the racing office. She pauses, reverses course, and darts into the bathroom. A moment later she emerges, returns to the double doors, and yanking one open, she enters the office lobby. Again she pauses. Men in cowboy hats, baseball caps, and racing helmets mill about, shuffle, or stand. Old men, tall men, young men, short men—every size and shape—men, only men, clutter the lobby. They cuss, scratch their private parts indifferently, yawn, belch and laugh, jostle and punch each other. "It's a boys club," she thinks, watching the antics. "It's a summer camp for bullies." Kallie glances across the room, and there, beyond the counter, against the far wall two prominent men stand and converse: the Hawk in uniform, and Willie Dudley, rotund and foreboding. "Let's do this, Kallie," she thinks as she stirs her apprehensive legs to move. One step, two steps, a third, each stride easier than the last. When she reaches the counter—her nemesis never out of view—she takes the rumpled summons from her hip pocket, lays it on the countertop, and queries, "Ah sir, Mr. Peterson, I'm here to see why you left me this note."

The sound of Kallie's raspy little voice strains to carry over the surrounding din, but it is heard by the intended ears. The Hawk turns, and locks Kallie in his telescopic sight; Willie Dudley folds his arms across his copious chest, leans against the wall, and stares at her. Neither man speaks; they just glower. Distance is no mediator; time,

Too Far A Dream

not a factor. The Hawk and Willie are eyeball to eyeball with the PIP. Seconds pass; no one blinks. More time passes; no one yields. Finally, like the rumble of magma welling from the pit of a volcano, Willie Dudley roars, "What'd ya say, PIP? I didn't hear ya! You're here to answer a SUMMONS?"

The rabble falls mute, and cowers; anyone standing near Kallie retreats; all activity ceases. The room is so quiet that the footsteps of a passing ghost would be detected. Kallie holds her ground, but offers no reply.

Willie waits.

The Hawk waits.

The rabble waits.

And then, Kallie cracks a devious smile. Taking all the wind stored in her miniature lungs she hollers back, "There might be a jockey out on the track that didn't hear you Willie, could you shout a little louder?"

Dreadful silence is the reply.

Beyond the counter, the Hawk gapes, his jaw hangs open, his eyelids flutter like butterfly wings.

Somewhere in the room, an ash drops from a lighted cigarette, it strikes the floor with a poof, the petrified crowd starts in alarm, and the leaning colossus bounds upright. "THE HELL YOU SAY!" he bellows, shaking the building with his reply. "Get your smart mouth into the hearing room—now, Phillipa!" Willie lifts his huge arm indicating the direction.

Kallie glances from side to side to make sure that all the quivering men are watching her—they are. Then she turns back to Willie, and chirps pleasantly, "Yup, everybody heard you that time, Willie. I'll be right there."

As Kallie saunters through the quaking throng, Bernadette Keats nudges her. Trembling, she warns Kallie, "You're dead PIP—dead."

"Not yet Bernie," she replies winking, "but if I don't come out in fifteen minutes, call the cops—no wait—they're the ones that called me in."

When Kallie enters the hallway that leads to the steward's office, the Hawk darts to intercept her; Willie, attempting to keep up,

307

rumbles behind, but like a steam locomotive on a steep grade, he chugs and gains little ground. "You got some guts, PIP, talking to the racing secretary like that; especially in front of all of the guys," the Hawk advises her in a tone of voice that expresses both trepidation and admiration. "He thinks you're a smart aleck, and that ya pulled some strings to train out here. He doesn't like you, and smart-mouthing him ain't gonna help."

"Sure it is, Jim," she snarls as they pass the cubbyhole assigned to the paddock judge. "If I don't stand up, he's going to bully me forever. And so are you. You've done nothing but give me crap since we first met."

"Maybe," the Hawk offers in timid agreement. "But still..."

"Maybe nothing! You're as bad as the rest of them—pick on the girl and see if you can make her cry. Yeah—big men, all of you, aren't you?"

Just before they reach the steward's offices, the Hawk stops, and gestures to Kallie that she should accompany him into a vacant room. An engraved brass placard on the open door reads: HEARING ROOM. The racing secretary trundles far behind. Kallie does as directed and enters the cramped, windowless cell. From the ceiling, a florescent light buzzes. A single, gray metal conference table with a gray, rubber, writing surface occupies the middle of the room. Arranged evenly around the table, six metal folding chairs—gray, and bruised from hard use—provide austere seating that only a spartan would enjoy. "Don't get me wrong, PIP," the Hawk whispers as they enter the room. "I ain't out to get ya. Really, I'm just doing my job. You gotta know that. It's tough out here. If ya cave in for even a second, the guys are gonna jump on ya, and then you're done—might as well pack up and go home. I'm just trying to help you..."

"Kiss it, Jim," Kallie snarls as she clanks down in a chair that faces the door.

"See—I don't even mind that you cuss at me; everybody out here does it. I know they ridicule me, crack jokes behind my back, and make fun of my glasses. I like it that the guys call me the Hawk; it's kind of like them calling you PIP. It's a good nickname—makes me feel proud..."

Too Far A Dream

Kallie is not swayed or moved by the Hawk's comments. She glares at him and thinks, "You pitiful, little worm. You're so full of crap."

"Sit down, Jim-bo," the racing secretary growls squeezing through the door, "let's get this thing started." The Hawk complies by taking a seat across the table from Kallie. Like a beached sea lion, Willie lugs himself around the table to a spot next to his henchman. Then, he takes two folding chairs, moves them close together, and eases down to sit, overfilling both seats. "Well, well, well... What have we here?" he quizzes sneering at Kallie. "Some smartass kid who thinks she runs the place. Ain't that so, PIP?"

Kallie sniffs compulsively at the stale air trapped within the tight quarters; she rubs her nose with her palm; then wipes away the dampness by brushing her hand against her thigh. With the self control of a hardened convict, she stares calmly at her accuser, but makes no reply.

"What's the matter, PIP, cat got your tongue? You got no smart answer for me? You're usually full of them." Willy scowls, and presses her sarcastically, "Ya aint' gonna start to bawl, are ya, PIP? Are ya gonna start bawling like a big cry baby?"

Kallie folds her arms across her chest; when she slips her hands into her armpits, her sinewy biceps swell within her short sleeves. She rests motionless before replying, "Am I here to answer some kind of charge Willie, or did you just call me in so you could pick on me?"

"Ah, there. See Jim-bo? I knew it wouldn't last. She just can't keep her smart mouth shut. Always with the lip, ain't ya Phillipa?" Kallie rubs her nose again, more vigorously this time; she re-crosses her arms, and sniffs. Willie, confident that she's ready to break into tears, leans toward the Hawk and grunts, "Tell the monkey what ya got on her before she bawls her eyes out."

But Kallie does not cry. Instead, she smirks and remarks caustically, "I think one of you guys could use a shower..." She looks first at the Hawk, then focuses her attention on the racing secretary, and says, "No, no... I think it's you, Willie—you need a shower."

Explosively, the racing secretary shoots to his feet; he bangs his hands flat on the table; the thunderous clap booms horridly.

309

Kallie stares in amazement, and wonders, "How did he do that? How'd he get up so fast?"

"That's it, Phillipa!" Willie, red-faced and jittering with rage, yells hammering the table again. "No more shit! I ain't taking no more shit from no piss-ant little girl." He wiggles furiously and jigs in place. "You're in big trouble you worthless piece of crap. Who the hell do ya think you are sneaking your horse into one of my stalls? We know what you been up to. You're done! Ooo…" he rants, "we got ya, PIP—you're a goddamn liar and a cheat, and I'm sick of your sass. Don't, don't get me pissed off…"

"Easy Willy, easy. Calm down," pleads the Hawk in an attempt to restore order. "Sit down, take it easy."

"Is everything okay in here?" Max Heppner asks, appearing in the doorway. "I heard some pounding. Is there a problem?"

"I got it under control, Max…" the Hawk answers.

Max Heppner looks at Willie who's red as a warning light, and still quivering with rage. The big man's shirt tails have come untucked from his trousers, and perspiration pours down his arms. "Okay Jim. Good. Take care of it…" he replies. Then glancing at Kallie, he shakes his head from side to side and thinks, "Oh yes, there is a problem." As he turns to leave, he adds, "Try to hold it down, Willie. If you need me, don't shout. I'm in the room right next door."

Once Max is gone, the Hawk snaps to his feet and pleads, "For Christ's sake, Willie, get control of yourself. Sit down, you're gonna have a freaking heart attack." As Willie descends to his chairs, the Hawk whispers to him, "Be careful. Watch what you say. You can't be spouting off like that. Now relax, I'll handle this." The Hawk remains standing, he takes two steps backward, leans with his back against the drab, ship-metal gray wall, and inhales a deep breath, composing himself. The racing secretary's anger ebbs, but it could erupt again without warning. Kallie waits. The Hawk tilts back his head, sighs, stares aimlessly at the ceiling, and wonders, "How do I do this without Willie killing her?" Kallie waits patiently. Finally, pushing off from the wall he steps to the table, and confronts her with his charges. "I gave you the summons because I found your horse stabled on the grounds, Miss Phillipa. Without an approved stall application, you cannot occupy stalls. The backside is private property, and you are trespassing. The track could prosecute you. Do you understand that, Miss Phillipa?"

Willie offers a condescending, "Harrumph."

Kallie, serene as an angel replies, "Yes sir, Mr. Peterson, I do."

"Good," the Hawk says, placing his hands on the tabletop, and then leaning closer to her, he gives solemn warning. "This is very serious, PIP. This ain't like breaking a rule, trespassing is a criminal offence—it's not handled by the stewards, you could go to court."

Her face shows no expression when she sighs, "Hum..."

"Ya better think about what you're gonna do here kid," grunts Willie. "Ya could go to jail. Sound good? You'd have to smart mouth me and Jim-bo from behind bars."

"Have the owners of the track ever prosecuted anyone for trespassing?"

"Um..." the Hawk replies hesitantly, "that's part of my job. As the chief of security, it's up to me to file the complaint."

"And do you take guys to court every time you catch them using stalls without authorization?"

"It don't happen that often..."

"Yes it does," Kallie rebuts sharply. "There are guys out here using twice as many stalls as they're supposed to. Do you want me to name names? Are you going to call them in; are you going to threaten them with jail, or are you playing favorites?"

"That's different," the Hawk retorts, stung by the charge. "Those trainers are out here earning a living—they got families to support. They applied for their stalls; they let me know when they ship in a new horse—there ain't no favors given to no one."

"It looks that way to me."

"You're wrong, PIP. Besides, those guys race their horses..."

"What," Kallie snarls sarcastically, "and I'm just out here for recess? I'm out here for the fun of it? You called me a sneak. Well— I'm not. I applied for a stall almost two weeks ago; it's on file, and it's time stamped..."

The Hawk is jarred; off stride, he fumbles, "Um—ah, ah..."

"Or maybe the rules have nothing to do with it. Maybe it's because they're men, and I'm a woman. You know, Mr. Peterson, maybe when you were a kid, they didn't have laws to protect women against discrimination, but they do now." With her arms still folded, Kallie rocks back on her chair, and squints menacingly at the Hawk. Before he can recover from her first salvo, she hits him with a second. "What do you think a judge would award a little girl for having to put up with harassment in the workplace, and sexual discrimination—three, four hundred thousand?"

Boiling, seething, Willie erupts. "You conniving little bitch! Are you threatening us?" he yells, pounding his fists on the table. "Like fuck ya are! Like fuck you're gonna tell us how to run the show! Nobody threatens us—no sir. You're just a no good little bitch—a sassy, little prom queen. Go back to the country club, you fucking…"

"SHUT-UP, Willie!" the Hawk shouts, restraining him from getting to his feet. "Keep your mouth shut; you can't talk like that!"

"He's doing a pretty good job of it," Kallie comments. "At least he knows how to use the 'F' word."

Willie rants, "YOU BITCH!" as he and the Hawk struggle.

"P-P-P-PIP stop it, please," he begs, gasping. "He's really pissed." Willie jostles wildly to free himself; like a cast horse in stall, he flails with all four limbs; the Hawk holds on. The table lurches, the unused chairs scatter, the Hawk pleads, "Willie cool it, cool down, we'll sort this thing out. For Christ's sake, com' on, quit fighting…"

Willie's agitation relents momentarily—just long enough for the Hawk to rush to the door and slam it shut—and then the racing secretary explodes again, "Ya ain't never gonna get any stalls out here; I'll have your fucking license; you'll never work in this business again. I'll blackball ya—you won't even get a job shoveling shit."

"We'll see," Kallie replies, taunting him.

"No! No you won't!" he curses. "I was a trainer for ten fucking years before I got stalls at the track. I had to train from the farm—lots of guys did—and you think you're gonna waltz in here and get a stall by threatening me—NO SIR! There ain't no stalls for ya here…"

"There are empty stalls all over the place. You're short of horses; you can't even fill the card. Last week you ran a race with four horses."

"Don't be telling me how to do my job, you little asshole." The buttons on his shirt strain as he gulps a deep breath, and shouts, "I don't need your horse—goddamn it—and I don't need your smart mouth. If ya want to race that nag of yours, do it somewhere else!"

Kallie glares coldly across the table at Willie—right dead center in his pupils—her stare could not be more piercing without being fatal. He stares back, but his madness is retreating; he blinks, then rests his broad forearms on the table in puddles of his own sweat. His breathing is rapid, irregular gasping. The Hawk sputters, his wind spent. Kallie hardly breathes at all. "Hum," she sighs, rocking forward on her chair to sit upright; she unfolds her arms and rests them on the table opposite Willie's. The Hawk, a haggard referee, plops into his chair. Like two boxers in between rounds, Kallie and Willie weigh the course of battle. For the moment, quiet rules.

"Oh shit. Was this a bad idea," the Hawk thinks, taking off his glasses to clean them. "There's no way this is gonna turn out good." He scrubs the lenses with a tissue from his pocket, and then hanging the frames on his nose, he hooks the wire bows behind his ears. "What do I do now?" he wonders. "If I charge her, or order her off the grounds, she sues us. If I don't do anything, it'll look like she beat us—SHIT—this is not good." The sound of Kallie clearing her throat interrupts his thoughts; he squints to focus on her, then on Willie; they both appear poised to resume sparring. "This is not good," he cringes silently.

"Are you going to act on my stall application, Mr. Dudley?"

"Ha!" he bellows, disbelieving his ears. "Haven't I made myself clear to ya; can't ya hear? No fucking stalls, PIP."

"That's not what I asked you, Willie. I asked if you're going to act on my application."

"Sure, yeah," he snarls, "when I'm goddamn good and ready. Does that answer your question?"

Kallie leans forward sliding her fists nearer to Willie's; her eyelids narrow to slits that reveal only her pupils; her nostrils flare

313

with each calculated breath—a mongoose is so disposed before it kills a cobra. Intimidated, Willie gives up an inch of tabletop—a trail of sweat marks his retreat. Her raspy voice gives way to disarming clarity as she cautions him, "Your time is up, Willie… According to the rules, you have seven days to act—not ten, not twenty. Seven days, that's all."

"Huh," he blubbers, "So what?"

Kallie inches even closer; her clinched fists enter no man's land. "So this," she mocks. "While you and Mr. Peterson call me in and accuse me of breaking the rules, you guys break them and don't care. Is it okay for you to ignore the rules?"

"What kind of bullshit are ya talking about? We ain't in violation here."

"Yes you are," she corrects him, sure and confident. "You didn't act on my application in a timely fashion, you've given stalls to horses with less qualifications, and you denied me my rights under the state-bred preference rule. That's three rules violations right there, and I won't even mention the harassment and sex discrimination—oh yeah—and Willie, you're rude too."

"Ha!" he yelps with a sarcastic laugh, "that's just a load of crap, PIP. Those ain't nothing but technicalities; we got plenty of leeway when it comes to interpreting the rules. I write the races, and if I think a horse is good for the card, I'm gonna let it in. And PIP, I don't give a fuck if ya think I'm rude…"

"Do you think the stewards would call them technicalities?"

Willy rumbles; he rocks back and forth from chair to chair, like tectonic plates along a rift, they split when he erupts. "Oh yeah—you bet!" he bellows, launching to his feet—the chairs crash against the floor; the Hawk is knocked off-kilter; Kallie is scorched by the fury and retreats for cover. "Ooo," he howls ascending to his full height, "that's it, asshole! No more 'mister nice guy'. I'm gonna have 'em jerk your ticket. Get up Phillipa," he yells, jabbing a porky finger in her shoulder. "I'm taking ya in to see Max Heppner, he knows how to deal with a smartass like you—oh yeah!"

Kallie chuckles, as much from embarrassment as from apprehension—the big man is out of control. The Hawk, regaining his balance, leaps and girdles Willie in an attempt to hold him from doing harm. "Willie! Willie!" he cries, his voice cracking under strain. "Willie!"

"No Jim-bo, no SIR!" he wails, tussling with the Hawk. "She ain't threatening me, she ain't gonna make no fool out of me..."

"We don't have to do this, Mr. Dudley. We can settle this. Max can't help you..."

"Like shit he can't, Phillipa!"

All of a sudden the door swings open. Kallie, defended by her chair, is pressed into the far corner; the Hawk and Willie are embraced in a polka; the table is askew, two chairs stand like pickets and three have fallen. "Did someone call my name?" Max Heppner— blazing scarlet necktie, stiff white shirt, and polished alabaster hair— asks from the open doorway.

"Not me," Kallie pipes meekly.

"Ya got to straighten this kid out, Max," Willie shouts, breaking free of the Hawk's clutch. "She's in here threatening us, says she's gonna sue us all, says I'm in violation of the rules." He lumbers around the table to face Max in the doorway, and plead his case. "Ya can't let her get away with it," he grunts short of breath, "ya got to pull her license. She don't belong out here. She ain't nothing but a smartass and a cheat. A disrespectful little smartass who thinks she owns the fucking place."

Max scowls, his thin lips form an angry frown, he glares at Willie and warns him, "Watch your language Mr. Dudley, there is a woman present."

The big man shrinks, and steps back cowering. "Ah-ah," he stutters, "ah, sure Max, sure. Sorry."

With the faultless wisdom of a regal eminence visiting a dungeon, Max enters the hearing room. Judge, jury, ax-man—ABSOLUTE POWER. If there were jail keepers, they would grovel; if there were inmates, they would beg; even the stale air bows before his over-powering cologne. Slowly, ever so slowly, he shifts his gaze from Willie, and casts it on Kallie. Cornered, she doesn't curtsy; she doesn't nod—noble heads greet eye to eye. "Miss Phillipa," he utters respectfully.

"Sir," she replies in kind.

Slowly—ever so slowly, he looks from Kallie to the Hawk. Still standing—his necktie rumpled, shirt wrinkled—the Hawk trembles, whipped and beaten. "Jim, what's this all about?" he inquires.

"Ah, ah," he babbles, "it's like Willie said. Honest Max. We called her in because she's been keeping her horse on the grounds, and then she says she's gonna sue the track for discrimination, and charge Willie with violating the rules." He collapses, exhausted and confused, into one of the few un-toppled chairs. "Honest Max," he sighs resigned, "I don't know what's going on. I ain't got a clue. It's a mess. Willie went berserk; started shouting; I had to hold him back." Max glances at the over-sized Willie, then back at the skinny Hawk. "Judging from their size," he thinks, "it must have been an uneven contest." The Hawk shakes his head from side to side, and adds, "Maybe you can make some sense of it—I can't."

Slowly, ever—so—slowly, the chief steward, rotates his gaze. Like the steady lamp in a lighthouse that illuminates a dangerous reef, he finds a wayward vessel: Kallie, buffeted, but still afloat. "Well, Miss Phillipa," he probes, "have you anything to say?"

She pauses to consider her response; softly, she leans into the corner, her shoulders bear against the cold cement blocks. She lifts her arms to fold them across her breasts, but her inner voice intrudes to stop her, *"No, no Kallie, crossing your arms is a defensive posture."* She stands upright weighing the effect that every pose may have: bold or timid, aggressive or meek, defiant or contrite? "How would the Baron stand?" she wonders, and then his words return to her: "You are a woman, Miss Phillipa, but you need not be meek." With a reserved, but confident gesture, she places her arms 'at ease' behind her back—her chin is level, but not jutting. Her shoulders are square, but supple. *"You've been here before Kallie,"* her inner voice advises. *"You picked this fight to earn their respect—you can't back down. Stay calm, breathe. And Kallie, there is a difference between being right, and being wise."* She takes a shallow breath, smiles piously, and replies, "I'm not going to argue with what Jim said about stabling on the grounds—I have been. It saves me about two hours a day that I'd spend driving, and it saves me the cost of thirty days board at the farm. That's money I can use for stakes payments and entry fees..."

"Those sound like fine excuses, Miss Phillipa. But you do know that you've been trespassing, don't you?"

"Yes sir, I do."

"And that it's against the law to trespass?"

"Yes sir, I do."

"Hum," he sighs thoughtfully, "that's not an offense I'd be involved in unless the track owners filed a complaint against you. Jim, is it the track's intention to file a complaint against Miss Phillipa?"

The chief of security snaps to attention, and replies, "I think this can be taken care of here, Max..." He glares a warning at Willie that says: We'll take care of this here!

"Like hell!" Willie grouses. "What about her mouthing off and threatening us? She said she was gonna sue us for..."

"That's something else, Willie," Kallie says, interrupting. "And I told you that I didn't think it was a good idea to get the stewards involved."

His interest piqued; Max questions her, "Why not, Miss Phillipa?"

"I don't mean to sound disrespectful sir, but you're not a lawyer, or a judge. The racing commission hired you to enforce the rules; you can't interpret them, except 'in conformity with applicable law'. Only a judge or the legislature can tell you what the law means, so you have to go by the book..."

"Yes, well, that's essentially correct."

"It is sir, I checked with the Attorney General, and it's in Chapter 7879 of the Rules." Max nods his head confirming silently, I'm sure it is. "What's happening here is that I'm having a disagreement with the racing secretary about how he's applying the rules. It has to do with the requirement that he act in a timely manner on my stall application, and his failure to comply with the state-bred preference rule." She stops and ponders whether to make her final charges. "And Sir— um—this is the part that's really—um—this is something that you can't decide, only a judge can..."

"Go on, Miss Phillipa."

"I believe the racing secretary and the chief of security are denying me my rights, and discriminating against me because I'm a woman—they've bullied and threatened me." She hesitates; her pious smile changes to a grim frown. "Sir," she continues, "the racing secretary called me a liar and a cheat; he made demeaning comments about my family, and he called me a F-ing bitch."

With a noise like a pestle crushing peppercorns in a mortar, the chief steward grinds his teeth, and snarls, "This is not something I want to hear."

"I could sue the track and the employees involved, and I might have the racing secretary charged with disorderly conduct, or maybe even fifth degree assault for touching me…"

The grave implication of Kallie's words strikes Max Heppner. His gray eyes crackle electrically; his cheeks flush; the muscles of his jaw twitch. He bristles, mulling over the options: *"She could win a discrimination lawsuit—shit—just bringing one would be a disaster; she'd probably name me too—Christ, it stinks in here."* He scowls at the racing secretary; Willy fidgets tucking his drenched shirt tails into his trousers. *"Seven days, he has seven days to act on an application—half the stalls are empty—if he's exceeded the time limit, he's going to pay for it. This could have been so easy if he'd just given her an approval—stupid, just plain stupid. I've got to make this go away."* He takes his reading glasses from his shirt pocket, and hangs them on his nose. Then, reaching into the front pocket of his creased khaki slacks, he takes out a pocket-sized copy of the 'Rules of Racing' and flips the pages. *"What the hell is the number of that preference rule?"* Desperate, unable to locate the statute, he glances to Kallie, and asks, "Miss Phillipa, what chapter is the preference rule?"

"Chapter 7876, subpart 7."

"Thank you." Max leafs through the pages to Chapter 7876. As he reads, his scowl deepens. "Mr. Dudley, are you in possession of a stall application filed by Miss Phillipa?" he asks, closing the rulebook and sliding it into his pocket.

"Yeah Max," he replies tersely, "I am. I ain't had time to act on it yet."

Calmly, and with self-assurance he removes his reading glasses; folding them, he holds them in his closed hand. "I won't be disrespected by you, Mr. Dudley, this isn't a circus, it's a hearing. You'll address me as Chief Steward Heppner. Do you understand?"

Intimidated, Willie quivers, and when he answers, "Yes Sir—sorry," his breathing comes in ragged gasps. The Hawk lifts an overturned chair from the floor, sets it upright and advises, by nodding, that the racing secretary should sit. "Um, thanks Jim," he grunts, smothering the chair with his wide bottom, then he shifts side to side to distribute his weight. After a moment, the racing secretary leans back, rests his arms atop his belly and sighs.

Max directs his attention to Kallie—her posture is unaltered—and he resumes his questions. "How long ago did you file your application, Miss Phillipa?"

"Fourteen days sir."

"Fourteen days. You're sure?"

"I got it time stamped by the racing secretary—I'm sure."

"Your horse is a two-year old state-bred maiden?"

"Yes sir."

"A non-starter—it hasn't raced yet?"

"Yes sir, it's a non-starter," she replies calmly, "but we have two official works, and I'm starting his gate approval this week."

The chief steward turns to Willie, and squinting, he asks, "Mr. Dudley, are there any open company, two-year old non-starters stabled on the grounds?"

"Um, maybe a few…"

"A few?" Kallie jabs sarcastically. "Maybe? Bertram Story has twenty stalls, and he's started only six horses all season. Everything in his barn is a Kentucky, or Florida-bred maiden. Half of them haven't even worked yet. He's using this place as a training farm—he gets all the stalls he wants, but us local trainers can't even get in the gate. It's not fair, and it's against the law."

"Bullshit! What a load of crap."

"Shut up, Willie, she's right," barks the chief steward. "She does have preference, and you're in violation on two counts of the rules, maybe more." He takes aim at the Hawk next. "Mr. Peterson, some serious accusations have been made about your conduct. Is any of it true? Have you, or Mr. Dudley threatened Miss Phillipa, or used obscene language at any time in your dealings with her?"

Jim Peterson replies with a muffled, "Yes."

"Yes what?" he growls.

"Both, sir…"

The chief steward sighs ominously and stares down at his wingtip shoes—the straight crease of his slacks reflects in the polished toes. Silently he stews, *"Is she that clever? It's just too neat, too perfect, and they're not that dumb. Has she planned this; did she set us up?"* He smiles invisibly as he answers his question: *"She has a good teacher—no one was better at scheming than my stepbrother."* Finally, without looking up from his shoes, he asks, "Miss Phillipa, could you please excuse us for a minute? You can wait in my office. And… will you close the door as you leave?"

Willie and the Hawk watch apprehensively as Kallie scuttles out. Max continues to focus on his shoes. She shuts the door, and wanders from the gloomy hearing room into the steward's office—the sudden, blinding daylight staggers her. "Good morning, Kallie," a familiar voice salutes her through the glare. She shades her eyes and sees Eddie Cantrell seated at his desk.

"Hi, Eddie," she says returning the greeting. "How you been?"

"Good, real good. Having a little trouble in there are you? It sounded like you guys were wrecking cars or something."

"Nah," she chuckles, "the boys were just telling me how the game is played. I don't know, maybe I'm a slow learner 'cuz I'm a girl, but I think it's being sorted out." Her eyes adjust to the light. Glancing around the office, she asks, "Mind if I sit down, Eddie? The chief steward asked me to wait for him in here."

Eddie responds with a cozy smile, "I sit all the time and no one complains. Grab that chair by Max's desk and pull it over here so we can talk." While Kallie goes after the chair, Chuck Wallace dashes to the hearing room. He knocks on the door; the door opens; he hands a document to the chief steward, and the door closes. "Something's up, PIP," Eddie reports as Kallie plinks down beside him. "Chuckles just delivered some evidence."

Straight-facing the news, she replies, "Not on me, I'm clean."

"You don't have to convince me, PIP. I don't know why, but I think it would be pretty tough to get anything on you—you just seem to be a couple steps ahead of everyone else."

A chill of apprehension grips Kallie, she's unsure of Eddie's meaning, and replies cautiously, "It sounds like you suspect me of something."

"I suspect you of good planning, studying, and I suspect that you work hard."

"Um-oh, okay. I think that's good, don't you?"

Eddie raises a feeble hand to the joystick of his wheel chair—an electric motor whirs, and the chair rotates to position Eddie facing Kallie. "I also suspect that you have some talent," he continues. "What's the name of your horse, Wicked Punch? Good horse. I was in the timer's booth when you worked him the first time. A very nice ride—smooth, quiet—there aren't many riders who make it look that easy. You're very good."

Embarrassed by the complement, Kallie trembles shyly. Thanks, Eddie. Um, really, thanks."

He stares intimately into her eyes—shared experience permits such a gaze. His voice is soft, soothing when he asks, "You were in 'the zone,' weren't you?"

Kallie blinks, but her focus is steady. "Ah-huh," she replies with a dry whisper.

"Was it what you expected?"

"Um…"

"It's like everything and nothing, all at the same time—speed, danger, comfort, peace—like free-falling through clouds, flight without fear, joy without memories…"

"It's just like that, Eddie."

"And then, you hit the ground," he says, his voice trailing off.

Kallie sighs, "Yeah, it's nice 'til then."

321

Eddie glances away, and looks out the sunny window. Helpless to prevent tears, his moist eyes sparkle. "I'm not sure I miss it. It was fun—being a jockey—but I think, in this chair, I'm less handicapped now than when I rode. I'm happier, I enjoy living a lot more, I don't worry about what people think." He looks back at Kallie who's shaken by his words, but betrays no emotional clue. Eddie's voice takes on a more melancholy tone as he talks on. "I don't worry about dying anymore. I was close; I was almost killed when I fell. I knew how bad I was hurt; I didn't think about it. I pulled it together and survived. It's funny—all I wanted to be is a jockey, but now, I wouldn't trade the life I have for that one. I know you've thought about it, I can tell by the way you ride—grace in the saddle, nerves of steel. Are you going to apply for a bug license? You're good enough."

"I have thought about it," she replies, "I've thought about it a lot. Ever since I was little I wanted to be a jockey. When mom brought my first horse home, all I did was ride. I pretended I was Gary Stevens, I even pretended I was you. That's the reason I came out here, to be a jockey. That's the real reason why I disguised my horse and used a bunch of fake names, so Jake Witzman would see that I could ride and recommend me for a license. I love to ride, but after being out here and learning what racing is all about, I think—no…" she pauses thoughtfully and corrects herself, "…I <u>know</u>, I like training more."

"You're a very good rider…"

"It's not the kind of life I want to live."

"You could be very successful as a jock."

"I can be a successful trainer, too."

"Training doesn't pay much," he replies, glancing at the door, and then he whispers to her, "Max and the boys are coming out."

Kallie stands up from her chair and resumes her 'at ease' pose. The chief steward, squinting from the sunlight, approaches; the Hawk and Willie follow him close behind.

Respectfully, she greets Max Heppner, "Sir."

"Miss Phillipa," he replies handing her a copy of her stall application. "The racing secretary apologizes for delaying action on your application, and although it's overdue, he's given you approval to occupy the stall your horse is stabled in. No complaint will be brought against you by the track's owners." The expression on his face is one of restrained pleading as he says, "I hope this will settle the issues of preference and due process we discussed."

Kallie stares at the application, her grin is so wide her tongue is visible through the gap in her front teeth, but she controls her excitement, and answers, "I won't press the other issues, sir."

"One more thing, Miss Phillipa, these two gentlemen have something to say to you." Max turns around and signals with his finger that they should approach. The Hawk steps double-quick; Willie plods as quickly as he can. "Gentlemen," he prompts them, "say what you have to say."

The Hawk recites his speech first: "Miss Phillipa, I sincerely hope that an apology from me will be accepted. My behavior was unprofessional, and I treated you unfairly. I'm sorry, I apologize." He extends his hand in a gesture of good will. Kallie hesitates; her inner voice chimes in, *"There is a difference between being right and being wise,"* and Kallie responds by accepting Jim Peterson's handshake.

Willie speaks next. "Miss Phillipa—um—I sincerely hope that an apology from me will—um—be accepted. My language was offensive—um—and unprofessional, and I treated you unfairly. I'm sorry." Max Heppner glares at him and Willie adds, "Um—I apologize, and I'm real sorry for poking ya with my finger." He holds out a flabby paw, and Kallie shakes it.

"Does that conclude our business, Miss Phillipa?" Max inquires.

"Yes," she replies, holding back her glee, "and thank you for intervening."

As Kallie leaves the stewards office, Eddie Cantrell calls to her, "Good luck PIP, think about what I said."

Later in the afternoon, Max Heppner walks from his office, and posts a notice on the bulletin board in the lobby. It reads:

NOTICE OF FINDINGS:

It is the finding of the Stewards that Willis Richard Dudley has conducted himself in a manner unbecoming a Racing Secretary. He has been found to have violated Chapter 7876.0100, subparts 3, and 7 of the Rules of Racing.

Willis Richard Dudley is hereby ordered to pay a fine in an amount of $250.00 for each of the two counts.

Signed: Maxwell Heppner, Chief Steward.

* * *

Fifteen: Bob and Sid

With the end of the race meeting approaching, Kallie cannot afford the luxury of dallying. During the next seven days, she readies Wicked Punch for his gate approval, and his final official work. For the first time in the long process of training, she begins to take shortcuts in an effort to compress her schedule—small shortcuts. She quits disguising Wicked Punch as Shady Character, and Two-dollarbilly. And at the training farm, she gives two of her more experienced rides to a novice galloper so she can get to the track half an hour earlier, and spend the time training at the starting gates.

Under normal circumstances it will take two weeks to school a young horse through the starting gates, and it's very dangerous work. For everyone involved, the starter, the handlers and the rest of the gate crew, the risks are enormous. But for a jockey, it's like sitting in a cramped, one hole privy with half a ton of dynamite in the crapper—you want to do your business, and get out before the load detonates. Most of the time, luck rides with the jock, but sometimes it doesn't, and a race meet seldom passes without the rueful visit of tragedy—it's not a matter of if, but when, it will arrive.

Kallie is patient and methodical in her task. The first day, she and Wicked Punch approach to within twenty feet of the starting gate—a huge, mechanical contraption on wheels; twelve chutes wide, made from tubular steel and gleaming, enameled sheet metal. Across the front of the behemoth are twelve trap doors with iron bars; lining the rear are spring-loaded shutters that lock in place. It's awesome, intimidating, and it's abuzz with activity. When a horse approaches, men scurry to assigned positions, and act with precision. Everyone is smoking a cigarette or spitting sunflower seeds. They bark at one another, but work together. There are no slackers on the gate crew. Kallie and Wicked Punch survey the scene calmly; they observe everything. They watch as an older mare, on the *Steward's List* to be re-schooled, fights to escape her lesson—a tightly wound ball of frightened muscle, she bays madly; her eyes wide and blind from horror, she crow hops in aimless circles. "Get another lead rope on her," Bill Hicks, the outrider stationed with the gate crew shouts from behind the spinning horse. A skinny, agile man, lunges from the right, and clips a second rope on the mare's bridle. "You got her, Butch?" Hicks quizzes from horseback.

"Yeah, got her," he yells while he and the header on the left struggle to quiet the frantic horse.

The anxious jockey coos, "Easy little girl, steady..."

"Good. Now walk her, and I'll come in from the rear. Ted, you and Joey flank her ass and lock her up." Ted and Joey do as told, but as soon as they link arms behind the mare's rump, she kicks out delivering a shot, point blank, to the chest of Bill Hicks' horse. Bill's horse exhales its wind, and the mare starts bucking. The jockey grabs a hank of mane, and sits tight. "The som-bitch kicked my horse!" roars Hicks. The mare bucks viciously. "The freaking whore kicked my horse. The som-bitch 'bout killed me..."

"Hicks!" the starter yells from the rail. "Quit yapping and get in there."

Hicks dashes to the rescue.

"Back off Hicks," the jockey shouts. "I'm not getting paid by the hour. We're going to do this right if it takes all morning."

"What ever ya say Squirrel," Hicks shouts, retreating, "You're the one riding that pig..."

"Butch, Freddie, let her go, I need some room to dance." The headers release their lead ropes, and Earl Donnbury trots the nervous mare in a steady loop large as a half a tennis court. Kallie and Wicked Punch watch. Once around the loop, twice around. As Earl the Squirrel finishes the second loop, he yells to Kallie, "Hey, hey you. You going to school that horse through the gates?"

"We're here watching, that's all—maybe tomorrow...."

"You're the PIP, right?" he asks cutting in, and riding a small circle around her. "Got to do it sooner or later PIP, might as well be today. I need your help. Come on. Trot along side of me."

Kallie hesitates, but Wicked Punch springs to action and follows the lively mare. "Oh crap..." Kallie gulps wondering, "Who's riding who?"

Too Far A Dream

Rising the trot, she and Punch quickly pull even with Earl the Squirrel, riding again on the large loop. He looks over and winks, and then in a tone as cool as a winter breeze, he says, "Nice to see you again, PIP."

"Yeah, hi Earl," she replies, her raspy voice parched.

"You got a good horse there, I've been watching him work—fast. Will he walk through the chute?"

"I think so...."

"Good." At the top of the loop, Earl whispers, "Walk now..." Wicked Punch does as told. Kallie's knees chatter when she sits on the saddle. Earl Donnbury gives instructions, "As we get close to the gate—about thirty feet away—take the lead, walk straight at the open hole. Quickly, but don't rush. I'm going to be right on your ass—don't hesitate. Go through like you mean it. It'll give my horse confidence."

"Okay."

"When you're through, trot and come around again—got it."

"Yeah."

"We'll do it a couple of times." The gates tower fifty feet ahead. "Hicks, get in front of the gate so the horses can see you on the other side of the hole." Bill Hicks gallops to the front and takes a prominent position. "Butch, Freddie, and the rest of you guys," he yells to the gate crew, "stand back, but keep loose."

"I don't like this Squirrel," the starter shouts.

"I'm taking this mare to reform school, Buckshot, not the penitentiary—trust me." The gates loom thirty feet ahead. "Go on PIP," the Squirrel says with a nod, "make your move."

This is not the time to pee, but Kallie wants to. *"Not now PIP,"* her inner voice scolds her. *"You got a J-O-B to do."* Kallie relaxes. A sense of order and rightness calms her. She feels the Squirrel's horse nudging Wicked Punch's rump; she glues her focus on Bill Hicks beyond the gate; steadily, assuredly she marches at the open hole. Ten feet, five feet, in and out. "Yes-yes-yes!" she squeals elated.

"Save it PIP," the Squirrel barks. "Trot on!" And away they trot to have another go. For Kallie, the second time is just as delightful. For Wicked Punch, it's *a walk in the park*. "Good, that's fine PIP," he says before Kallie can break to trot again. "Fall behind, and park by the rail. This time I load and go." He stands up in the irons and trots the big loop. Drawing near, he shouts at the gate crew, "Close the hole, we're loading…" Two men scurry to the front trap doors. "Wham! Clank!" they sound, slamming in place. Joey takes the headman's post; he darts inside the chute, and standing on a tiny perch at the front, he prepares to steady the horse's head. Twenty-five feet from the gate the Squirrel walks the mare and yells to the starter, "Buckshot! Ring the bell and open quick, she's still pretty sour."

Poised with an electric control switch in his hand, Buckshot yells in answer, "Will do Squirrel, but if she acts up again, we do it my way!"

Freddie and Butch—one at a rear shutter on either side of the hole—stand ready.

Ten feet away, and Earl the Squirrel glances at Kallie and Wicked Punch looking on from the far end of the starting gate, and hollers to them, "Thanks PIP, I owe you one." He stares straight ahead, sits deep in the saddle, into the privy he goes. The shutters close. An instant becomes infinite. The starting bell blares. The trapdoors blast open.

"Haw! Go-go!" Joey shrieks. Aluminum horseshoes claw the track. Muscles uncoil. Limbs flail. Dirt explodes everywhere, and away streaks the Squirrel aboard a hurling powder keg with hair.

As placid as a cow that's done grazing, Wicked Punch looks on. "Well, I've seen enough," Kallie whispers while rubbing his supple neck, "Tomorrow we'll walk you through again." And tomorrow, and for several days after, she does.

Thursday August 14th, two hours past midnight. In the Belleview warehouse district, the steamy air of dog days hangs like choking smog; the cobbled stone streets and avenues are clad in sweat. Above the kitchen entry at the rear of the Gasthaus Jägermeister a neon sign flickers its message: Closed. A half block away, on the corner of Commerce Avenue and South 24th Street, a stoplight flashes a silent warning. From two blocks away, in the rail yards along the river,

Too Far A Dream

comes the clank and rattle of boxcars being coupled—the muffled drone of a diesel train engine swells and fades. From farther off rolls the mournful sound of a barge horn wailing an alert to floating traffic up river. Commerce Avenue is empty, 24th Street, deserted. The still night wears like a heavy coat.

The kitchen door swings open and a muted silhouette emerges from the Gasthaus—Morgan Marie Jasperson has finished her shift. Dressed in her waitress uniform, she walks alone across the parking lot to Commerce Avenue and heads south. At South 24th Street she turns left. Ahead of her loom the abandoned brick, and stone warehouses that line the rail yards—imposing vaults without currency—beyond them lies the river. She walks one block, turns left onto Waterfront Avenue and ambles north toward the crumbling Steinkeller Brewery. A block later, she's gone full circle and reached the brewery and the far rear entrance of the Gasthaus' parking lot. Morgan stops and waits motionless beyond the glow of a buzzing street lamp—its feeble light hardly penetrates the cloak of gloom. Ahead, tucked obscurely in a seedy loading bay of the ruined brewery is a rusty, sub-compact station wagon; only its rear end is visible—an eyesore punctuating overwhelming blight. The buzzing street lamp flickers, falls silent and dims to a snuffed ember. "Right on time," she whispers, crouching like a soldier under fire, "just like clock work."

Hidden by shadow, disguised by shade, Morgan sneaks to her car. She opens the hatchback, and from underneath her sleeping bag she takes a tattered pair of cut-off jogging pants. The street lamp buzzes, and then beams anemic light—swarming mobs: moths and flying insects dive helter-skelter at the artificial flame and sound a "ping" when repelled by its glass shield. She reaches underneath the puffy skirt of her waitress' uniform, and pulls off her pantyhose and underwear. "Oh God," she moans relieved, tossing the undergarments into the car, "I know a man invented these things; a woman would never come up with anything so painful." Leaning against the bumper, she steps into the cut-offs, pulling them up under her skirt; she unbuttons the collar of her stained blouse, and then standing, she removes her skirt and crumples it into a tight bundle. As she climbs inside the unlit car, she takes her work clothes with her, and sighs from fatigue, "Oh boy, do I need a beer right now." Morgan knows where everything she owns is; rummaging through her belongings to find a hidden cooler, she grumps, "I've been waiting all night for this." She pushes the cooler nearer the open hatch, crawls out of the car, opens the cooler, takes out a can of beer and a pack of cigarettes, and sighs as longingly as a spurned girl with a crush, "If I only had some ice—oh well, warm beer is better than no beer." She lights a cigarette, opens a can of beer and gazes through the sweltering night at the Gasthaus parking lot—squiggly heat radiating from the asphalt desert distorts her view. "Ah," she sighs, sipping contentedly, and rubbing her stinging eyes, "beer never tasted better."

A long, low white sedan cruises slowly along Commerce Avenue; it pulls into the Gasthaus parking lot, circles the lot once and stops. The headlights go off, the engine stops. The dome light goes on as the driver's door opens; a dog yaps, and a man gets out. Morgan sits with her feet dangling from the hatchback, she gulps her beer, drags on her cigarette, and spies unnoticed. The car door creaks, and bangs shut; the dog yaps again, and the man, leading a leashed dust mop, walks to Commerce Avenue, turns south, and disappears behind the untrimmed hedgerow that borders the sidewalk. The dust mop yaps in the distance.

"Belch!" Morgan replies, answering the dog, then she crushes her empty beer can and pitches it overhand toward the gangly shrubs beside the brewery. "Plink!" it reports hitting the soot-stained limestone wall beyond. She takes a long, last drag on her cigarette and flicks the lighted butt twirling at the parking lot. She opens another beer, and sips.

The dog yaps in the distance. The barge wails sorrowfully from the river.

"Camping out ain't so bad," she muses, comforting herself, "A hell-of-a-lot better than living at home, or getting beaten up by some drug dealer's girlfriend—Christ it's hot, I'd give anything to have a cold shower." She un-fastens two more buttons of her blouse and pulls the collar wide open. The distant sound of the dog's yapping echoes from the limestone ruins along Waterfront Avenue—it's a wheezing sound like a flock of sheep with emphysema. Morgan lights another cigarette, and blows a smoke ring, a wispy phantom that floats in the listless air. "A queer and his faggot dog..." she whines sarcastically, spitting out a tobacco fragment.

A train's whistle blares in the rail yards. The dog yaps from somewhere nearby—too near for comfort.

Cautiously, Morgan slides from her rusty apartment, and takes several hesitant steps toward Waterfront Avenue. Peering south down the empty avenue she sees nothing. She brushes her dark hair from her shoulders; she holds her breath; she listens—nothing. She returns to her hatchback, sits alert, and waits. In the parking lot, a car door squeaks, the dome light in the white sedan goes on. Morgan turns startled, and watches. The dog yaps from inside the car. The door slams, the light goes out. "Good riddance," she thinks placing her beer can on the dirty pavement, and then adds aloud, "Ooo, nature calls..." Softly, she treads to the gangly shrubs beside the brewery and slips in behind them; she takes down her jogging shorts, squats and sighs, "Ah." (Morgan is not the only guest that frequents this toilet—the stench of urine is thick enough to taste.) Her business finished, she stands, pulls up her shorts, and then pats the fabric against her groin to dry herself. She returns to the hatchback and stares at the parking lot. The white sedan has not moved. The dog is quiet. A cigarette lighter flashes in the shadow behind the Gasthaus; an ember glows; a puff of smoke drifts from an invisible mouth; the burning cigarette waltzes side-to-side approaching—it never leaves the shadow, and dances on silent feet.

Morgan knows where all her belongings are—she's at home. She picks her beer can from the ground, and sits in the open hatchback. Reaching deftly behind her back, she feels among her rumpled wardrobe for her folding pocketknife. She finds it. The burning cigarette comes closer. At the edge of the shadow it emerges, followed by a man wearing tennis shoes. Morgan studies him calmly. He's thin, with thin hair. Five feet, ten inches tall, "maybe six feet," she thinks. His clothing fits like old pajamas—loose and un-constricting. The dark hides his features. She clutches her knife and sips her beer.

"Hi," the man says from ten feet away, and then stands motionless awaiting a reply.
Living on the streets has taught Morgan to suspect every visitor. "Hi," she answers cautiously. Absent from her voice is any emotion that may betray interest or a weakness.
"Kind of hot tonight, isn't it?" he asks, taking the cigarette from his mouth and dropping it to the ground.
"It's August…"
The man grinds the smoldering butt with the sole of his sneaker, and replies with disarming warmth, "Yeah, I don't think it will snow tonight." He walks half the distance to her, and stops. Something bulges from under his left arm. "I was out walking my dog…"
"I saw you," Morgan interrupts curtly—her fatal hand ready to act.
"…I noticed you back here when I was over there by the dumpsters." Morgan glances at the overflowing dumpsters near the back of the parking lot. The buzzing street lamp is right there casting dim light from overhead, but volunteer elms, buckthorn and thick brush conceal the trash in darkness. "My dog likes to do his job by the bushes. It's kind of—you know?—like his place. Anyway, I saw you and thought you might like some company, maybe something cold to drink. I've got a six-pack, do you want to share it with me?"
"<u>Cold</u> beer…" she thinks, tossing her warm one into the grungy loading bay. "Yeah," she answers eagerly, "a cold beer would be good." The tense grip on her knife softens. As the man approaches, Morgan is able to see his features more clearly—middle aged, with a flat chest and a weak belly. "Somebody's daddy out cruising," she says to herself when he offers her the beer. Her knife is idled; she accepts the beer, and pops the ring-top. The hiss of airbrakes in the rail yard mimics the sound of the pressure released from the can when it opens. She sucks the foam, and gulps. "Oh Christ, does that taste good, or what," she sighs, wiping her cooled lips on the rolled up sleeve of her blouse. The man pulls another can from the plastic retainer of the six-pack, and sets the others on the ground just outside the hatchback. Standing three feet away from Morgan, he stares as she swabs her forehead with the cold can, and then leers—the collar

of her blouse is open wide; her dark hair is swept back exposing her naked shoulders; her brassiere is dimly visible, and her pale skin oozes beads of perspiration. Morgan nestles the can in between her breasts and shivers provocatively, "God that feels so-oh good."

Scarcely containing his drooling interest, he replies, "It looks like it feels great—wish I could be that beer...." Morgan shies at the comment; lowering the chilly can to her lap, she wiggles her head swishing her hair to conceal her bare shoulders. The man glances away. With a manicured fingernail, he taps the lid of his beer can nervously as a distraction, but leaves it unopened, and then he asks, "What's your name?" Morgan knows better than to be forthcoming, and assumes an aloof attitude—looking off at the buzzing street lamp and sipping beer—but she does not rebuff him. He sees that she's uneasy, and laughs in an attempt to reassure her, "We're having a drink together; I'm harmless; I've got kids your age—a daughter that's nineteen. Come on, we might as well be friends—you know—make some conversation, shoot the breeze a little. Besides, we got four more beers to drink, it would more fun if I knew your name." There's a comforting honesty in his manner and voice when he volunteers, "Um—look, if it will make you feel better, my name is Bob. Come on, say it—Bob."

Morgan's suspicion eases, and she smiles. "He's cool," she thinks, but she does not give her name. Instead, she replies politely, "Nice to meet you Bob, your beer couldn't come at a better time—thanks. Mine was like drinking warm piss, the ice in my cooler melted, it doesn't last long in this heat." And then she lies, "My name is Sadie, but everybody calls me Sid..."

"Sid," he says, repeating the name as if it were the first word in a Spenserian sonnet, "Sid, Sid—I like that—Sid."

"Easy to remember, huh Bob? Look," she says, gulping the last of her beer, "you got another one of these little fellas?"

Bob bends down and retrieves the remaining cans. "Sure, I got four of them," he says, slipping the unopened can into his pants pocket. And prying another can free from the plastic fastener, he offers it to Morgan, "Here ya go, Sid."

"Thanks, Bob."

"Mind if I sit down, Sid?" he asks flexing like a gymnast doing shallow jumping jacks, "My knees are killing me. That mutt of mine about ran my legs off. He's a good little hound, but he needs some schooling—maybe a lot of schooling. He's real friendly though. I call him Moses—you know?—from the Bible. Because he barks like he has a lisp. I read somewhere that Moses had a lisp—funny huh?"

"It looked like you were chasing a dust mop," Morgan replies, patting the edge of the hatchback as an invitation.

Groaning softly, Bob plops down beside her and puts the remaining beers between them. Morgan opens her can and sips. Underneath Bob, her knife is trapped. The street lamp flickers and dims. Neither Bob, nor Morgan speaks; neither moves. For a moment, the night is dead quiet—pregnant with potential. The light buzzes and flashes to life. "It gets kind of dark back here when that happens, huh?"

"That's a good thing, Bob..." she replies, "Good things happen in the dark." He turns apprehensively, looks at Morgan, and is greeted with a jaded expression: lifeless eyes, a joyless heart, and discarded conscience. He's confused, unguarded and unprepared. "So Bob," Morgan asks as coldly as a banker calling a loan, "What do you want to do now?"

The initiative transposed, he stumbles, "Um, ah.... Are we talking business?"

"You got it, Bob. What are you here for? Are you thinking about having sex with a little girl? Do I remind you of your daughter?"

"No! Shit no!" he gasps, jogged by Morgan's comment. "God—that's a filthy thing to say. I figured that maybe you were working, but you don't have to talk so dirty—Christ, you're so young."

"Sure Bob, I'm just a little girl..."

"No, really. That's disgusting. I'd never let my kid talk like that."

"Yeah, so, do I have to pay you for the beer, or do you want something else, Bob?"

"You're just a kid..."

Morgan leans toward him fluttering her made-up eyes and murmurs, "And I got bills to pay. Don't be shy Bobby—I know you were cruising, admit it." Like kneading taffy in her fingers, she fondles his groin. "I forgive you—tell your little girl what you want." Replaced by swelling lust, the sting of shock fades. Bob stutters, "Um, okay, sure. Yeah sure, I'll tell you what I want. I figured that maybe I could get a blow job or something…"

"That'll cost ya thirty bucks, Bobby," Morgan coos, reaching for his zipper.

"Thirty bucks!"

"I swallow…."

Shouting, "Jesus Christ!" he bounds to his feet to confront her, "You got to be joking. I can get a hummer for twenty downtown, and those girls are real whores, not some slut working out of a car in a piss hole."

Morgan knows that negotiation is part of any deal—she has a product, Bob wants it—price can be compromised. "I tell ya what Bob, I can do better…." she says calmly. Then, getting up from the hatchback, she embraces him and strokes his flaccid belly. "I got a better price for you." She glances down; Bob's interest protrudes within his pants. She unzips the fly, edges her hand inside and closes it around his erection. "For a hundred bucks, we can go to a motel— I'll fuck you in the shower and do the blow job for free…" She clutches his penis more tightly and rubs it against her tattered shorts. "I'll even let you spank me for being a bad little girl. Is that better, Bobby?"

His penis quivers in Morgan's grip; he answers tentatively, "I've only got seventy-five…"

"Seventy-five is better than nothing," she thinks before replying, "Okay, but I want to see the money now." Morgan releases her hold on him, takes a step backward, and watches as he reaches his hand into his pants pocket. Bob takes out the unopened beer can. "Money Bob, not beer…" she reminds him—they are the last words she utters. Bob swings viciously, smashing the unopened can against her face. The beer explodes. Two colors paint the instant: white foam and suds as the can splits open; red gore as Morgan's cheek erupts—like a doll without a spine she falls in a heap—her blood spatters the weeping pavement. Her attacker bends over and grasps her forelock; he looks into her open eyes; sense, judgment, control are absent from her stare. He releases, and Morgan's head flops back and thumps the ground.

"Filthy slut," he snarls, "you ain't worth no seventy-five bucks." He reaches in between her breasts, grabs Morgan's blouse and brassiere like a suitcase handle, and carries her into the blackness of the loading bay—a deposit of trash is treated with more dignity—he drops her flat. Morgan sprawls motionless. Bob goes to the hatchback. Yanking out Morgan's sleeping bag, he returns, and crouching, spreads the shabby bedding between her legs. He rolls her onto her belly; kneels between her thighs; tears at the back of her blouse collar—the buttons pop—Morgan's limp arms stretch backward and shed the blouse and sleeves. He yanks at her bra; the delicate fabric shreds. It's cast aside. "I'm going to hump you like a dog you little bitch," he sneers, ripping out the crotch of her jogging shorts. Stripped and helpless, Morgan doesn't stir. Bob is ready. As he penetrates her, he tugs at her hair, smears her broken face against the filth and litter on the ground, and taunts, "How does this feel—fucking whore—see how much Bobby loves you?" He grunts in spasms approaching a frenzied climax. "Bitch!" he groans, "Do you like it? You want it all? Here it comes—filthy slut!"

Morgan doesn't hear him; she doesn't feel him finish. Bob withdraws; fumbles to his feet, zips his pants, and then straddling her, he ridicules her before fleeing, "Was that fun princess? Now be a good girl, and sleep tight—fucking slut."

Unconscious, naked and alone, Morgan leaks her attacker's vile fluid.

At nine o'clock in the morning, Thursday August 14th, Dorchester Downs sizzles. On the east side of barn D-3, ventilation fans strain, sucking the stifling air from overheated quarters. The lush summer grass bordering the shed row is withered and dying—a desiccated carpet of amber thatch that's turned crisp. Lined up at the wash stall, sweating horses drip; one after another, they take their turn under a spray of cold water—on a day like this, none protests their morning shower. In front of stall number twelve, Kallie paces. She glances at her wristwatch—the crystal perspires. Hoping it will cool her down, she rolls the short sleeves of her soggy T-shirt over her pale shoulders—exposed to the sun, they blush—nothing helps in the heat of dog days. She turns toward stall twelve and stares impatiently. Wicked Punch is tacked and ready to go. She glances at her watch again: 9:03.

"Morning PIP," a man's voice calls from the alleyway. "Nice suntan..."

Kallie stops pacing, turns round and sees Earl Donnbury twirling his riding stick swaggering toward her—a fresh cock in a hennery exhibits itself with less pluck than this strutting rooster. "Hello, Squirrel," she replies, rolling down her shirt sleeves.

"Been farming long?" he quips when he stops to pose before her. "My grandfather used to have a tan like that—a farmer tan—you should get to the beach more often, even it out a little."

"The beach? Ha! I don't even own a swim suit..."

"Shame," he comments as he tosses his twirling stick in the air, and nabs it spinning before it reaches the ground. "On a day like today, a beach and a couple of cold beers is all I want out of life—well, that and a lot of money, and maybe a good looking woman too." He looks her up and down, and comments, "I think you'd look good in a swim suit..."

"Dream on, Squirrel, that's not a picture you're going to see anytime soon."

"Too bad, PIP. After you helped me at the gate, I thought that maybe we made a connection."

Kallie glances at her watch again, and whispers, "Where is she?" And then she replies to Earl, "Nope, no connection Squirrel—none. What are you doing here, anyway?"

Earl Donnbury taps his riding stick on the silver conchas lining the side seam of his engraved leather chaps, and replies, "My agent said you needed someone to break your horse from the gate."

Perplexed, she answers, "Yeah, I do. But I never talked to your agent..."

"A good agent knows these things," he boasts. "He's been watching your boy. Said he got a bullet work, and was just a tick short of matching Alydarling. He figures we could cash a check on him."

"You're too late, Squirrel," she says, pacing again, "I got Bernie Keats coming for the ride."

"Keats isn't coming, PIP—I had a chat with her. I told her that your boy's too much horse for her; she owed me something and it was time to pay up, she understood, so she gave the ride to me. She spun you, PIP."

"Spun me? No way!" Kallie grumps disbelieving what he's said. Now it's Kallie's turn; she looks the diminutive jockey over. Pacing before him, she's a terrier quartering a mouse—a mouse with a reputation for mayhem. "How could he do that?" she wonders, "Why would he do it. He's the best; he only rides winners." And then it strikes her: "HE WANTS THE RIDE!" Earl Donnbury is incisive, calculating, bold, sometimes reckless, and while others contrive success, his reputation is genuine—he's the leading jock, no one wins more often; his demeanor is honest—he need not boast, his record brags for him—and his bluster? It's a badge he's earned, and displays prominently. "Shoot! Earl the Squirrel wants the ride—I don't believe it. This is too good," she giggles to herself, "he thinks we're going to win the first time out—God! I didn't dare ask him, but he's asking me—*don't cave, Kallie, don't make it easy for him, you've worked too hard. You're a trainer—you're the boss.*" She stops pacing and faces him—nose on line with nose—a foot apart. She heaps as much weight into her raspy voice as she can when she asks, "Do you want the ride, Earl?"

"That's why I'm here, PIP…"

"Do you really want it?"

"Yeah," he replies with arrogance in his voice that implies, "and you're lucky to have me…"

"Good," she says, her face stern as steel, "then this is the way it is. It's all about money, Earl—cashing a check—I want my horse to win. I'm not going to pay you for the gate approval or the work—you'll only get paid from the win purse." Kallie narrows her eyes to slits and continues, "You might ride the horse, but you got to follow my instructions about training—you're a good jock, and I'm not going to tell you how to ride, but I lay out the plan. Punchie's a tough one; get to know him. He likes to fight, and he hates to loose—don't ever doubt him, but don't trust him either—if you let him, he'll kick in and win every race by ten lengths. That's too much. Winning by a nose is good enough. Win the race, but save the horse."

"Sure PIP, not a problem—I know my job."

"I mean it, Earl," she says, stepping back, "and don't call me PIP—I'm you're employer, our relationship is professional, and our arrangement is strictly business. From now on, my name is Miss Phillipa."

Stunned, he asks, "You're joking, aren't you?"

It's a rare fool who challenges Earl Donnbury head to head—defeat is the most common outcome—but Kallie is no fool. Her terms are clear, backed by conviction, and Earl wants the ride.

"Did it sound like I was joking, Earl?"

"She's serious," he thinks, assessing her grim expression, "Oh man… I heard about what she did to Willie and the Hawk, and that she has Max the Ax in her pocket. But shit, the guys weren't kidding—she's tough!" Slowly, a contrite smile—a sincere smile—fills his lips, and he says, "No, no it didn't sound like a joke. I'm sorry, Miss Phillipa. You're right. You and me are a team, but you're the captain. Okay? Do you want me to school Punch? Do I get 'first call' when you enter?"

Satisfied that her point has been made, and her terms accepted, Kallie nods, yes, and reaches out her sweaty hand. They shake, consummating the deal. "He's in the stall, ready to go," she says turning, leading Earl the Squirrel to stall twelve. Earl begins twirling his stick confidently, but respecting his employer, he follows at her shoulder, and listens attentively as Kallie gives instructions. "Back track him to the gate at an easy trot—it's hot today and I don't want to be pumping fluids into him all night. He's been walking through the chute for three days, and yesterday I stood him in a couple of times…" Opening the stall door and leading Wicked Punch out by the reins into the scalding humidity and searing heat, she adds, "but I didn't close him in." She tugs at the nearside stirrup pulling it down. "Walk him through two or three times, and then have Butch or

Freddie head him, and stand him with the gate closed. If he's okay with that, then have them open the gate—don't spring it—and walk him out."

Standing next to Wicked Punch, his left hand holding onto the mane, and grasping the cantle of the saddle, Earl bends his knee anticipating a 'leg-up,' and asks, "Do you want me to take him around then?"

"Yeah, an easy two miles," Kallie replies, tossing the reins over Punch's head—he's confused, and turns his head to see who's mounting; it's not Kallie, and he steps aside apprehensively. "Easy big boy," she reassures him as she bends down to throw the Squirrel aboard. Earl releases his hand-hold, grabs the reins and then a generous hank of mane. Wicked Punch stands steady, but stares suspiciously back at the unfamiliar rider. "Ready Earl?" she asks, clutching his calf with both hands.

"Good to go boss…" Earl jumps; Kallie lifts. It's a short flight with a quiet landing in the saddle. His misgiving grows, and Punch grunts anxiously. "Easy Punchie," Earl whispers, offering a soothing pat, "Steady big boy." Punch is comforted—somewhat, but not enough. He humps his back, squeals and kicks out behind. "Oh yeah," yelps the Squirrel gleefully, "that's why I want to ride this horse—he's got attitude!"

"Yeah," Kallie concurs, "I learned about that when I broke him."

Walking Punch across the crunchy grass of the alleyway, the Squirrel chuckles sympathetically, and asks, "Hit the dirt a few times, did you?" Lagging behind, Kallie groans a wordless reply. In the morning sun, the scarlet polo wraps look like a quartet of rambling pomegranates; the matching saddle towel is their banner. "Miss Phillipa, are you going to meet us at the gate," he shouts, continuing on his way, "or you going to wait here?"

"I'm taking my truck. I'll meet you there…"

As Earl the Squirrel and his mount amble toward the bridle path, and the track beyond, Kallie jogs to her pickup truck. When she swings open the door, the cell phone mounted to the dashboard is chiming; she lunges for the phone, and pipes excitedly, "This is

Kallie—hello…" She hears static, a harsh sounding click, and then an emotionless male voice.

"Kallie May Phillipa?" the voice asks.

She doesn't recognize the man's voice, and replies cautiously, "Yes, yes that's me—who is this?"

"Miss Phillipa, are you familiar with a woman named Morgan Jasperson?"

"Ah, ah, yes," she stutters, "I know her—who is this, and why are you asking about Morgan?"

"Miss Phillipa, this is Deputy Lyle Heart with the Dorchester County Sheriffs Department…"

"What—what—what's this about? Has something happened to Morgan—is she okay? Why are you calling me?"

"I'm sorry, Miss Phillipa, I can't release that information over the phone," Deputy Heart replies, and then, into his dull voice, creeps a grave tone. "We found your name among Morgan Jasperson's belongings—you were listed on a Red Cross identification card as the person to contact in the case of emergency…"

Kallie scrambles through the memories of their friendship. "Tenth grade," she gasps silently, "we filled out those cards in health class in tenth grade. Oh God, Morgan!"

"…And nothing else we found identified a next of kin. Do you know if she has any next of kin we should contact?"

As if by instinct she cries, "No, no one—her mom, but she's in treatment, I think… I don't know where, and her dad's gone…."

"Hum, not good," sighs Deputy Heart.

Stunned, reeling, she fears her worst fear, and blurts terrified, "Is Morgan hurt? She's alive isn't she? Can you tell me anything?"

"She's been attacked and injured pretty bad, she's still unconscious," is his bland reply. "It looks like it will be a while before we can interview her. Can you come to the county hospital and give us some information?"

Kallie thinks quickly, "Half hour at the gate; another half to get Punchie back to the barn, cool him out, feed and water—two hours…" Her schedule composed, she asks, "Who is this again?"

"Deputy Lyle Heart…"

"Will you be there, should I ask for you?"

"Yes, I'm assigned to the case. Go to the trauma entrance and ask for me, they'll have me paged."

"I won't be able to get there until after eleven. Is that okay, Deputy?"

"That's fine, Miss Phillipa, thank you. Good bye."

Kallie closes the faceplate of the phone. And then rushing at the allowed speed of ten miles per hour, she drives to the top of the home stretch where the starting gates are located. From the rail she watches Wicked Punch, the Squirrel, and the gate crew go about their tasks.

If horses used words to express their feelings, Wicked Punch would ask, "What's the big deal, boys? Sure I bite, and kick, and fart fire—that's what racehorses do—right mom? It's part of my J-O-B. Ho-hum, how long do I have to stand in this thing?"

11:18 a.m. In a crowded 'intensive care' dormitory at the Dorchester County Hospital, enclosed within the privacy curtain surrounding Morgan Jasperson's bed, Deputy Lyle Heart speaks very plainly to Kallie about her injured friend. Breathing in fragile gasps, her eyes squeezed shut from swelling, unconscious, Morgan sleeps through the story. It's a woeful tail, reported flatly, without embellishment, and few established facts: "We believe she's been living in an abandoned car. A passer-by found her in a loading dock at the brewery on Waterfront Avenue—he's not a suspect." Kallie restrains a sob as Deputy Heart continues, "She's been assaulted physically, and there is clear evidence that she's been raped. The crime lab has taken DNA samples of her attacker's semen; we've also recovered what we think is the weapon used in the assault, and some other physical evidence was recovered at the scene. At this point, there is no reason to suspect that drugs were involved. It looks like it was a crime of opportunity—it happens a lot to the homeless, they're easy victims—she's lucky to have survived. Do you know any of the people with whom Miss Jasperson has been associating? Miss Phillipa?"

Before her, Morgan lies limp and pale; she is unconscious, but Kallie is comatose. Overwhelmed by sadness; her stunned gaze fixed upon Morgan; silent regret haunts her. "Why didn't you call me Morgan?" she wonders. "We were best friends, I could have helped you. *You could have,*" her inner voice bites, "*but you didn't, Kallie. You could have called her.* I didn't know anything was wrong. *Yes you did, the signs were always there; you ignored them.* She pushed me away; she didn't <u>want</u> to be my friend! *Bravado, or courage, Kallie? What would the Baron think? What would Dad say? You pick fights and <u>pretend</u> to be brave—you do it only to get your way. But you show no courage, the bravery of quiet moments—when you're frightened or doubtful—the courage to be selfless, to sacrifice for someone when it gains you nothing at all....*" Kallie weeps, and apologizes silently, "I'm so sorry, Morgan. How could I let this happen to you? I was your friend."

"Miss Phillipa?" Deputy Heart asks, nudging her back from her stupor, "Do you know if Miss Jasperson has any friends we should contact?"

"No. No sir. Morgan didn't have anyone she could call a friend..."

"Hum, that's too bad," he mutters, turning to leave the room. "Someone should be here to help her through this—it's going to be tough." He pauses at the door, looking back, he adds sympathetically, "Especially if the rape results in a pregnancy... Poor kid. I wouldn't want anyone I knew to deal with it alone."

Kallie stares at Morgan's battered face—swollen black eyes, splayed nose, puffy blue lips—and whispers a promise, "Don't worry Morgan, you won't be alone." She clutches Morgan's unresponsive hand, and sobs quietly, "It's not your fault—I let you down. It won't happen again."

*　*　*

Victor John Faith

Sixteen: The Hot Pepper Squirts

Last Sunday, August 24th, after a bullet work from the gate—three furlongs in thirty-five seconds flat—Wicked Punch was issued a gate approval card. Now, Kallie can enter, and her horse can race, but she and Punch are behind schedule. This late in the meet—there are only twelve racing days left—most other horses Punch's age have three or four starts, and if they've been lucky, they have a win. If the race Kallie needs for her colt, a *Maiden, Special Weight Allowance*, isn't in the final condition book, their chances of getting a race—and a win—diminish. Or, if it is written, and a late preference date makes Wicked Punch, *Also Eligible*, but excluded from starting, then they're no better off. Should either bad case occur, or worse, he gets a race, but fails to win, she'll have to ship her horse to another track to break his maiden. Kallie will have to leave home. She'll have to get a license, and insurance in another state; she'll have to support herself—pay rent, buy food, have transportation and money for gas, and then, she'll have to feed her horse, pay for shoeing, veterinary care, and hire a jockey. This is a dose of responsibility better taken with family nearby. Kallie is worried.

It's early morning, Thursday, August 28th. Overnight, a petulant thunderstorm dragged a cool front out from Canada. At dawn, a tattered cloak of shredded clouds obscures the sky. The August heat, chased by bracing chill, lingers south on the Great Plains, but not here. On the backside, people scurry about in sweatshirts, and shiver. Another day of work is underway.

After an easy gallop of two miles, and a bath, Wicked Punch rests quietly in his stall. A hundred and twenty days of unblemished training, done. He's fit; his bay coat glistens like a lacquered walnut desktop; his muscled chest is pronounced and bulging; his haunches are defined in promontory tissue cleaved by rifts; there's enough daylight under his gut for a child to pass upright—he's a fearsome competitor. But yet, he's kind, and eats his hay serenely as Kallie studies the condition book. Outside his stall, seated on an overturned bucket, she pages forward and back marking races. Punch hears her strained voice, but he's deaf to her turmoil.

"If I enter the *special weight* on Sunday and he looses, I'm stuck with the *maiden claimer* on Friday—I could loose him for ten thousand bucks—and that's kind of soon to run him back. That only leaves the special weight on the fourteenth, the state-bred claimer on the eleventh, and the *allowance* on the twentieth. But if he wins Sunday, I can drop into the *stake*, or that *starter handicap* in two weeks—it's open company, but he could do it. Shoot," she grouses, slapping the condition book closed, "this is so complicated. How could anybody figure out the best dates? What do you think Punchie?" she asks, glancing over her shoulder at Wicked Punch. "Are you good enough to run in open company against Kentucky and Florida breds? Do you want to run in a handicap?" Wicked Punch nickers contentedly, and Kallie replies for him, "What am I talking about? He'd better be good enough—there aren't going to be any other state-bred horses in the derby. We might not get another chance; I have to enter the special on Sunday, and hope like hell he wins." That decision concluded, she groans, standing up from the bucket, and slides the condition book into her hip pocket. "Good thing I'm not riding today," she whines, stretching her right leg, "this cold weather really makes my knee stiff—Ooo, ouch." And then she thinks of her battered friend, and observes, shuddering, "Count your blessings, Kallie. It could be a lot worse—thirty stitches, and a mangled face—I wonder if she remembers what that asshole did to her... God! I hope they catch him. Nobody deserves to have that happen—if she's lucky, she won't remember—poor kid." She looks in at Wicked Punch; he's standing in the corner of his stall munching a last mouthful of grain. "Eat up good, Punchie," she says, pushing up the long sleeve of her sweatshirt to glance at her wristwatch. "Eight o'clock, another hour before they start taking entries—I just hate killing time—maybe I should go to the kitchen. Lets see, Thursday," she muses, gazing off at the cloudy sky, "Thursday, yeah, Tex-Mex scrambled eggs—yum! That stuff is so good. See ya latter Punchie, I'm running up to have a snack." Not exactly running. Kallie is eager, enthusiastic and spirited, but while the rest of her dashes to the kitchen, her less than able limb struggles to keep up.

9:00 a.m. Agents, owners, trainers, jockeys and hangers-on clog the lobby of the racing office. The motley, and the manicured rub elbows and back slap. After downing a double serving of Tex-Mex, Kallie belches, and presses through the crowd.

"Howdy PIP," a man, tipping his scuffed and soiled cowboy hat, says while giving way so Kallie can pass.

"Morning Jack," she chirps, "Aren't you kind of chilly in a short-sleeved shirt?"

"Nah, I'm from Montana—this is a winter shirt."

"PIP, PIP," a whiskered trainer without teeth asks, "Ya ain't gonna enter that big horse of yours, are ya?—I don't wanna hook that monster."

"Maybe Vinnie, or maybe not. You'll have to wait and see..."

"A couple of bullet works—mighty impressive PIP," another adds, shaking her hand.

"They look good on paper, Joel, but you don't get a paycheck for a fast work."

A jockey, carrying his helmet and wearing a paisley kerchief, waylays her, asking, "If the Squirrel spins ya PIP, will ya give me the call?"

"Mister Donnbury has the first call, Mickey—I've got it in writing."

"Yeah, but..."

"No promises Mickey, excuse me."

Behind the long counter, Chuck Wallace sits at his desk. He sees Kallie making her way through the crush toward the entry cubicles beyond. He springs from his chair, and bounds for the cubicles, but before he's half way there, an imposing voice booms, "Stay put, Chuckles. I'll handle this one." Willis Richard Dudley hoists himself to his feet and plods forward.

"Oh—oh..." a feeble voice within the mass sighs. "This ain't gonna be good."

"Willie wouldn't dare pull anything on the PIP," someone whispers anxiously.

"Best-a luck PIP," the toothless man lisps.

Kallie steps inside the cubicle and closes the louvered shutters behind her. Willie plugs the enclosure opposite her. A narrow laminate shelf separates them. The ragged and the resplendent gather outside to eavesdrop. Willie whispers, "Hello Miss Phillipa. Can I take your entry?"

"Yes, Mister Dudley," she replies politely. "The second race on Sunday..."

His voice barely audible, he interrupts, "The state-bred maiden special weight going six furlongs?"

"Yes..."

"Tough company. You sure?"

"I got a tough horse..."

"Okay. Your entry?" he asks while marking the information on an entry form.

"Wicked Punch," she whispers, "he should have a zero date."

"Ah-huh," he murmurs softly, "I'll have to check. Colt or gelding?"

"Colt."

"Allowance?"

"I've got to take the full weight—a hundred and eighteen pounds."

"Any special equipment?"

"None."

"Permitted medications?"

In a hushed tone, Kallie answers, "Bute only, no Lasix."

"Good. And have ya made arrangements for a jockey?"

"Earl Donnbury."

"Willie smiles doubtfully, and replies, "He might have another engagement."

Kallie reaches, and tenderly covers his huge paw with her dainty hand. "He doesn't," she assures him, "I have a written contract for his services."

He wiggles his head from side to side, and replies with a subdued laugh, "Yeah, I'm sure ya do, Miss Phillipa; I'm sure ya do. Any other entries for ya today?"

Withdrawing her hand, she smiles and answers gamely, "No sir, the one is all I need."

"Okay then," he says, folding the entry form and sliding it into his shirt pocket, "that's all there is to it, Miss Phillipa. It wasn't that bad, was it? Ya gonna stick around for the draw?"

"No, I have to help put up a load of hay—I'll check the overnights when I feed this evening."

"Good luck, Miss Phillipa…"

"Thanks a lot Willie. Really—thank you."

Like a bung popping from a barrel, Willie unplugs the cubicle and disappears from her view. Kallie pauses a moment—she knows what awaits her outside. With pluck and verve, she swings open the shutters and strides into the disparate throng. Nosey men pester her.

"What happened PIP?" asks one.

"We all thought he'd kill ya," comments another.

"You're one tough bugger," pipes a third.

"Boys, boys," she laughs, restraining them, "nothing happened. Willie and I kissed and made up—that's all." And as she saunters from the lobby, she glances back and comments impishly, "And you know, he isn't a bad kisser…"

Later that evening, dirty and covered with hay, Kallie stops by the racing office to get the schedule of races for Sunday—the overnight sheet—it reads:

Second Race: Allowance. State-bred, Maiden Special Weight, 6f. Purse $12,600 (Plus $5,290 from the breeder's fund). For Maiden colts and geldings 2 years old. Weight 118 lbs.

Post Position	Jockey
1. Lastfastone	Keats

Too Far A Dream

2. Snoshovel   Estrada
3. Pinkpeppermint   M. Evans
4. Wicked Punch   Donnbury
5. Jackpine Sam   Rousham
6. Momsmarvel   D. Smith II
7. Jacques Rocket   Brisbois
8. Likelyvillin   l'Forte
9. Alequint   Escobar
10. Polka Dancer   Davis

"Yes!" Kallie shouts, gleefully dancing a limping jig, "The four hole—that's the best." And as she dances, she sings, "*I got a happy feeling, a feeling 'bout you; you're a magic racehorse, with lightening studded shoes...*"

The longest three days in a horseman's life occur between the time he enters his horse in a race, and the moment the starting gate springs open—confirming or crushing his hopes.

Thursday night, Kallie sleeps fitfully. Everything that could go right in Sunday's second race, and everything that could go wrong, clutters her dreams: Wicked Punch leads the race by so wide a margin, the other horses surrender; heads hung low in shame, they walk across the finish line, defeated—theirs was a vain effort from the start. He duels with the favorite; neck and neck they jostle around the far turn, the rest of the pack missing in their dust; the duelists rampage down the stretch—head to head, nose to nose—neither yielding an inch until the wire. The photo confirms it: Wicked Punch by the length of a proud lip. And then there are night starts: Kallie jerks when Punch conspires in the starting gate, he casts his jockey skyward, concocts shenanigans, incites riot, revolt takes hold, and the equine rank runs amuck—hoofbound chaos reigns! She thrashes, called before the stewards to hear the sentence: RULED OFF! GO HOME PIP! DON'T COME BACK—NOR YOUR HORSE NEITHER! She twitches tormented, and moans.

At five-thirty, Kallie's alarm clock screams. She bolts upright. Her wadded blankets launch; soaked from sweaty trauma, they splash on the floor. She teeters on a cusp between wakefulness and sleep, staring—delirious one blink, alert the next—and groans, "Oh God, what a night." She kills the squealing clock, and then wraps her arms around her rumbling stomach and gripes, "What the hell did I eat to have dreams like that—the peppers in the Tex-Mex? Oh God, help me! It's Zapata's revenge—oh God, I need a toilet..." Dashing, she makes it in time. Slam goes the door; up goes the lid; down goes her head; out fly the peppers. "Ah-ugh! I-eee! Oh-ooo no."

"Are you okay in there pal?" Anthony asks from outside the bathroom.

"Oh-ooo Daddy, I think I'm dying..."

Standing in his pajamas, Anthony leans his head against the door and listens—the sounds from within are woeful, sickly and inspire pity. "Are you throwing up, honey?"

"I was," comes her shaky reply, "but now I got the squirts. I-eee!"

"Are you nervous because of the race?"

"It's the freaking Tex-Mex, Dad. I've been poisoned—ah-ugh!"

"Ooo, ugly," he grimaces. "Anything I can do to help? Should I get mom up?"

"No-ooo—thanks. Let me croak in peace."

"Maybe I'll make some coffee," he offers, slinking away. "Maybe a cup of joe will fix you up."

"I—ooo, ah—don't think—ugh—so...."

Anthony pads lightly down the stairs. At the front door, he peeks between the drawn window shades; beyond the meadows, eager rays of dawn shimmer from the scarped limestone heights. "Looks like it cleared up last night," he tweets happily, "it's gonna be a sunny day." When he enters the kitchen, Waggs and Goldie lift their heads inertly and yawn; they stare quizzically, but surmise the intruder is benign and resume their repose. "Yeah boys, don't get up. God forbid that I was a robber, I could clean the joint out before you'd move—great watch dogs." Without ceremony or haste he brews coffee. The dogs snore. The coffee pot chugs. Anthony sits at the table.

Kallie stumbles in, ragged listless languid, she flops on a chair, plunks her dizzy head on the table, and moans, "Ooo-ouch."

"Not feeling so hot, pal?" he asks chuckling, "The jalapenos cleaned out your pipes?"

"I feel like the *Roto-Rooter* man worked on my butt," she replies timidly, "God, does it sting! I should sit on an ice cube. How am I going to do my chores? I'll die."

"Beer..."

"Huh?" Kallie asks, moving only her lips.

"Beer. Best cure in the world for the hot pepper squirts."

Kallie shivers, and then groans, "I think I'm going to be sick again..."

"No, really, shrimp," Anthony assures her, "drink a bottle of beer—it'll settle your stomach, and keep you from getting parched. It always works for me—grandpa Stuie swears by it." He glances aside and adds, "Of course, he always takes a second dose. Stay put, I'll get ya one."

"I'm not going anywhere, Dad..."

"No," Anthony sighs sympathetically, "it doesn't look like ya are." He goes to the refrigerator, takes out a bottle of beer, unscrews the cap, and hands her the bottle. "Drink up pal," he says winking, "I guarantee it will work..."

Kallie lifts her head, sips the tonic and replies smiling, "A beer never tasted better..." Later, by telephone, she makes arrangements with Winston to have Punch hand walked for an hour, and fed—breakfast and dinner. Then, she goes to bed. At noon she takes a second dose and sleeps away the day. By six in the evening, her recovery nigh, she has a third dose—a wonderful bliss accompanies the cure. She sleeps, unperturbed, throughout the night.

* * *

Victor John Faith

Seventeen: Riders Up!

Saturday morning, Kallie rubs her eyes awake. An exuberant stretch coupled with a vigorous yawn completes her wake-up ritual; she springs from bed refreshed. The bathroom is her first stop, but her visit is less urgent than yesterday's. Next it's the kitchen, she gulps coffee and gobbles eggs, and then out the door she hustles. Her day is routine. Chores at the training farm finished, she goes to the racetrack to exercise Wicked Punch—an easy gallop of two miles. Next, she roars to the Baron's to clean stalls, sip tea with the Baron and Charlene, and then she's back at the racetrack by five to feed Wicked Punch, and supervise the veterinarian who administers ten milligrams of 'bute'—routine, everything, except for the churning nervousness in her stomach, and the surprise barbeque attended by three generations of Phillipas in honor of Kallie's maiden outing. Hope flows freely, and so does the beer—Kallie does not imbibe.

Sunday, race day, bright sunny blue sky. Post time for the second race is 1:26; the grandstands open to the public at noon, and the Phillipa clan makes its prompt appearance. Grandpa Stuart leads the way, and strides through the turnstile like a marshal leading a parade, clinging to his arm is a trophy woman ten years younger than him. Behind them follows Reggie wearing a floral sundress that flows like translucent gauze in the mild breeze; her hair—blonde gossamer—drapes across her bare shoulders like an unfurled skein of spider's yarn. Celeste walks with her. Always giddy, she chatters, "Can you believe it? John really wants another baby—cripes! I thought Grant was going to kill me when I delivered..." She glances at Jason, Madison and Grant bouncing and skipping at liberty—the gleeful choir of young Phillipas sings, and replies to the rebounding echo with shouts and whoops. "Three's plenty, don't you think, Reggie?"

"One was enough for me," she replies casually. And then, as they enter the front courtyard of Dorchester Downs, she exclaims, "My God! Isn't this a beautiful day, Seal? I love August. And just look at this place. Don't you think it's beautiful? That kid of mine is so lucky..."

"I'm happy for her too, Reggie."

If there were Grand Tetons nearby to judge scale, the highest peak would be the main spire of Dorchester's grandstands. Robust and lofty, it extends to a height extreme enough to be snow capped, but there is no snow, this spire is clad in gleaming copper, and a proud flag adorns its summit. On either side of mount Dorchester, two lesser pinnacles rise, but they are not modest little cousins, and if compared with notable western ranges, they would be found prominent in every measure. The grandstand's broad, unmarred façade of raw sienna stucco is preeminent, and cantilevered balconies windowed with silvered glass mark the higher elevations of its extravagant face. Dazzling banners, hung from remote escarpments, welcome regal guests. At the grandstand's foot, vendors, sporting festive regalia, hawk tidbits from high-wheeled carts. "Corn dogs!" one yells; "Programs! Tip-sheets, get your programs!" cries another; "Beer, cold beer!" barks a third—a carnival of tempting goodies abounds. The Phillipas are tempted, but ramble on. Cobbled stone boulevards lay underfoot—crew-cut turf of vibrant green, carpets any unpaved open space. And begonias, a profusion of begonias in full bloom, begonias of every shade and hue, ring the sequestered parade paddock—here, gentlemen and ladies, and horses of paladin blood will joust competitively. "Did my new Rolex get in the picture? Is my gown the most splendid; are the colors flattering to my skin?" Whinny, whinny, neigh, the tournament is nigh.

Anthony and John carry the train. Jostling and joking, they tease each other. "She's my daughter."

"Yeah, but she's my niece—and my little squeeze."

"Ten bucks says she won't let you in the winner's circle for the photo...."

"Why? I combed my hair, and I polished my boots! She'll let me in."

"She won't."

"Will too."

"Won't."

"Will." They amble and gawk and quibble.

"Boys," Reggie scolds them, "If you don't stop bickering we're going to leave you behind."

Anthony and John glance mischievously, and continue with heightened vigor, "WON'T NEITHER!"

"WILL TOO!"

"WON'T."

"That's it," she grouses. "Seal, let's take the kids to the playground. Stuie, do you and Rose want to join us?"

Grandpa Stuart pretends he's tempted, but offers regrets, "Um, um no, not me—maybe later—but Rosie can. I better look after my sons."

Busy on the backside, Kallie polishes her horse. A brush in each hand, she lays every hair in tidy place. If his hide was tanned, and she added boot wax to her buffing, Wicked Punch would shine like a marine sergeant's shoe. She grooms to calm her nerves, and to pass arrested time.

Earlier this morning, the track veterinarian made a fitness exam—flawless health—Punchie passed. Then, after an hour of walking in hand, Wicked Punch got a bath, walked half an hour more to dry, and returned to stall number twelve for breakfast. His mane has been pulled. Whiskers trimmed. Tail banged. Bridle cleaned. Everything is ready. A distracting click comes from the public address loudspeakers as the microphone in the racing secretary's office is turned on. A man's voice rolls along on the warm breeze. Kallie cocks her head to listen.

"Attention horsemen! First call for race number one. Bring your horses to the receiving barn for the first race."

Kallie trembles; her bladder winces. With an equal measure of joy and dread, she exhales a sigh that quivers, and wonders, "Oh God, what am I doing?"

Old horsemen pay little attention to the secretary's page; tough and jaded, their first race, a consummated event made dim by years of routine, they don't even feel a blush. They have grooms who tend to the duties in the barn, and a trainer has other business to do—

important business—they have rich clients to dote on. But to an untested, maiden horseman like Kallie, the page is terrifying. She's fresh and green, and all alone; a one-woman stable with one homebred horse. Her spirit sags, and doubt visits. "Is this a silly dream?" she moans bewildered. "What is it about girls and horses, why do we love them? What ever got in to me that made me want to do this?" Her stomach feels like she's swallowed a wiggling snake. She groans, adding, "I don't think I can do this..."

During the past two years, Kallie has paddocked many horses for Winston Chase; she's made the mile and a quarter jaunt from the backside to the receiving barn; sweated time in the walking ring under the vigilant eyes of the track vets and security guards; attended her charge, restraining it with all her strength to the saddling pavilion; witnessed the horse race well or poorly, and then, borne the brutal antics that a savage race incites, delivered on her by a half ton of crazed muscle on the long walk home. But this is Wicked Punch. This is her horse. This is her first outing. A hundred appearances playing a bit part do not prepare one for the leading role.

Kallie knocks her pig-bristle grooming brushes together freeing the collected grime, and as she ambles to the stall door, the fluffy bedding straw rustles underfoot, and smells sweet as buttery porridge. She leans against the stall door, drops her brushes into a grooming tote outside, and stares pensively up the vacant shed row to the faraway prairie. The noonday sun has passed zenith. Its soothing rays caress grassland, woodland, and urban land alike. A lilting melody floats on the aimless breeze; lyrics come from somewhere unseen, Kallie strains to hear.

"I got a happy feelin',
a feeling about you;
you're a magic racehorse,
with lightning studded shoes...."

"Leo! That's Leo's voice," she chirps, her glum mood altered by the cheerful song. "I haven't seen that old turd in weeks." She cranes her neck and squints her eyes. Just a glimpse, that's all she gets as Leo trots his pony horse, and tows a strapping gelding through a nearby cross alley—his song swells and fades. Kallie dwells a moment, and then she joins the chorus: "You're entered at a mile, and gonna come in first; I'll see you in the test barn, where beer will quench our thirst!" Embarrassed, she giggles, and offers an admiring comment, "Damn Leo, you got guts. You got a one horse stable that never wins, but you keep trying—and you're always happy, or playing a prank, or teasing someone—just out having fun. *Could be Kallie, that's what it's all about*," her inner voice advises. *"It's business yes, but not serious business. Enjoy this moment, this day. This is the only first race you'll have.* It is," she sighs wistfully, "never, in my life, never will this day happen again."

In the expansive parking lot outside the front entrance to the grandstands, yellow shuttle buses disgorge their loads of pedestrian cargo. Cars, racing like cattle through stockyard chutes, roar helter-skelter along rows of already parked vehicles searching for luck and a vacant parking space. People of every sort—high and low born, and a mass of middle born—dash for the turnstiles. Clamor, hubbub, hullabaloo; a carnival of misfits meld in the occasion—it is the betting public that funnels through the admission gate.

Beyond a foreboding wrought iron fence, across a wide lawn, at the far end of the grandstands, is the VIP entrance. There, under a sumptuous canopy, is the valet station; toward it, a splendid Jaguar treads on rubber paws. Its engine purrs with confidence. Its carnivorous grill of chrome teeth sparkles. From bonnet to boot, its feline pelt glistens, and when it pads to a stop, it seems to crouch. A smartly clad parking attendant grasps the polished silver door lever, and Albert, the Baron Verrhaus, emerges. "Treat her kindly, son," he says, handing the keys and a generous tip to the eager valet, "she's a rare cat."

"Totally! Absolutely Sir—I love this car, I see it around town. I've always wanted to park it—it's a classic. Do you want me to polish it or something? No extra charge, Sir...."

"Thank you, Thomas, but no," he replies, glancing at the valet's name tag that reads, Tommy. "She's temperamental about who grooms her." And then, striding with no less confidence than his cat, he saunters round the ornamented bonnet to the passenger's door, opens it; a woman takes his hand, and with the kindness bestowed by a genteel nature, he assists his friend from the car. Dowdy, but dignified, Charlene Fauxhausen stands in the shade of the canopy wearing baggy slacks of tropical weight khaki wool; an ivory colored linen smock embellished with buttonhook closures, and a silk scarf—a turban, white as alabaster—rolled, and tied around her graying hair. So attired, she could mingle with rajahs in the Punjab, or give comfort to Scheherezade. And she wears sneakers.

"You look very handsome in that fedora hat, Albert," she whispers, clutching his elbow, and patting him on the forearm. "I used to enjoy it so when our families went to the races. You always drew such attention in your summer whites, every girl wanted you—I'm very happy we're together Albert—you look so young today."

His smile reveals a fondness that years of joyful partnership bring, and he whispers in reply, "I never thought I'd return—perhaps, I let myself grow old too soon. I'm sorry for that. You're the dearest thing in my life, Miss Fauxhausen, and the most beautiful."

As the stately pair walks arm-in-arm into the Turf Club—exclusive to those with both wealth and panache—the din of frantic prattle hushes. Like Daphnis and Chloe, Albert the Baron, and Charlene his friend, charm the moment. Charlene blushes radiantly, and nudges him softly, "You see Albert? You're still the captivating boy I remember. How do you get all these people to mind you?"

Replying with a wink, he says, "You flatter me Miss Fauxhausen, I'm nothing more than a shepherd in a tailored suit...."

Big enough to house a colony of bats; the enormous cavern within the belly of the grandstands is flush with railbirds. Flocks of them circle television monitors; they flit and flutter, and gossip about fractional times, speed figures, and track bias in a language peculiar to their breed. Their plumage is odd too: ball caps, slouch hats, cowboy hats, chapeaus—all off kilter, and worn to spite good taste; T-shirts, sport shirts, dress shirts, work shirts, in an array of colors that stretches the spectrum until it squeals. A collection of rabble, riff-raff, ruffians, simpering fops, and affected nabobs—so varied, but so alike—their wagers plump the purse. And there are plain folks too.

Victor John Faith

Moms and dads, aunts, uncles, brothers, sisters, cousins, second and third cousins, unrelated friends, and a barge load of strangers milling—all of them intoxicated by the sights, sounds, aromas, and the expectation of cashing a winning ticket.

In the midst of this aberrant spectacle the Phillipa men carouse; each of them carries a beer cup large enough to contain a gallon—sloshing, sudsy beer, cold and refreshing. They roam, chomp on pretzels big as bread loaves, exchange views, speculate, cipher the odds, and calculate wagers. "*Snoshovel* is going off as the two to one favorite," mumbles John, his mouth full of salty bread, and mustard. "He's got the second hole, and he ran third last time out. Maybe I should play him in an exacta box."

"Could be a good bet, John-boy," replies Grandpa Stuart, glancing at the program notes, "Wicked Punch is going off at twelve; the morning line has him picked to come in third. I'm gonna put twenty on his nose—I got guts, and a good feeling about it. How about you, Anthony, what you gonna do?"

"Tough one Dad, the bullet works give Wicked Punch the edge—he's definitely the fastest one in the field, and Donnbury is riding—but he's never started. Might be a longer shot than the experts think, and I hate to say it, but Kallie's never raced before either. I just don't know. If I bet on Wicked Punch to win, it's going to be a courtesy bet. Maybe I'll bet him heavy to show."

"Braaack, buck-buck-buck," clucks John, chiding him. "That's such a chicken-shit bet—you got loads of money you cheap bugger. What would Kallie think if she found out you bet him to come in third? It would break your little baby's heart, and I'd have to pound on you."

"What? Pound on me, why?"

"Well—I don't know—because you're so damn cheap, I suppose." Just then, on the overhead television monitors, the horses for the first race appear in the saddling paddock. Hurriedly, John gobbles the last of his pretzel, chases it with half a gallon of beer, and dashing for the exit to the paddock, he blurts, "I'm gonna bet *Tinkertinker* in the first race—BELCH!—I want to get a look at him. Come on boys…"

"Right behind you, brother."

"Hold up, Johnny," shouts Grandpa Stuart, traipsing laggardly after them, "I got him in the daily double. Hold up, I don't want to spill my beer."

On the backside, the loudspeakers crackle; Kallie, pacing in front of Wicked Punch's stall, perks her ears to listen. The voice of the assistant, racing secretary growls: "Attention horsemen! Get your horses ready for the second race. Horses in race number two, to the receiving barn."

"This is it, big boy," Kallie whispers breathlessly. "Time to bridle you and go." In an instant, the bridle is on and the reins are looped and knotted around Punch's neck. After clipping a lead rope to the snaffle, she grabs a girth channel, and a red, terrycloth towel monogrammed with her initials from her grooming box. And then she begins her long walk to the receiving barn—the first stop on a journey of hope. Alone, she and Wicked Punch amble along the alleyway that converges with others at Nearco Lane. As they leave the cluster of backside shed rows, another horse and its groom approach from the left, and form a second file twenty yards behind; soon another joins them, and another, and then two more—contestants slated for the second race—with a single cause and joined purpose, they unite. In a tidy column, they march past the track kitchen—barbecued chicken and spanish rice is on the lunch menu; the aroma nearly halts the parade, but onward they march. Beyond the high, whitewashed fence and hedgerow that encircles the main track, the squad continues round the far turn. From far a field, a solo trumpet heralds a call to post. Unseen by the present company, the proud horses of the first race enter the track, and urge explosive cheers and hopeful salutes from a city of fans. Kallie's pulse quickens at the sound. The squad marches onward. At the top of the stretch turn, the whitewashed fence ends, only the outer rail remains. Everything is in clear view: across the infield, as far away as the moon, is the starting gate—tiny horses dance around it. Down the stretch, the grandstands loom; near the summit, in rarified air, miniature people flap their arms in jubilation. Just ahead is the receiving barn, a hundred yards distant. On either side of a gap in the chain-link security fence surrounding the compound, two uniformed guards stand—one is the Hawk, the other, a cop of lesser rank—the grooms and horses must pass between them and present credentials. Kallie's heart cartwheels, her bladder answers with a somersault. "Stay calm, remember to breathe, stay focused on the job," she chants silently.

So far, the walk has been easy; Wicked Punch, a consummate gentleman; the other horses, nonchalant, but now, as the parade nears the receiving barn, an urge to commit high jinx infests them. The second in line—a maiden gelding, but with four starts, no virgin at racing—snorts, kicks out, and then dog-trotting, attempts to rush the lead. Wicked Punch cow-kicks at him, pins his ears, and makes his reply clear: *"Not today you pugnacious lightweight. Be satisfied to watch my tail."* Then, he repeats his warning with a provocative cuff. The one-two combination nearly sends the gelding and its groom sailing back to the kitchen for lunch.

"Easy boy!" scolds Kallie, reinforcing her remark with a tug on the lead rope, but Punch ignores her; he's fit to dance, and dance he does—a high stepping lively polka. The rest of the parade joins in; it's like a wedding party set loose on barrels of free beer—delirious revelers sally and hop madly. Dust and dirt, launched by prancing toes, flies. Tethered to her horse, Kallie bounds ahead shouting, "Steady boy, STEADY!"

A choir, whooping, hollering, replies in Spanish, English, and in terror, "Whoa!"

"AQUI! Atención."

"Quit it, you piece of shit!"

The last twenty-five yards to the receiving barn are done at a dash; the column, at double-quick, zooms. Kallie, first in line, careens through the gap, and yelps to the Hawk, "WICKED PUNCH SECOND RACE PHILLIPA!"

"Get him walking PIP; he won't have any gas left for the race."

"He's got a tank full Jim, and it's pure octane!"

The Hawk waves his arm and replies gasping, "Phew! Yeah, I can smell the fumes."

Time spent in the receiving barn, is time spent in limbo—too late to turn back, too soon to move on. The interior is lofty, dark and cool. Sparrows flit, and visit among the rafters. Along the sidewalls are stalls for the outriders' horses, in the center is a walking ring. Like a carrousel with a mute calliope, the animated horses for the second race prance quietly around the ring; a somber troop of officials observes in silence. If the organ piped to life, it would sound a dirge—soft, reflective chords, the only music for the task: collecting wits, and mending frayed nerves.

As she leads Wicked Punch on endless revolutions, Kallie's mind wanders. She recalls afternoons, August afternoons, with sunny cloudless blue skies, afternoons like this one. She gallops Cashman through meadows choked with timothy grass and wild asters, her childhood friend Morgan, aboard chubby old Mary, capering behind. They frolic on hidden trails, shaded by the craggy bluffs; meander through oak sheltered ledges; trod on fallen leaves that look and crunch like cornflakes, and under the wings of soaring eagles, they gaze at the cultivated prairies far below—wonderful afternoons, forever gone.

"Lead 'em out PIP."

"Huh?" she grunts, jerked back to the present, "What?"

"You're up, PIP," the Hawk repeats softly, motioning with his clipboard, "Take 'em out." Kallie completes a final revolution, and as the parade follows her out of the barn, the Hawk shouts, "Good luck, horsemen."

In the center of the entry courtyard overshadowed by mount Dorchester is the parade paddock. It's a recessed park, sequestered within a broad crescent of descending terraces that grant coliseum viewing to the general public. Arborvitae, cut neatly as a castle wall, forms a fortification for the park within. Inside the wall, a whitewashed, cross-buck fence stands as a second deterrent to any overzealous commoner. There is but one gate; a vigilant sentry in a snappy uniform guards it—only the privileged, their equerries and squires may enter.

The park is vacant now. Almost everyone is attending the outcome of the first race, and the trainers, grooms, and horses for the second race haven't arrived from the receiving barn. The entry gate is closed; the sentry stands 'at ease' before it. Alone in the courtyard, the Baron and Charlene walk with pride and purpose toward the parade paddock. Charlene clutches his arm as they descend the terraces; his cream-colored suit glows—a nimbus within a cleft of clouds. As they approach the gate, the guard adjusts his hat with praetorian ceremony, and stands to attention. Every freshly polished, brass button on his uniform, and there are dozens of them, gleams. The Baron winks at Charlene, and whispers, "I haven't seen that much macaroni on a policeman's hat since we were in Düsseldorf."

"May I help you?" the guard asks dismissively. The warmth of the afternoon is building under the dark crown of his spangled hat; he's hot, thirsty, and cranky.

Cordially, the Baron replies, "Yes, I think you may. Could you open the gate and allow us to enter?"

"The paddock is a restricted area," he snipes.

"So it is, but..."

"I can't let you in without a license, or without prior authorization."

Calmly, and without appearing peeved or overbearing, the Baron asks, "Do you have a list of invited guests?"

"Yeah," he replies, shuffling through the pocket beneath his holstered weapon, "sorry."

"Kallie May Phillipa has invited us to join her in the paddock for the second race. Do you see our names on your list?"

"Don't know," he grumps, perusing the list, "It looks like she's invited about twenty people, and all of them are Phillipas. Who are you?" he asks, still staring at the list. But before the Baron can respond, the guard interrupts, "No wait, here's a different one, Albert Verr—verr—Verrhaus, Baron." His jaw falls slack, and he starts to quiver. The paper in his hand shakes as he realizes who it is he's waylaid. "Ah—Baron Verrhaus, are you him?"

"I am he, and this is Miss Charlene Fauxhausen."

"Ah, um, well Baron, sir, I didn't know," he bleats, swinging open the gate. "Go ahead, walk around, and enjoy yourselves."

With the smallest morsel of terseness in his voice, the Baron replies, "I'm quite sure that we will—thank you." And, as Charlene precedes him into the parade paddock, he pauses and remarks in confidence to the sentry, "Perhaps, on a warm day like today, a summer issue cap would be a better choice..."

The guard says nothing in reply, but he stews silently, "Rich bastards, they're all alike. They think they own the place."

Serenity rules the paddock in between races; it's an uncanny stillness that portends riot. The tote board on the façade of the saddling pavilion projects the odds for the second race with illuminated bulbs—gibberish to the uninitiated, but vital intelligence to the railbirds. The Baron and Charlene ramble through a crisscross of pedestrian lanes lined with gardens; they wonder at the glorious blossoms—intoxicating petals of crimson, vermilion, carmine, nestled in baskets of verdant foliage. They mosey across the lawn—persian carpet, green as emerald, made from grass—neither speaks, the mood is too precious to disturb, until the Baron, giddy as a child at a circus, whispers to his awed companion, "I think I'll plant some begonias next year. They're not perennials, but they're just as beautiful as my roses, and I wouldn't have to spray for aphids."

Charlene swats him on the sleeve, and teases as they continue to walk, "You've babied that rose garden for years, Albert. Between your roses, the horses, and that old car of yours, I almost never see you, except in the winter when you prowl around the house like an old bear—growling. You love your roses; pruning, and nipping buds, grafting, and when one of those stubborn plants <u>does</u> flower, you cluck for days like a hen with a brood of chicks. I just can't imagine you growing begonias"

"They might suit me; they're quite delicate..."

Stopping at a point on the lawn, marked with a bronze placard laying flush with the mowed grass, Charlene adjusts the scarlet tearose he wears in the button hole of his lapel. "They're effeminate, Albert," she coos, "You're not a fragile little flower; you're a man. A man with a personality that prickles." She looks down at the

Victor John Faith

placard, it reads: *PP-4*. Similar markers dot the lawn at even intervals around the perimeter of the paddock. Beyond the markers, the turf is well trod—off limits, only horses may parade on this trampled grass. Glancing back at the Baron, she remarks with certainty, "No, roses are the only flower for you. I needn't remind you that you're the one always saying: *bury the weak and let the tough hang.*" She winks lovingly and cuddles his arm. "Both you, and your roses have improved by years of suffering."

    Before the Baron can reply, the sound of approaching hoof beats intrudes on their conversation. Coming toward them along the bridle path that leads from the receiving barn to the saddling pavilion walks Kallie; at her shoulder, towering well above her head, is Wicked Punch. Behind them amble, shuffle, dog-walk, prance, saunter, and strut the rest of the horses for the second race. Kallie leads the column into the saddling pavilion and strides, with deceptive calm, to Punch's designated post position, stall number four. She leads him in, and brings him about to face front. The other horses, one by one, take their assigned places in the open fronted, copper roofed pavilion. "Remember to breathe, Kallie; stay focused," she pants from behind a mask of nonchalance. "This is no big deal; I've been here before; I can do this." She stares beyond the paddock at the banners draped from the grandstand's ramparts—her tongue is dry as a camel's whisker. She gazes at the faces gathering on the glass-clad balconies; they gaze back, and every face looks only at her—thousands of them. She scans the spectators cascading through the grandstand doors, they spill into the courtyard, jostle, push and shove, competing for the best view from the terraces, and they all look at her—at least a million doubtful eyes stare at her. Then, a herd of owners and their jealous guests stampedes the gate and clogs the parade paddock—there is not a lowing cow among them—they're active, animated, they mingle and moo, sport their designer hides of the latest color, and glide in footwear made from snakes. Kallie trembles. And then, a calming, cozy sensation greets her when she sees friendly faces wandering among the owners—Phillipa faces, a half dozen proud and happy Phillipas meander, and wave frantically at her. She waves back—inconspicuously.

"Anthony!" a voice calls from below an uplifted cream-colored fedora. "Anthony, Regina, we're over here," the voice and hat beckon from the far side of the parade paddock. The Phillipas reply with a ceremonious whoop, and dash to the waving hat.

Kallie squints until her cheeks hurt; finally, she sees them. "Yes!" she giggles, "They made it. Thank you, Sir. Thank you, Charlene." Quickly, she returns her attention to Wicked Punch—moisture has returned, and quenched her parched tongue—she whispers a last instruction to him: "Run fast, run safe, come in first. We gotta do this Punchie; we can't break the Baron's heart."

The paddock judge, the identifier, and the chief steward appear at the entry gate, the sentry swings it open, and they march with dispatch toward the pavilion. Kallie winces, and thinks, "Oh God, this is it," but she doesn't think long. "WHAM!" The whole pavilion rattles as the horse in the next stall kicks the backboards. Kallie jumps out of her tennis shoes. Wicked Punch snorts, farts an atomic blast, and retaliates with a wood splitting kick so strong it knocks a bus over in the parking lot. The other horse rears up, flails its front hooves, and screams profanities.

"Whoa, whoa!" shouts its groom, dangling from the lead rope coiled around the horse's nose.

Wicked Punch squeals, stomps his hooves and paws the ground defiantly. "Easy Punchie, easy," Kallie pleads, struggling to maintain control. "Save it for the race."

From the balconies, the terraces, the paddock, a million eyes focus on the brawl. Like an insulted rough-neck eager for a scrap, Wicked Punch curses his rearing neighbor; the neighbor jeers him with obscenities. The pavilion shakes, "WHAM WHAM WHAM!" as Wicked Punch transforms the backboards into kindling. The neighbor pounds down and bares his teeth. "Wee-ha!" Punchie neighs, displaying a cocky grin. Kallie, wedged between them, bobs and dodges. Among the million, two eyes are most keen: Max Heppner's. Spying the ruckus, he shouts, "Number three. Move out; take him for a walk!" His order is terse, decisive, meant to be obeyed. "You too Phillipa—now!" Eager to comply, Kallie clips a shank around Punch's nose. She expects trouble, but none comes. Her horse stands firm. So does the neighbor. They posture menacingly, and assay one another with narrowed eyes. Their sweaty coats glisten. Their muscles ripple. Tufts of froth hang from their underbellies. A dreadful moment passes, and then Wicked Punch prances—he passages. Lifting his knees, he bounds proudly and floats free of gravity, yards above the ground. "Very pretty passage, PIP," the chief steward remarks as her horse prances within the enclosure of the saddling pavilion. "If he can't run, maybe the Baron will buy him for a dressage horse."

"Oh," she replies panting, "he can run alright, Max, but getting him to stop, that's a problem I haven't solved yet."

The chief steward laughs, and replies, "I can see that, but try to get him walking, or you'll have to saddle him on the fly."

"On the fly? Oh God," she gulps, "I've never done that...." She gives a stout jerk on the shank, but it's no good. Wicked Punch prances on.

Gathered around the *PP-4* lawn marker in the parade paddock, the Phillipa clan, the Baron and Charlene fret. "Is she okay, can we help her?" Reggie quizzes anxiously.

"You needn't worry, Reggie," Charlene offers, consoling her with a hug. "We've seen Kallie handle a lot worse. She's tough; she knows exactly what she's doing; she'll be fine. Isn't that so, Albert? Albert?" The Baron's attention is fixed on the tote board; Charlene nudges him softly, and asks again, "Albert?"

"Yes?"

"Isn't that so?"

"Yes, absolutely, she's very capable. Have you been watching the odds? Wicked Punch is getting a lot of play—somebody just put a small fortune on his nose."

Anthony glances at the lighted board above the pavilion, and jerks in surprise. "Wow!" he exclaims, "When we came in here, he was going at twenty to one, now he's back down to twelve."

"But look at the win pool. It went up an even five hundred in a single tick."

Charlene looks suspiciously at the Baron and inquires, "Albert, do you have someone wagering for you?"

"No, honestly," he stammers, "No one. I'll place our bets before we go to the horseman's box. Maybe the jockey's agent—I don't know." The tote board flashes again, and the odds on Wicked Punch drop to eight. "The backside money, or maybe the crowd—that dual with the three horse must have impressed them."

"Shoot!" grouses John, "I was looking forward to a big payday. A twenty dollar bet's only gonna pay a hundred and sixty."

"That should about cover your bar tab, Johnny..."

"Close, Reggie," he replies with a shy smirk, "I've got to hit the daily double to cover it all—dad and your husband left their wallets at home."

"They always do..."

Just then, a momentary hush grips the milling herd. Like cattle catching the scent of a pack of wolves, they turn in unison and watch as the jockey's valets, carrying racing saddles and pads, enter the lawn on their way to the saddling pavilion. The herd steps back; the valets pass. (Only three people are authorized to handle the racing tack after the jockeys have weighed in: the valet, the trainer, and the jockey. If anyone else should have contact with it, an objection could be claimed, and the jockey and the tack would return to the scales to verify that the assigned weights have not been tampered with.)

Still prancing confidently, Wicked Punch drags Kallie behind. The three horse has already retired to its stall. "Hey, PIP," shouts the chief steward, "put him in, and saddle up."

She expresses a nasty scowl, and retorts silently, "Easy for you to say, Max." When she nears stall four, she digs the treads of her tennis shoes into the dirt, and tugs on the lead rope. Punch saunters in. "Thank God," she gasps, short of breath. "Now stay quiet, Punchie." He lowers his head contritely, winks, curls his upper lip and "WHAM, WHAM," he chops some more firewood. "Oh Shit!" Kallie shrieks, jerking the lead rope.

"Watch your language, PIP," the chief steward barks, glaring through narrowed eyes. Kallie shrinks timidly. Wicked Punch smirks defiantly.

Three stalls to her left, John Shenman, the identifier begins to verify the entrants. Standing in front of the first horse, he studies a list on his clipboard; glancing over the rim of his reading glasses, he remarks dryly, "Bay with black points." Then, he lifts the horse's upper lip, and examines the encoded lip tattoo. "*Lastfastone*, match," he confirms, marking the list. His assistant clips a numbered badge to the bridle, and then they move on. "Gray, no markings, *Snoshovel*," he says from two stalls distant, "Match," and on goes the badge. "Bay with black points, *Pinkpeppermint*, match," he utters from the next stall, and again the badge follows. He approaches stall number four. "WHAM!" the pavilion rattles as Wicked Punch engages his wood splitter.

"Knock it off, Punchie!"

"Hold him steady, PIP. I want to live long enough to retire…"

"Sorry, John," she apologizes, clutching the lead rope as tightly as she can. Sweat runs down her sinewy arms and drips from her clinched fingers. "He's kind of fired up. That three horse pissed him off. He wants to run."

"I thought he already did that out front here," he replies with an impatient lift of his eyebrow. Then, examining her horse more closely, he adds, "He's kind of lathered; let's hope he has something left for the race…

The portent of John Shenman's remark causes her to shudder. "He's wasting a lot of energy…" she thinks, and then determination revives her. Without hesitation, she grabs a handful of skin on Punch's neck, and squeezes—this is how a cowboy twitches an unruly horse—he relents, and stands still. "Easy boy, steady," she commands in a low, soothing tone.

John Shenman peers over the top of his glasses, and observes calmly, "That's a good trick, PIP. Bay with black points; Wicked Punch, match." The assistant clips on the badge, and on they go. "Bay with black points; *Jackpine Sam*, match…"

No sooner does Kallie release her twitch, than Earl Donnbury's valet dashes into the stall. "Hi-ya PIP," he chirps, starting to work. "My name's Charles Barnes." Blink once, the numbered saddle towel is on. "Everybody calls me *Chilly*." Blink again, the felt pad is on. "Earl says you're running a live one…" Once more, and up goes the tiny racing saddle. Kallie slides the girth channel in place around

Punch's barrel; she grabs the girth, tugs, and buckles the billets. "...he said ya got a good shot." Last, on goes the elastic, over-girth; the valet drapes it across the saddle and holds one end saying, "Grab your end and pull." Kallie takes hold of the loose end, grunting, she stretches it down around Wicked Punch's chest and hands the billet to Chilly; without releasing the tension, he slides the long billet through a dee and passes the free end back to Kallie; she buckles it and tucks the surplus into a row of keepers that run along the center of the over-girth. "Nothin' to it, hey PIP?" he asks, patting Wicked Punch's neck. "That's all there is; we're done here."

Kallie releases a gust of breath, replying, "Yeah, that was so slick—God, am I nervous."

"Don't be, PIP, all the smart money's on you. The Squirrel never misses on the daily double—he's got the first half already. Good luck!"

"Thanks, Chilly. We might need a little luck." Charles Barnes winks at her, and then, as quickly as he appeared, Earl's valet is gone. Wicked Punch stands quietly. Kallie savors the brief moment of calm. She nods her head and thinks, "Yep, the smart money *is* on us—every extra penny I have is riding on your nose, big guy." Her horse nickers, and nuzzles her affectionately. "Good boy," she coos. He curls his upper lip, and snorts. "Ugh! Boogers," she yelps, hopping a step backward from the blast, and then giggling from embarrassment, she whines, "This was a clean polo an hour ago; now look at it." Her new red polo shirt is a sea of wrinkles, and contains as much salty liquid as an ocean. Her hair is mussed, her jeans are stained, her tennis shoes, scuffed. "Ooo, I'm gonna look like a hag in the win picture. Why can't I ever look like a lady?" she pleads to the rafters, "Just once, that's all I want."

"LEAD 'EM OUT!" a booming voice commands. Both Kallie and Wicked Punch crane their necks to locate the sound. It's Willey Dudley. His enormous gut sags, then heaves as he shouts again. "Number one, lead 'em out!"

Lastfastone, lead by his groom, walks from the number one stall and heads for the lawn in the parade paddock; following behind is

Victor John Faith

Snoshovel; next is Pinkpeppermint, then Kallie May Phillipa leads out Wicked Punch and the rest of the card.

Hidden away outside of the parade paddock, beyond the plebian risers, far removed from the hubbub, but near enough to vicariously share the spectacle, a lone figure stands: an insignificant female, badly marred; a battered woman, no more than a girl. The afternoon sun adorns her; the breeze befriends her. Her black hair, a disheveled skein, is ragged, and her attire is in the only fashion purveyed by charity, but she is not pitiful, she is pretty, and full of joy. Morgan Marie Jasperson smiles, watching alone. Ever so far away, the one horse strides into her view, the two horse, the three horse, and then Kallie and Wicked Punch prance in like tiny figurines on a toy carrousel. Morgan beams, and shouts to Kallie, casting her affection, and her best wishes across the expanse of earth that separates them, "You go for it, girlfriend! You're the best. You can do it."

The phrases, muted by the rallies' din, reach Kallie—a distant cheer, barely audible—indistinct, friendly words from far away. She searches among the immense crowd; a frail hand waves above an unseen soul. "Morgan," Kallie whispers hopefully, "Have you really come out to see me race?" And then, she's back to work.

"There she is, there's Kallie! Oh God—I can't believe it. I'm so proud. That's my little girl," cries Anthony, "that's my daughter—I changed her diapers."

The nabobs and tall-hats in the near vicinity stare; if their expressions had voices they'd comment, "How ordinary."

"Truly common."

"Working class."

"Not one of us—surely...."

"Take it easy, Tony," Reggie whispers, "You'll embarrass her—she'd hate to see her father bawling."

He fights to restrain his blubbering. "I can't help it darlin'." His eyes threaten a thunderstorm of tears. "She's all grown up—I've never seen her that way—my little shrimp is a woman."

Reggie too, struggles to prevent a sob. "The years went too fast, didn't they Tony?"

The Baron's comforting words infiltrate their embrace. "It's a good thing that's happened, Anthony. You've done a fine job as a father, but now, the job gets more difficult. Now you and Miss Phillipa may become friends."

Perplexed by his comment, Anthony asks, "What? I don't understand. What do you mean?"

The Baron pauses before answering. With his expression grim, he appears to be weighing a serious reply. "We love our children because we must—we can't send them back to where they came from—we don't have a choice." Each of his words is well chosen, his voice measured and calm. "When they become adults, sometimes, we find out that we don't like them very much, and they don't like us at all. It happens in families. Parents and their children don't speak; sisters and brothers grow apart; brothers squabble over petty things, and never see each other again—it's tragic. This is a gift you're being given today, an opportunity to love a child as your equal—that's the difficult part, because we tend to continue treating them as children. They resent that. But today, and for the rest of your life, you may experience the joy of having a friend."

Charlene squeezes the Baron's arm adoringly, and in an uneven, but supportive tone, adds, "Albert is right, Anthony. He's had no children, but he knows about families, and how they can fall apart." Then, reaching in a gesture of kindness, she caresses Anthony's hand in hers, and sighs, "And he knows about making, and keeping friends. Both you and Reggie are very lucky, Anthony."

It's odd how, sometimes, honest words prove to be predictive. No sooner has Charlene finished adding her advice to the Baron's, than a familiar voice enters the conversation. "Hello Albert, I thought it must be you wearing the summer whites; no one else would be that picky about an old tradition."

The Baron turns to see his elder stepbrother approach. "Hello, Maxwell," he replies, becoming more rigid than is usual for even him. The chief steward reaches his hand in a gesture of greeting; the Baron responds by coolly accepting the handshake. Then, in deference to

371

protocol, he asks, "Are you acquainted with my friends? Shall I introduce you to them?"

"Yes," Max Heppner answers—his porcelain hair gleaming as brightly as his starched white shirt. "I'd be pleased to meet your friends, Albert, but I already know Doctor Phillipa," he says, greeting Reggie with a handshake, "and of course I remember Charlene Fauxhausen." He pauses; his voice croaks asking, "Do you remember me, Charlene?"

"Dear Maxwell, yes. We used to be very close. Albert mentioned that you two had spoken. What was it, four or five weeks ago? You haven't been forgotten." She kisses him warmly on both cheeks; the chief steward melts like vanilla icing on a warm muffin.

"Hum," intrudes the Baron.

"No Albert," Charlene arrests him, saying, "I'll make the introductions." Cradling the chief steward's arm, she starts, "Everyone, this is Albert's older brother, Maxwell Heppner," and then she introduces the Phillipas. "This is Anthony Phillipa, Dr. Phillipa's husband; John his brother; Grandpa Stuart, Anthony and John's father, and this is Rosie, Stuart's fiancée. Oh—and John's wife, Celeste is at the playground with their children."

"A brother?" Reggie asks, nudging the Baron. "You don't even look alike...."

The Baron frowns. "My mother married his father."

The chief steward nods his gleaming head respectfully, and remarks with gentility and grace, "It is truly an honor to meet you, ladies, gentlemen. I'm well acquainted with your daughter. You must be very proud. Did you enjoy the first race?"

Giddy, all the Phillipas answer, yes. The Baron remains rigid. Somberly, he relies, "Those were kind words, Maxwell...."

"Albert," he responds politely, "you're not the only gentleman in the crowd—we shared the same family, and, for a while, we were happy." He sighs deeply. "Forty years is a long time for us to be enemies."

The Baron is stunned by the remark. "We were young," he thinks. "We quarreled over a girl, we vied for father's respect—it may have been silly, but I'm blameless for the grudge." Charlene looks tenderly at him; her expression reminds him of the words he's just spoken to Anthony—two old men stand face to face, a lifetime lost between them. "Tragic," he utters quietly. His terse demeanor softens, and with regret in his voice, he replies, "We went different ways in life—that doesn't make us enemies."

"No it doesn't, but can we be friends after so long, Albert?"

Charlene steps in and answers for him, "Yes, yes we can. Too many years have been wasted." The Baron purses his lips, and nods a rueful affirmation. "We're all too old to have this go on any longer. We were a family once, we can be friends again." The chief steward and the Baron both acknowledge Charlene's determined perception; their eyes reflect a willingness to lay their differences aside. And then, she offers the unexpected gift: "You've never been to Albert's house, Maxwell. Would you like to join us this evening after the races for a cocktail and dinner? It would delight us both. Wouldn't it, Albert?"

Forty years of harsh winter thaw when he answers, "Yes, please do come."

"I'm honored, Albert—thank you Charlene. May I invite my wife to join us?"

"Your wife?" Charlene jerks startled. "I had no idea. Do you have children?"

"Three. All girls, all grown now, and one grandchild—a boy."

The Baron removes his hat in the manner of an honorary salute, but before he can speak, Earl the Squirrel swaggers in to join them, and announces, "Hi-ya folks, I'm the PIP's Jock—Donnbury, Earl Donnbury." He is the tallest standing five-foot man on earth, and crows with all the pluck of a bantam rooster in jodhpurs. "Hi-ya Doc, Max." He glances around at the unfamiliar faces fixed on him, it's as if he is awaiting their applause, but none comes. "I'm gonna get the PIP in the winner's circle—put your money down now folks. We're gonna be eating porterhouse tonight—it's guaranteed."

Cocky little bugger, ain't he?" Stuart whispers aside to John.

"He rode the winner in the last race. Paid sixteen and change on a two dollar bet."

"How much you got on the daily double, son?"

"Twenty..."

"The combined odds should be better than sixteen to one," Stuart says, continuing to whisper. "Anthony and I will back it up with a big win bet."

Meanwhile, Kallie trudges around the perimeter of the parade paddock; Wicked Punch prances airborne. The cleft between his hind limbs is covered in meringue; his nostrils blaze red; his coat gushes sweat. The announcer, giving expert commentary on the condition of the horses, notices and reports:

> "Wicked Punch, the four horse, is in fine form; he has two bullet works, but this is his first race, and that fracas in the saddling pavilion wound him up pretty tightly. It looks like he ran his race before they put the saddle on him. He may be there for a small piece of the purse, but he won't be in the money."

Kallie glances at the tote board; instantly, the odds on Wicked Punch start to climb: eight to one, twelve to one, sixteen to one. "The smart money's on us," she thinks, as the announcer continues:

> "Jackpine Sam, the five horse is the long shot in the race. He's failed badly in three prior attempts, and I don't expect much from him today."

Back on the lawn at PP-4, the chief steward looks at his wristwatch, and gulps, "Oops, I better run."

Earl the Squirrel twirls his riding stick confidently, and jokes as the chief steward darts through the milling nabobs, "Yeah, Max, I was wondering why you were hanging around. Don't you have a race to run?"

Max slams on his brakes; turf squirts from his heels skidding to a halt. Slowly, ever so slowly, he turns his head, and glowers. "Careful with your lip, Donnbury," he growls through a crevice in the crowd,

"I'll be watching to make sure you ride clean—I'd love to set you down for a few days."
"Okay Max, sure."
"That's not good," groan John and Stuart.
"Definitely, not good," adds Anthony.
"Nah! Ignore it; that's nothing to sweat," the Squirrel wisecracks, twirling his riding stick behind his back. "Max and I joke like that all the time. He knows I always ride a clean race—clean to the finish line. Your money's on a sure thing—don't worry."
"What do you think boys? He seems confident."
"Confidence is good," replies Anthony.
"Yeah, dad, I like confidence. What do you think, Baron?"
The Baron surveys the Squirrel from tassel to toe. Earl is aware that a man that matters is studying him, but he's not intimidated. Instead he inflates his chest, and postures like a cock sparrow during mating season. His racing togs are pressed and preened—Kallie spent a week's pay on the scarlet silk jersey alone. His patent leather boots, shiny black with red cuffs, have never trod on dirt. He's attired so gaily, he could fit seamlessly into a carnival ball. The Baron concludes his assessment; in a somber tone, he prods, "Mister Donnbury, is your stick an ornament, or can you use it?"

The Squirrel gazes up at the Baron; a cunning smile fills his lips as he answers, "Sir, what Francois Baucher said about the spur applies as well to my stick, and I'm not a monkey with a razor."

The retort takes the Baron by surprise. He pauses, and then he laughs. "That's very good, Mister Donnbury, very well said, a clever turn on the phrase."

"What did that mean?" the three Phillipa men ask.

The Baron grins. "Gentlemen," he answers, "It means we have a jockey we can wager on."

Just then, Willie Dudley's enormous voice booms, "RIDERS UP!"

Earl Donnbury jogs from PP-4 onto the forbidden lawn. Kallie and Wicked Punch approach. The Squirrel waits. They stop. The Squirrel dashes in beside them. Kallie grabs his lifted calf. He jumps. She throws him on. They're up, and away. "Any instructions boss?"

"Ride hard, ride fast, bring the whole horse back to me."

Knotting the reins, he crows, "We're locked and cocked and ready to rock."

"I hope we are..."

"Good luck, Miss Phillipa."

"Good luck, Mister Donnbury."

* * *

Eighteen: Twenty to Win

There are a hundred and thirty-one man-sized steps between the parade paddock and the entrance to the racetrack. Every step seems like a mile. Kallie covers the distance in forty-five seconds. At the outer rail, she hands Wicked Punch and the Squirrel over to the pony rider who leads the pair onto the track. The Squirrel stands in the irons, and away Wicked Punch trots under the pony rider's mindful control.

Track side, in front of the grandstands on an elevated platform, a man wearing a top hat, a red surge blazer, and English hunt boots, lifts a brass hunting horn to his lips and plays the rally to post. For the moment that he plays, the rabble pays polite attention—only that moment—and then the boisterous fans resume their riot. The track announcer's voice blares from a hundred loudspeakers:

"THE HORSES ARE ON THE TRACK!"

Ten contestants parade to post. The bridle path from the paddock is empty. Kallie dallies at the rail, alone. Her mind is a whirl of memories: a doomed delivery and an orphaned foal; a shadow, revealed by lightening; cracking bones, blackness, and then a dire prediction; a friend lost; endless sleepless nights, and redemptive hope in the lessons of an able teacher. *"You've come a long way, Kallie,"* her inner voice sooths, *"Even if Punch fails, it's a victory—you're one race closer to winning."* And then the Baron's advice revisits her: "One day at a time; a little bit every day."

So deep in thought, Kallie is unaware that she's been sobbing. Someone clutches her hand—a tender caress—and asks, "Kallie, are you okay? You're crying."

She stares through her tears; even blurred, the face is familiar, "Morgan…"

"You shouldn't be crying, girlfriend. Today's your day. You've wanted this your whole life—maybe this ain't the derby, and you ain't a jockey, but you're gonna make it there someday. I just know it. You and Wicked Punch are gonna get there somehow."

As the two friends embrace, Kallie weeps, "I'm just so tired Morgan. I've worked so hard. Every day, the guys out here gave me shit—every day was a fight. And it's dangerous, I was so scared sometimes..." She laughs unevenly, catching her breath in between embarrassed sobs. "I peed my pants once, Morgan—cripes! How bad is that?"

Morgan hugs her more tightly and whispers, "It's okay, girlfriend; the doctor told me I did worse than that when I got beat up. You're tough, ya just gotta keep fighting."

"Why, Morgan?" Kallie asks, her tears subsiding. "Why?"

"I don't know, I really don't." Her voice is filled with determination when she adds, "All I know is, I'm not going to be a victim ever again. Not my mom or dad's, not some guy's. Nobody's gonna push me around. If I'm gonna last, I gotta play the game smart—I gotta be a fighter."

"It's a silly game, Morgan."

"Yeah, it is, and we're silly to play it, but we're stuck with it." The pronounced scar on her face distorts her smile when she adds warmly, "Good luck today, girlfriend."

Kallie balks as they separate, and asks, "Aren't you going to be with us if we get in the win picture?"

"Not looking like this, honey. I couldn't face your parents."

"They love you...."

"There's too much they don't know about me—I can't. I'll be way up in the bleachers waving to you."

She pleads, holding Morgan's hand, "Please, stay? I told them you had an accident. It's okay. Please, Morgan."

Morgan gazes down at the crushed limestone of the bridle path; she cuffs at it with the toe of her worn shoe, and replies, "You should have told them the truth—all of it. It's ugly, what happened to me, but I'm responsible for my life. If I believe that, maybe I can change it." Kallie squeezes Morgan's hand and tugs gently, but Morgan will not stay. Her request is filled with sadness when she says, "Don't ask me to do this, Kallie—not now, not yet. I'm just not ready."

Too Far A Dream

In the belly of the grandstands, at the head of an enormous line at one of the many mutuel windows, four eager men clamor. Each holds a program, and a wad of currency. John is first in line. Holding his program next to his mouth, he leans into the window and whispers to the mutuel clerk: "Dorchester Downs; race number two; the four horse..." He glances at a television monitor behind the clerk, the odds for the second race flash on the screen. His eyes focus on number four reading: 16. He calculates instantly. "Let's see," he thinks, "A two dollar bet will pay thirty-two and change—cool." And then he continues entering his bet, "...Twenty dollars to win."

With several deft key strokes, the clerk punches the wager in, and the totalister machine spews out a ticket that reads: DcD. Race 2, #4, $20W. "Here you go sir," the clerk chirps, handing the ticket to John. "And good luck."

Grandpa Stuart is next in line. His ticket reads: DcD. Race 2, #4, $50W.

Now it's Anthony's turn; he peals out three crisp twenty dollar bills, and handing them to the clerk, he says, "Second race, twenty bucks across the board on number four." His ticket reads: DcD. Race 2, #4, $20WPS =3 Bets, $60.

Finally, the Baron steps to the window. While the other men were in and out quickly, the Baron takes an inordinate amount of time placing his wager. When he does emerge, he carries four tickets in his hand. One covers the wager he placed for himself: DcD. Race 2, #4, $2W. And the other three tickets are bets he placed for Charlene: DcD. Race 2, #4, $100W; DcD. Race 2, #2+3+4, $50 EXA Box = 6 Bets, $300; DcD. Race 2, #4 2 3, $100 TRIFECTA. "Well, that was fun," he thinks, ambling to rejoin the Phillipa men. "It's been a long time since I made a wager."

"What'd ya do, Baron, bet the farm on the race?" quips John when the Baron approaches.

"I didn't, but if Charlene's wagers pay off, we may be able to retire the mortgage—she likes to play the exotics." He fans himself with his fedora, and asks, "Gentlemen, is anybody thirsty? Shall we have some beer?"

Jubilant would be too strong a word, but John is tickled by the invitation; he likes beer—it's what makes him who he is—and when it comes to moderation, he has as much of that virtue as the devil has pity. In answer to the Baron, he slaps him on the back and asks, "Do bears shit in the woods? You're buying, aren't you, Your Highness?"

The Baron laughs at John's high jinx, and offers a snide rejoinder, "I'd enjoy it very much, John, but I don't know if I have the funds to buy beer in a quantity sufficient to abate your appetite. That would drain the exchequer." Stuart and Anthony snicker, and nod agreement.

John's puzzled, he's not sure what exactly the Baron said, but then, after a moment, he understands. "Oh—I get it," he replies, squinting playfully at him. "You just gave me a shot, you zinged me, didn't you?"

"He got ya good, Johnny..."

"Take it like a man, brother."

Just then, the track announcer's voice rumbles over the loudspeakers:

"THE HORSES ARE APPROACHING THE GATE."

A whoop erupts from the crowd. Collective panic sends the betting public into motion—time is running out—they stampede the mutuel windows—lines a hundred feet long are compressed by half as eager gamblers squeeze the daylight out of their ranks. The Baron and the Phillipa men make a narrow escape. Had they delayed long enough to gasp a breath, the wind would have been squeezed out of them by the crush. Scurrying through the grandstands toward the beer concession, John shouts to a barmaid thirty feet in the distance, "Four barrels of your finest draft, sweetheart. My buddy here is buying!"

On the second level of the grandstands, is a section of seating reserved for horsemen only. Friends and family will be admitted when accompanied by a licensed owner or trainer, but only for the race in which the licensee has an interest running. Reggie occupies a seat in the second row, one seat in from the risers. Next to her is

Justin, then come Grant and Madison, Celeste, Rosie and Charlene. Four seats to Charlene's right are empty; the rest of the horsemen's section is packed. Reggie fidgets impatiently; growling, she wonders aloud, "Where the heck are those men? They'll never find us with all these people walking around. We're not going to be able to save their seats much longer."

"Albert waylaid them probably," Charlene replies. "If I know that old man at all, he's eating his second hot dog by now—he just loves them."

"So do I!" pipes Justin.

"Me too," adds Grant, "with mustard and onions and sauerkraut..."

"That's just how Albert eats them."

"Aunt Reggie, can we get some hot dogs? I'm starving."

"Maybe later, Justin. After the race."

"No, they're at the beer wagon," Celeste grouses. "With John, beer always comes first, then maybe a pretzel, more beer, and then I have to drive home."

With a sympathetic laugh, Rosie contributes, "He gets that from his dad..."

"Aunt Reggie, can we get a pretzel?"

"Hey everybody," Kallie shouts, weaving in and out of the race fans clogging the front aisle. "Choice seats, huh—where are the guys?" She plunks into the empty seat next to the risers, and groans, "Boy, was that horse of mine being a dink. I thought I was going to get killed..." She leans close to Reggie and whispers, "but I didn't pee my pants—thank God—I thought I was going to, but I didn't." As Kallie and Reggie share the secret aside from the rest of the company, a man, two rows up from Kallie calls her name, she turns around to answer, "Hi-ya Winman. What's up?"

His tobacco stained teeth shine like polished amber when he smiles and says, "I got that bet down for ya." He stands, reaches around the horseman in the row between them, and hands her a mutuel ticket. "Ya got some guts, PIP," he adds, lifting the wide brim of his cowboy hat, "either that, or you're plumb nuts. I hope it pays off."

Kallie winks to Winston as she takes the ticket. "You told me to bet what I could afford to loose, that's what I did."

"Yeah, I said that, but..."

"If you're gonna play, you gotta pay, Winman." She glances at the imprinted numbers on the mutuel ticket, they read: DcD. Race 2, #4, $500W. "Thanks a lot Winston, I owe you."

Winston retakes his seat. Nudging Juan sitting next to him, he complains quietly, "I'm paying that gal way too much."

"THE HORSES ARE AT THE GATE," bellows the track announcer's voice.

An anxious hush grips the diverse hoard. Many cultures, classes, races, genders, ages meld; they are all gamblers now. They clutch their bets with fervent resolve—only defeat can pry the value from their tickets.

"IT'S POST TIME AT DORCHESTER DOWNS..." The foundations beneath the grandstands quake from the volume of the report. "LASTFASTONE, LOADS ABLY; FOLLOWED IN TURN BY SNOSHOVEL; THE THREE HORSE, PINKPEPPERMINT, IS CAUSING A RUCKUS, AND REFUSING TO ENTER..."

A cadre of meek voices squeaks through the pause, "Coming through, excuse us, pardon me—oops, sorry, that will dry off in a second, it's only beer.... Ya still with us, Baron?"

"Hurry up," yips Reggie, recognizing the voices and seeing the truant men approaching. "Where the heck were you? They're loading the horses—I don't believe you guys. Hurry up," she growls, continuing to snipe, "Sit down." The four tardy men squeeze into the saved seats next to Charlene; Reggie glares at Anthony, and rails on, "I'll deal with you later cowboy, and John, you're such an instigator sometimes..."

"It wasn't me, it was the Baron's fault. He wanted to have a beer..."

"John Phillipa, that's a load of crap," Reggie barks, squinting at him, "Only a worm would blame someone else."

"Honest, I'm innocent..."

The bantering would continue, but Celeste enters the fray, "Cut it out you two," she scolds them. "Behave! John—quiet—now."

Kallie fidgets on the edge of her seat. Her attention is focused on the tiny men and horses far across the track infield. Her ears are jarred by the announcer's thunder:

"THE FOUR HORSE HAS BACKED OUT TO JOIN PINKPEPPERMINT, WE'LL HAVE TO WAIT ON THOSE TWO; JACKPINE SAM IS IN; SO IS MOMSMARVEL, THE REST OF THE FIELD IS SET TO GO; ONLY WICKED PUNCH AND PINKPEPPERMINT REMAIN..."

She strains to hear the muffled sounds of the gate crew chattering in the background of the broadcast, only fragments are audible: "Watch it Smittie! Oo-ouch!" WHAM, WHAM! "You okay Fred? ...busted finger! Push the pig! Look out..." WHAM! "...pig's in..."

"What's happening Mom? I can't see."

"Just a second, Justin..."

"PINKPEPPERMINT IS IN, WE WAIT ON WICKED PUNCH. THAT ONE HAS YET TO LOAD..."

Kallie labors on the sounds of the gate crew. She hears the Squirrel's voice. "Get back, he'll walk in..." She thinks anxiously, "He will, listen to the Squirrel..." BANG! "Clear, Buckshot!"

"Ready?"

"Ready!"

"THEY'RE ALL IN LINE..."

"Oh God, oh God, oh God..." Kallie chants. The starting bell rings. The gates explode. The horses lunge for freedom. The crowd gasps, spawning a whirlwind that sucks litter into the air.

"Aaaaand—they're RACING!" cries the announcer. "IT'S A CLEAN START FOR ALL EXCEPT LIKELYVILLIN, THAT ONE IS LEFT BEHIND." He pauses in his commentary for the horses to clear the six furlong chute and enter the main track, and then he starts the first call: ON THE OUTSIDE, PRESSING THE EARLY LEAD IS JACQUES ROCKET WHO LEADS PINKPEPPERMINT CHARGING ALONG THE RAIL; TAKING COMMAND OF THIRD IS WICK-ED PUNCH, FOLLOWED HOTLY BY SNOSHOVEL." The announcer grabs a deep breath. "AND THEN IT'S A SARDINE CAN OF HORSES WITH LIKELYVILLIN AT THE REAR—THAT ONE TRAILS BY FOUR..."

"I knew we wouldn't get the early lead," Kallie whispers to Reggie. "We didn't want it. The Squirrel is going to save him." And then she gushes, "It's part of our plan."

Reggie doesn't hear a word—she's screaming, "Go—go—go!"

The field streaks past the eighth pole. Kallie glances at the timer, flashing on the infield tote board, "Eleven seconds," she gulps, "that's too fast... Easy Squirrel, easy!"

"MIDWAY THROUGH THE BACKSTRETCH, IT'S JACQUES ROCKET MOVING IN TO THE RAIL. BY A LENGTH, HE HOLDS THE FIELD AT BAY. ON HIS HEELS, IT'S WICK-ED PUNCH BY A WHISKER OVER PINKPEPPERMINT WHO LOOKS TO SHAVE THE OTHER'S BEARD. ONE LENGTH FARTHER BACK IS ALEQUAINT WHO HAS A SLIGHT ADVANTAGE OVER MOMSMARVEL." The announcer grabs a quick deep breath. "STRUGGLING DOGGEDLY, A HALF LENGTH BEHIND, THE EARLY FAVORITE,

Too Far A Dream

SNOSHOVEL IS HELD AGAINST THE RAIL BY LASTFASTONE. FAR OUTSIDE THOSE TWO, IS POLKA DANCER WHO'S LOST HIS INVITATION TO THE BALL. THEN IT'S FIVE LENGTHS BACK TO JACKPINE SAM. LIKE-LY-VILLIN IS THE TRAILER..."

They race by the first quarter marker. Kallie stares at the clock. "Twenty-one and two! That's too fast." She bounds to her feet and shrieks, "Hold him Squirrel, hold on!"

Infected by the blistering pace, rabid fans roar approval from the grandstands—there's a real race going on. On the tarmac below, they rush the fence guarding the outer rail. Lawn chairs are trampled. Spilled beverages drench the pavement. Food is mashed under careless feet. At three eighths, the clock reads: 34.18. The announcer's voice booms:

"MOVING INTO THE FAR TURN, JACQUES ROCKET IS GIVING WAY; ALONG THE RAIL IT'S PINKPEPPERMINT AND WICK-ED PUNCH WHO CONTEND. GAINING SMARTLY, SNOSHOVEL HARRIES BEHIND THE LEADERS AND IS JOINED IN COMPANY BY ALEQUAINT AND MOMSMARVEL VYING FOR FIFTH..."

Atop Wicked Punch, Earl Donnbury rides invisibly. Under light restraint, his mount glides around the turn. The Squirrel has not yet cocked his stick—he carries it in reserve. The wind howls through his helmet as they zoom past the half-mile post in 44.32. Mike Evans rides Pinkpeppermint. They hug the rail, and force the pace. The challenge was made in the saddling pavilion, and the lesser horse now seeks revenge. Two contentious spirits bump and jostle, but keep their steady stride. "Gimme some room Squirrel!" shouts Evans, "It's too tight."

"Shut up and ride, Mike!" the Squirrel fires back.

Pinkpeppermint pins his ears and nips at Wicked Punch's jowl. Punch replies by extending his neck and holding his head out of reach. If they could be translated into words, Wicked Punch's thoughts would be: *"That's as close as you're getting to me today."*

"...LIKELYVILLIN HAS BEATEN TWO AND APPEARS TO BE GAINING SHARPLY. JACKPINE SAM TRAILS THE FIELD BY FOURTEEN AND IS BEYOND STRIKING DISTANCE—THAT ONE IS DONE..." The announcer grabs a hurried gasp of air and continues: "ROUNDING THE FINAL TURN AND HEADING FOR HOME, IT'S WICKED PUNCH BY A HALF BEING PUSHED WIDE BY PINKPEPPERMINT LEAVING ROOM FOR THE FAVORITE SNOSHOVEL WHO'S CHARGING ON THE INSIDE. IT'S THOSE THREE, FOLLOWED BY ALEQUAINT AND— LIKELYVILLIN WHO'S NOT OUT YET..."

A world of people flies to its feet. Frantically, they thunder: "Go, go, go!"

High atop the grandstands, just below the snowcapped summit of mount Dorchester, is the stewards' observatory. Noise does not carry this high. Inside the silent room, Max Heppner, Eddie Cantrell, and Phillip Brown view the race through binoculars. "Fast race," comments Brown.

"Real fast," replies Cantrell. "It looks like the PIP knows what she's been doing, huh Max?"

Muttering without emotion, the chief steward answers, "I never doubted her, Eddie—not for a minute..."

"Sure, Max—never..."

At a lower elevation, in the horsemen's seating, Kallie and Reggie are on their feet, yelling; Justin and Grant jump and shriek; Madison bawls in Celeste's arms, and Rosie hollers. Charlene stands next to the quiet Baron and clutches his waist. John, Anthony, and Grandpa Stuart flail and shout, "Come on Punchie, come on!"

Charlene whispers, "You ought to be very proud, Albert. Your student has learned well..."

Too Far A Dream

"I never doubted her, Miss Fauxhausen," he replies confidently, "Not for a minute."

With an eighth to go before the finish, Kallie peeks at the clock: 59.47. "Holy shit!" she gasps. "They can't keep going like that. Put them away Squirrel!"

Leading by a length, Earl Donnbury cocks his arm. Wicked Punch stretches like a cheetah chasing a gazelle. Donnbury fires his weapon. Wicked Punch explodes. Two lengths; three lengths; four lengths so fast his tail ignites and leaves a trail of smoke—a bullet with hooves, seeks its target. The announcer, his voice straining, raised in pitch an octave, screams the stretch call:

IT'S WICK-ED PUNCH TAKING COMMAND ON THE OUTSIDE—HE LEADS BY FOUR. INSIDE, ITS SNOSHOVEL, PINKPEPPERMINT AND LIKELYVILLIN DUELING NECK AND NECK—SECOND PLACE MONEY IS ON THE TABLE AND THESE HORSES WANT IT. FIGHTING FOR DAYLIGHT, ALEQUAINT IS ON THEIR HEELS HELD TO THE RAIL BY POLKA DANCER WHO WON'T GIVE UP..." With less than a sixteenth to run, the announcer doesn't breathe, he keeps on shouting, "IT'S WICKED PUNCH PUTTING THE FIELD AWAY—HE LEADS BY EIGHT..."

Kallie glares at the clock: 103.67. There's a stampede on the track and another in the stands. Hooves pound. Feet stomp. Dirt, and litter is kicked skyward.

"*WI*CKED PUNCH BY NINE, BY TEN."

Everything shakes—noise inflates the air. Beer foams. Soda fizzes. The racket shatters puffy clouds overhead.

"WICK-ED PUNCH, WICK-ED PUNCH—THAT ONE WILL WIN BY TWELVE!" The horses whiz to the wire. "SNOSHOVEL, PINKPEPPERMINT, LIKELYVILLIN,

Victor John Faith

ALEQUAINT, TOO CLOSE TO CALL—IT'S WICKED PUNCH, THAT WINS IT!"

Kallie falls dead in her seat. All the other Phillipas dance. The Baron smiles proudly. Charlene weeps.
The announcer's voice returns, it's softer, calmer: "Hold your tickets; the finish is not official. The stewards will examine the photo for place and show."
Kallie opens her eyes. She's uncertain whether it's day or night, winter or summer—whether she's dreaming or awake. Fixed in her sight, across the track, the lights on the tote board glare. She looks at the fractional times and mutters, "That's fast." She stares at the finish time: 109.98, and stammers, "Way too fast." She scans the odds. Wicked Punch went off at sixteen to one. Her mouth hangs open; she calculates, "Sixteen times five hundred," and then she stutters, "Eight—thousand—dollars. Holy shit!" She continues adding the numbers. "Sixty percent of the purse—that's another seventy-five hundred, plus the breeder's money. Eight and seventy-five, that's fifteen five, plus thirty-two more.... Eighteen thousand, seven hundred—I-eee..." The unexpected always happens during gleeful moments—her nervous bladder, held fast by a strong will, refuses further restraint. "...eee—ooo—shit, shit, shit!"
"What is it Kallie?"
"Nothing mom," she scowls. "I peed my pants—I don't care any more—I'll deal with it..."
"You gotta get down to the winner's circle..."
"I know mom. Get dad—right now."
"Sure, ah-huh, okay." The assignment is equal to sending a chicken into a den of foxes. Reggie slips past Kallie, and then elbows her way through the reeling fans massed in the front aisle. "Anthony!" she pleads, "Anthony!" The men are hugging, back-slapping, exchanging praise, comparing mutuel tickets. "Tony—I need you!"
"Darlin'..."
"Come here, I need you."

"I need you too, baby!" he pipes joyfully, and continues to celebrate.

"No, listen to me. It's an emergency. Kallie wants to see you."

"Oh-oh," he groans. Then, steadying his huge cup of beer, he steps over the row of seats in between the second row and the front aisle. The other men resume their revelries. "What? What is it?" he asks, joining her in the chaos.

"Come on..." she orders, grabbing his shirt sleeve to drag him along. In an instant, she's delivered him to Kallie.

"What do you need, shrimp?"

"Give me your beer dad," she whispers.

"Why?"

Squinting, she growls quietly, "Just give it to me—now." He understands the message and passes her the beer. With self-assuredness and calm, Kallie sits in her seat. She lifts the huge cup above her head, and spills the contents down her scruffy polo—the crest of the wave splashes into her lap. "I-eee!" she shrieks, bounding to her feet. "Dad! How could you do that? Ah-ugh, I'm soaked! Damn, damn! How is this going to look in the picture? Cripes, Dad!"

Confused, he stammers, "Huh? What the... I didn't do anything."

"You're supposed to pour the beer over the winner after the game!"

Just then, the announcer's voice blares over the loudspeakers—the world falls silent.

"LADIES AND GENTLEMAN, THE STEWARDS HAVE EXAMINED THE PHOTO FINISH FOR PLACE AND SHOW. THE RESULTS ARE OFFICIAL. NUMBER FOUR, WICKED PUNCH WINS; NUMBER TWO, SNOSHOVEL IS SECOND, AND NUMBER THREE, PINKPEPPERMINT IS THIRD—LIKELYVILLIN AND ALEQUAINT SCORED A DEAD HEAT FOR FOURTH. POST TIME FOR THE THIRD RACE IS IN TWENTY-FOUR MINUTES."

Victor John Faith

The Baron glances at Charlene's wagers, and giggles fiendishly, "A hundred dollars to win," he croaks in disbelief, "fifty on the four, two exacta combination, and the four, two, three trifecta—gads, what a payday!"

John is reeling, and chimes in, "I'll second that Your Highness. I get more than three hundred for the win, plus the daily double. That should be worth about four hundred and eighty."

Far across the track, near the six-furlong chute, the contenders in the second race have finished their run-out. One by one, they turn around and canter easily back to the finish line.

"Hurry up!" shouts Kallie, elbowing her way through the crowd. "We gotta get down to the winner's circle, the horses are coming back... You too, Winman! Com'on Juan!" The Phillipa clan, the Baron and Charlene, Winston Chase and Juan hustle along in single file behind her. They dash down two flights of stairs to the tarmac. Pushing and shoving, "Excuse me; coming through; pardon us; stand aside please," they charge toward an enclosed semi-circle next to the rail, trackside.

The winner's circle is the most coveted and sublime quarter acre of ground on earth. A trainer can try a lifetime with a hundred different horses and never step foot in front of the camera here. Kallie is lucky. One start, one win. The camera waits on her. She scurries to the entry—her train of guests is coupled closely behind. "Good win, Kallie," the security guard tending the gated entrance remarks, "Remember to show off that pretty smile of yours."

Kallie slaps his outstretched hand in a high-five salute. Giggling, she replies, "I dreamed about this for so long, Andy—it's like it's not real."

"This is as real as it gets..." he says, ushering the clan and guests in. "Quick, have all your people get on the platform." He glances up track, and adds, "It won't be long before Punchie comes home to mama."

If one expected splendor in the winner's circle, they wouldn't find it. For all the prestige the space endows, its appearance is humble: a semi-circle of groomed sand that juts inward toward the grandstands; at its center, along the outer rail of the track is an elevated platform with potted shrubs placed at the corners—that's it, that's all.

Kallie gets everyone situated on the platform. Anthony and Reggie are at center stage; the Baron and Charlene are at stage right, the rest of the clan and friends overspill into the wings; Celeste has to wait outside with the children—no one under the age of sixteen is admitted, it's too dangerous. "Now stay put everyone," she barks nervously. "The Squirrel has to weigh out, and then we'll bring Wicked Punch in. This won't take a second." She jogs out onto the racetrack and waits.

Spaced at safe intervals along the outer rail, trainers and grooms await the return of their horses. Jackpine Sam is the first to arrive. "¡Aquí, ven acá!" the groom shouts as the horse comes to a halt before him. The stout groom holds the reins and bridle; the jockey leaps off striking the ground with a puff; the trainer releases the girths; the last place jock grabs the tiny saddle and pad, and trundles off to be weighed out by the clerk of scales. Next come Polka Dancer, Momsmarvel and Lastfastone, but no Wicked Punch. Then, Jacques Rocket, Alequint, Likelyvillin, and Pinkpeppermint return. Anxiously, Kallie stares toward the clubhouse turn. Snoshovel, the second place finisher, pulls in beside her. As Miguel Estrada dismounts, he congratulates her cheerfully, "Nice win PIP. Fast race, really fast."

"Thanks Mickey. Have you seen my horse?"

Miguel Estrada flops the racing saddle over his forearm, and replies, walking to the scales, "The Squirrel had some trouble getting him to stop—ran another five furlongs—should be here soon. I hope you had some money on that boy."

"A little," she answers timidly. "I made enough to buy burgers tonight…" As Mickey weighs out, Snoshovel departs to the test barn, clearing her view of the track. Wicked Punch comes into sight two hundred yards away. Earl Donnbury stands in the irons; Wicked Punch trots slowly. Kallie watches the pair draw nearer. When they're fifty yards distant an uneasy sensation grips her; she studies his stride intently—its rhythm is haphazard, uneven. "Is he off?" she wonders, "He looks sore, or is he just tired?" Slowly, the Squirrel guides

Wicked Punch to Kallie. Her horse is drenched in sweat, his bay coat is soaking black; tufts of foam drip from his underbelly; his nostrils are flared, blood red; he pants furiously. Kallie's stomach turns into a meat grinder consuming itself. "God, he looks terrible," she cries as the Squirrel tosses the reins over Wicked Punch's head, and dismounts.

"So do you," he quips, noticing her soaked polo and blue jeans.

"What happened? Trotting up, it looked like he was off."

With able quickness, the Squirrel removes the racing saddle, and then answers, "Fast race... Let me weigh out first, PIP." He slings the saddle over his arm, dashes to the scales and steps on.

"Official," the clerk of scales reports.

In an instant, he's back. Holding the reins, awaiting the news, Kallie trembles. Earl Donnbury throws the saddle on Punch's back, and does up the girths. A quick leg-up and the winning jockey is remounted on the winning horse. She leads them into the winner's circle. "Ready?" the photographer quizzes. Everyone poses. "Poof!" An incredible flash of light illuminates the assembly—John blinks. That fast, it's over. Their images are recorded forever.

As the Squirrel dismounts again, Kallie grabs his arm, and presses her inquiry, "What happened Earl, was he limping? I thought he was..."

"I'm not sure," he answers hesitantly. "He wouldn't stop; I couldn't pull him up; he just kept running. On the backstretch, he switched to the inside lead and I heard a pop—I don't like that sound—might have been the splint bone. He wobbled and switched back to the right, and then he trotted. It felt kind of iffy."

Kallie turns and stares at Wicked Punch's left forelimb. Her throat is dry, her voice more raspy than normal when she replies, "He's not standing off on it..."

"Adrenaline. Ten minutes—if he's hurt, he'll start showing it by then." Kallie lets go of his arm; her lips quiver; her eyes beg for information. Earl Donnbury can offer none. "Have the vet in the test barn look at him—see what he thinks." Although he knows the rules set for their relationship at the outset, and no one could accuse him of being tender, he takes an unusual liberty. Embracing her, he whispers,

"I'm real sorry PIP, but I got rides in the next couple of races—I gotta get to the locker room and shower. Don't worry; Punch is a good horse. If he's okay, he'll be a great one—he'll get you to Churchill, and maybe the derby. I'll stop by and see you in the morning. Good win, boss."

Stunned, Kallie watches Earl Donnbury dash past the scale, and then disappear down a flight of stairs that leads underground. She takes a private moment to compose her thoughts. Her family and friends mill about the winner's circle wondering what to do next. "Dad," she says finally, "take everybody up to the Turf Club. Order steaks—the best. I'm buying today."

Anthony laughs and comments, "Oh, big spender!"

"No, I'm buying," shout John and Stuart in unison.

Sternly, and with no nonsense, Kallie barks, "Knock it off bigshots. I've got work to do, so don't argue with me—it's my treat. Go on, get going, I'll join you as soon as I'm done."

"Sure, shrimp."

"Yeah."

"Okay, PIP."

The clan, Charlene Fauxhausen, Winston Chase and Juan mosey toward the exit and the charbroiled meat that awaits them at higher elevations. The Baron dallies on the platform. "Mom," Kallie calls to Reggie before she can leave, "can you come with me to the test barn? I'll need some help there."

Reggie responds immediately. She too, noticed unevenness in Wicked Punch's trot. "It could be something, but probably not...." she thinks, joining Kallie as she leads her horse onto the track for the long walk to the test barn. They walk behind the platform. The dirt underfoot is moist, loose and comforting. The breeze is soft. They pass under the lingering gaze of Albert, the Baron Verrhaus; he smiles—respect, pride and admiration fill his speech, "Miss Phillipa," he starts solemnly, "A life is what we lead between winning and loosing—loosing is hell. When we win, we go to heaven for a moment." Slowly, as if performing a holy sacrament, he lifts the scarlet tea rose from his lapel, and with an underhand throw, he tosses it to Kallie—it floats for a lifetime ending in a one handed grab—a souvenir to cherish. "You'll race for a wreath of roses someday, my dear friend," he whispers, watching her retire.

During the walk to the test barn Wicked Punch begins to limp. While giving urine in the test barn, he favors his left forelimb. The joint capsule of the knee begins to fill with fluid. The tiniest little thing can come between a hero, and lasting fame; the race was too fast, and Wicked Punch was too fast for his fragile bones. The x-rays reveal his injury. "Wicked Punch has a stress fracture beginning at the distal end of the cannon bone, and it progresses proximally," the attending track vet reports. "And he has compression fractures to the second and third radial metacarpal bones—his knee is gone, Miss Phillipa."

Reggie examines the x-rays, and concurs. "It's over, Kallie. He'll never race again," she pronounces gravely. "I'm sorry. It was a great race, but sometimes, they only have one race in them. I'm sorry to tell you this."

"But Mom, you can do surgery. You can save him. I can't put him down…"

"They're very serious injuries, Kallie. If you love Wicked Punch, you'll have to consider what's humane for him."

* * *

Epilogue

A week before Christmas day, six years after Wicked Punch's only victory, Albert, the Baron Verrhaus is seated behind his writing table in the library of Spring Ridge cottage, proofreading a letter he's just composed. The letter reads:

> *My Dear Ms. Phillipa-Donnbury,*
>
> *In the opening paragraph of his famous book, Henry Thoreau wrote: "At present I am a sojourner in civilized life again." I find that I am also a sojourner—civilized, and comfortable, perhaps, more so than is good for me. Although my health is fine, I tire easily, and the stuffed chair in my library bears a deep imprint as testimony of my affection for sitting these days—I wish my saddle bore the same impression. With spring yet two months away, Nimbus is showing discontent with me that he's not being ridden; he wonders if you'll return and put him to work. His tack is cleaned and waiting for you.*
>
> *Miss Fauxhausen and I spent Thanksgiving Day with your parents. We had a lovely time; the meal was splendid—you must miss your father's cooking—but the holiday wasn't the same without you. We know that your schedule doesn't permit you to return home often, however, if you and Earl are able to come for Christmas we would be delighted if the two of you would join us. Tea is served at the usual hour, and Miss Fauxhausen has promised to bake some of those date-filled biscuits we both love so much. You still drink tea, don't you?*
>
> *Sitting here at my desk, I'm moved by the recollection of our first meeting so long ago—seven years. Has it been that long? The library was tidier*

> then. I haven't oiled the wainscoting recently, or cleaned the windows, and the dust, layering the trophies atop my bookshelves, nags me. Like a conscience that won't be quiet, it's an unpleasant reminder that honors won, to endure, require constant tending. I've grown neglectful of such things lately, but from the latest news about you, I know that you have not. Continue to dream my dear friend. I learned from you that even an improbable dream, pursued seriously, is not silly.
>
> With warmest regards,
>
> Albert Verrhaus

Four months later. Overcast misty early morning. A cool, light breeze blows from the southeast. On the backside of Loblolly Race Course in Arkansas, tethered to a hitching post outside a neatly kept shed row, a handsome pony-horse stands quietly. A young woman scrubs a stack of feed buckets in front of an eight horse stable—seven bay heads with black muzzles watch her; a five-year old child lingers at her side. A nanny goat wanders freely nearby. In the tack room at the far end of the shed row, sipping black coffee, Kallie leans over an insignificant metal table facing the door; an open diary lies before her. She stares at it. Pressed between the dog-eared, yellowed pages is a fragile, dried rose—its scarlet blush is gone, its fragrance, vanished. She smiles wistfully, and then as reverently as one would treat a bible, she closes the diary and fastens its hasp. The child wanders in. "Aunt Kallie," he intrudes politely, "Mom wants to know if she should get the filly ready."

Kallie rests her coffee cup on the table, walks out from behind it, and picks the child up in her arms. Hugging him playfully, she answers, "Thank you, Peter. Tell mom I'll be set as soon as I tack my pony. Have her do up the filly's legs in polos, and put the cavesson on. We're just going to jog her today." Gently, she returns Peter to his feet, and then mussing his dark hair, she asks, "Have you fed your nanny goat yet?"

"First thing, Aunt Kallie. Everyday. Honest."

"Good Peter. In no time at all, you'll be old enough to start rubbing horses."

He stares down at his scuffed tennis shoes, dejected, he admits, "But I want to be a jockey, like the Squirrel…"

"Okay… that's possible," Kallie agrees nodding, "but you've got to quit growing so fast. You're almost as tall as me."

"I am, but you're a little shrimp, that's why they call ya PIP."

"What?" she growls teasing, "You bugger! I'm going to tell your mom you said that…." Peter flees howling. Kallie makes a futile dash after him. "Come back here!" she shouts, but he's too quick, and scurries through the shed row to the protection of his mother. "Morgan!" she cries, feigning anger, "Morgan. You have to teach that boy some manners."

Giggling and braying, "Mom, mom, help! The P-P-Pipsqueak is after me," he launches into Morgan Jasperson's crouching grasp.

"Sorry Kallie," she says, tightly cuddling her child. Then, standing up, she pinches Peter's ear tenderly, and tells him, "She's little Peter, but she's really strong—so watch out. Now go and get the rake, and groom the walkway. We want it to look pretty around here for our clients…" As Peter runs for the rake, Kallie and Morgan exchange a friendly smile, and then, it's back to work.

Kallie ambles into the tack room. In a moment, she emerges carrying a saddle and bridle, and wearing her riding vest and helmet. Morgan glances at Peter who's started his chore; raking feverishly, pea-sized clods of clay obscure his feet. She enters a stall with a name plate on it that reads: *Raspberry Punch*. Her practiced hands do the work capably—four scarlet polo wraps from fetlock to knee. Kallie saddles her pony, mounts, and waits by the hitching post. From the shed row, Morgan leads a fine-boned three-year old bay filly from its stall—tall, lean, wearing a coat that shines like lacquered mahogany and accessorized with a braided ebony mane, the elegant three-year old strides as smoothly as a skater in knee-high scarlet stockings.

"She's feeling good today, Kallie. That win on Sunday charged her up—girls always love to get their pictures taken."

Kallie smiles, but remains silent. Watching as Morgan brings Raspberry Punch up on her right, she wonders, "When will you have your picture taken, Morgan? No one ever notices the scars anymore." And then sighing, she answers her own question, "The scars have healed, but not the shame..."

"Got her?" Morgan asks, handing Kallie the leather lead that's attached to the filly's cavesson.

"Yep, got her," she answers, cueing her pony forward. "When I get back, I'll gallop *Spike*...."

"I'll have him ready."

The route from the backside, to the race track at Loblolly, meanders through a hodgepodge of alleys lined by ill repaired barns that squat on weak foundations—they all need painting, some need siding, most need new roofs, all have stood longer than expected and threaten imminent collapse, but the mood among the inhabitants—both beasts and men—is congenial, and makes this a cozy slum. Giant pine trees, as old as the red clay they grow from, enclose the ground, and its dwellings in a shady tent. Sons and daughters enter the family business here—racing. And a strapper, a trainer, and an owner may all share a family name, although sixty years may separate the apprentice from the progenitor.

Raspberry Punch is in for light work today: an easy jog around the track under the kind and watchful eye of a seasoned pony. Kallie takes it easy too. The slow, methodical undulations of the horse beneath her are soothing, and the neighborhood is sublime. She sniffs the air—sweet fragrance—she draws a nose-full, "The dogwoods are blooming," she whispers, rubbing her pony's neck, "They smell just like the lilacs at home, don't they, boy?" Her pony-horse nickers an affirmative reply, and plods onward.

To reach the racetrack, a horse and rider must ascend a long, gently sloped, earthen gangway that rises to the elevated backstretch. Trainers, owners, and early morning railbirds share the same path. As Kallie and her pony lead Raspberry Punch in a slow walk up the gangway, an over-the-hill gallop boy trudges on foot before them.

Too Far A Dream

Kallie overtakes the man—his helmet cover is tattered and in need of mending; the protective ribs of his riding vest protrude like a skeleton's; advancing age and hard falls have played meanly on this man. Kallie glances down from atop her horse, the man glances up from foot... "Leo?" she wonders aloud.

"PIP?"

"Leo!" she yelps joyfully.

"PIP!" he chirps, his weary eyes gleaming, his wizened cheeks filling with a vernal blush.

"Leo, you homely old shit!" "What are you doing here—you haven't been here all winter have you? Shit, it's good to see you."

Leo Sands, the sometimes gallop boy, sometimes one horse trainer, quickens his pace to keep even with Kallie. Walking on her left, and sincerely glad with the accidental meeting, he replies, "Good to see ya too, PIP—heard you were here. I just got in from the *bushes* yesterday. I'm gonna lay-over here a couple of weeks, then go to Kentucky for a month, and then ship up to Dorchester for the summer—did ya just call me an old shit?" he scowls playfully. "Ya still got that smart mouth ain't ya?"

Kallie laughs. As they continue to walk toward the track entrance, she apologizes, "Sorry Leo, I didn't mean it—you know—you always bring out the worst in me."

"I ain't homely either, and I ain't old..."

"Fresh as a daisy—pretty as a school girl...."

"Yeah," he mutters agreement.

"How'd you do in Texas?"

"My best meet ever. I got two wins."

"You only got one horse."

"There ya go again," he grouses, before rebutting, "He's a real good horse." Nearing the track, Raspberry Punch is getting rambunctious, and starts crow-hopping. Leo gets a glimpse of the animated filly, and asks, "Is that the little girl ya won the Memorial Handicap with last Sunday?"

"Raspberry Punch..."

"That was a huge win—she home-bred?"

"By my stallion, and out of one of the Baron's mares. I've got a two-year old, full brother to her back in the barn. *Spiked Punch*, remember that name. He's got some talent too."

His shoulders slump. Wheezing, he ambles, remarking, "I can't believe your luck, PIP. I'll never see a payday like that—a hundred and fifty thousand bucks, what a paycheck. I run for a five thousand dollar pot, and you're up there winning six figures—don't seem fair, just not fair, and ya got her brother to boot." He slows to unfasten the safety clasp of his helmet; taking it off, he fluffs his thinning hair, and asks, "When is this one gonna run again, I'd like to see her go."

"Three weeks…"

Leo shows confusion, and wonders aloud, "How ya gonna do that, the track closes here in a week and a half." Kallie winks, and then he understands. "You're gonna run in the distaff on derby weekend, ain't ya?" he blurts in amazement. He quickens his pace. "You're gonna run in the biggest filly race in the world—holy shit, PIP!"

"She's eligible, her payments are up to date…" she replies, mindful that in racing, luck can change quickly, and that with one bad turn of an ankle, she could be groveling and Leo riding on top. She whispers, so as not to appear to be boasting, "The early odds have her running first or second—the Baron would be proud."

"That figures, PIP. I never met a gal whose dreams came true more often than yours." He takes a moment to catch his breath, and then asks, "How is the old Baron, anyway?"

Kallie stares at the in-gate twenty five yards ahead. Snap shots of galloping horses flash through her field of view. "He died just after Christmas last year," she answers.

"Um, um, I'm sorry, PIP. I liked him. He was a nice guy. I know ya respected him a lot."

"I did," she replies soberly. "I really miss him, Leo, but I don't cry—he hated it when I cried. I could get tossed from a horse, be in a heap on the ground and he'd look at me and say: *It's unseemly for a student to cry in the company of her teacher, Miss Phillipa. Now get back on your pony and we'll try it again.* And I did get back on, again and again and again. I won't let him down by bawling now."

Kallie has reached the in-gate, but before she enters traffic, she turns to Leo, who's paused along the way, and offers him an invitation, "Meet me in the kitchen later, Leo. I'll buy you coffee. We can catch up on gossip—about eleven..."

"Sure, if you're buying, PIP. I'll be there."

And with that, Kallie, her pony-horse, and Raspberry Punch trot onto the narrow backstretch. She enters the outer traffic lane. A female jockey, standing in the irons and leaning backward to prevent her mount from running off, yells to her as she passes, "When are you shipping out for Churchill, PIP? We're a six pack behind and a joke or two short..."

"Next week!"

A bug boy jogs along side and comments, "God—what a beautiful girl. Really nice ass..." Kallie stares crossly at him. He laughs cheerfully, and adds, "I meant the filly, PIP—it's a joke. Don't tell the Squirrel I said that."

Raspberry Punch, kicks out behind and farts; Kallie nods at her as if to ask, 'Did you hear that?' and then replies to the bug boy, "I won't mention it, Dougie, but Earl's horse might."

"Not worried about that, PIP," he crows, breaking company to resume a livelier gallop. At the top of the stretch, guiding his mount handily around the turn, Dougie cocks his stick and gently urges the horse onward; away they zoom in a quick lick home.

Her thoughts detached, Kallie watches. Like a rapid heart pumping, the distant hoof beats echo from the grandstands. "Not a good idea, Dougie," she thinks. "You're going to get nabbed. A stunt like that cost me a pack of smokes once.... But it was worth it." And then she daydreams. She imagines the feeling, the incredible feeling she had when galloping Wicked Punch—the wind screaming past her ears; her light body jostled by the undulating muscles and pounding hooves below her; her burning thighs and calves, and her paralyzed fingers. She drifts deeper into fantasy. The grandstands are packed with race fans, cheering, jumping, stomping, waving, shouting madly fans; the wire ahead in sight, she gulps air unconsciously, moves invisibly, rides impeccably—Wicked Punch flies flat-out in a blurring charge for the finish line and his one gallant victory.

Victor John Faith

"WICK-ED PUNCH, WICK-ED PUNCH—THAT ONE WINS!" She stands in the irons and lifts her arm to salute the wild fans. A voice calls her name. A single rose follows the voice in flight. She makes a one-handed grab; her fingers close; the charm is hers. She sees the smile behind the voice, her teacher, and dear friend. Her daydream ends. The gray sky hangs low, and the grandstands are quiet. There is only a mournful echo in the mist.

Raspberry Punch nickers, and then she farts. "You're feeling good today aren't you *Berry*?" Kallie whispers to the filly. "You're going to make your daddy really proud—you're just like him." Kallie reaches, and rubs the neck of her pony-horse; she laughs playfully, and says to him, "Your little girl wants to run... Should we show her how you used to do it, huh Punchie?"

Wicked Punch, Kallie's pony-horse, squeals, expels a gentle fart, and then takes his daughter, and Kallie in a proud gallop down a lane made of silly dreams.

The End.